UNDER
A SKY
OF
MEMORIES

UNDER A SKY OF MEMORIES

SORAYA M. LANE

Published by Lake Union Publishing, Seattle

www.apub.com

Amazon, the Amazon logo, and Lake Union Publishing are trademarks of Amazon.com, Inc., or its affiliates.

ISBN-13: 9781542031974
ISBN-10: 1542031974

Cover design by The Brewster Project

Cover photography by Richard Jenkins Photography

Printed in the United States of America

"I ask for my boys what every mother has the right to ask—that they be given full and adequate nursing care should the time come when they need it. Only you nurses who have not yet volunteered can give it . . . You must not forget that you have in your power to bring back some who otherwise surely will not return."

—*First Lady Eleanor Roosevelt*, American Journal of Nursing *editorial, August 1942*

PART ONE

CHAPTER ONE

Kentucky, USA, August 1943

EVELYN

Evelyn lifted the hair from the back of her neck, grateful for the temporary relief. There was no wind to cool her skin, only the reprieve of her hair no longer sticking to her for a blissful few seconds. Her head was starting to pound, and she would have done anything for a glass of water and some shade, but instead she was standing in an enormous group outside, waiting to board one of two railroad cars. She glanced down in dismay as she realized her uniform was damp, and saw that sweat was starting to trace a wet mark across the fabric. She hated to think how she'd look by the time they reached their destination, wherever that might be. It seemed their superiors preferred to keep them in the dark until the very last moment.

As she looked around, Evelyn was grateful she wasn't the only one suffering from the conditions. The heat was sweltering, and most of the women looked like they were about to expire; their hair clinging damply to their foreheads and their cheeks flushed pink.

"Ladies first!" someone yelled out from the train. "It's time to board!"

Evelyn shuffled forward, exchanging smiles with a pretty woman she'd talked to a few times during their stay in Louisville, where they'd been doing their specialist flight training. *Dot?* She wracked her brain. *Yes, definitely Dot.* The training had been intense and, aside from the sheer number of men and women there, there simply hadn't been much time for socializing; she felt they'd barely had time to get to know anyone at all.

"I feel like you could fry an egg on my forehead," Evelyn complained to Dot as they ended up side by side in line, noticing the way the other woman dabbed at her forehead. "I've never known heat like it."

"Me neither," Dot replied. "I can barely breathe the air's so hot. How are you keeping your makeup on?"

Evelyn smiled. "I think we have to just give up on makeup for the time being. All the powder in the world won't stop our foreheads from shining now."

She wanted to give poor Dot a hug, she looked so forlorn. Makeup was the least of Evelyn's worries, but from the way Dot was fretting, her appearance was obviously very important to her.

"How red do I look? Is it terrible? I feel like a tomato."

Evelyn patted her shoulder. "You look lovely. Trust me."

Dot didn't look convinced, but Evelyn noticed that the anxious dabbing had stopped.

They shuffled forward again, and Evelyn couldn't help but be happy they were leaving Kentucky behind. The heat had been stifling on more days than she could count, with some of the girls passing out during training. And although she was grateful they were wearing pants for their work, she would have done anything for a skirt while she waited, to catch even a whisper of a breeze against her legs.

"Come with me," Evelyn said, gesturing to Dot when they were finally on board. "Let's sit here by the window."

They tucked in tightly beside each other as more nurses, medics, and officers piled into the railcar. She hoped they weren't going

4

to be cooped up like chickens for too long; the humidity was even more unbearable inside. An officer leaned over them to shove a window open, but when the train finally started to chug forward, the open window suddenly didn't seem like the best idea.

"Close it!" someone yelled.

Evelyn glanced at Dot, who was holding a handkerchief to her mouth and trying not to cough. Her own throat was beginning to choke up a little, but it wasn't until they started to move faster that the coal smoke billowing in made them all start to splutter.

"Close those damn windows!" someone yelled again, and as Evelyn scrambled up to attempt it herself, a woman who looked completely unflustered appeared beside her and stood on tiptoes, pulling with her. Her hair was perfectly coiffed, swept over and pinned at the sides, with soft curls falling over her shoulder, and her high cheekbones made her look more movie star than nurse.

"Thanks," Evelyn said.

"My pleasure. I'm not about to arrive anywhere in a uniform covered in soot."

Evelyn studied her, wondering how anyone could look so put together when she herself was such a hot mess, her hair in damp tendrils around her face. She'd seen this woman during training and noticed how beautiful she was, with her big blue eyes and porcelain skin, but with hundreds of them stationed there, they'd never properly met. There was something about the way the woman had managed to breeze so gracefully through training, always smiling and always with the most impeccable posture, which had made her impossible not to notice.

"Evelyn," she said, holding out her hand. "And this is Dot."

"Vita," the other woman said warmly, her hand soft as she shook first Evelyn's and then Dot's. "It's lovely to meet you girls."

"Do you have any idea where we're going?" Evelyn asked.

Vita shook her head. "No, but I have a feeling we're about to find out."

She perched beside them as their commanding officer stood, clearing his throat loudly.

"Ladies and gents, I suggest you get used to the conditions because it's going to be a long ride," Captain McKnight boomed, smiling as he surveyed them. He was perhaps as old as Evelyn's father, although he had the bright-eyed, square-shouldered disposition of a much younger man. "We're heading to Camp Kilmer in New Jersey, which will be your final training destination before you're sent offshore. So settle in and try to get some shut-eye before we change trains."

New Jersey? Evelyn shut her eyes for a moment, trying to picture a map in her mind. But that would have to be . . .

"How long is the train ride, sir?" Vita called out.

"Twenty-four hours, give or take," the captain replied.

Evelyn slumped back in her seat, hearing Dot's groan and knowing exactly how she felt. *How will we all survive twenty-four hours of this?*

"I'll see you later, ladies," Vita said, rising and giving Evelyn a beaming smile. "I'm going to find somewhere cooler to sit, but I'm sure we'll be crossing paths in New Jersey."

Evelyn almost laughed, but she was so hot and tired she didn't bother. *Somewhere cooler.* Unless Vita persuaded an officer to physically fan her, she doubted there was anywhere on board that didn't feel as unbearable as a desert in the middle of the day. But there was something about Vita's attitude that was contagious, and Evelyn found herself smiling back at her anyway.

"Have you ever met her before?" Dot whispered, once the other woman had gone.

Evelyn turned to look at Dot. "I've seen her around, but we've never spoken. Why?"

"She terrifies me," Dot confessed. "I mean, she's just so . . ."

"Beautiful? Intimidating?" Evelyn finished for her.

6

"Exactly," Dot sighed, fanning at her face with her hand. "We were in the same training group together, and she didn't just look picture-perfect all the time. She was fearless too. I was so worried about getting everything wrong, but she tackled it all head on, even the physical course, and she was always first to call out an answer." She shook her head. "I suppose that's normal for someone like her, though—to have an answer for everything."

"You mean someone so pretty?" Evelyn asked.

"Someone from *money*," Dot whispered. "There were rumors she's some wealthy heiress, but you didn't hear it from me."

"Well, she seemed friendly enough," Evelyn mused, even though it made total sense that Vita came from money. It would explain her confident demeanor. "Although girls like her can . . ." She stopped herself from saying what she thought.

"What?" Dot asked, looking worried. "Girls like her can what?"

Evelyn shook her head. "Well, it's just that some girls do this because they like the idea of an adventure, that's all. I hope she takes it seriously once we're posted." What she meant was that if Vita did come from a privileged background, then Evelyn only hoped she had the stamina when the going got tough.

The next moment, they heard laughter and then Vita's unmistakable drawl drifting from the adjoining railcar.

"You know what?" Evelyn said, wishing she hadn't been so quick to judge Vita. "I take that back. I'm actually pleased she's in our squadron. I have a feeling she'll be good for morale, even if she's a hard act to follow."

Dot's eyes were wide, as if she were still anxious about what Evelyn had said before. Evelyn reached out to pat her hand.

"I didn't mean to worry you," she said. "I, for one, can't wait to get to New Jersey. We're so close to receiving our orders now."

Dot nodded, and Evelyn saw the way her fingers went to her throat, fingering her necklace.

"Is that a ring you have there?" Evelyn asked.

"Yes." Dot's fingers froze. "My engagement ring. I didn't want to leave it behind."

Evelyn leaned forward and Dot held it out to her. "It's beautiful, Dot, absolutely beautiful. I bet your man is missing you terribly."

Dot just smiled, and when she didn't say anything further, Evelyn simply closed her eyes, trying to follow the captain's orders and get some much-needed shut-eye. Right now, it seemed like the only way to make the journey halfway bearable. And if she didn't sleep, she was only going to start fretting about her sisters and her father. Leaving them behind had been the toughest thing she'd ever done, and she was only ever one step away from running straight back home to be with them again.

Evelyn stepped quietly downstairs and found her father sitting at the table in the kitchen, his boots by the door and his shoulders slumped forward. She'd just put her little sister Katie back to bed, holding her after a recurring nightmare about their mother had woken her yet again, and the house was otherwise quiet, with her other sisters already long asleep.

"Hello, Father," she said, touching his shoulder as she passed.

His hand found hers, palm closing over it for a moment, although he said nothing. Evelyn took out a bowl and ladled some stew, placing it in front of him. This was how they always were now; he'd barely spoken since her mother passed, his smile no longer bright, his eyes no longer sparkling. He never left the house without dropping a kiss into her hair or pulling her close for a hug, but there was a fog of sadness hanging over him that had never lifted.

"Dad, I need to talk to you about something. About the war," she said, sitting across from him, her hands tightly clasped. She lifted her gaze, forcing herself to look at him.

His eyes were steady, warm, as he blinked back at her, and she cleared her throat. She shifted, not sure how to say what was on her mind, even though she'd been practicing saying it inside her head all day.

"There's a shortage of nurses, Dad, and I would like to train to be one," Evelyn told him. "Rachel is already older than I was when I took over the house, and Clare is old enough to help out. I know you need me here, but our country needs me too."

He blinked at her, his expression giving nothing away.

"I've done my best—for three years now I've looked after you all, and tried to become like Mama, but I . . ." She swallowed, not wanting to say that she needed a break and that she just couldn't do it anymore. "I want to do something meaningful for our country, and I would very much like to be a nurse. There's even a new program for nurses to train to airlift soldiers to hospitals."

When her father still didn't say anything, she reached for his hand. "I want your blessing, Daddy. I won't leave you if you say no, but this is important to me. I want to be part of something, instead of just trying to fill Mama's shoes each day."

She quickly brushed the tears from her eyes. She missed her mother so much—the pain so raw, so visceral, that sometimes she'd drop to her knees, a gasp catching in her throat as she rocked back and forth, crushed beneath the memories, beneath the longing.

"You're just like her, Evelyn. So like your mother it almost breaks me sometimes."

Her breath whooshed in and out as she stared at him, not used to hearing this many words fall from his lips in a week sometimes, let alone in one evening.

"I've let you take your mother's place when it should have been me," he said, staring into his bowl.

Evelyn stood and went to him, bending low and wrapping her arms around him as he held her too, and she was certain he was crying quietly just as she was, her tears damp against his shoulder.

"You have my blessing," he said. *"Just make sure you teach your sisters how to cook before you go."*

They both smiled and she sat back down across from him, her heart beating fast as she thought about what to do next. She would miss her sisters like mad, but if she didn't get away from home, she'd become so stifled beneath the weight of those who depended upon her that she doubted she'd ever emerge. And they would survive without her, just as she'd learned to survive without her mother.

———— ✒︎⁓✒︎ ————

The next morning, after a night's fitful sleep and a change of train, barely able to breathe through the stuffy, smoke-filled air or stretch enough to get comfortable, Evelyn suddenly forgot all about her aching body and her homesickness. She leaned forward, nudging a still-sleeping Dot as she pressed her nose to the window and watched in wonder as Camp Kilmer came into view. She squinted at the rows of wooden barracks, appearing more like a small town than a training facility.

"It's amazing," she whispered to no one in particular, her fingers spread out across the glass as she watched in wonder. "I've never seen anything quite like it." It was much bigger than where they'd been stationed in Kentucky, and she had a feeling it was going to be even more intense.

"Are you sure this is it?" Dot whispered.

"This is it," Evelyn said, as the faded sign announcing Camp Kilmer came into view, the name painted on timber in front of a small wooden building.

The low murmur in the railcar had turned into something much louder now, and Evelyn felt her own exhaustion change into nervous energy as the train slowly rolled to a stop. When she turned to Dot, she saw the other woman was anxiously fiddling with her necklace again, and she placed a hand on her shoulder.

"It's going to be great here," Evelyn assured her. "There's absolutely nothing to worry about."

Dot nodded and ran a hand over her hair.

"And you look lovely, by the way," Evelyn whispered with a grin. "Trust me."

Dot's cheeks went red, but her smile lit up her face. "Thank you. That means a lot."

"Gather your things and meet for roll call on the forecourt!" Captain McKnight instructed, his loud voice putting an end to their whispers.

Evelyn fumbled for her bag and stood pressed against Dot as they slowly shuffled forward, edging closer to the door. It was too small a space for so many men and women, especially given the heat, but she had a feeling they'd forget all about their cramped traveling quarters once they were in their barracks.

She saw Vita then, moving through the train and getting to the door just ahead of her, and Evelyn caught the woman's smile and her gaze.

"After you," Vita said, waving her ahead, and Evelyn hurried forward, gulping as a gust of wind blew around her. It was warm but not hot, and she suddenly understood the true meaning of a breath of fresh air.

They were all divided up by gender and then into small groups, and as Evelyn looked around, it dawned on her just how many of them there were in the 807th Squadron. She attempted a rough head count and came up with at least ninety; no wonder she'd barely met half of them at Bowman Field. It had been such a blur of military-style training to prepare them for their new flight-based roles—much more challenging than her previous training to become a nurse—and she couldn't believe so many of them had made it through to the next stage.

She turned her attention back to their commanding officer as he stood in the center of their semicircle, his voice carrying easily to her at the back of the group.

"Camp Kilmer is a highly specialized training facility, set on fifteen hundred acres. There are many troops training here ahead of their deployment, and you will all be assigned a barracks where you will remain for the next week or so. You will find a post office, telephone center, chapel, library, and theater on-site, as well as a large hospital," he told them. "Over the next few days, you will be given final medical exams, and your gear will be checked. You may write letters home and mail them, or call your loved ones, but make no mistake about it—you must not reveal anything about your location or your orders. Are we clear?"

"Yes sir!" Evelyn replied, along with the rest of her squadron.

"Good. Then I suggest you try to get some sleep and rest while you're here. And remember . . . the soldiers you see around you? They could be the very men you're entrusted to airlift for medical treatment one day. Your deployment as members of the Medical Air Evacuation Transport Squadron is vital to the war effort, and we are truly grateful to have you all here with us completing your deployment training."

Evelyn nudged shoulders with Dot, her stomach doing cartwheels as she digested where they were and what they were about to embark upon. Even the fact that there were so many men at their camp was enough to make her nervous—so many soldiers training all around them, so unlike the life she was used to at home with her three sisters.

This is our last stop. Once they were cleared, their next trip would be by ship, and none of them had any idea where they would be sent. But one thing Evelyn did know: the captain was right. They were joining a new program that would airlift thousands of critically injured soldiers to hospitals, meaning fewer mothers would lose their sons and wives their husbands, and she'd never, ever been so proud of something in her life.

12

CHAPTER TWO

DOT

"Come on, you can do it."

Dot blew her hair off her face, using the back of her hand to wipe the dirt from her skin. Her entire body ached, her legs screaming in pain and barely able to carry her to the finish line. She hated to think what she looked like. Her grandmother had brought her up her entire life to believe that sweating was unladylike, which had led her to never exerting herself for fear of looking a hot mess. And now here she was with the stuff dripping off her forehead!

"I don't think I can," she panted, trying to keep her composure, using her sleeve to dab her upper lip. "I don't think I can do this." *This isn't what I signed up for! Why did I think this was a good idea?* But she knew why. She'd been trying to impress her fiancé's family by being chosen for such a prestigious deployment, although it hadn't helped her standing with them at all in the end. If they could see her now, she was almost certain they'd be horrified.

"It's the last one, Dot." Vita clasped her hand, tugging her along beside her, her smile far too bright for a training course so grueling. "I'm not finishing without you, and if we don't pass the physical training, we'll never receive our final orders."

Evelyn was ahead of them, already having crossed the finish line, her final training exercise done, but she was calling out encouragement, cheering them on. Dot groaned, forcing herself to keep moving forward, knowing if she so much as stumbled she'd never be able to drag herself upright again. What good would it do her to be sent home? That would be even more of an embarrassment than a broken engagement. Although she couldn't understand why they all needed such vigorous military-style training for a job that involved working inside a plane!

"You've passed the medical, you've been cleared to travel," Vita said, puffing beside her. "And we are going to have the time of our lives tonight, so you cannot give up!"

"Tonight?" Dot slowed, but Vita just tugged her along, insistent.

"Come on!"

Vita didn't elaborate, and Dot didn't have the energy to ask again as she focused on the finish line. Vita was right, there was no way she was going to have spent those torturous weeks in Kentucky in vain; she had to pass this final hurdle. And the only thing worse than giving up would be being last. She glanced behind her and saw two other red-faced nurses puffing away, their hands on their hips as they doubled over. She dug deep, brushing her hair off her face and squaring her shoulders as she marched forward. If everyone else could do it, then she needed to do it as well.

And then, like a miracle, she heard her name called by the soldier holding the clipboard at the finish line, and she collapsed to the ground, not caring who was watching. She'd made it. She'd actually made it! She was actually going to be part of the MAETS!

"We did it!" Evelyn was on her knees beside her, her eyes wide with excitement. "This is it, Dot. We're officially in the squadron!"

"And we're officially about to have the best night of our lives," Vita murmured.

"What . . ." Dot started to ask again, before they all turned as Captain McKnight cleared his throat and everyone fell silent.

"Congratulations on finishing your training," he said. "I'm pleased to let you know that you'll all be receiving a twelve-hour pass, starting at six p.m. tonight. But make no mistake, your barracks will be checked at six a.m. to ensure you're back on base, and no curfew exceptions will be made."

An excited murmur started to spread amongst their group, and Vita grinned and mouthed, "I told you so." Dot had no idea how she'd known already, but she didn't have long to wonder, because the captain was speaking again.

"Tomorrow night we'll be shipping out, so make the most of your recreation time. It could be the last pass you'll have in a long while."

Vita held out her hand and Dot pulled herself up, smiling as Vita's arm looped around her shoulders on one side and Evelyn's on the other. The last week had been amazing, with Vita and Evelyn both taking her under their wings when they'd been assigned to the same group. Just being with Vita had made Dot feel more confident, especially given the attention they were receiving as a group. There wasn't a soldier they passed who didn't want to stop and say hello to their beautiful friend, and she was hoping a little bit of Vita was going to rub off on her. And if she was more like Vita? She couldn't help but wonder if perhaps things might have worked out differently with Peter.

"Ladies, are you ready for an amazing night out?" Vita asked. "I'm thinking we start with drinks and then dinner, and then we can head to—"

"Honestly, I'm not much of a drinker," Dot interrupted. "We could always just have a quiet dinner and then come back for an early night?" She cringed, hating how pathetic she sounded. But going out with the girls might lead to questions, and the last thing she wanted was to be asked about her personal life. She instinctively touched the ring at her throat, knowing she needed to take it off

15

if she didn't want to field questions about her engagement. She'd always found comfort in the ring's weight, the feel of it against her skin, although lately she'd started to wonder if she was stupid to wear it at all anymore. It was just another way of holding on to the past.

One thing's for sure, I'm not telling these amazing girls that I was jilted the night before I left for Kentucky. It was embarrassing enough that Peter's entire family knew how easily he'd cast her aside, let alone anyone she worked with. She blinked away tears, hating the way he'd made her feel—that she wasn't good enough for him, that it was her fault he'd ended things with her.

"No drinking?" Vita laughed so loudly she snorted, which made Evelyn start to giggle beside her.

"I just mean that we all need a good sleep, that's all."

"Over my dead body you'll be coming back to base to sleep, Dot," Vita said. "You're not coming back here until five minutes to six. In the *morning*."

Dot hesitated, her nerves slowly starting to fade as she watched Vita. A night out in New York would be exciting, she supposed, and it wasn't like she *had* to tell them her engagement was over. Would it be so bad for them to believe she was still betrothed? She nervously wrung her hands together. They'd all made such a fuss over her diamond ring, and if she told them the truth now? She shuddered just thinking about the look on Vita's face if she found out Dot had been lying.

"It'll be fun, Dot," Evelyn said, leaning around Vita. "What do you say? The three of us, out on the town?"

Dot hesitated, but Evelyn looked so hopeful and Vita *was* very persuasive. And besides, it wasn't every night she had the chance to explore a city like New York.

"Well . . ."

"Come on, Dot! We have a couple of hours to rest and get ready before we get our passes. Please say you'll come," Vita begged.

"Of course I'll come," she finally relented, smiling back at her friends despite her nerves.

"Yay!" Vita took her hands and twirled her around, much to the amusement of the soldiers passing by. And then they all three linked arms, Vita in the middle, and Dot wondered why she'd ever thought to say no. "This is going to be the best night of our lives, ladies, just you wait and see."

Vita was good for her, a breath of fresh air like no other, and if she was going to have a night out with anyone, why wouldn't she want that person to be Vita?

Evelyn caught her eye and winked, and Dot found herself laughing, despite her insecurities. If these fun, vivacious women wanted to be friends with her, then why shouldn't she at least try to let her hair down a little? She had no idea why they'd befriended her, but it wouldn't be the worst thing in the world to relax and have some fun.

If only you could see me now, Peter. I'll show you exactly what I'm capable of, just you wait and see.

———— ◦⌇◦ ————

"Are you ready?" Dot could see Evelyn standing behind her in the small mirror as she finished her lipstick, and she moved to the side so they could share.

"Almost," she replied, smacking her red lips together and smiling at her reflection. Despite feeling too tired earlier to do anything, she was full of nervous energy now, and she fluffed her hair one last time before turning away to find her purse, hoping she looked fashionable enough.

"Let's go, girls!" came a call from the door, and there was Vita, banging on the timber as she leaned into the doorframe.

Dot sighed, taking in Vita's long legs and perfectly styled hair. Vita was model-beautiful, and although Dot felt very pretty all dolled up, she doubted anyone would so much as look at her over her gorgeous friend.

"How do we look?" Evelyn asked, doing a spin so that her full skirt flared out around her.

Dot joined in, doing the same, and they both laughed when Vita started clapping her hands.

"Stunning! Now come on, I don't want to waste a minute of our leave."

Vita marched out the door and spun in a half-circle before linking arms. "This is our one chance to party before we ship out, girls, so be prepared to have the time of your life tonight. We're dancing till dawn, until our feet won't hold us up a second longer."

"You still wishing you were catching up on sleep tonight instead of this?" Evelyn whispered, but not quietly enough to stop Vita from hearing.

"Sleep?" Vita snorted, before Dot had a chance to reply. "You can sleep when you're dead! This is going to be the best night of your life. Trust me!"

Dot brushed her hands over her dress, feeling how soft it was compared to the scratchy fabric of her uniform trousers or her wool jacket, their hair in soft curls instead of neatly pinned back. She would have preferred to have a coat over her shoulders, but she didn't have anything suitable—it was the only dress she'd packed, and she'd decided she'd rather be cold than drab. And with Vita and Evelyn beside her, she could see she'd made the right decision.

"Come on, it's time to kick up those heels and find some fellas to dance with!" Vita announced, and Dot found herself immediately caught up in Vita's enthusiasm. "Although, make no mistake, I'll be claiming the best-looking one for myself!"

"This is all I've ever wanted," Evelyn said, her tone wistful. "I've never just been a girl out on the town with friends, with nothing to worry about except for making curfew. Thanks for organizing tonight, Vita."

Dot wanted to ask more, but before she could, Vita had her fingers between her lips and had let out the loudest whistle she'd ever heard. She almost died, it was so embarrassing—but it worked, because the next thing a car headed in their direction and slowly ground to a halt, sending out a plume of dust that made Dot cough. She'd have never done something so unladylike, but it seemed that Vita could get away with anything and still seem amazing.

"Come on, girls, let's go!"

It seemed that, thanks to Vita, they now had transportation.

New York City, here we come.

CHAPTER THREE

VITA

"Wasn't that just the best cheesecake you've ever eaten?" Vita asked as they tumbled out of the restaurant door to look for a taxi. She looked back at Reuben's Restaurant, pleased she'd been able to take her friends there. She'd read months ago that they had the best cheesecake in New York, when she was lying on her bed and dreaming of being anywhere but home, and she'd vowed to visit if she ever found herself in the city. She twirled around in a circle on the sidewalk, feeling like a little girl in a candy store. Being away from home, away from her parents and their expectations of her—she'd never felt so free.

It's been worth it, she thought, smiling. The pain and tears, the threats of disownment from her mother, it had all been worth it in the end.

"Where to now?" Evelyn asked.

Vita let out a loud whistle again, laughing at the mortified look on Dot's face. "You might hate it, but it works. Look who's stopping for us!"

A taxi pulled up and she hurried down the pavement, opening the back door for her friends and then slipping in beside them.

"Where to, ladies?" the taxi driver asked, his eyes meeting hers in the rearview mirror.

"21 Club, please," she said, leaning back in the seat, her hand splayed on her stomach from eating too much.

"How do you know all the best places to go, anyway?" Dot asked.

"Because before I was a nurse, my entire life revolved around my *social* life," Vita said, surprised at how easily she'd spoken about her past. She'd decided to keep her upbringing to herself when she'd entered the MAETS training program, but something about being with Dot and Evelyn had made her let her guard down. "Knowing how to have a good time is what I know best."

It only took minutes to reach their destination, the taxi pulling up to the curb and letting them out almost adjacent to the iron gates that marked the entrance of 21 Club. Vita went ahead, smiling as the door was opened for them, the music from the live band washing over her body the moment they were inside.

"Come on, let's go get a drink!" she called back, grinning at the looks on both women's faces, their eyes wide as they all shimmied over to the bar.

"What are we drinking, girls?" Vita asked, leaning against the bar as she looked over at them.

"Ah, I don't really drink alcohol," Dot said, and Vita caught her looking nervously in Evelyn's direction. She had no idea why Dot was so anxious about everything; she'd seen Dot's hands physically shaking earlier in the day, so she'd decided to make it her personal mission to make her relax and have some fun.

"You'll be fine. Come on, just one glass? You're safe here with us," Vita promised.

"How about champagne then?" Dot asked, with a nervous-looking shrug.

"Champagne it is!" Vita announced, clapping her hands together.

Before Vita even had a chance to order, let alone pay, a handsome soldier in uniform leaned between them. She stepped back, winking at Evelyn before turning her attention to the man.

"Let me buy these, ladies," he said.

"Well, aren't you a gentleman," Vita said with a grin. "But we're just fine paying for our own drinks, thanks."

He laughed, but didn't seem to mind her rebuff. She probably should have just let him pay, but she was enjoying her little surge of independence, a thrill running down her spine as she leaned forward to order their champagne herself.

Vita passed the glasses to her friends, her first sip sending an easy kind of feeling through her as her friends chatted. She was excited about shipping out, getting further away from everything she wanted to leave behind, but she was also happy simply to be away from base for the night.

"Would you like to dance?"

Vita looked up, locking eyes with a man in an Air Force uniform, his thick blond hair brushed back off his face and his piercing blue gaze almost impossible to avoid. She grinned. He was a pilot, and she sure was a sucker for a handsome pilot.

"You asking me, or one of my friends?" Vita asked, knowing full well he was asking her, but glancing over her shoulder anyhow.

But he wasn't put off. She was waiting for his cheeks to stain a dark pink or his words to come out in a nervous stutter, but to her surprise he just leaned in a little closer.

"I'm asking you, beautiful."

Vita fanned at her face, as if she couldn't believe it.

"Sorry, but I'm kind of busy here," she said. "Maybe you could come ask me again later, with some other fellas who can dance with my friends."

He shrugged, as if to say it was her loss, but she had a feeling he'd be coming back sooner or later. And if he didn't? She glanced around the room. There were plenty of handsome men for her to dance the night away with, even if he was the most handsome one.

"The poor fella, he looks heartbroken!" Evelyn cried when he walked away. "You could have given him one spin around the dance floor, Vita."

"Oh, I'll give him a spin, don't you worry. I just like to play hard to get."

"Vita, that's terrible! You should have just said yes," Dot said.

"You wait, he'll be back. Besides, I'm here to have fun with you girls, not leave you for a man straight away."

The words had barely passed her lips when he returned, this time with two other pilots. Vita laughed, shaking her head as he walked closer with his hand outstretched. She had to give it to him; he wasn't easy to turn down.

"I'm Bobby," he said, his fingers closing around hers when she lifted her hand. "And I believe this dance is mine?"

"Vita," she replied, looking back at her friends to make sure they were alright before letting him lead her away. They both gave her a thumbs-up, smiling shyly at his friends, and Vita let Bobby pull her gently into his arms, the song conveniently turning slow the moment they joined the other couples on the dance floor.

"You know, I've seen you before. You're with the 807th Squadron, aren't you?"

She nodded. "I am. And you're . . ."

"One of your pilots," he said with a grin. "Have you heard we're shipping out tomorrow?"

"Any idea where?" she asked, tipping her head back a little to study his face.

"They like to keep us all in the dark about these things, in case you haven't noticed. But . . ." He leaned in closer and she found herself holding her breath, waiting for him to tell her something, thinking that he must have secret information to share. His breath was warm against her cheek, his hand flat to her back as he pulled her into his chest a little, before he whispered into her ear: "What will be, will be."

"Ugh!" she groaned, pushing him away slightly in annoyance, only to be caught by his hands and tugged back closer again.

"What?" he asked, ever so innocently.

She slapped at his chest. "I thought you were going to share some top-secret information with me!"

"Darling, I have no clue where we're going. They don't tell pilots anything, either. But one thing I can tell you?"

She stared up at him, not sure whether he was teasing her or being serious.

"What is it?"

"That this could be our last night of fun in a long while, so we need to make the most of it," he whispered into her ear.

Bobby started to move them slowly around the dance floor then, and Vita found herself leaning closer to him despite his teasing, her head finding its way to his shoulder as his arms encircled her. He was right, they did need to make the most of the night, and there was nothing wrong with being in the arms of a handsome man, for one song at least. He smelled nice too, his cologne just strong enough to notice, and she felt an unfamiliar tremor run through her as his warm hands moved against her back.

Tears unexpectedly filled her eyes as she wondered if her brother had had a night like this before he'd shipped out. Or had the army been in such a hurry to send them off that he'd never even had the chance to dance?

The song changed, the music more upbeat now, and as Vita stepped back to rejoin her friends, blinking away her tears, Bobby's fingers found hers.

"Where exactly do you think you're going?" he asked, raising an eyebrow as he held up his hand to spin her. "Surely you'll give a guy one more dance?"

"One more then," she said with a smile, remembering her promise to her brother, remembering how she'd vowed to live every day with enough enthusiasm for the both of them. He'd have been the one encouraging her, pushing her forward and telling her to have the night of her life, just like he'd been the one to encourage her to become a nurse in the first place, when it had only been a whisper of an idea.

She saw both Evelyn and Dot dancing nearby, both still smiling from ear to ear. "You know what? I want to dance for so long I can't feel my toes."

His mouth turned into a wide smile and he winked at her. "That can most *definitely* be arranged."

Vita tipped her head back and laughed, as he suddenly twirled her before pulling her straight back in with a gentle thud to his chest, his eyes catching hers in the longest of holds before he twirled her away from him all over again. Her breath was ragged as they moved from song to song, her legs starting to burn as they danced the night away, lost in the music around them and the band's upbeat tunes, forgetting about everything else.

This is what being with a man is supposed to feel like. At home, her mother had always been insistent about choosing suitable young men for her to be interested in, and Vita hadn't been drawn to any of them. But Bobby? He was the type of guy who was interested in fun, someone who wanted to party the night away before their deployment and who'd probably be dancing with a different nurse the moment she rejoined her friends. Bobby was exactly the kind of distraction she needed—he looked like he'd be even less interested in something serious than she was.

Just as her hair started to stick to her neck, her face hot, the band announced they were taking a break, and she found herself standing in front of Bobby, her breath ragged, as the other couples made their way off the dance floor. He held out his arm, and she took it without hesitation.

"For a girl who didn't want to dance with me . . ."

She laughed. "Trust me, I did want to dance."

"Well, you could have fooled me."

Vita waved to Evelyn when she saw her, and then Dot, both of them looking flushed and happy as they made their way toward the bar.

"Can I buy you a drink?" Bobby asked, moving in front of her, his smile somehow twinkling all the way to his eyes.

"How about you come find me later, if your dance card isn't full?" she said, blowing him a kiss. She liked him, but she wasn't about to spend her night with one man when she only had such a short time to enjoy herself.

He took her hand and lifted it, pressing a slow kiss to her skin, before walking backward still smiling at her. Vita stifled her own smile as Evelyn and Dot came rushing over to her.

"Oh my God, he's gorgeous!" Evelyn exclaimed.

"Gosh, he certainly seems to like you," Dot said. "Were you dancing with him for *all* those songs?"

"Well, we're not all engaged to be married, are we? I can dance with whomever I like!"

Dot looked crestfallen at her retort, which made Vita feel terrible. "Let me get us all more drinks." She grabbed Evelyn's hand, forcibly turning her friend away from Bobby's retreating figure, and marched them back toward the bar. "We have champagne to drink, ladies. Glass after delicious glass of champagne."

"Honestly, I think I've had enough," Dot protested as they neared the bar. "I was already feeling giddy before that dance."

"Nonsense, we've only just started," Vita said, pushing past some soldiers to order their drinks. She glanced over her shoulder at her friends. "These drinks are on me."

It would have been so easy to spend the night dancing and chatting with Bobby, but she'd never had close friends before, and

26

right now making friends was far more important to her than a few hours of fun with a man. When she'd refused to marry the man her mother had lined up for her, her social life had imploded. All those girls she'd thought had been her friends since childhood? They weren't exactly impressed with her decision to turn her back on her perfect little society life, or perhaps their mothers wanted them to have nothing else to do with her. And when she'd left home to start her nursing training? She may as well have run away and joined the circus for all the feathers she'd ruffled. But now, she felt like she'd found the people she was supposed to be with; the way Evelyn had befriended her when they'd arrived at Camp Kilmer, her smiles so warm and her conversation so easy—she was the type of friend Vita had always wanted and never had. And Dot had been just as friendly, in her own, shy way. The one thing they had in common was that they seemed to like Vita for who she was, not for who her family was or the money she'd grown up with. To them, she was just Vita, and it was the first time in her life she'd had that.

When she finally had their drinks, she passed them back to the girls and they made their way to a table that had just been vacated, sitting down and resting their weary feet.

"You know, that pilot you were dancing with looks very familiar," Dot said. "Has he been on base with us?"

Vita nodded. "He's actually going to be flying with us. His name's Bobby."

"Bobby the gorgeous," Evelyn sighed, making them all laugh. "My tongue would be in knots if he asked me to dance!"

"I propose a toast to adventure," Vita said, grinning at Evelyn as she held her glass up high so they could all clink theirs together. "We've got the adventure of a lifetime ahead of us, girls, and I just know we're going to be great friends. I don't know about you, but I can't wait to receive our orders tomorrow."

"To adventure," Evelyn echoed at the same time as Dot, and Vita bumped shoulders with her as they downed their drinks.

"This place is incredible," Dot said as they all sat and looked around. "I don't think I've ever been anywhere quite so fancy."

"It was actually the most famous prohibition bar in its day, and they still have the camouflaged doors and revolving bars here that they put in to fool the authorities," Vita told them, leaning in. "The secret wine cellar is actually next door, so the proprietors could swear hand on heart that there was no alcohol on the premises."

She was about to keep talking when a hand cupped her shoulder from behind. She glanced at Evelyn, who nodded, seeming to confirm that it was Bobby.

"You ready for that second dance yet?" he asked as he leaned down and whispered into her ear.

She saw the way he winked at her friends, but she wasn't going to fall for his charms that easily. She had a feeling that was what he was used to.

"How about you pull up a chair and join us for a drink instead?" she asked.

Vita hadn't expected him to sit, but the next thing he was pulling up a chair and waving his friends over, turning their little group into a fun party of eight. It was exactly the kind of night she'd hoped for, meeting new people and feeling like she didn't have a care in the world, for a few hours at least.

"I can't stop thinking about tomorrow," Dot moaned, wringing her hands together in her lap. "Where we're going, what it will be like. Does anyone know *anything*?"

"If you're that worried, then you obviously haven't had enough to drink," Vita replied, holding up her glass again and gesturing for them to do the same. "Unless you'd actually rather be sitting at home instead of being here?"

Dot shook her head. "Of course not."

Vita grinned and nudged Dot's glass closer to her, even though she did wonder if Dot *would* actually prefer to be at home than out partying. She couldn't quite make her out—whether she was just shy or perhaps just insecure about being outside her comfort zone. Or maybe she just didn't want to be out on the town when she was engaged to be married. "To whatever tomorrow brings," Vita toasted, holding her own glass high and winking at Dot. Whatever Dot's reasons for being unsure, Vita was determined to bring out her friend's wild side.

"To tomorrow," everyone repeated, including Bobby, who lifted his beer and clinked glasses with them.

"We have eight hours left now, girls, and we're going to make the most of every minute," Vita told them, leaning toward Evelyn and Dot. "And wherever we end up, wherever they send us and whatever happens, we have to promise to look out for one another. If we have each other, we'll be fine."

"So long as we don't miss curfew tonight," Dot cautioned.

"Find this girl a fella to dance with, would you?" she asked Bobby. "She's spending far too much time worrying when she could be having fun."

They all laughed, and when Bobby held his hand out to Vita, she went to take it. *What's the harm in one more dance?*

"Gotcha!" he said, laughing as he pulled his hand away before she could clasp it, as if it were the funniest thing in the world to trick her like that.

Vita rolled her eyes, leaning forward to take it the next time he offered. "Do that again and I'll find someone else to dance with."

This time he took her hand in his, grinning from ear to ear, but his little antics only solidified her thoughts that he was most definitely a one-night thing. She only hoped he was more mature when he was in charge of flying a plane.

CHAPTER FOUR

EVELYN

"Evelyn, are you alright?" Dot asked, her hand covering the small of Evelyn's back and moving in comforting circles.

Evelyn groaned, leaning deeper into the ship's railings as she battled waves of nausea. "I think I had too much champagne last night."

"Don't talk to me about champagne," Dot muttered. "Or the fact that I stayed in a bar until five in the morning, either!"

"Girls, you're missing the band, they're playing on the pier." Vita leaned beside Evelyn as she joined them, peering down at her. "What's wrong? You do look a little unwell."

"It's all your fault," Evelyn said, hauling herself upright and closing her eyes, thankful the sun was only just beginning to rise. "I blame it all on you."

"We both blame it on you!" Dot joined in.

Vita just laughed at them. Evelyn felt like death, her eyes burning and her head pounding, not to mention her swirling stomach, but somehow Vita appeared completely unaffected by it all. At least Dot had the decency to look green.

Vita had hauled them back to their barracks the night before, despite how unsteady they'd been on their feet, at two minutes to 6 a.m., just in the nick of time, and although she'd felt great during the evening, Evelyn would have done anything to turn back the clock now they were on board. The day had been almost unbearable, going through the arduous steps of rechecking their gear and working through checklists, and then having a few hours of precious sleep before they were summoned from their beds at midnight. And then it had been hauling their barracks bags, with their musette bags and gas masks slung over their shoulders, for a mile to meet their train, which hadn't departed for some time, followed by the ferry ride they were on now, and the closer they got to the pier, the louder the brass band became, which wasn't conducive to helping her pounding head.

As the ferry finally stopped moving completely, Evelyn felt her stomach start to settle somewhat, and it eased almost completely as they stepped off and were shepherded directly toward the gangplank of an enormous ship that she guessed would be taking them all the way to their final destination.

"Listen up, the 807th!"

Evelyn and the rest of the squadron came to a halt, as Red Cross volunteers darted between them giving out hot cups of black, tar-like coffee and warm donuts. She readily accepted both, the donut just what her stomach needed, washing it down with the piping-hot coffee, her bag dropped at her feet.

"You'll all be boarding the *Santa Elena* presently," Captain McKnight told them. "You'll be travelling with a few thousand troops, so boarding will continue for another twenty-four hours, give or take. It's going to be tight; she was formerly a cruise ship built for a few hundred, not thousands, so as such, space is limited. Nurses and doctors, you'll be in the staterooms; medics, you'll be bunking in the ship's holds. And before you think you're hard done by, keep in mind that enlisted soldiers are two to a bed, and will have to take turns sleeping."

Evelyn digested the news, her donut suddenly dry in her mouth as she stared up at the enormous ship looming in front of them. She chewed, lifting the coffee cup to try to wash it down.

This is it. Once we step onto that gangplank, we'll be leaving America behind for months. She blinked back tears, the thought of not seeing her sisters for so long making her lose her appetite completely. Some days she was so determined to do what she'd set out to accomplish, and others, like right now . . . She quickly wiped at her cheeks with the back of her hand. *I love you, girls. I love you, Dad.* What she wouldn't do to be curled up with her sisters listening to the wireless or wrapping little Katie in her arms.

"Has anyone heard where we're going yet?" Vita whispered beside her, not seeming to notice her tears. "I saw Bobby when we boarded the train last night and they were still clueless, too. Wouldn't you think they'd at least tell the pilots?"

Evelyn had no idea either, but as she looked at the other ships in the harbor and saw the Statue of Liberty coming into sight as the fog lifted, she knew that wherever they were going, it was a long, long way from home. Vita was still talking, but Evelyn couldn't hear her, her mind still drifting back to her sisters and wondering if she'd done the right thing in leaving them.

"Do you ever wonder how long it'll be until we see all this again? Until we're home?" Evelyn asked.

She looked back over her shoulder, drinking in the scene of New York stretching out around her. The Red Cross ladies with smiles as big as could be; the troops starting to arrive, duffel bags sprawled at their feet; and the band winding into another song. There were no families saying goodbye here, no sweethearts crying into shoulders; they must have been left behind on train station platforms, just like her family had been so many weeks ago. Everyone here, other than the volunteers on the pier, was going to be piling onto the same ship she was, jammed like sardines in a can.

"I don't have a lot to come home to, so I'm not so worried about that," Dot said quietly.

"What do you mean? What about after the war, when your fiancé is home?" Vita asked.

"Of course. I just, well . . ." Dot's voice trailed off.

"If you're talking about your family, then I understand," Vita said with a groan. "I just about caused another war when I left home, so if you don't want to talk about family, then I get it."

"My mother and father actually died, when I was young," Dot murmured, her eyes brimming with tears. "I was just a little girl when I found out they'd drowned. Their car was hit by a truck and they ended up in the lake. I still remember my grandfather scooping me up in his arms, and my grandmother whispering to me and making me cup after cup of hot cocoa, telling me I'd be fine because they would look after me."

Evelyn wiped away her own tears. "My mother died too, a few years ago now. The pain never seems to get any easier, does it?"

Vita was silent, but her gaze was warm, compassionate, as she watched them.

Evelyn heard Vita start to talk, but she turned away, needing a moment, needing to put her memories in the little compartment in her mind where she hid them. It hurt too much to talk about what she'd lost, or what she'd left behind.

"Evelyn?" Dot's hand was warm in hers, clasping her palm. "Evelyn, come on, we need to move up."

She turned, squeezing Dot's hand before taking her first, shaky step up the gangplank after her. She'd already decided how much she liked Dot, but having that shared sense of loss suddenly made her feel even closer to her new friend.

"Just think of all the men we're going to save," Vita said, her voice quieter than usual as she stood behind them. "Whenever I think I can't do it, I just remember what it's all been for. We're doing something that matters, something real, and nothing is more important than that." She cleared her throat. "I lost my older brother, the only member of my family I've ever loved with all my heart, and I keep thinking that if I can help even one brother get home, one husband, one son . . ." Vita's voice trailed off, then cracked as she dropped to a whisper. "Then it's worth it. It's worth *everything*."

Evelyn blinked away tears as she followed her friends, realizing just how much they'd all lost, what they'd all had to leave behind to even make what they were doing possible.

Vita was right, and that's what she had to keep reminding herself: their job was to do everything they could to save as many lives as possible; to send as many men home to their families as they could. They all had experience as nurses, but this was something else entirely, something so few nurses had been accepted to be part of.

Now all Evelyn had to do was somehow stop fretting about her family, or else she'd be no use to anyone. She only hoped the words she'd whispered to her sisters as she'd left them at the train station were true.

"Evie!" Katie cried, her voice cutting through the air as Evelyn walked, the smoke from the steam engine curling in the air, suffocating the station.

She turned, even though she knew she shouldn't. But hearing that little voice, a voice that had called her name ever since they'd lost their mother; it tugged at a heartstring that Evelyn couldn't ignore.

"Evie!" The little body came hurtling toward her, escaping from their father's grip and leaving him on his knees as he watched his youngest daughter run to his oldest.

"Katie, you know I have to go. It's time," Evelyn whispered, but even as she said the words, she felt the pull back to her family, drawing her into the familiar fold of all she'd ever known.

"Evie, you can't leave me. Please don't leave me," Katie begged.

Evelyn held Katie at arm's length, dropping to her knees so she could look her in the eyes; eyes that were filled with tears, brimming to the point of overflowing. She gently removed her sister's thumb from between her lips, feeling more mother than sister to her, which made what she was about to do so much harder than it should have been.

"Katie, I love you so much, but you're going to be fine without me," she said, fighting her own tears now. "You and the girls are going to look after Dad, and I'm going to help all those soldiers. Our men need nurses, and it won't be forever."

"But I need you," Katie whispered.

Evelyn sighed, drawing her in for one last hug, inhaling the smell of her hair, committing her warm little body and the way it folded into her to memory. It would have been so easy to choose her sisters, to believe that they couldn't survive without her.

"I'll be home in no time, pumpkin," she said, using the nickname their father had always used for Katie before their mother had passed. "And I'll be so exhausted from all the men I've nursed, it'll be you tucking me into bed each night and singing me to sleep."

Katie hugged her even tighter.

"This is not like Mama," Evelyn whispered into her ear. "You'll be seeing me again, I promise."

"Pinky promise?" Katie murmured, holding up her little finger.

Evelyn used her own pinky to clasp her sister's, solemnly swearing, "I promise," in reply. "I love you," she whispered, dropping one final kiss onto Katie's hair as she rose, collecting her bags from where she'd dropped them and turning before she changed her mind. She didn't look back at her father, or turn to see which of her other sisters were sobbing; she just kept on walking until she was on the train.

That's when her own tears began, like raindrops silently falling down her cheeks all the way to her chin. And if the doors of the train hadn't shut, the wheels slowly starting to turn, she would have fled straight back down those steps to scoop Katie up and never have thought about leaving home again.

PART TWO

CHAPTER FIVE

SICILY, OCTOBER 1943

EVELYN

The sky was alive with activity, and as Evelyn lifted her hand to shield her eyes from the bright sunshine, she couldn't hide her smile. Even with her uniform clinging to her damp skin and the heat so intense she could barely breathe, the sight of all those planes coming in just to see them was truly something else.

"Ladies, keep moving!" came a call from up ahead, and Evelyn immediately saw a furious-looking general marching toward them. "I want you all assembled inside promptly. And whatever you do, do not wave or give any form of encouragement to those pilots!"

It was impossible to hurry along without keeping an eye on the sky though, with some of the pilots flying so low she could actually see their smiles. One gave her a thumbs-up and a big grin, and she responded with a shy wave despite the warning they'd received, blushing furiously as she ducked her head and hurried along with the others. Half the time she felt much older than her years, after so long looking after her family, forgoing dances and fun for chores and childcare. But when it came to men? She put her palms to her flaming cheeks. She was woefully naive about the opposite sex, leaving her feeling more child than grown woman.

"Apparently they all defied orders so they could come and take a look at us," Vita whispered in her ear, linking their arms as they walked toward a non-descript gray building. "Seems like word traveled fast about all the nurses arriving from Bizerte."

Evelyn glanced at her. "You're serious? They actually flew here just to see us?"

"How many American women do you think pass through here?" a medic ahead of them called out, obviously having overheard their conversation. "You'll be the highlight of their week, if not their year."

Evelyn opened her mouth to respond, but promptly shut it when Vita let go of her to blow kisses to the next pilot circling over them, waving dramatically to him. Evelyn groaned; Vita was a lot of fun, but sometimes she was just outright embarrassing—more overexcited puppy than level-headed nurse.

"Ladies!" a voice boomed, and Evelyn dragged Vita along with her, not wanting to get in trouble within minutes of arriving. It had been a long, slow journey from their desert camp in Bizerte, and she was ready to collapse.

As they paused outside, waiting for the rest of the group to enter the building, Evelyn took one last look at the sky. It was filled with circling P-47 Thunderbolts, P-38 Lightnings and C-47 Skytrains, and knowing the show was all for them made her heart beat just that little bit faster. Were they really such a novelty? She'd seen the excitement from the British soldiers when they'd arrived at their previous station, all so thrilled to see a real-life American girl, but to defy orders and fly planes just to catch a glimpse of them? It was almost impossible to believe.

The general who'd hurried them along earlier was standing at the front of the room now, stroking his bushy mustache as he waited for them to assemble. He looked much more relaxed now they were inside the building, and Evelyn took a moment to look around her, taking in the bland interior and cold gray walls. She had no idea what she'd expected, but it couldn't have been more different than their temporary quarters at their previous camp, where they'd been stationed after their ship had docked. There, they'd sweltered under canvas and had an outdoor latrine dug for them, whereas this seemed so much more permanent.

"Welcome to the 807th MAET Squadron," he boomed, his voice carrying easily to the back of the room, where Evelyn stood. "We are very pleased to have you here in Catania! Although I know it's been a long journey, you will be assigned your flight teams today before being billeted to your new accommodations. Tomorrow, many of you will have your first assignments, and as such you'll be expected to report for duty at daybreak. I suggest you all make the most of the next twelve hours and take the chance to have a well-deserved rest."

Evelyn glanced at Vita and saw her attention was focused behind them, out the door, but Dot was hanging on the general's every word, always eager to please. She was anxiously holding on to her necklace, something Evelyn had often noticed she did when she was nervous.

"Your new flight team will consist of one nurse and one medic, with a flight surgeon overseeing you," the general continued. "As the registered nurse on board, you will hold primary responsibility for the welfare of all patients, and you will be expected to transport up to twenty-four patients on each flight. Whatever medical attention those troops need will be up to you, and largely you alone, to administer. Their fate is in your hands, from when you collect them until you safely deposit them at the closest hospital."

Evelyn nodded along with the other nurses, doing her best to focus even though her attention was waning. They'd spent weeks training for their new posts, at Bowman Field Base and then at

Camp Kilmer, so none of this was news to them; they were all very much aware of their responsibilities and what their job entailed.

"Following the successful delivery of your patients to the closest hospital, you will be expected to find your way back to base here on a transport plane, and as such it's important you always pack your overnight bag and take it with you. You will need to be resourceful to ensure your prompt return at all times, but there may be instances where you're required to remain in place for a night or even two. Are there any questions?"

The room was silent, other than the shuffle of tired feet and the shifting of bags on shoulders.

"Since there are no questions, please wait for further instructions from your squadron leader. The work you're doing here is vital to our Allied soldiers, so on behalf of the United States Army, I'd like to sincerely thank you for your service. I have been told by our president himself that with this new initiative we may well save thousands of men who would otherwise not survive their injuries, so do not for a moment underestimate your contribution to the war effort."

A shiver ran through Evelyn as she looked at the men and women around her. Up until today, it had all been theory and practice, and the odd bandaging of minor wounds on the beach at Bizerte, but now it was real. Come morning, she would likely be boarding a plane and taking charge of her first flight-load of injured soldiers, and the responsibility that came with it was a sudden weight on her shoulders. She'd nursed previously, before her flight training in Kentucky had commenced, but her local hospital hadn't exactly prepared her for war.

"I hope we're billeted somewhere better than this old place," Vita muttered as she pushed slightly ahead of Evelyn. "It's like a mental asylum in here. Just looking at the walls makes me shiver."

Evelyn resisted the urge to nudge straight back past Vita, used to reprimanding her little sisters for not being patient or waiting their turn, but instead she held her tongue, *and* her toes.

"It was actually a military school prior to this, not an asylum," Dot said, her voice so low that Evelyn was surprised Vita even heard her. "Although more recently it housed German soldiers."

"If only these walls could talk then, huh?" Vita said, grinning as she edged her way past a handful of medics to get even closer to the front.

"She's something else, isn't she?" Evelyn muttered. "I think she's even more confident here than she was on home soil."

Dot gave her a shy smile. "I'd give anything for even a dollop of that confidence though, wouldn't you?"

They both laughed and waited their turn, stepping forward every few minutes, the air becoming more and more stale by the second—a combination of the number of people crammed in one room and the temperature itself. It was like being back in Kentucky all over again.

A few minutes later, she reached the front of the line and ran her eyes over the pages of paper, looking for her name. *Evelyn Ravenswood.* She was paired with a medic named Tom, who she vaguely thought was a blond with a Southern accent, but couldn't be sure. Her flight surgeon was Nicholas Alexander, and she committed both names to memory before stepping away and following the slow-moving crowd back outside.

A light breeze caught her skin and she raised her face skyward, enjoying the relief, closing her weary eyes for a moment. She felt like they were burning in their sockets, so tired and itchy from the sand and far too many hours of being open when all they wanted to do was slide shut.

"Come on," Vita whispered in her ear. "You can stare at the sky and dream of flyboys later."

Evelyn laughed, wishing she had the energy to tell Vita that she most certainly wasn't daydreaming about boys, but instead she simply trailed after her and hauled herself back into the army truck.

———— ⚬⚬⚬ ————

An hour later, Evelyn spun around in amazement, her jaw almost sliding to the floor as she stared out an enormous window. *This is something else.*

"I thought we were being treated well when we had our tent and cots at our last camp, but this—*this* . . ."

"Is the most beautiful view I've ever seen," Dot finished for her.

They were standing shoulder to shoulder, bags dropped at their feet, and drinking in the most incredible water view Evelyn could have ever imagined. Nothing had prepared her for the beauty of the Mediterranean, the water so blue and vivid it was almost hard to believe it hadn't been created by an artist's brush. She couldn't have dragged her eyes away if she'd wanted to.

"I could almost believe the world wasn't at war, standing here," Evelyn said with a sigh, turning as she heard Vita behind them. "This villa, the view, the sleepy feel of the little village as we drove through. It's like we've been whisked away from war and discovered a little slice of paradise just for us."

"While you two have been fawning over the view, I've chosen my bed," Vita said, sinking into a sofa by the window. "I dare say the rooms aren't as impressive as the outlook, but we'll be comfortable."

Evelyn wondered, not for the first time, just how posh Vita's home and life had been before she'd joined the MAETS, because *she* thought the villa was heavenly. She looked around, marveling at the fact they were so far from home, in a town as far removed from middle America as one could get. There had been times she'd wondered if she'd ever be able to leave home at all, to leave all her responsibilities and everything she knew behind, which made the experience now all the more surreal.

"How do you feel about your first flight tomorrow?" Dot asked as she joined Vita on the sofa.

Evelyn followed their lead, sinking into the soft leather and reaching down to remove her shoes. She wriggled her toes and sand sprinkled the floor, a reminder of what the earlier part of their journey had been like. Before they'd boarded the trucks from their last camp, they'd had to walk for the better part of three days, sometimes in ankle-deep sand while being attacked by biting flies, and now that she was idle, Evelyn's skin had started to itch all over again.

"Evelyn?"

"Sorry, what?" She looked up and saw her friends watching her.

"The inaugural flight tomorrow, how are you feeling about it?"

"Fine," she replied, not about to confide in anyone that she was so nervous her knees were in danger of knocking. "We've been training for this for months; we'll take to our jobs like ducks to water."

That made Vita laugh, but Dot looked like a ball of nerves, her slender arms wrapped tight around her body.

"Come on, let's crawl into our beds and get some sleep. I don't know about you two, but I could sleep for days." Evelyn stood and held out a hand to Dot, who grasped it and pulled herself up, giving Evelyn a warm smile as she righted herself.

"Is it just me, or do you have butterflies beating their little wings like crazy in your stomach too?" Dot asked.

"There's at least a hundred flying inside me right now," Evelyn whispered back. "Queen Bee might not have them, but I *definitely* do."

Vita laughed at them as she passed, her shoulders straight, her glossy chestnut hair somehow still in place. How was it even possible to look so good after the journey they'd had?

Evelyn picked up her shoes and her bag and crossed the cool tiles, and not for the first time she staved off thoughts of her sisters, wishing she could stop worrying about them for just one day.

They're old enough to look after themselves. They're going to be fine.

Only it didn't matter how many times she told herself that, it didn't stop the knot inside of her that said she should never have left them. She only hoped that once she was flying every day, she'd be so busy that she'd worry less about home and more about the men she was going to be charged with transporting.

Evelyn touched the locket she wore around her neck and lifted it to kiss the gold. She didn't need to look inside to see the tiny photo; she'd stared at it for so many hours it was committed to her memory forever.

You keep watch over us all, Mama. Keep us safe.

And as she blinked away the familiar brush of tears, she dropped the locket back against her skin and fell straight onto her narrow bed, her eyes falling shut before she even had a chance to change her clothes, let alone bathe away the dust that coated her skin.

CHAPTER SIX

VITA

Vita shut her eyes as the plane jolted unexpectedly, gripping her seat tightly as the plane shuddered and shivered mid-flight.

"First time on one of these?"

She was tempted to lie, but when she prized her eyes open and saw the warm, smiling face of the medic staring at her, she couldn't bring herself to do it. Not when she and Eddie were going to be working together in such close quarters for weeks, if not months.

"Yes," she admitted. "Unless you count the smaller planes we used for training."

"We'll be fine," he said with a grin. "Every ride gets a bit easier than the last."

"It's different than I imagined, that's all. I expected less shuddering and more smooth sailing I suppose."

They both laughed, and she slowly released her grip on the seat, taking a deep breath. "How many times have you flown before?" she asked. "You look so calm and collected." There was something about him that reminded her of her brother, his steady demeanor and the easy way he made conversation making her feel as if Andrew was somehow there.

She was waiting for him to answer when suddenly the loud, roaring sound of the engine that had filled her head since takeoff cut out entirely. She balked, looking around for a moment as she thought what a relief it was on her ears. Until she realized what the lack of sound meant, and she re-gripped her seat. Panic clawed at her throat as she fought the urge to scream.

"What's happening?" she gasped. "What . . ."

Eddie's face turned as white as a sheet, and if she hadn't been paralyzed with fear she'd have leapt up to sit beside him. She was well past the point of feigning confidence now, and his lack of speaking was making her even more terrified.

Suddenly Bobby yelled out from the cockpit, and she wished that she hadn't somehow ended up flying with him. "Hold tight, slight problem up here. I just gotta get the engine started again!"

The engine has stopped? Vita shut her eyes, trying to keep down her breakfast as she prayed that he was as capable of flying the damn aircraft as he was of dancing the jitterbug. Her food was threatening to come straight back up as she rocked quietly back and forth, and held on to her seat like her life depended on it. What on earth had she signed up for? They were supposed to be taking simple flights back and forth from base to evacuation point; she'd never once thought their equipment would fail! How did engines just stop working mid-flight?

We're going to die. Oh my lord, we're going to die!

Rrrrroar.

Oh! Thank God! Her heart leapt as the engine roared back into life, the loud, vibrating noise like music to her ears after the deadly, terrifying wall of silence.

"Hang in there," Eddie said, his voice carrying to her despite the roar, the color returning to his face. "We'll get there in one piece, don't you worry. These pilots know what they're doing. Trust me."

"Is this normal?" she whispered.

"Normal, no. But it does happen from time to time."

Her nerves were completely gone; she couldn't imagine how anyone could get used to something so terrifying! But Vita forced herself to nod and feigned confidence again, flashing a quick smile while still clinging tightly to her seat, and she didn't let go until they began their descent into Algiers, her legs wobbly as she tried to unwind them. She didn't even want to think about something like that happening ever again!

"Tell me, do you have a sweetheart waiting at home for you?" Eddie asked.

Vita looked up, staring at him. She'd been thinking how big brotherly he was, and he was thinking of her like that? "No. And before you—"

"This is my wife," he interrupted, taking a photo from his breast pocket and holding it up so she could see the pretty, dark-haired woman. "I miss her like crazy. You have anyone you miss like that?"

Vita ignored her burning cheeks, liking the way he'd interrupted her before she'd had time to say what she was going to say.

"My older brother," she said, surprised how easily the words came. "He died soon after his deployment. You actually remind me of him."

Eddie nodded. "How about we agree not to talk about what we left behind then? We can just talk about easy things to pass the time."

"Deal," she agreed, liking Eddie already even though she'd only known him a short time.

The plane finished its descent before they could talk more, the roar of the engine too loud to make conversation over, and as soon as they were stationary, she followed Eddie's lead and unbuckled herself, gathering up her things as quickly as she could. She'd never thought she'd be so happy to get out of an aircraft; she couldn't wait to feel solid ground beneath her feet.

"We'll be wheels up within the hour," Bobby called out from the cockpit. "The quicker we're back up again, the safer we are. Got it?"

Vita's eyes brushed over Bobby's as he looked back and her skin flushed, but she didn't give away just how well she knew him, or how traumatized she was from the engine failure. The last thing she needed was for him to have any idea of how rattled she was; it didn't exactly go with the Vita she'd presented to the world, or the Vita he'd danced all night with back in New York. And besides, her job was far too important to her to risk anything inappropriate; she wasn't doing anything that might have her sent home.

"Yes, Captain. We'll see you soon," she said brusquely.

Eddie grappled with the door, and soon they were out, sand billowing around them as they surveyed their surroundings. It reminded her very much of being at the base in Bizerte when they'd first arrived off the boat, only busier. Much, much busier.

"Wow," Vita muttered, staring at the enormous canvas tent ahead of them; as many ambulances were arriving as were leaving. "Nothing quite prepares you for reality, does it?"

"You can say that again," Eddie muttered, and they walked together, her matching his long stride into the campsite. "Stay focused when we walk in, and don't get lost in the pain of seeing so many men. It's easier when you just keep your mind on the job."

It was nice to have Eddie with her rather than working alone, especially when it was all so new to her. She smiled as she saw him waiting for her response, and she gave him a quick nod. That was another reason he reminded her of Andrew—he was always the first to make sure everyone else was okay before worrying about himself.

It seemed to take only minutes for everyone to hear of their arrival, and as she looked from bed to bed, injured and dying men as far as the eye could see, Vita's heart sank. Even if each team in their squadron airlifted twenty-four men every single day, it was only ever going to be a drop in a lake compared to the number of men who needed them.

Twenty-four men I'm going to save today, Mother, Vita thought bitterly. For all the arguments they'd had about her joining the MAETS as a nurse, for all the tears and threats, it suddenly dawned on her that even one planeload of men was worth it.

"Vita?"

She spun around, seeing Eddie's questioning gaze. "Sorry, I was lost in my own thoughts. It's quite something seeing all these men here."

"From the way they're looking at you, they think you're *quite something* too," a doctor said.

Vita grinned. "Well, anything I can do to brighten up a soldier's day."

She laughed along with the doctors and orderlies who had gathered, knowing she didn't need to play the part of the pretty girl who liked nothing more than to please men, but finding it too easy a role to slip back into. That was the girl her mother had wanted her to be, but she didn't need to be that person anymore. She'd fought hard for her freedom, and if she wanted to prove herself, she needed to remember that. All the men she met, all the soldiers she cared for, she wanted them to see her as the capable nurse she was, not as the pretty heiress.

"Here's the list of men you'll be transporting today," the same doctor said. "Some of them are fragile, but getting them out of here is their best chance at survival. You have no idea what this new initiative means to us all."

"Well, let's get them moving then, shall we?" Vita replied, swallowing the lump in her throat, the weight of what she was doing making it almost impossible not to feel emotional. "There's no time like the present."

Vita walked briskly back to the plane with her list, climbing on board and preparing for her patients. She took a breath, leaning against the cool steel frame for a moment as she took stock of the situation, not wanting anyone else to see her moment of self-doubt at what she was about to do. *You can do this.*

"This is just like your training, Vita," she mumbled to herself. Only it wasn't. Because nursing patients at home hadn't come with so much responsibility. These were men with no other hope, men who might otherwise die or face horrible amputations if they didn't safely airlift them. She ran her eyes over her supplies, mentally taking in the bandages and gauze, the vials of morphine and piles of blankets—all at her disposal if she needed them.

"How's it going back there?" Bobby called, still in the cockpit.

"There's more men than we can transport, that's how it's going," she called back brightly, belying her nerves and hoping he hadn't heard her muttering to herself. "But we'll be ready to take off again in no time."

She took a moment to drink it all in, finding it hard to believe that she was actually there, that she was finally putting her training to use. The plane was enormous, much bigger than anything they'd ever trained on, and she looked silently over the rows of bare, metal beds on each side, space for men to fit from the floor to the ceiling. It was basic but practical, and she could hardly believe that it would soon be full to overflowing with troops; troops who were in desperate need of medical care. She knew from what they'd been told at Camp Kilmer that the mortality rate for patients at mobile field hospitals was dire at best, which meant they truly were a lifeline for these soldiers. *A game changer*, that's what Captain McKnight had told them.

"Hey, Vita," Bobby called out.

She turned, listening to him as she counted her morphine vials again, mentally taking stock.

"Mmm-hmm," she murmured.

"Why don't you come up here and say a proper hello, while we're all alone?"

Vita bristled, furious that he'd even suggest something like that when she was about to open the plane to so many injured soldiers. But before she could berate him, there was a call from outside.

"Knock, knock."

She stuck her head out and saw the first passengers, on stretchers and being carried by orderlies, and she decided to deal with Bobby later. Eddie was right behind them, and between them they allocated each patient a space, ushering the orderlies carrying them inside and ensuring they were as comfortable as could be while they were transferred from the stretchers onto the hard, built-in beds on board, before carefully strapping them in. The temporary bunks were four beds high, covering almost every inch of wall space, and by the time they'd loaded all the patients there wasn't a bed spare.

Vita made notes on the manifest, focused on her work now and refusing to be upset by the sights in front of her. These men needed her to do her job, and that's exactly what she was going to do. Bobby might see her as just that fun party girl from New York, but if that's all he thought she was, then he'd sorely underestimated her.

She marched to the cockpit and cleared her throat once she was done. "I've double-checked the manifest and we're ready to go," she said, meeting his gaze when he looked up at her.

"Vita, about before . . ." he started.

"I'm good at my job, Bobby," she said, "and nothing and no one is going to jeopardize that, so don't you *ever* make a suggestion like that again. Are we clear?"

She turned on her heel before he could answer. Bobby had been fun for a night, but even a gorgeous Southern charmer wasn't going to distract her from what she was here to do. Or get away with treating her as anything but a capable nurse.

Vita settled herself into her seat, swapping glances with Eddie as the plane rumbled to life again. They were all under her charge on board, which meant if anything happened to any of their patients during the flight, it would be her responsibility, and it dawned on her that this was nothing like working in a hospital back home. It was one thing to know in theory what a soldier's wounds might look like, and quite another to actually look at so many faces, almost all of them etched with pain, and see it firsthand. Once they were in the air she'd need to check each of them and administer morphine as required, and tend to splints and bandages. But for now, she just wanted them in the sky and on their way to safety.

What she hadn't been expecting, though, was the loud cheer that erupted through the aircraft as soon as the wheels lifted off the ground; the whoops, slaps against metal, and general cries of happiness caught in her chest. She blinked away tears as she smiled through them. She hadn't expected to feel so emotional, either.

"We'll have you all safe soon enough, boys," she murmured, as they all settled in, some crying out in pain as they were rocked from side to side. She cleared her throat and swallowed away her emotions, wishing they didn't remind her of her brother, of what might have happened to him if he'd been airlifted out. "You're being flown by the best."

And as the plane leveled out and her nerves about her maiden flight slowly started to disappear, as she realized she had to do something to take the soldiers' minds off their pain, Vita broke into a quiet song, the lyrics to "We'll Meet Again" leaving barely a dry eye amongst the war-hardened soldiers in her care. Little did they know how much the song meant to her, too.

"You alright, Vita?" Eddie asked, his eyes searching hers.

She nodded, her chin high as she fought her tears. But when Eddie patted her knee in an unexpected display of kindness, she couldn't stop one sliding silently down her cheek.

"Hello, stranger."

Vita stifled her yawn when she realized someone was talking to her, and she turned in her seat and saw Evelyn taking a space nearby. She'd settled in well before anyone else, expecting to be one of the only nurses on board the enormous transport plane, but now that she looked around, it was starting to fill up with a handful of other nurses and medics who were all headed back to Sicily, too.

"How was your first day?" she asked Evelyn.

"Exhausting, but in a good way. You?"

Vita smiled. "I actually feel invincible after today. Our engine stopped mid-flight, and as terrifying as it was, it was kind of amazing, too. It made me realize what we're part of, I suppose—what we're risking."

"Your engine stopped?" gasped Evelyn, sounding alarmed. "I think my heart would have stopped right along with it!"

"Trust me, I think mine *did* stop," Vita confessed. "After today though, I'm only pleased we didn't have to overnight. I just want to get back to the villa, curl up in a real bed, and wake up to that view tomorrow morning."

"Me too. I think I held my breath the entire flight back, terrified one of them would die on me. But to be honest, they were just so grateful to be leaving, I think, and I only had to administer morphine and check a few wounds."

"It seemed more about managing pain than anything else."

They sat in silence after that, Evelyn holding a book that had a well-shared, scuffed appearance, and Vita staring at her bag, trying to decide whether to reach inside for the letter or not. She was starting to feel like it would burn a hole clean through the fabric if she didn't at least glance at it to see what Mother dearest wanted to tell her. But the moment she thrust her hand into the bag and slid her fingernail beneath the seal, slowly opening the embossed cream paper and skimming the words, she wished she'd left it to rot.

"Letter from home?" She heard Evelyn's question but couldn't drag her eyes from the words.

"Mmm-hmm."

Dear Victoria,

I hope this letter finds you well, although I'm sure you've had quite the sudden shock living without the comforts of home. If you weren't so stubborn, I'm certain that you would have returned by now, but of course we all know how much you like to be controversial, don't we?

We had a meeting with our family attorney today, and your father and I are in absolute agreement that it's time for your little sojourn to come to an end. It's one thing to refuse a suitable engagement, but we see it as an absolute betrayal to disobey our orders and leave home. You could be here knitting for soldiers or helping with the postal service, my darling, there's no need to go gallivanting off to foreign shores just to prove yourself! And on the subject of engagement, Seth has been very understanding despite your terrible behavior. Thankfully he believes it to be nothing more than a flighty disposition on your behalf, and has chalked it up to your being a few years younger than him, and he's willing to take you back if you return promptly.

Which all leads me to our ultimatum: If you don't follow our orders and return home, we have instructed our lawyer to remove you from our wills, and ordered that no moneys will be payable to you from the family estate now or in the future. You have given us no choice, Vita, and although neither of us wants to cut you off, this is unfortunately what it has come to.

Your poor father is beside himself with worry, and we want to assure you that things will return to normal immediately, should you return promptly. However, if you don't, then nothing will ever be the same again, Vita. Just imagine what your life will be like after the war without the luxuries you're so accustomed to? Without your family?

Come home, darling, and we can put this rebellious little adventure behind us all, never to be spoken of again.

Your loving Mother.

Loving Mother? Vita's hand shook as she held the paper, biting back the scream that filled her lungs. How dare she! How dare she continue to make this about herself, when there were so many men needing help, needing their sacrifice? *Like Andrew,* she thought, seeing her brother so clearly in her mind's eye. Didn't all the Andrews of the world deserve to have women volunteering to care for them, to do anything they could to save them? The work she was doing was so important, and that was clearer to her now than it had ever been, yet still her mother was acting as if she'd committed some naughty little act of rebellion akin to sneaking out with a boy or going to a party in the wrong neighborhood.

"Vita? Is everything alright? It's not bad news from home, is it?"

She took a deep breath and carefully refolded the letter, trying to hide her trembling fingers.

"Ah, no," she managed. "Just a letter from my mother, and she always knows how to rile me, that's all."

She was grateful that Evelyn didn't ask why she'd held onto it without opening it for so long, or any other questions for that matter, because talking about her family wasn't something she had any intention of doing. They wanted her to be the perfect heiress; to marry the perfect man, go to all the right parties, and do just enough for the war effort so that all her mother's friends would clasp their hands together and swoon over her dedication. But the longer she spent away from home, the more removed she felt from her perfect little life—a life that she might never be going back to, from the sounds of it. Even more ridiculous was the fact that her mother thought Vita could somehow just return to America at will, even if she wanted to. Was she supposed to hire a private ship to sail back home on, in the middle of a world war?

Evelyn reached out a hand and patted her leg, as if she could sense something wasn't right, and as her friend shut her eyes, Vita silently tore the paper into tiny pieces, dropping them into her bag and wishing she could blow them straight out the window into the ocean below. She only wished she could blow her memories from her mind too, because every time she shut her eyes, there they were, haunting her whenever her mind was idle.

"You're not going, and that's the end of it."

"I wasn't asking permission!"

Blood pounded in Vita's head, her body trembling as she clenched her fists and faced her mother, who was sitting with her cup of coffee perched on her knee and her back ramrod-straight.

"Excuse me?"

"You heard me, Mother. I've made my mind up, and telling you was a simple courtesy, nothing more."

Vita kept her chin high, knowing that her mother would sense any weakness within her.

"Sweetheart, what your mother is trying to tell you . . ." Her father entered the room and she swiveled to look at him, her heart softening slightly when she saw him. He was the opposite of her mother in so many ways, but when it came to pleasing his wife, it was like there was a collar around his neck, forcing him to submit.

"Father, I was counting on you to understand," Vita said, trying to sound like she wasn't pleading, even though in truth that was precisely what she was doing. "You stepped out from under your own father's shadow to build your business, you've made your own decisions in life, surely you understand that I want to make something of myself, to experience a future that isn't predetermined?"

He drained his tumbler of scotch. "Vita, in this instance you need to listen to your mother. She knows what's best for you; she runs the household."

Vita looked from his florid cheeks to her mother's wide smile. Hatred thrummed through her, pulsing like a living, breathing thing.

"What's best for me? What, so she can turn me into a coward just like my pathetic little brother?" she seethed. "You want me to hide away from the war here like him, while all his friends bravely fight for our country? Is that it?"

Her mother rose and strode across the room so fast, with such fury, that Vita didn't even see the slap coming. But she certainly felt the sting, sharp and violent, her skin screaming out even though she stayed stoically silent, not about to give her mother the satisfaction of crying or even lifting a hand to her cheek.

"You ungrateful little . . ."

"Bitch?" Vita finished. "Is that what you were going to call me? After you raised your hand to hit me?"

Her father came toward them, and Vita softened, ready for his embrace, ready to walk into his arms and listen to his soothing words. But his arms found her mother instead, held the woman who'd hit his

59

daughter, who'd tried to control her life as if it were a perfectly choreographed play since the day she was born.

"You're not to speak of your younger brother that way," her father said, and she knew then that she'd lost his support the moment she'd mentioned her sibling. "Would you prefer him to die in a blaze of glory like Andrew did?"

Vita swallowed, carefully choosing her words this time, knowing she needed to appease her father if she ever wanted him on her side. She dropped her gaze. "No, Father. I would do anything to bring Andrew back, you know that." She'd loved her big brother, with all her heart.

Tears burned so hard against her lashes but she refused to acknowledge them, swallowing away the emotion and ducking her head slightly, to make her father see that she wasn't trying to defy him, that she still felt the pain of losing her older brother.

"What is it you want, then?" her mother asked.

"I want men like Andrew to receive the care they deserve. I want to make sure that they're not left to . . ." She fought for the right word. ". . . to suffer when they could be airlifted to a better hospital, to an actual hospital equipped with everything they might need to save their lives."

What she wanted to say was that her younger brother, who was no doubt cowering in the kitchen, was a weak, knock-kneed imbecile who didn't deserve a reprieve from war or anything else in life. Or that the last thing she wanted was to talk about Andrew, about her older brother who'd bravely volunteered and left without anyone's permission. Andrew, who'd been so proud when she'd told him she wanted to do something useful, something more than knitting, for the war effort.

She had her father there, though; she could see the shift in him, the silent acknowledgment of her words.

"Father?" she finally said, searching his face, hoping she'd made him change his mind.

But the only eyes that met hers were her mother's, and they were as cold and unforgiving as ice.

"You walk out of this house without our permission and you'll regret it," her mother whispered. "Don't test me, Vita."

Vita bit back the hatred inside of her and turned on her heel, walking straight out the door before breaking into a run. She slammed her shoulder into her brother as she passed him, taking in the shocked look on his face before going through her bedroom door and shutting it behind her. She locked it and then pressed her back against the timber, sliding all the way down to the floor and sinking into the carpet.

She didn't know what a life without her family would look like, but it appeared she was about to find out.

CHAPTER SEVEN

DOT

She couldn't move. Dot balled her fists, trying to stop her arms from trembling as she stood, frozen, on the grass. She'd managed a few steps, but her legs were suddenly immobile and nothing she could do would make them work.

I can't do this. I can't get on there again. I can't go through that all over again.

"Dot?" came a voice from behind her, a voice she recognized even though she couldn't bring herself to turn. What would Vita think, finding her standing there, so pathetic she couldn't even do her job?

"Dot, what are you doing out here alone?"

There were other people moving about, but when she saw Vita, everyone else seemed to disappear.

"I can't do it," she whispered, her eyes meeting Vita's as she tried so hard not to cry. "I can't be here. I just want to go home. I know it's pathetic, but . . ."

Vita stepped in front of her, gently taking her hands and holding them, and Dot grasped hers tightly.

"Honey, you *can* do it. Tell me what you're worried about. What happened?"

Tears slid silently down Dot's cheeks then, the floodgates well and truly open, her bottom lip trembling as she opened her mouth to speak. She hadn't expected Vita to be so kind.

"I couldn't sleep last night," she whispered. "I couldn't stop thinking about them, about, about . . ."

Vita opened her arms and pulled her in for a hug, and Dot clung to her. If they were seen they'd be reprimanded—they'd been told to board immediately—but Dot needed a friend and she didn't want to let go of her.

"You need to tell me what happened," Vita said, standing back. "I can't help you if you don't talk, and we don't have long."

Dot's shoulders heaved, and Vita took hold of her hands again.

"Why didn't you talk to us last night? You could have told us, Dot. We're all in this together."

"You were both asleep when I got back," she murmured. "And then I just lay there for such a long time, seeing it all, over and over."

"Did something happen on your flight?" Vita asked.

"I, I . . ." Dot's breath shuddered out of her, and she struggled to get the words out. "I don't think I was prepared to be in charge of so many men, to see so many injuries, to . . ."

"What's wrong?" Evelyn was suddenly with them, leaning in close, her arm around her. "Captain McKnight's on his way over to see why his planes haven't taken off yet. We need to get moving."

"I had to pin a man's tongue to his shirt button to stop him from choking!" Dot gasped, the words finally spilling out. "It was either that or let him die, but he kept howling like a dog in pain, it was so awful!"

The memory was so visceral, made her so afraid to close her eyes in case she saw it all over again.

"Oh, sweetheart, that's awful!" Vita gasped.

"I bet you saved him though, Dot," Evelyn said quietly, her voice filled with compassion. "It might have been traumatic, but he's alive, isn't he? All those men we're airlifting, they all survived, none of us lost any of our patients, and that means they have a good chance of making it home. Can you imagine what his mother would say if she knew how brave you'd been? How quickly you thought on your feet to save him?"

Dot's tears had slowed now, and as Vita gently wiped her cheeks she stood there and tried to pull herself together. Evelyn was right. She needed to focus on her patients' families—that was how she was going to cope with any horrors she had to face. She took a deep breath and thought of her grandparents, of how proud they'd be seeing her do such an important job. But her thoughts were overshadowed by Peter, hearing his voice in her head, telling her what she was and wasn't capable of, that she could never do something so brave even if she wanted to.

"If you don't get on that plane, it'll stay grounded. There's no one else trained to take our place, our troops need us," Vita whispered gently to her. "Perhaps you could write down their names, in a journal maybe, even just their first names? That way when you don't think you can do it anymore, you can look at all those names and remember how many lives you saved."

Dot blinked at her. "You really think I could do that?"

"I know you can do that," Vita said. "Now, come on, we're supposed to be wheels up by now. I believe in you, Dot."

Dot gave her a quick hug, before nodding and collecting her bag, which she'd dropped at her feet. She glanced over her shoulder at her friends as she rushed away, raising her hand in a wave before they parted ways and hurried off, too. She broke into a slow jog, forcing her feet forward, Vita's words ringing in her ears.

If you don't get on that plane, it'll stay grounded. There's no one else trained to take our place, our troops need us.

Vita was right. If not her, then who? There was no one else trained to work in the air like them; if they couldn't fly and transport patients, then those troops would never find their way to better hospitals to receive care.

They might not be assisting with gruesome surgeries or amputations like other nurses stationed near the front lines, but the weight of responsibility in the air was enormous, more than she'd ever expected. When she'd first signed up, it had been about proving herself to Peter, who'd made her feel as if she wasn't capable of doing anything more than sitting at home. But now that he'd ended things, she was going to prove to his entire family exactly how capable she was. Instead of sitting at home and crying into her pillow, she'd held her head high and made something of herself, and she couldn't turn back now. She'd felt lost without him, as if she'd never amount to anything, but if she got on that plane, if she pushed past her fears?

"Dot, come on!" her medic called, peeking his head out from behind the open door. "What's the holdup?"

You can do this. Vita believes in you, Evelyn believes in you. Screw what Peter would think. Just because he'd been older than her and from a family with more money than hers, she'd let herself believe that his opinion mattered more than her own, that his *mother's* opinion was more worthy because of her social standing. But Dot was part of something bigger now, something more important, and she had to keep reminding herself of that.

"Coming!" she said, taking a moment to absorb the interior of the plane with its row of metal beds on each side. She breathed, imagined it filled with patients again, patients she was going to ensure made it to hospital, no matter what. She squared her shoulders against her fear, her chin jutted high.

"Come on then, buckle up."

She sat down, careful to do her belt up as the plane shuddered into life. She guiltily thought of how easily she'd let Evelyn and Vita think she was still engaged, to save herself the shame of admitting she'd been jilted, and she tugged at her necklace, vowing to remove it when she was back at the villa. She was going to tell them, she *had* to tell them. If they found out later, then what would they think of her?

You can do this, Dot, she told herself. *Because if not you, then who?*

Vita's words were ringing in her ears as they started to taxi down the runway. Now all she had to do was remember them if she lost her confidence again. The last time she'd been this strong was when her parents had died, when her entire world had fallen apart. When Peter had finished with her, she'd fallen to pieces, but she was not going to let that happen now. Not again.

She yanked at her necklace, wishing she had the strength to rip it off and throw her ring away as easily as her fiancé had discarded her that day in his mother's sitting room.

"I'm sorry, Dot, but I just don't feel that way about you anymore."

He may as well have slapped her, the shock was so great. She swayed on unsteady feet, gripping her teacup as if her life depended on it. She instinctively sat, her back as rigid as the hard fabric-covered chair she'd dropped into.

"I'm sorry, you're . . ."

"Breaking off our engagement," he said matter-of-factly. "I know you've had a terrible time these past few months, and I'm loathe to add to it, but I can't pretend any longer."

Pretend? She forced herself to put the cup down and folded her hands tightly in her lap. "But your mother, your sister," she began. "I think of them like my own family. What will they think? I mean, I thought I was . . ." Her words trailed off, suddenly too painful to utter. She'd thought of Peter's family as her own; she'd thought she finally belonged. Without them, she'd be truly, completely alone.

"Obviously Mother won't be happy, but in time she'll understand." Peter sounded impatient, as if Dot were something he needed to be rid of.

How long had he been practicing this speech for? All this time she'd been so excited to have him home on leave, and yet he'd been waiting to call things off. She suddenly stared at the ring on her finger and she extended her hand out, not sure what to do.

"Please, keep it," he said. "It was given as a gift and I certainly don't expect you to return it."

Dot nodded and folded her hands again. She should have hurled the ring at him, but if he was telling her to keep it, perhaps he might change his mind? Perhaps he wasn't thinking straight.

"I'm sorry, Dot. Truly, I didn't mean to hurt you."

She stared after him as he hurriedly left the room, the man she'd expected to marry, the man she'd spent months waiting for, who she'd thought was going to give her the family she'd always longed for, the security and love she'd so desperately wanted.

"Dot? Where's Peter?"

His mother stood in the doorway, crossing the room when Dot looked up and revealed her tears.

"Oh, Dot, what's wrong? You look so terribly upset."

"He's called off our engagement," she whispered, pressed to the older woman's chest. "He's met someone else. He said he's in love."

His mother looked crestfallen for all of a few seconds, before regaining her composure and turning a cold stare on Dot. "What did you do? My son would never behave this way without reason."

"What did I do?" Dot pressed her eyes shut and quashed her tears, before facing the woman she'd thought might become like her own mother one day. Everything they'd asked of her, she'd done—from *hosting teas for suitable young women from their social circle to taking cooking classes to ensure she could look after their son and be the perfect housewife.* "I did nothing. How could you think that? What could I possibly have done?"

"Well, dry those eyes and pull yourself together," Peter's mother said brusquely. "Nobody wants to see your tears."

Dot swallowed, staring at her teacup again, sitting untouched on the table. Of course no one wanted to see her tears; they were a family who cared about appearances and status, not feelings.

And just like that, she was alone again. If Peter didn't want her anymore, she was certain she'd never hear from anyone in his family ever again.

CHAPTER EIGHT

VITA

After three weeks of almost-daily flights, the longest days Vita could have imagined, and a bone-deep tiredness that had them all falling into bed each night as soon as they'd eaten, everything had suddenly come to a grinding halt.

Vita stretched and looked out at the endless expanse of water from their villa window, suddenly feeling like a bird in a gilded cage. In the beginning, she'd have done anything for some time off to spend lounging around and resting, but after days of doing nothing, she was bored. Not to mention she hated to think of all those troops in desperate need of being airlifted; how many would suffer or die just because they couldn't get to them?

"Surely this weather can't last," she muttered to no one in particular.

"Want to play another game of cards?" Dot asked.

Vita turned and sighed, crossing the room and sinking into a chair at the table. "Alright, but not rummy again, can't we play something else?"

Dot shrugged. "Cheat?"

"I suppose so." She wasn't particularly enthused about playing any card game, but it beat pacing back and forth, staring out the window at the rain and the thick cover of clouds.

When the front door clicked, Vita set down her cards and looked up, waiting to see who it was. Evelyn hurried into the room, taking off her wet jacket and shaking out her blonde hair, leaving a small puddle on the floor.

"Any news?" Vita asked.

"Other than an update on how many men we've transported since we arrived, I found out absolutely nothing," Evelyn said with a sigh, sinking into one of the hard-backed chairs at the table. "We've moved some sixteen hundred men these past few weeks, would you believe, and not one of them has died yet."

"Imagine how many more need us," Vita grumbled. "It's ridiculous that we're still stuck here. Surely it's not impossible to fly in this? It doesn't look that bad to me."

"Just because you survived a near-death experience when your engine cut out, you're suddenly invincible now?" Evelyn snapped back. "I spoke to some of the pilots at headquarters, and they said they wouldn't want to go up in this no matter the reason, it's just too risky. But we're to report tomorrow morning, just in case it clears. It's not like any of us want to be sitting around doing nothing."

Vita straightened, ignoring Evelyn's little snipe. They were all worried about the number of injured waiting to be transported, not to mention bored, so it was hardly a surprise they were getting on each other's nerves. "Did they actually say we might be flying tomorrow?"

"Apparently there's a chance of the weather clearing, but we're to report each morning from now on just in case. There might be more news later, when they've heard from the control tower." Evelyn's sigh was loud. "I feel like we've trained for this incredible new program, and then our legs were taken from under us just as we got started."

"Well, tomorrow sounds promising to me, but I know exactly what you mean. Being grounded is unbearable." The longer Vita sat around, the more she stewed about her mother and fretted over the threats she'd made, so she didn't want to be idle for any longer than necessary. Not to mention she couldn't stop thinking about the men she'd airlifted so far; some of their injuries were nightmare-worthy, and the more soldiers she cared for, the more she *wanted* to care for. And she also couldn't sleep. It had started as soon as her brother died; from that moment, she'd tried to keep her days as busy as possible so she'd fall into bed each night and sleep. Because if she didn't, she'd only lie awake thinking of him; of what his life could have been, and how she'd ever be able to live the rest of her own life without him.

After three long days of being grounded, she was ready to climb the walls.

"Come on, deal me in," Evelyn said. "We may as well make the most of our time off, because I have a feeling that once we start flying again, there'll barely be time to catch our breath."

"Tell me about it," Dot said. "I bet they'll have us doing back-to-back flights just to make up for it."

"I did see Bobby down there though," Evelyn said.

"Oh? What did he have to say?" Vita asked.

"Don't tell me you've had a quarrel with lover boy?" Evelyn said. "I thought you'd be loving seeing him each day!"

Dot giggled, but she stopped when Vita gave her a cold, hard stare.

"I have no interest in Bobby," she retorted, hating that her cheeks were burning. "He doesn't seem to know where to draw the line between fun and professionalism."

"Sounds juicy," Evelyn said. "Tell us more!"

Dot burst out laughing along with Evelyn, and no amount of glaring at her helped this time, not now that she had Evelyn giggling with her.

"He was a bit of fun, that's all," Vita said, ignoring their laughter. "I'm not about to go throwing my life away for a man, so Bobby can ask about me all he likes, but nothing is happening between us." She still hadn't forgiven him for his behavior when they'd first arrived, and she certainly wasn't going to get entangled with a man and end up dependent on him, either. It would be as bad, if not worse, than being dependent on her parents.

"You know I'm only teasing, don't you?" Evelyn said, her hand closing over Vita's at the table. "He just asked after you—I think perhaps he was wanting to know if you're interested, that's all."

"Well, I'm not," Vita said with a shrug. "We've had nothing but a professional relationship since we've been here, and whether he likes it or not, that's the way it'll be staying."

"Doesn't it seem like a lifetime ago when we left America?" Dot asked. "I mean, I still want to cry thinking about that physical training course, but that last night when we had our twelve-hour pass . . ."

All three of them sighed at the same time, which made them laugh all over again. "It was a great night," Vita said. And she hadn't been lying about Bobby; he was gorgeous to look at and dancing with him had been fun, but he was also a jerk. "Perhaps we could have a night out here if we're ever allowed out of our ivory tower?"

"Without the drinking this time," Dot said. "I've never felt so sick in my life."

"Take that," Vita announced, smugly placing her last card on the table and grinning at her friends. "That's what you get for teasing me before."

The other two groaned as Vita stood and gave a little bow. "Now, who wants coffee? I don't know about you two, but I'm almost starting to like the taste of it."

She walked through to the kitchen, her eyes drawn to the view again. It wasn't such a bad place to be stuck with nothing to do, but the trouble was, they all knew how desperately they were needed now. A few weeks had changed everything for her; she'd started out desperate to do something, anything, and get away from home, but it was so much more than that now. For the first time in her life, she was doing something that mattered.

We'll be back in the air soon, she thought, taking out three cups and reaching for the coffee. *Don't you worry, boys, we're still coming for you.*

"Vita, get out here!"

She turned at Evelyn's call and rushed back to the living room, her eyes falling on Eddie standing by the door, his cheeks flushed as he took off his wet hat. And then she saw who was coming in the door behind him. *Speak of the devil, if it isn't Bobby.*

"What is it? Is something wrong?" she asked Eddie, not bothering to acknowledge Bobby. "What's happened?"

"Nothing's wrong, we've just come to tell you that they've made an announcement. A big announcement, in fact," Eddie said. He pushed his dark hair back off his face, his tall, lanky body braced against the wall. Eddie was almost the exact opposite of Bobby; one was blond and broad-shouldered, the other dark and resembling a beanpole.

"Well, spit it out," Vita said impatiently.

"They're sending a big group of us up together. At least thirteen nurses and as many medics."

"So thirteen planes are heading up?" Evelyn asked, her eyebrows raised as she traded glances with Vita. "Or do you mean . . ."

"I meant that at least twenty-six of us are going up in the one plane. It's a C-53D Skytrooper, much bigger than our regular planes. They said they're picking their best nurses for the flight, but they didn't tell me any more."

"What?" Vita stared at Eddie, wondering if she was imagining the entire conversation. Her eyes flicked to Bobby. There was no way they'd send that many of them up at once. "That would have to be a third of our squadron? Are you sure?"

"They said they have so many men to evacuate that they need a big group of you up together," Bobby said, his eyes meeting hers. "The general was here just now; came in a car and stayed all of fifteen minutes before leaving again. Evelyn just missed him. He was less than impressed when he found out we hadn't been flying these past few days, and the order came directly from him."

"This all sounds like a bad idea to me." Dot was still sitting at the table, and Vita watched as she nervously worried at the edges of her cards.

"We'll be fine, Dot," Vita said, not about to let Dot sense how uncertain she was. An order was an order, and if they were chosen then they'd just have to do it.

"Of course we will," Evelyn muttered. "But she's right to be worried; it's never been done before. I can't believe they'd put so many of us up together on one plane. They must be desperate to get those soldiers airlifted."

Vita's pulse started to race. She wasn't going to argue that it wasn't terrifying, but she also found it all rather exciting.

"You're to report at daybreak," Eddie told them. "The jeeps will be here outside the villas waiting to take you."

"So we're all going? All three of us were chosen?" Evelyn asked.

"I was told to pass the message on to everyone in this villa," Eddie said with a grin. "They said they wanted the best, and your villa was second on the list. I'd say you've all made quite the impression."

"Come on then, ladies," Vita said, secretly delighted they'd been handpicked. "Let's have that coffee and make the most of our last afternoon off. Eddie, do you want to join us?" She looked at Bobby, knowing she couldn't avoid him forever. "And you, Bobby? Would you like a coffee?"

"You know how to make coffee?" Bobby asked with a grin. "Or do you have a servant hiding here somewhere?" He looked around, seeming to find his own joke hilarious. She just rolled her eyes, even though inside she was bristling. How had he not noticed how hard she worked when they were flying together? How she singlehandedly looked after all her patients?

"Not today, Vita," Eddie said, shaking his head at her as if to tell her not to bother with Bobby's teasing. "I have more calls to make. I'll see you in the morning."

She walked to the door as they left, noticing how Eddie waited, his eyes searching for her as Bobby hung back. She nodded, letting him know she was alright. He'd never asked her about Bobby, but Eddie noticed things, and when Bobby wasn't looking, he often strutted around and ran his fingers through his hair, peering at her over pretend aviators as if he were Bobby. She'd always end up in fits of laughter, wishing Bobby could see what a good impression Eddie did. They'd become close in their short time together, and she'd found herself drawn to him—she liked that he was committed to his wife and clearly not interested in anything other than friendship with her.

She watched as he slowly disappeared down the cobbled path.

"Vita," Bobby said, looking like he was about to reach for her but then shoving his hands into his pockets instead.

She stared into his bright blue eyes.

"What happened, on our first flight together," he began. "Look, I just want to say how inappropriate that was. I can see that now."

She could barely believe what she was hearing. Despite saying some truly awful things to her over the years, no one in her family had ever apologized to her. Remorse wasn't something she was used to receiving.

"Thanks, Bobby," she said. "That actually means a lot to me."

"Friends then?" he asked, taking a step away as Eddie called out to him from the next villa.

She laughed as he jogged backward, his hands held in a gesture of prayer as he waited for her answer. "Friends," she agreed.

"Vita, shut the door!" Evelyn yelled out.

"Alright, alright," she muttered, closing the door and smiling to herself before turning around.

Evelyn and Dot both looked up at her expectantly, but she just shrugged and joined them at the table.

"Who's up for a second round of Cheat then?" Vita asked.

Dot groaned, and Vita put an arm around her shoulders. "If you're worrying about tomorrow, stop it. It's going to be fine, Dot. Don't think about everything that could go wrong, just think about how far you've come. I'm so proud of you."

Dot leaned into her.

"You're a fine nurse, do you hear me? Don't ever doubt your abilities. And let's not forget that we've already transported more than fifteen hundred patients without losing a single one. It makes me think we kind of know what we're doing!"

Evelyn smiled at her across the table and Dot gave her an impromptu hug.

"Alright, alright, that's enough. Let me deal the cards already, would you?"

She sat back as Evelyn and Dot started to talk excitedly about what the morning would bring, her mind drifting to Bobby. She was so proud of herself, first of all for dancing all night with someone her mother would wholeheartedly disapprove of, and secondly that she'd been confident enough to turn down his advances since then. It was just another step up the ladder of finding her own way, of demanding her independence. Six months earlier, she'd been on the cusp of an engagement, and now she was on her own, on a different continent to the rest of her family. *I'm free.* For the first time in her life, she was finally free.

Vita walked in silence, her mind full of things to say, but none of them finding their way to her mouth. It seemed too hard, or maybe she just couldn't be bothered making small talk any longer.

"So, tell me about yourself?" Seth asked, and she tried not to recoil when his knuckles brushed hers as they walked. There wasn't anything wrong with him, it wasn't like he was terrible to look at or rude or obnoxious, he just wasn't . . . She sighed and tried to tell herself not to be so sensitive. He just wasn't the kind of man she wanted to spend time with, and especially not one she wanted to think of as husband material.

"I don't know what to say," she said, feeling like it was the most honest thing she could tell him. "I like horseback riding and reading, and . . ." She glanced at him, wondering if he even wanted to know how she felt. "If I'm perfectly honest, I would have liked to go to college, actually. I love to learn."

He seemed to mull her answer over, his smile giving her hope.

"Would your father not allow it?" he asked.

"Unfortunately not," she replied, staring off across the field, wishing she were on horseback right then and there, cantering with the wind whipping at her face and making her forget everything. "He couldn't see the point, despite the fact that both my brothers were encouraged to study, and my mother didn't like the thought of me furthering my studies at all. She didn't even approve of me finishing my final year of high school."

Seth looked at her, and in that moment his smile was so kind and his eyes so warm, she had the most overwhelming sensation that he was going to tell her that he'd let her go. That he liked the fact she was ambitious and eager to keep learning. That if they were married, he'd make it a priority for her since it obviously meant so much to her.

"He's right, you know," he said, offering his arm as if she were just waiting eagerly to take it. "You'll be going from your father's home to your husband's, so there's little point in spending all that money on a fanciful idea. I can see why he thought it a frivolous waste of resources."

If her heart were capable of dropping, it would have thudded all the way to her toes. Just when she'd thought he might be different, when she'd thought there was a glimmer of hope that he believed in women doing more than just what the men in their lives told them to. But she wasn't going to whimper and dampen down her dreams; it only made her all the more determined to tell him what she wanted.

"I dreamed of studying the arts, of learning more about history and . . ." Her voice trailed off as she saw the disinterest in his gaze. What was the point? She'd already argued enough with her parents; there was no point in having the same argument with anyone else. And she dared not tell him she'd once dreamed of studying law, because she doubted women were even able to do so in the first place.

"Victoria, you can get all those books out of the library, you don't need to go to college," he said. "A woman full of that much information would become tiresome, anyway."

Vita, *she thought silently.* If you knew me, if you cared, you'd know that everyone calls me Vita. And you'd also know that there is nothing tiresome about having a conversation with someone who's studied what they love! Someone with knowledge to share!

She kept walking, feeling as if the life was draining out of her with every step.

"I know your parents have spoken to you about marriage, and I wanted to tell you that I think we'd be a wonderful match," he said, not even noticing that she'd withdrawn from him. "I think we could build a life together, and I'm sure we'd be so happy together. I mean, it

wouldn't be such a change for you, moving from your family home to mine, and . . ."

He stopped walking as his voice trailed off and he fumbled for her hand, and she numbly let him take it. He stared into her eyes and she could see that he actually believed his own words, that he thought whatever it was he felt for her was enough to get married. He actually thought it was what she wanted. She stared at his hand holding hers, hating that it was clammy, wishing he'd let go.

The worst thing was, this wasn't her. She was loud and brave and fun; she wanted to marry someone she loved, someone who truly saw her for who she was, someone she could talk to about her dreams and not be put in her place. Someone she could be that loud, brave woman with.

She'd already shouted a version of this very argument at her mother, who'd retaliated by giving her a swift slap across her cheek, leaving an angry red welt there. Her mother thought she was fanciful, a romantic who had no concept of reality, but she knew what it really was: her mother wanted to crow about whomever her only daughter was marrying. All she cared about was the size of the diamond, and how big the bank balance of her potential in-laws was.

Vita prayed that he wasn't going to ask her to marry her right then and there, worried she wouldn't have the nerve to say no to him. She stared at her small hand in his beefy one.

"Victoria," he said, clearing his throat.

She did her best to hide her grimace, pulling back slightly.

"Victoria," he began again.

"Oh, Seth," she said dramatically, holding one hand to her stomach. "I've come over feeling terribly unwell, my stomach is cramping terribly." She lowered her voice. "Sorry, I fear it's a woman's issue."

It was unkind; the poor man blushed a deep red and started to stutter as he attempted to get his words out.

"I, well, I suppose—"

"Would you take my arm?" she asked, playing the part of the help-less female. "I think it's best if we turn around. I'll keep hold of you."

She leaned against him and felt the nudge of something hard in his jacket pocket, and her heart sank. It was a ring box, she just knew it. Which meant that there was only so long she could stall before he did ask her, and she needed to prepare what to say. Or else she needed to convince her father to change his mind.

"I'll come over tomorrow," he said quietly, patting her hand as they neared the house. "If you're feeling better, of course. I won't intrude if you're still, ah, under the weather."

She smiled up at him and silently slipped away, intending on never being tucked into his side ever, ever again.

CHAPTER NINE

EVELYN

For some reason Evelyn had barely been able to sleep. She'd had the strangest sense of foreboding, worrying about the flight, and combined with worrying about the early start and sleeping in, it had all contributed to a disastrous night. Now all she wanted was to curl up beneath the covers again.

A loud honk sounded out then, and she parted the curtains, looking out to see a handful of trucks gathered and waiting for them outside the villas. But they weren't the only things gathered in the half-light.

"Girls, you have to see this."

Dot rushed straight over, peering out past her. "What are they all doing out there?"

"I have no idea," she said, stepping back to let Vita look at the group of children waiting beside the trucks, as if the vehicles had arrived to transport the children somewhere instead of a dozen nurses and just as many medics. "But I'd take a guess on them wanting chocolate or chewing gum."

"Or cigarettes," Vita said breezily. "But that's one thing I'm not sharing."

"Come on, other nurses are already heading down there," Dot said, and they both reached for their bags at the same time, putting them over their shoulders and across their bodies. The long strap of the musette bags made them easy to carry, and Evelyn mentally went through everything she'd packed in case she'd missed something.

Vita went out first, but she turned around before she'd even taken a step. "We need our field coats, it's freezing out there."

They took her word for it, hurrying back in for their coats. They were bulky to carry when they didn't need them, which was why they often didn't bother taking them, but Vita was right, it was cold and the last thing they needed was to be sitting around shivering, especially if the rain started again. They also had galoshes to pull on, which they picked up at the door, not about to ruin their smart leather shoes in the mud.

As soon as the door was shut behind them and they were on their way down, the sound of children's calls and laughter filled the otherwise-silent early morning air. The village was largely asleep, the surrounding villas shuttered for the night still, but the barefoot children seemed not to notice.

"Where are their parents?" Vita murmured. "Poor little things."

"Maybe they're street kids," Dot said. "Look at their clothes, and their little feet are caked with mud."

It didn't stop them from smiling though, and as Evelyn neared them she took out the lone stick of gum she had in her pocket, happy to share what she had. She noticed some of the soldiers were leaning out over the truck windows and passing things out, too; war hardened a man in so many ways, but not, it seemed, toward the smiles and innocence of children.

"*Cioccolato!*" the children cried, holding out grubby hands. "*Cioccolato!*"

Evelyn passed them her piece of gum and bent to kiss the cheek of a pretty little girl before climbing into the truck, and as it rumbled away, the children running as fast as they could beside them until their little legs could run no farther, she had the strangest feeling it was a farewell of sorts.

"Doesn't it make you want to scoop them all up and take them home with you?" Evelyn mused, craning her neck and straining her eyes to see the children in the distance.

"Feed them, yes," Vita said, frowning. "But never once has it crossed my mind that I'd like to take them home with me."

Evelyn nudged Vita with her shoulder. Trust Vita to make them all laugh so early in the morning with her heartlessness!

"So, what's the news, fellas?" Vita asked, leaning forward and attempting to sweet-talk the soldier driving them. "Are we gonna be wheels up this morning or was this early start all for nothing?"

"No idea, ma'am," he replied, seemingly unaffected by Vita's charms. "But there's a mighty big Skytrooper waiting on the field, so . . ."

"That's us," Evelyn said. "We must be heading up after all."

They all three looked at one another, and Evelyn saw the same mix of excitement and nerves that she felt inside, reflected in both her friends' faces. There were ten other nurses packed into the trucks, and just as many medics, and the idea that they were all going up together was surreal to say the least.

It was only minutes before they reached headquarters, and they were directed immediately to the front of the building, their squadron leader standing with a clipboard, and Bobby and another two pilots standing to his left. Evelyn had always thought Bobby was handsome, but seeing him in uniform with his aviator sunglasses tucked into his jacket, he looked even better than she remembered. His blond hair was cropped short, his skin golden, and his blue eyes so piercing they almost matched the Mediterranean, but the way he winked at every pretty nurse made her wonder just how reliable he was. Perhaps that's why Vita kept insisting he'd been nothing more than a bit of fun.

As the sky continued to lighten, Evelyn glanced around at the other nurses. They looked striking, all in their powder-blue uniforms, even with galoshes on and their slate-gray coats draped over their shoulders. She was surprised the medics weren't as well dressed for the cold, with only a handful of them wearing warm jackets, but it was too late to go back for them now.

"Good morning!" Captain McKnight called out, his voice cutting through the chatter and silencing everyone immediately. "This is a historic morning, sending so many of you up in one plane, but the army is begging for transportation and we have to get as many men airlifted as possible today, in case the weather closes in again. You have all been specially chosen to work together, and we expect to start doing more large-scale flights like this to catch up on the backlog, before resuming our usual service. We have a terrifying number of men in desperate need of airlifting."

There was barely a shuffle of feet as he cleared his throat and continued on. Evelyn expected everyone was filled with as much nervous anticipation as she was.

"If you could all please form a line and we will begin the process of adding each of you to the manifest and weighing you, along with your bag. You're making history today, ladies and gents. Mark my words, your service to your country has already been invaluable. Heck, it's why we need you up there as soon as can be."

Evelyn swelled with pride, feeling a catch in her chest as she digested his words.

"I shouldn't have eaten all that bread last night," Vita whispered. "Between that and my magazines, I'll probably be too heavy to board!"

"No talking, ladies!" someone barked.

Evelyn shot Vita a look and stifled her smile as they slowly shuffled forward. She'd only just been able to close her bag it was so full, with a change of clothes, some makeup, and her book, along

84

with a candy bar she'd been saving, but with a long flight ahead of them she was happy to at least have something to read. And the others had magazines, so they'd no doubt share those around, too.

Evelyn stared up at the enormous Skytrooper with the huge wingspan as they edged closer, squeezing Dot's hand beside her. *It's amazing.* She could barely believe her eyes, or the fact that so many of them were going up in one flight. She had to crane her neck to look up at it, to really take it in, and even though it was a transport plane today, she could imagine how menacing it was when it was fitted with ammunition.

"Imagine how many soldiers we'll be collecting today," Dot whispered. "All those men that we'll safely transport to hospital."

"It's going to be incredible," Evelyn replied. "Although I still don't know if it'll make up for all the days we've been grounded. It's something, though."

Vita moved ahead of them, and Evelyn watched her laugh with the poor soldier who'd been charged with weighing each of them before they were allowed to board. Evelyn patiently waited her turn, happy to receive a tick of approval when she finally stepped forward. She couldn't imagine how embarrassing it would be to be turned around.

And then it was time to walk up onto the big gray plane. She grinned as she took her first step, listening to the excited hum of nurses and medics around her, her boot steady on the metal stair. Within the hour, they'd be wheels up and flying toward Bari to collect perhaps a couple of hundred injured troops and transport them to hospital.

This is going to be the best day of my life.

"Up you go, ladies. Mind your step."

Once she was standing in the open doorway of the enormous Skytrooper, Evelyn paused and looked back. The sky was light now, a pinky tinge to it that swirled with patches of gray, and she only hoped the weather held long enough for them to get the patients to the closest hospital. Even if they were grounded straight after and had to overnight somewhere, at least they would have done their best.

Dot was right behind her and they took a seat together, Evelyn's bottom already uncomfortable on the metal, and she adjusted her belt to make sure it was secure. When she looked up, she saw Bobby standing outside the entrance to the cockpit, arms folded and his eyes glinting as Vita sashayed past, even though they'd supposedly agreed to be just friends.

"I saw that look he gave you," she whispered to Vita when she sat down.

"What look?" Vita asked, as innocent as could be as they all removed their galoshes.

"The one where he looked like he could eat you in one bite," Dot muttered. "I saw it too."

Evelyn laughed. "My thoughts exactly." She blushed just thinking about a man looking at her like that!

"Well, he can look all he likes, but he's not getting anything," Vita said with a shrug.

"And that's exactly how she always gets what she wants," Evelyn replied with a sigh. There was so much more to Vita than met the eye, yet she seemed able to play the pretty-little-nurse card at the drop of a hat. "Honestly, Vita, you could sweet-talk your way out of murder." Evelyn was perfectly fine talking to the soldiers in her care when it came to treating them, because she was confident in her nursing abilities, but when it came to anything else, she felt well out of her depth.

They were silenced by the crew chief reading through his checklist, and soon he joined Bobby, the other pilot and the radio operator in the cockpit. The plane was already running, the engine vibrating beneath their seats, and they all sat quietly for a short time as the noise became louder and louder. Before they knew it, they were taxiing down the makeshift runway, and an excited hum of chatter began the moment they were in the air.

Evelyn stared out the window, marveling as she always did at how magical it was to be soaring through the air like a bird; she still couldn't quite wrap her head around how such a big machine was even capable of actually flying. The only thing that always worried her was that they weren't marked with a white cross; they had no protection in the sky, because their planes were dual-use and therefore didn't qualify as medical aircraft.

"Look at this," Dot said beside her, holding up a magazine. "Have you ever seen anything like it?"

Somehow, *Vogue* had managed to create the most beautiful wedding dresses from silk parachutes for a story, and Evelyn had to agree that they looked jaw-droppingly good.

"When are you getting married, Dot?" Vita asked from beside them. "Because I think you'd look beautiful in one with a sweetheart neckline. Have you thought about dresses yet?"

"Ah, well, after the war ends," Dot said, and Evelyn didn't miss the tears brimming in her friend's eyes as she spoke, obviously missing her fiancé terribly. Evelyn reached out and patted her knee, leaving her hand there when she saw how fragile Dot still looked. "I'd hoped to get married when he was home on leave, but it just, well, things didn't turn out that way. I . . ." Dot's voice trailed off, her cheeks reddening, but even though she looked like she was going to say more, she didn't.

"It's all so romantic," Vita swooned, hand to her heart. "Who could want anything more than to marry for love, am I right?"

"There'll be plenty of time after the war," Evelyn assured Dot, seeing her falter and wondering if it was too hard for her to talk about her man when he was so far away. "You'll be so pleased you waited, especially if there are no rations and you can have an amazing cake and buy a new dress."

"What's he like, your fiancé?" Vita asked. "I want to know how you fell in love."

"Oh, well, he's great. He's very successful and he couldn't wait to sign up to serve," Dot said, her face lighting up as she spoke. "I suppose I was just looking forward to being part of his family, that's all, since I don't have my own parents."

"Where's he stationed?" Vita asked.

"Ahh, Europe somewhere."

"Dot, when you say *was,* what do you mean?" Evelyn asked, confused about what Dot had said and the way she was wringing her hands together. "Are you worried he's not going to make it home? Or that his family aren't going to welcome you into the fold?"

"No, I didn't mean that," Dot mumbled. "I'm sure he's just fine. And they're fine too; they're a very suitable, well-to-do family."

Then she cleared her throat, before starting to thumb through her magazine again, seeming to put an end to the conversation. Evelyn was certain she was crying now, but Dot didn't look back up and she didn't want to press her. Besides, what did she know about affairs of the heart? She hadn't even had a boyfriend before! It wasn't like she knew what it was like to be in love and then parted by war; she could only imagine what Dot must be going through.

Evelyn was going to ask Vita about Bobby, but the plane gave a sudden lurch and distracted her. She looked out the window again, reassured by how clear the sky was, and stared at the island and the rolling hills disappearing beneath them, as they edged northeast.

"Must have been a bird strike," Vita muttered, as if she were the authority on all matters aviation. Mind you, she seemed to be an authority on most things, so Evelyn shouldn't have been surprised; Vita was a lot of fun, but she always had a very high opinion of herself.

Evelyn took her book from her bag and tried to get comfortable in her seat, turning the well-thumbed pages of *A Tree Grows in Brooklyn* as the women around her knitted, talked, and flipped through magazines, and the medics mainly talked amongst themselves or read letters that looked like they'd been folded and opened more times than they could count. She was just happy to relax for a moment, and prepare for the carnage of transporting so many wounded soldiers.

———— ❦ ————

One moment Evelyn had been on the verge of falling asleep, her book perched in her hand as she unsuccessfully tried to keep her eyes on the words, and the next thing it was soaring through the air past Vita and landing with a soft thud on the floor of the plane. And Evelyn was suddenly very much awake, all thoughts of slumber long gone.

The plane gave a sudden lurch again, making her grateful she hadn't eaten before they'd taken off, because she knew the contents of her stomach wouldn't have survived.

"What the hell's going on?" Vita gasped beside her.

Evelyn reached for Dot's hand and then Vita's, and they both clasped hers tightly, their fingers all colliding and not letting go.

The sideways lurch was followed by a moment of steadiness, and Evelyn looked around at the other nurses and saw a wall of collective terror staring back at her. Even the men looked green, and she noticed they were all holding tightly to their seats.

"Maybe it was just a moment of turbulence," Dot said. "You know, a little patch of bad weather? Or what was that thing you said about birds earlier?"

"Bird strike," Vita whispered. "I said I thought it was a bird strike."

Evelyn immediately looked out the window then, and her heart sank as she saw gray clouds swirling. Gone was the blue sky and rays of sunshine of earlier; it looked almost angry now. And she doubted very much they would encounter a second flock of birds to strike, if it had even been that in the first place.

"I'm sure we'll be fine," she said brightly. "It'll be nothing our pilots can't handle."

As they continued to hold hands and the plane made smaller jerking movements that made Evelyn's stomach dip every single time, it was the final shuddering lurch that told her things most definitely weren't going to plan. Because this wasn't so much a rough patch as them being whipped around like a blade of grass caught in a whirlwind.

"I don't think we're going to make it," Dot whimpered beside her, as Vita stayed uncharacteristically quiet. "Do you think we're going to make it?"

"Shhh," Evelyn murmured, as she would to one of her sisters when she was trying to comfort them. "Shhh, we'll be fine. Just sit tight."

But as she stared out the window again and then shut her eyes at the next shudder, she doubted very much that they were actually going to be fine.

"Evelyn!" Dot cried.

The plane jerked sideways and Evelyn's fingers slipped from Dot's as she gripped her seat, her stomach lurching again and her head pounding.

Oh no.

It was worse than she'd first thought. The clouds were ominous now, swirling closer and closer, as if they were flying into the perfect storm, and the waters below were looking murkier by the second.

"We're going to crash," Dot sobbed beside her.

Evelyn shook her head, trying to find the words, but instead all she found was the terrified gaze of Vita staring back at her when she turned, as if she were silently pleading with Evelyn to save her.

Please, Mama, if you're up there, save us. I don't want to die.

90

CHAPTER TEN

EVELYN

Within seconds, the plane leveled out and the bumps disappeared, and Evelyn stared at the ceiling of the cabin, almost believing that her prayer to her mother had worked. She carefully let go of her seat, her fingers aching from gripping so tightly to the metal.

The cockpit door thrust open then and Bobby appeared, his face so white he looked more ghost than human. Evelyn instinctively reached for her seat again, her breath coming in shallow pants as she stared at his face. She barely recognized the solemn-faced pilot staring back at her.

"Hope you're coming out to apologize for the bumpy ride!" one of the medics called out, leading to an eruption of calls and chuckles from the men. They clearly all thought it was a great joke being shaken like stones in a jar.

Evelyn looked around and saw that not one of the nurses was smiling or making so much as a sound. *They can tell*, she thought. They could all see the change in Bobby, the pilot who was better known for wolf-whistling and charming nurses than looking solemn about war. The medics might not have noticed the change, but to all the women on board, it was blatantly obvious. This was the man who'd danced in New York like it was his last night alive, and winked in a way that made any girl blush. But this was not that Bobby.

"You'll have noticed we're flying at a much lower altitude now, to combat the thick fog we've ended up in," he announced, his voice lower than usual. "We're expecting the conditions could get worse before they get better, but we want you all to sit tight and know that we're doing our best up here."

A murmur ran through the group, and Evelyn looked around, studying all the faces around her. Some she knew well, some were still strangers to her, but collectively they all had the same echo of fear in their expressions.

"What's the control tower saying?" Eddie called out. "Do we have to turn back?"

"We've contacted the control tower repeatedly, but we're not getting any reply at this stage," Bobby replied.

"Why not?" Vita cried beside Evelyn. "How can they just not answer you?"

Bobby ran a hand through his hair and then stumbled as the plane groaned and lurched, but he was standing straight and steady again within seconds, still looking much calmer than she felt. Either he had a particularly good poker face, or he actually believed he was capable of keeping them safe. Or perhaps it was a mix of both.

"We requested an updated weather report as soon as we reached the Peninsula, but we didn't have the correct codes for classified information, so our request was refused."

His admission sent a ripple through the cabin.

"How can they refuse us?" someone called out angrily. "You need to try harder!"

Bobby ducked his head and Evelyn felt like the entire cabin was holding its breath as they waited for him to answer.

"Without the correct codes, they have to treat us as an enemy aircraft. It's, ah . . . Well, it's supposed to be for our safety. It's a fairly new rule, and they didn't give us the codes before takeoff." He shook his head. "We're as dumbfounded as you are, trust me."

Evelyn swallowed and shut her eyes as she digested the reality of the situation. It was going from bad to much, much worse.

"We've changed course again, and now that we're getting closer to Bari we're asking the station to activate their beacon to help guide us in for landing," he continued. "We're hopeful they'll assist us, despite the lack of codes."

"And what if we don't get them?" someone else called out. "Will we be turning back? What's the plan if we can't get help?"

"Look, we're going to try changing course again slightly," Bobby said, sounding tense. "We're all capable pilots, so we suggest you sit tight and let us do our jobs and get you there safely. I need to get back to the cockpit, but we all wanted you to understand the situation."

Dot whimpered beside her, and Evelyn lifted her arm and tucked it around her, holding her close. It was like having her younger sisters with her, and as much as she'd wanted to get away from them, suddenly all she was craving was the sweet smell of Katie's hair and someone to curl up beside in bed. Those things that she'd moaned about, things that she'd felt were tethering her to something she hadn't asked for, were suddenly the things she missed the most.

"Are we going to make it?" Vita's words seemed painful, each one choked out, but Bobby heard her. *Everyone* heard her, and waited for his reply.

With a quick glance and a call behind him, he suddenly hurried forward, dropping down low in front of Vita. Evelyn had seen two different sides to Bobby now, but she hadn't been expecting this third one, this tender one; one that perhaps he'd reserved just for Vita.

"I'm going to get us out of this," Bobby said, his voice low. "We're going to land safely, all we need is some time to figure it out. The control tower will come back to us, I know they will. We gotta keep the faith, that's all."

Evelyn liked his confidence, but she still wasn't convinced; and from the look on his face, she didn't think he'd managed to convince himself either, not completely.

In the only display of public affection she'd ever seen between Vita and Bobby since New York, he touched her hand and brushed a kiss to her cheek, and it was then that Evelyn's stomach truly dropped. There must have been some small part of him that didn't believe his own words, because otherwise he wouldn't have risked both their jobs to comfort her so openly. And she couldn't help but notice how tightly Vita appeared to clutch his hand, too.

Evelyn looked away from them and immediately wished she hadn't. A movement outside caught her eye, clouds starting to move fast, but she had barely registered what she was staring at before a yell came from the cockpit, loud enough for every single one of them to hear it.

"I can see tornadoes rising! Bobby, get back here."

Bobby's face said it all, his skin ashen-white as he gulped and bent to look out the window, hovering as if he didn't know whether to run back as quickly as he could to his copilot who was yelling for him, or stay and reassure all his passengers.

"Eddie," Bobby finally said, his voice steady as everyone seemed to be holding their breath and waiting to be told what to do. "Get another couple of medics and start distributing the life jackets. I want everyone else to remain seated and strapped in. Do it as quickly as you can."

"Life jackets?" Evelyn asked, her mouth feeling like it was full of cotton candy as she tried to open it, her words dry in her throat. "You think we could be going down?"

Bobby's fixed smile didn't convince her for even a second. "It's just a precaution. I told you all I'd keep you safe, and that's exactly what I'm doing. I'd rather you all have a Mae West ready to wear, just in case."

Despite Vita's whimpers, he turned and started to walk quickly away from them, holding the metal rail overhead to steady himself, as Eddie and another medic hurried to the rear of the plane. Evelyn understood why Vita was scared, but she knew exactly where she'd prefer Bobby, and that was behind the controls in the cockpit, not whispering sweet nothings in Vita's ear. He might be arrogant sometimes, but he wasn't called their best pilot for nothing, and she could see now that he was most definitely capable.

"Ahh, Bobby," Eddie called out.

Evelyn's head swiveled, along with everyone else's.

"I gotta get back in there, Eddie, you—"

"There's only twenty-two life jackets."

Bobby marched back past them all, as if he could singlehandedly fix the crisis, and Evelyn saw the change in him, the rising panic that he was barely keeping a lid on.

"That can't be right! We have twenty-six passengers as well as the flight crew, so—"

"There's no mistake, I've counted twice," Eddie said, and Evelyn saw the way Bobby started to shake his head, as if he didn't believe it.

"Dammit!" Bobby yelled, at the same time as the biggest blast Evelyn had ever heard roared through the air around them, and slammed the plane sideways. Eddie and some of the other medics fell, and she stared in disbelief as Bobby hit the ground, then crawled like a toddler, on his hands and knees, straight past them, all in his haste to get back to the cockpit.

"We've been hit! Bobby, get in here! It's a direct hit!"

We've been hit. Evelyn's body turned to ice as everything seemed to slow around her. The sound of screams and cries, the sensation of the plane lurching again, dropping again, and then evening out, the ache in her neck from being thrust unexpectedly to the side and then back again, her ears still painfully ringing from the blast.

Someone is shooting at us. We have no contact with the closest tower. The weather is closing in. We don't have enough life jackets. Evelyn wasn't one for theatrics; she was the calm one, the collected one, the one others turned to when they needed help or clarity. But this, this . . .

She opened her eyes, barely even realizing she'd shut them in the first place, and slowly looked around. There were nurses crying and out of their seats, fighting and sobbing as they tried to get their hands on a life vest; medics arguing loudly over what should be done, about who should distribute the vests and who should get them; a medic yelling that he'd take over the radio himself and force someone to give them the goddamn information they needed.

But she knew then what no one else seemed to understand: if they went down in a blaze of glory, no amount of life vests would save them. One or two of them might get lucky, but chances were, they'd all die. She wasn't about to share her moment of clarity with anyone else, but she *was* going to try to talk them down from their hysteria and get them back in their metal bucket seats.

Evelyn cleared her throat and spoke loudly. "Someone can take mine," she said. "I have every confidence in our pilots, and the best thing we can do is follow orders, stay calm, and keep our belts on just like Bobby told us to."

There was a murmur nearby, from the nurses and medics who were still seated, but there was still just as much squabbling. Evelyn didn't unbuckle herself, but she did raise her voice even more, straining to be heard. She caught Dot's hand again, pressing their palms together as she spoke.

"We need to sit tight and let our pilots get us out of this. You all heard Bobby before, he's going to keep us safe, so we need to do our bit and stay quiet and calm for them so they can do their job. We're highly trained nurses and medics, and we need to behave as such, and we certainly don't need to be squabbling over life vests."

Some hung their heads and others returned to their seats, a few still clinging to the Mae Wests they'd claimed and weren't about to give up, but at least they were quiet. She'd been so desperate to leave home, but now she felt like she was right back there, scolding her sisters for their behavior and trying to make them see reason.

But just as she had everyone relatively quiet, as she thought her attempt at leadership had worked, a loud whistling sound was followed by a jolt that slammed her back hard in her seat and sent the entire plane into hysterics again.

"We've taken a direct hit to the tail!" one of the crew yelled out. "Brace for impact! Brace yourselves!"

Evelyn knew enough about planes to know that it wasn't looking good now. They were either being hunted down by the enemy in the sky or from the ground, and she had the most devastating, sinking feeling that the pilots had no idea where they were, let alone how to get them out of whatever mess they'd flown into.

So much for staying calm.

CHAPTER ELEVEN

DOT

No. *No, no, no!*

Dot wrapped her arms tightly around herself as she rocked back and forth in her seat, trying not to think about it, trying not to imagine what it would feel like when they crashed, how painful it would be or how long it would take for . . . She swallowed and squeezed her eyes shut. *To die.*

The panic inside the plane was too much for her; she couldn't stand the crying or the screaming, she just wanted to yell at everyone to stay quiet. But she didn't, because she couldn't have yelled if she'd tried, her voice always too quiet, her confidence confined to her own mind just like it always was.

Evelyn was her strength, and as her friend reached for her again, as she had so many times since their flight had taken off, she leaned closer to her, clutching her hand and seeing that, on the other side, when she eventually peeled her eyes open, Evelyn was holding Vita's hand, too. A sob erupted from her chest without warning, clawing its way out as she leaned forward, as bile rose with it and threatened to choke her.

"Brace!"

The command came fast, and as her fingers slid from Evelyn's, as she leaned forward with her elbows on her knees and her palms on each side of her head, a pinging sound echoed out and the plane seemed to spiral, the bullets shattering any hope she had left that they were going to survive—along with whatever was left of the tail of their plane. She could barely imagine what their mighty Skytrooper must look like, with holes gliding straight through her as if she were as insignificant as a bird in the sky. And it was cold, so unbearably cold, as they'd seemed to climb higher and higher, trying to evade whoever was shooting at them, the freezing-cold temperature at such a high altitude almost impossible to bear. She felt like even her eyelashes were turning to ice.

Thump.

They flopped to the side and then back again, and Dot kept her arms tucked tight to her side, staying in position. *I don't want to drown. Please, just don't let me drown. Anything but the water.* She'd had nightmares all her life about how her parents had died; she couldn't go through the same fate herself.

Memories washed over her, catching her, refusing to let her scramble away as she begged someone, anyone who might be listening, to not let her drown.

"Oh my God!"

"Look!"

Dot should have stayed in position, she never should have looked up, but she did; and she wished she hadn't. The sight was like a boot to her chest, constricting her airways, too heavy to breathe past, and she knew then with absolute certainty they were going to die.

The German aircraft was coming for them, his menacing gray nose facing them as he lined them up, and no amount of climbing altitude or sideways maneuvers were going to help them, not now. Especially not limping through the sky after so many bullets as good as paralyzing them.

They were a transport aircraft for this flight, which meant they had no way to defend themselves, no ammunition on board to fire back at the enemy. And suddenly Dot wondered if this was how her mother had felt, how her father had felt in the moments, *in the seconds*, before they'd died.

Dot instinctively tried to unbuckle herself then, panicking as she thought of her mother. If she hadn't become trapped, her mother might have made it out of the car, would have at least had a chance of swimming, of staying alive; and if Dot ended up on a sinking plane she wasn't going to be fighting with her belt as she tried to survive.

"Dot, what are you doing?" Evelyn cried. "Don't you dare undo that buckle!"

"I have to. I have to get out of here," she sobbed.

But Dot didn't have a choice in the matter in the end, as the plane swung to the side, and more bullets echoed and they started to fall. Her stomach seemed to drop faster than the rest of her body, and Dot fought not to be sick as they were thrown around like ragdolls, the speed at which they were descending making her ears hurt and her toes curl tightly in her shoes.

But then there was a moment of calm, as if they'd managed to pull back and steady the plane, as if they weren't free-falling and about to nosedive into the ocean.

Until Dot heard the loudest screeching noise she could ever have imagined, her sweaty palms slipping from her seat to cover her head again as she dropped low to brace.

Boom.

And then they were all thrown back, and her head slammed against the side of the plane as it screamed against the ground after impact and came to a terrifying, crashing halt, and a man's body went flying down between them all, like a toy, feet first into the door of the cockpit, and the sickening sound of bone snapping and the almost unhuman scream was enough to make even the strongest of backbones crumble.

More screams cut through the air, calls for help, cries of pain or terror or maybe both. She squeezed her eyes shut, didn't want to open them and confront the horror of what was happening.

I want to go home. It was the first thing Dot thought, the only thing that ran through her mind as she clung tight to her seat, as she tried to find her breath and still the panic inside of her. Only what was left at home for her, other than an empty house? She felt the weight of her ring on the chain around her neck, against her skin, and she wished she'd ripped it off weeks ago. There she was, pretending to everyone that she had a fiancé to return to after the war, when in fact all she had left were shattered dreams and a broken heart. It was a lie she should never have told in the first place, one she'd held on to because she hadn't wanted it to be true, but she vowed to be truthful with her friends if they survived.

She'd missed a chance earlier when they'd first boarded the flight, but she wasn't going to miss one again.

"Dot? Dot, are you alright?"

"I'm—I'm fine," she managed, opening her eyes as Evelyn tugged at her arm. "I . . ." *Am I fine?* She looked down, half expecting to find injuries but not seeing any. She held up her hands, turning them over and inspecting them, but the only thing she could see that was different about them was how vigorously they were shaking, the tremble starting at her wrists and filtering all the way to the tips of her fingers. She looked around, hardly able to believe what had happened to them, seeing everyone crying and scrambling to move.

"Vita? Vita, look at me."

Dot heard Evelyn talking again and forced herself to focus, to see through the fog in her mind and help. There were cries from all around them, and the man—who was the man who'd flown past her? Or had she imagined it? It was like trying to make sense of a dream.

"Eddie!" Vita's scream was piercing, and as she looked from Vita down the center of the plane to the cockpit, she saw that she most definitely hadn't imagined the man. He was lying, his leg bent at an unusual angle, and Vita was struggling to break free from her belt, Evelyn leaning over her and freeing her before she half fell, half ran to her medic.

"We need to get off this plane," Evelyn was saying, and she grimaced when Dot grasped her hand tightly. "Dot, I need you to focus with me."

Dot looked out the window, trying to get her bearings. "Where are we?" she asked. "Where did we crash?"

"I don't know." Evelyn was on her feet now, and Dot was in awe of how calm she looked, clearing her throat and yelling instructions. She could barely register what had happened, let alone try to command others, but she numbly followed Evelyn's orders.

"I need you all to listen," Evelyn shouted above the commotion. "We need to get everyone off this plane as fast and as safely as we can."

There was a murmur that started low and built to a panic within seconds.

"Could we explode?" someone cried.

"Oh my God, get us off here!" came another frantic call.

"We need to stay calm," Evelyn ordered. "We don't know where we are or what the situation is yet."

Dot was watching Eddie now, lying on the ground, his face contorted with pain, but as far as she could tell, he was the only one with serious injuries. There were plenty of gashes across faces and no doubt bruises beneath clothes, but it looked like everyone else could at least move without assistance. It was a miracle no one had died.

There was banging then, and suddenly the door to the cockpit, which must have shut of its own accord during the crash, was flung open, and a frazzled-looking Bobby came out ahead of the other members of the crew, tripping over poor Eddie.

"Where are we?"

"Are we going to explode?"

"Is help coming?"

The questions came thick and fast, but Bobby didn't reply and neither did any of the other members of the flight crew. Instead they pushed past everyone and wrestled with the exit door, and it was as if everyone held a collective breath waiting for it, until it eventually thrust back and fresh air swooped into the cabin.

"Come on, Dot, we need to get out of here."

Dot followed Evelyn, jostled by other nurses and medics as she stood on wobbly legs and they slowly filed out, taking Bobby's hand for a moment as he offered it, another pilot helping her to the ground, his hands quick to find her waist and guide her down.

But she barely registered that he'd touched her as she walked a few yards from the plane, slightly apart from the others as she looked around. She'd never quite seen anything like it; they appeared to have landed on the edge of a lake, the plane precariously perched with its nose pointing into the water, as if it had skidded all the way and managed to stop at just the right moment. It was teetering as the medics climbed out, and she could barely stand to watch, expecting it to go up in a ball of flames any second now before they were all out.

But it wasn't the water and the crashed Skytrooper that surprised her so much as their surroundings. There were hills all around them, buffering them every which way she looked, and they were covered with dense trees, a thick forest by the looks of it, which she was certain was not the landscape in Bari where they had been headed.

Dot looked at the others, huddled together and no doubt relieved they'd all chosen to wear their thick wool coats when they'd left that morning. They all looked as dumbfounded as she was, all turning and staring at the scene around them.

And when she finally met Evelyn's eyes, as she saw the disbelief in her friend's face, she said the only thing that was running through her mind.

"Where are we?"

Evelyn shook her head. "I have no idea, but not where we're supposed to be, that's for sure."

So, then, where in God's name are we?

CHAPTER TWELVE

VITA

"You must have some idea of where we are?" Evelyn asked, standing with her hands on her hips beside Bobby, as Vita watched them. "How far off course did we end up?"

Vita's teeth were chattering, her hands shaking so violently that she'd tucked her arms around herself. She didn't like the way Bobby was constantly raking his fingers through his thick blond hair; it made him look nervous, and he never looked nervous. Bobby was fun and loud and confident; Bobby was the life of the party; but this Bobby looked as ominous as a general about to send his men into battle. She chewed on her bottom lip so hard she tasted blood.

"Honestly, the visibility was so bad up there, and then trying to outrun that enemy plane through thick clouds before we started to spiral, I . . ."

"So we're lost then?" Evelyn asked him. "We're actually completely lost?"

Vita hunched forward, not wanting to listen to their conversation but unable to pull herself away. *I should never have come here. Mother, you were right. I should have stayed at home, I should have known I wasn't cut out for this. I should have known my place.*

A loud groan sounded out then, and she turned, her stomach lurching as she stared at Eddie, her poor, poor medic Eddie, lying on the ground. She'd treated wounds far worse, but something about seeing *her* medic lying there instead of a stranger, with his mangled leg, wasn't something she could stomach. She bent forward and dry-heaved, continuing to retch even though nothing came out. *It's because he reminds me of my brother. It's because he reminds me of you, Andrew.* Suddenly all she could see was her brother lying there, injured, waiting for someone.

"Vita!" Dot urged, waving her over. "Come over here, I need your help."

She wanted to move, but her feet were stuck in place, as if the mud had a hold of her shoes.

"Vita!" Dot called again. "Eddie needs you, come here."

Dot was usually the timid one, but it was as if they'd had a role reversal, as if Vita were staring down from above and watching everything rather than being part of it.

But something about Dot's pleading gaze and the way Eddie's head turned toward her made her take flight, and she hurried the few yards over to them. What was she thinking? This was not the time to get stage fright! "How is he?" she asked, although she barely recognized her own voice.

"He's going to be fine," Eddie said, grimacing as he changed position.

She exchanged gazes with Dot, who didn't look quite as optimistic. "It's a very bad break, but once we finish this splint and get it stable, I'll be a lot happier."

"What do you need me to do?" Vita asked. She felt like she'd been frozen, numb to everything, and now she was slowly starting to defrost as she crouched between Eddie and Dot. "Does he need more pain relief? Eddie, how bad is the pain?"

His sweat-lined brow told her all she needed to know.

"He's had as much as I can give him," Dot told her. "Can you keep this splint steady while I wrap the bandage one more time?"

Vita did as she was told, happy to have a job to keep her busy, her eyes darting to Eddie's face constantly, hating that he was in so much pain.

"Does it look as bad as it feels?" Eddie asked, grimacing as he looked up at her.

"Oh, it's nothing, just a little scrape," she said, flashing him a smile. "I'm sure you've had hangovers far worse."

He grunted, which she took as a laugh. "Hangovers, huh?"

"Just enjoy the morphine," she whispered, swallowing her emotion as she kept up her brave face. "I've heard it's one hell of a ride."

"We just have to hope we can get airlifted out or find a field hospital close enough to take him to," Dot whispered to her. "Surely we won't have to wait here too long, do you think?"

"About that," Vita said, glancing down nervously at Eddie, who was lying back down now, and wondering if she should even say it in front of him. The poor man needed to have hope that they were being rescued soon; the last thing she wanted was him worrying.

"About what?" Dot asked.

Vita looked back at Bobby, the other pilot, and Evelyn, who was still standing with her hands on her hips and very much taking part in the conversation with the men. Vita had never realized quite how capable she was, but Evelyn was showing just how useful she was in a crisis.

Vita lowered her voice, not wanting anyone else to overhear them. "The pilots seem to have no idea where we are. Bobby's trying to sound confident but . . ."

"As in they don't know how far from Bari we've landed?" Dot asked, looking confused. "Or they don't know the exact coordinates to transmit?"

Vita inhaled deeply, then slowly let it go. "I think more like they don't know what country we're in, let alone the coordinates."

The fear on Dot's face mirrored her own, and she watched as her friend wrapped her arms around herself, the exact same position Vita had taken earlier as she'd listened to Bobby and Evelyn talking.

"Vita," Eddie said, reaching for her arm. "You're certain they don't know where we are?"

"I'm sure they were just joking, I'm—"

"Vita," he said, his voice lower now. "Tell me."

She nodded. "I'm certain, Eddie. That's what Bobby said."

"You don't think we're going to be rescued any time soon, do you," Dot said. "I can tell by the look on your face. You think we're doomed."

Vita's mouth went dry. Dot had said exactly what she'd been thinking, as if she could read her mind. "I don't know what to think. Honestly, I just—"

"*Vita.*"

Bobby's voice made her turn, and she fought the sudden urge to throw herself into his arms. But she didn't. *Couldn't.* Because how would that be any different than running back to her family for help as soon as the going got tough? Besides, Bobby looked terrible. His mouth was drawn into a tight line, his forehead bulging with a pulse she'd never seen before, his jaw clenched; she clasped her own hands as she stared back at him.

"What's happening?" she asked, jutting her chin higher and hoping she looked more confident than she felt.

"We're going to do some reconnaissance," he said, marching straight past her toward the plane.

"Reconnaissance?" she repeated. "As in you're just going to wander off and see what you can find? You can't be serious?" She stared out into the dense forest.

Bobby half turned to look at her, but he didn't stop walking. "That's exactly what we're going to do, unless you can think of something better?" As far as firsts went, this was another; he'd never been terse with her before.

She bristled but kept her mouth shut, not wanting to start an argument. She hadn't expected him to be quite so curt, but when she looked at Evelyn and then the other pilot, whose name she didn't even know, she saw they looked as grim-faced as Bobby. They were all just scrambling to figure out what to do; they couldn't exactly sit and do nothing.

Vita stood and awkwardly waited for Bobby to reappear, not liking the fact that he was in the plane again, certain it was going to blow up at any second, even though none of the men seemed concerned by it now that they'd given the aircraft a good once-over. She half expected it to erupt into a ball of fire while she was staring at it.

But when Bobby emerged, she froze, seeing the weapon in his hand and forgetting all about her earlier fears. Suddenly his curtness seemed the least of her worries. "What are you doing with that?" she asked.

"It's the only damn weapon on board," he swore as he climbed from the wreckage and marched toward them. "One single goddamn Tommy gun to protect us all with!"

"I think I should come with you," Vita said as he came near. "To keep Evelyn company. I don't think it's right that she goes alone."

Bobby seemed to consider her, and she stood her ground, somehow keeping her composure. Deep down she wanted to stay close to him, to keep him in her sights, but she wasn't about to admit that to him.

"You're sure you want to come?"

"When have I ever struck you as someone who likes to be left behind?" she said with a smile.

Bobby nodded. "Of course. But you and Evelyn need to stay quiet and follow orders. Are we clear?"

She exchanged glances with Evelyn and they both nodded their agreement.

"We're clear," Vita said, as Bobby strode over to the rest of their group. They were all huddled in small groups, and their worried, drawn faces turned to listen.

"I'm going to lead a small reconnaissance party into the forest to look for help," Bobby said. "Unfortunately, we don't have much information on where we are or which direction to go at this stage, so we suggest you all rest and stay as sheltered as possible. We'll return just as soon as we can."

There was a murmur amongst everyone gathered, until Bobby started to speak again, and then they fell silent once more. Vita watched him along with the others, admiring the way he'd taken charge, a side to him she hadn't seen before. She barely recognized him.

"Our first priority is to find help so that we can radio our location to the closest control tower," he continued. "We ask that you all stay calm and sit tight, and trust in us to get you to safety. I give you all my word that I'll do anything and everything in my power to get us out of here. For your part, I need you all to be careful with rationing any food and water you have. It could be a long wait for help."

Bobby turned on his heel then, and Vita quickly dashed over to Eddie before following him.

"Dot will look after you, won't you, Dot?" she said, squeezing his hand and smiling down at him. "I'll be back just as soon as I can."

She gave Dot a quick hug then hurried off after the others, not wanting to be left behind. Bobby clearly hadn't wanted to answer any questions, and she had to run to catch them, but within minutes she'd fallen into step beside him, her eyes searching the landscape. She'd never seen anywhere so mountainous; mountains rose all around them, and everything was so lush and green.

"Do you even know how to use that?" she whispered from beside Bobby as he slung the gun over his shoulder.

He seemed to find her observation amusing. "Yes, I know how to use a gun, Vita. I wouldn't be carrying it if I didn't."

She had so many more questions, but Bobby was walking fast again now and it took all her concentration to keep up with him and watch her footing at the same time. They were entering a denser area of forest now, and the ground was scarily uneven.

She stifled a cry as her ankle twisted as she went over a rock, gritting her teeth and refusing to slow down for even a second. All they had to do was keep going until they found a way to make radio contact with a control tower, then they might be home before nightfall and they could put all of this behind them like it had never happened in the first place.

———— ⊱✿⊰ ————

Thirty minutes later, Vita was starting to see just how naive she'd been in ever thinking they could make it home by nightfall, if at all. Her feet were already aching, and she'd been scratched repeatedly by branches, but she refused to let out so much as a whimper. Oh, if only her mother could see her now. She glanced at the angry red welts on her hands and arms, and quickly looked away.

"Stop!" The command was barely a whisper, but the sharpness of Bobby's tone made her halt immediately.

He was holding his hand up, and Vita huddled behind him, bunching up between him and Evelyn. Her breath was loud to her own ears, her heart beating so boldly that she could hear the rhythmic echo inside her head, but it wasn't loud enough to drown out the distinct sound of twigs breaking, of footfall over dry leaves. It seemed they weren't alone in the forest, after all.

She instinctively reached out a hand, thinking Bobby was going to take it but finding her palm slipping against Evelyn's instead. She clasped it, and Evelyn held hers just as tight.

And then the sound she'd been dreading came—the click of guns, black barrels pressing through the greenery ahead of them as four men stepped out of the forest. No matter how brave Bobby might be, his single gun was nothing against four men who looked like war-hardened soldiers. They all held guns and had spare rifles slung across their backs, with daggers at their hips and wearing a mismatch of hats all emblazoned with red stars. She tried not to stare at their crude, coarse-looking clothes, with pants that ballooned out and buttoned at the knees like knickerbockers, socks, and homemade-looking sandals strapped to their feet. Their garments might have been strange, but their stance was familiar; they were protecting what was theirs, and she didn't doubt they'd shoot if they needed to. She also guessed that the hats marked them as some sort of group or regiment, although she couldn't be sure.

One of them said something in a language that Vita didn't recognize, but he immediately switched to English when he saw their dumbfounded expressions. Heavily accented English, but she was grateful to be able to understand him at all.

"Americans?" he asked.

She swallowed, too scared to move in case it made any one of them squeeze the trigger. She edged closer to Evelyn. Were they supposed to be truthful, or pretend to be another nationality?

"Yes, we're Americans," Bobby said, answering for them all without hesitation. "We crashed our plane and we're looking for help."

The men stared back at them and Vita hoped he'd done the right thing in admitting who they were. There was something about the steadiness of their gazes, the calmness of their demeanors as they watched them, that unnerved her.

Bobby obviously felt nervous too, because he immediately took his hand off the Tommy gun and held both hands in the air, his movements slow and steady.

"Please, can you tell us where we are?" he asked.

"Where you are?" the man asked, looking at the others in his small group as they laughed, as if it was so amusing for an American to be asking them that question. Only, Vita had no idea why it was so funny.

"You're in Albania," he finally said. "You really didn't know?"

Vita's heart sank all the way to her toes. *Albania?* She didn't even know where Albania was on a map, or whether it was friendly or enemy territory!

"We really didn't know," Bobby admitted, and if Vita wasn't mistaken, there was as much defeat in his tone as there was in her heart.

"Where is the closest airfield?" she forced herself to ask.

"The airfield?" That made the men chuckle again. "It's been taken by the Germans. Didn't you notice them shooting at you? Bang, bang!"

Bobby grimaced, but Vita wasn't going to be put off so easily. If they were going to survive, they at least had to feign confidence.

"Sir, please, we need to know which direction to go. We need to radio for help, we need—"

"If you want to be safe, you come with us," the Albanian said, gesturing to his men. "You're lucky we found you; it was either us, the Germans, or"—he spat on the ground in disgust—"the others whose names we do not speak."

Vita swallowed. Someone worse than the Nazis? She didn't even want to know who he was talking about. But she was heartened that they at least seemed to hate the German army as much as they did.

"*The others*, meaning your own countrymen?" Bobby asked carefully. "Your own country is at war, amongst your own people?"

The man nodded, and Vita saw the pain in his face, the loyalty to what he believed in, what he was fighting for. She'd seen it before, in the faces of the men she'd transported to safety, that deep passion to fight for one's country, side by side with one's countrymen. But this man was also fighting *against* his.

"So you are, how would you say it, *partisan* fighters?" Bobby asked.

The man nodded, and Vita felt Evelyn's grip on her hand tighten. They were going to have to take this man's word for it that they weren't in danger.

"We were going to shoot you down, before you crashed. We have a machine gun in the woods, and we were watching. But I saw the white star on the fuselage, and I ordered my men not to shoot."

"You know the American symbols?" Bobby asked, sounding as surprised as Vita felt.

"I have seen in newspapers. We don't want to shoot Americans or British. You are not our enemies."

Vita could see the movement of Bobby's Adam's apple, and watched as he fisted his palms. It was the first time she'd ever seen him look so unsure of himself, or perhaps it was the first time he'd truly thought he was in danger of losing his life.

"Come," the man said, gesturing at them to follow. "Come with us. You're lucky we found you. Others would have just slit your throat."

"We have many more survivors at the crash site," Vita said, doing her best to ignore his last comment. "We need to go back for them." She didn't care what anyone said; they weren't leaving Dot or Eddie, or anyone else for that matter, behind.

The man nodded, and Vita watched as he held his hand out to Bobby, at the same time as the men behind him lowered their guns and let them hang over their shoulders instead.

"Hasan Josef," he said.

"Bobby Redfern," Bobby said, shaking his hand. "And this is my copilot Ralph, and two of our nurses, Vita and Evelyn."

"Josef," he said, shaking hands with Ralph but simply smiling at her and Evelyn. "Come, my dears. And welcome to the land of the eagle."

Vita instinctively looked toward the sky, half expecting to see an eagle soaring. Hours earlier, they'd been at their villa in Catania, and now they were suddenly in a country rife with danger, with no way to get home, an airfield overrun with Germans, and a group of men ushering them to God only knew where. For all she knew, *they'd* slit their throats the moment they got the chance.

A thrill ran all the way down her spine and back up again. She hated herself for thinking it, but as far as adventure went, it didn't get any more exhilarating than crash-landing in a country she'd barely heard of before.

"Come, my dears," Josef said again, scrambling ahead with one of his men to walk beside Bobby.

She glanced back at the strange men following, hating that she couldn't keep an eye on them, that they were behind her with weapons while she had no way to defend herself.

"It's all going to be fine," she whispered to Evelyn, squeezing her hand. "We'll find a way to safety, I just know we will."

"You're still so certain about that?" Evelyn asked. "They could be taking us anywhere!"

"If they wanted us dead, we'd be dead already," Vita said. "I think they'd have killed us immediately if that's what they wanted, don't you?"

Bobby looked over his shoulder at them and gave them a sharp look, but it was Josef who surprised them. Vita had naively thought he wouldn't hear what she was whispering to Evelyn, but clearly he'd heard every word.

"You don't come with me now, you won't survive the night," he said, stroking his thick, bushy mustache as he considered her. "You need us to help you."

"How . . ." Evelyn began, clearing her throat. "How is it you speak such good English?" Her voice was shaky, but Vita was impressed that she'd spoken up. "It's very good."

"Albanian Vocational School," he said. "Only one hundred and fifty of us learned English there before it was, how do you say, forbidden?"

Vita listened to them talk, her feet moving of their own accord, pushing past the pain of her heels, the blisters that she could almost feel growing as her feet sweated and rubbed back and forth against the leather.

"You're certain we should go with them?" Evelyn whispered one last time, her lips so close they almost brushed Vita's ear as they walked.

Vita leaned into her and slipped her arm around her, hugging her tightly to her side. "Honestly, I don't see what choice we have. I'm sure it's going to all work out fine. We just have to keep our faith, that's all."

CHAPTER THIRTEEN

EVELYN

Evelyn was barely keeping it together inside, although she hoped that to Vita and everyone else she seemed perfectly calm about what was unfolding. But the truth was that she was only seconds away from having to double over and be sick all over the forest floor, and she doubted she'd ever forget what it had felt like to see the hard nose of a gun pointed directly at her. She hadn't been able to drag her gaze from the cold, black metal.

You've lived in a nightmare before. You can survive this. You can survive anything.

She was usually so good at cheering herself along, telling herself all the right things to keep her mind from wandering, but there was also doubt that crept into her mind, that refused to be quieted no matter how positive she tried to be.

A loud droning noise thrummed above them then, and she hurried along after the others, snatching quick glances overhead in between watching her footsteps. There was no mistaking the looming gray aircraft buzzing back and forth, no doubt combing the area for their wreckage, and it was only so long before they found it. The sight of the German planes sent a shiver through her that ran all the way from the top of her spine to her tailbone and back again. She wasn't entirely comfortable with Josef and his partisan crew, but she was far more comfortable with betting on them than on the Nazis, who were undoubtedly out for blood. She didn't even want to think of their fate as women in a prisoner of war camp—or worse. She only wished she knew more about Albanian politics.

Within minutes they were back at the wreckage, and she saw for the first time what Josef would see, what anyone would see who stumbled upon them all. There were so many of them, and everyone they'd left behind was sitting in small groups, huddled together against the cold. The wind was bitter, although she was flushed and warm from their walk, and she realized how fortuitous it was that they'd prepared for the cold. Without their warm coats, many of the nurses would have been violently shivering by now. Evelyn looked around and noticed that many of the medics weren't as warmly dressed though, and she worried how they'd cope if the temperatures continued to plummet through the night.

"This is everyone?" Josef asked. "All of your, how do you say, *survivors?*"

She watched Bobby nod. "Yes. This is everyone."

"The injured man, you have a stretcher for him?" Josef asked. "It's a long walk to our village and we have no mule."

Bobby looked to her and she nodded. "Yes, we have a stretcher to use, and medical supplies on board as well. We'll bring them to your village with us."

Josef nodded. "Very good."

"Wait there," Bobby told Josef and his men, who had their hands braced on their guns again, although this time at least they were holding them low, pointed to the ground instead of up and at the ready.

Evelyn followed closely behind Bobby. She was impressed with the change in him, his voice carrying clearly to everyone and his easy stance not giving away for a moment that he might be uncertain about what he was asking them all to do. She was starting to like this version of Bobby much more than the partying, playboy one. This Bobby would protect them or die trying, of that she had no doubt.

"The man behind me is Hasan Josef; he's a resistance fighter who's kindly offered to take us to his village," Bobby said. "We're sitting ducks out here, and any minute now the Nazis could discover our location and come looking for us, so we need to move quickly. Those planes you hear overhead certainly aren't friendly. I, for one, don't want to be here when they find our aircraft."

"Did you radio for help?" someone called out.

"Where are we?" asked another.

Bobby was still for a moment; perhaps his voice caught in his throat, because barely a word came out.

"We're . . ." he started, looking back at the small group of partisans as if he couldn't believe it himself, before clearing his throat once more. "Well, it just so happens we're in Albania."

The collective gasp echoed how Evelyn was feeling, and when she caught Dot's eye, she saw how terrified her friend was and wished she could just go over and throw her arms around her. Only a day earlier, they'd been lying side by side on her big bed at the villa, flicking through magazines and moaning about how bored they were. Now, she'd have done anything to wind back the clock, to just be two nurses waiting expectantly for their next routine flight and reminiscing about home.

"I need you all to carefully go back to the plane and take your personal bags if you don't already have them with you. We will be gathering and taking what medical supplies we can easily carry, too. I know there's not a lot on board, but every provision is worth saving and taking with us."

"So we're just leaving the plane? How will our rescue flight know where to find us if we're not here?" called out one of the nurses.

"At this stage, we have to focus on keeping ourselves safe," Bobby finally said. "The priority has to be staying alive."

Evelyn knew the words that were on Bobby's lips, even though he never uttered them. *There's no rescue flight coming for us—not yet anyway, and maybe not ever.*

She felt movement behind her then and saw that Josef was walking forward, his men fanning out behind him, and she spun around to Vita, who looked as nervous as she'd ever seen her.

"Vita, why don't you introduce Josef to everyone? Make sure they all know we can trust him," Evelyn said, before hurrying after Bobby, who was headed back toward the plane.

"Bobby!" she said, breaking into a run. "Bobby, wait a moment."

He turned to her and she saw fear in his eyes that had been absent earlier, as if she were peering through a facade, although it was gone as quickly as it registered.

"You truly think this is the right decision?" she asked, her voice low as she kept up with his stride.

"I do. Do you?"

She nodded. "I honestly don't know, but I also don't see we have any other option," Evelyn sighed as she followed him around the back of the plane. "What can I help with?"

"I need to activate a charge back here which will set off an explosion," he explained. "We need to destroy all the classified equipment, the parts that send coded signals."

"So the enemy can't access it?" she asked.

Bobby nodded, but his mouth was drawn into a solemn line.

"What is it?" she asked.

He gave her a long look before turning away and muttering, "Because it also means no one can find us, unless we can manually radio our coordinates to a control tower. This is it for us in terms of anyone finding us. I don't see that I have any choice, but . . ."

She digested the weight of his words as she watched him work. *We're truly alone once he does this.* That's why he looked so glum.

Because once he set this chain of events in motion, no one, not even their own countrymen, would be able to find them.

Which meant they were going to be truly, *entirely* alone, in a country where no one would ever think to look for them.

———— ❧ ————

Evelyn had let herself wallow for a few moments as Bobby set the box on fire, but the moment she was in front of everyone again, she fixed her smile and straightened her shoulders, pretending she was playing a part, just like he was. In truth, she liked being the one others relied on, because it gave her something to do. She just hadn't realized how much she thrived in that role until she'd left home and had to figure out who she was without a family to care for. She wondered if mothers felt that way when their children left home—the mother hen with an empty nest, so used to being the center of everything until they just weren't anymore. Suddenly the only way she felt like she could cope with the hand they'd been dealt was to make herself indispensable to Bobby and their group.

"Come on, keep going," she said, cheering on some of the nurses who were starting to lag behind. It was Dot who caught her eye though, her limp pronounced as she struggled to keep up.

"Are you badly hurt?" Evelyn asked.

Dot grimaced. "I'll be fine, don't worry about me. It's just my ankle."

"Are you sure you don't want me to take a look?" Evelyn said.

Dot's determination was obvious before she even uttered another word. "I'm fine. I don't want any special treatment."

Evelyn knew better than to press her, and she saw the way Dot glanced back at Eddie.

They kept walking, on and on, up a hill and through a tree cover so dense she started to get disoriented, the lake long behind them now. If she suddenly had to flee back to the crash site, she wasn't so sure she'd be able to find her way; it was like walking through the corn maze her daddy had always taken her to around harvest time when she was a little girl, only this one was green and thick with trees and bushes. It had started to rain now, and from the looks of it, the rain had preceded their arrival, too. The overhead branches were swaying slightly in the wind, and rain was catching and falling from leaves, landing in big plops around them. Evelyn's shoes were squelching, full of water and sloshing with every step, and her pants were now so wet they were starting to feel more like a second skin than fabric, but still they kept walking. Up ahead, Josef was laughing and talking with some of the men, which gave her confidence in his intentions at least, and as she turned to look back, the rear was still being brought up by two of the medics who were carrying Eddie between them on a stretcher, their faces drawn in tight grimaces from the exertion.

The terrain became slippery then and Evelyn fell forward, her hands bracing her fall, nails sliding against the dirt as she tried to right herself. But just as she thought her legs couldn't keep going, as her shoulders slumped at the prospect of hauling herself back up, she caught a glimpse of a building at the bottom of the hill. A large, sad-looking building, but the only one that she could see, and it was the first clearing she'd spotted too.

"Dot," she said, reaching back a hand and clasping her friend's palm. "Come on, we're almost there. We can do it."

She hauled Dot up with her and they kept holding hands, steadying each other as they made their way down after the others like goats on a hillside. Eventually, despite falling twice, making her pants almost as muddy as they were wet, they were standing in dirt, staring up at a large two-story building built of timber with a very basic stone roof. Evelyn turned and looked for the rest of the village, having expected a large cluster of homes and perhaps small shops and other facilities, but it certainly didn't match what she'd pictured in her mind. There was nothing else; just this one building in the middle of nowhere, surrounded by trees.

"Do you think this is it?" Dot whispered to her. "Their entire village, I mean? Or aren't we there yet?"

Evelyn dropped her hand, trying not to become lost in the shock of what she was seeing. "I think maybe this is it," she whispered back. She knew little if anything about Albania, had no concept of what their culture or customs were, but she was starting to realize that it was in fact a lot more basic than what an American would ever expect. In fact, it was nothing short of surprising, and she hadn't exactly had a privileged upbringing.

"Come, my dears," Josef said, gesturing enthusiastically as people from inside started to peer out at them. "Come inside! Leave your bags here." He gestured to the area alongside the building that was covered by the roof overhang.

Evelyn put a protective hand over her musette bag. It was everything she had, and the last thing she wanted was to leave it behind.

"Can't we just take our things with us?" Dot murmured. "We don't even know these people. And why does he keep calling us all *dears*?"

Evelyn watched as Bobby and the others in front of them placed their things on the ground, and she instinctively knew the only polite thing to do was to follow suit, as much as she didn't want to. "We have to do as he says. We can't insult the locals. They're our only hope of surviving and it might be part of their customs. If they say we leave them, then we leave them." She also wondered if, logically, there simply wasn't enough room inside for so many people as well as all their belongings. How were they even going to fit? How many people already lived in the building?

"Vita, are you alright?" Evelyn asked, placing her hand on her friend's shoulder as she approached her from behind.

Vita almost jumped out of her skin. "Sorry, I was a million miles away. Do you really think we need to leave our bags? I feel like this is all I have left."

Dot looked hopeful, as if Evelyn had the power to make decisions, but she was forced to shake her head.

"We're here, and we're alive, so that means we need to keep our chins up and do the best we can. And we follow orders," she told her. "We get a good sleep here tonight, we figure out where exactly we are in relation to help, and we form a plan. But we can't do that if some of our strongest nurses start falling apart at the seams. Do you understand what I'm saying? Trust in Bobby and what he's doing for us. Can you do that?"

Dot nodded, and Evelyn saw recognition in Vita's gaze, too. She also saw how many other nurses had gathered and were watching her, listening to her, their eyes full of uncertainty. They all needed to trust in Bobby; he was their pilot and he was used to making quick, intelligent decisions in the air, which meant it was an easy choice to turn to him.

"We leave our things here just like they've asked, we stay strong, and we do everything in our power to keep making the most of a very bad situation," she continued. "If we hadn't come here, we would have been out in the rain all night huddled near the plane, so this is most definitely a blessing. We stay together and we stay strong."

"You're right," Vita said, moving to stand beside her. "You're absolutely right. We all need to stay strong, because if even one of us starts to slip, it'll bring everyone down and the doubts will start creeping in."

Evelyn was relieved to see Vita stand tall, her chin lifted defiantly, like the old Vita, like the Vita who'd stolen them all away for a night of dancing and drinking and staying out long past bedtime at Camp Kilmer. They all needed to see this Vita; she'd always been so good for morale.

As the rain started to pelt down, wetting their hair and streaming down their faces, Evelyn noticed the change in many of the nurses, their indecision turning to resignation as they stared at the house before them. They needed to get out of the rain, because if they didn't? They'd all end up with hypothermia, not to mention they had no idea which way to go or where to hide.

"Come, come!" Josef said, enthusiastically waving them toward a staircase that extended down one side of the building's exterior wall. "Out of the rain!"

Evelyn waited until the first small group had gone up, not certain the staircase could, or *should*, hold so many people at once. She glanced down as she finally walked up, holding the thin handrail as some women below caught her eye. They wore simple, long black dresses, their heads covered in scarves so that their hair wasn't exposed, and as they tilted their faces up, she saw they wore face veils as well, and it made Evelyn conscious of her messy hair and bare cheeks. Would they have to adopt the local custom while they were here? She guessed the women were Muslim, although she wasn't certain because it wasn't a religion she was overly familiar with.

"This—this is the toilet," Josef said as they passed an open door.

Evelyn glanced in, surprised to see a simple hole cut in the floor, with no wash basin. It was so unlike anything she'd ever seen before. She saw Vita physically recoil, and she prodded her from behind to make her keep walking, not wanting their guests to see them as being disrespectful. She'd have a word with her later about not insulting other cultures.

"You all stay here, get warm," Josef said, his smile as big as his mustache as he gestured to another door. "We keep you safe."

The other partisans had dispersed, and Evelyn followed the rest of her group into a large, basic room. There was no furniture or anywhere to sit or sleep, just a threadbare rug covering a small part of the wooden floor and a fireplace at the end, the walls stained black around it from no doubt years of fires burning. Thick smoke curled through the room, choking her as she inhaled, the smoke only getting worse as Josef threw a few more logs on. If only there were a proper chimney.

But it's something. It was dry at least, and even as her eyes started to tear up and burn from the biting smoke, she was grateful for having a roof over her head, and she peeled off her coat and sat as close to the fire as she could. Within seconds a man brought in a candle on a small dish and placed the flickering flame on the fireplace mantel. It wasn't until he'd left and shut the door behind him that the room seemed to come to life. They'd been in silence since walking in; most of them too scared to say anything until they were finally alone.

Evelyn looked to Vita, who was bent over the fire trying to stoke the flames, something she doubted her posh friend was used to doing, and then surveyed the room. Someone needed to say something to boost morale again, but just as she was about to stand and address everyone, Vita cleared her throat, flashing her full-wattage smile.

"Welcome to the Ritz!" Vita said with a grin. "We're all going to be just fine here tonight, especially once Bobby gets this fire going for us all. Isn't that right, Bobby?"

Bobby was suddenly beside her, taking charge of coaxing the flames and looking much more capable of the job than Vita had.

"I suggest we all get a good night's sleep," Evelyn said, smiling at her friend as she joined her in addressing the group. "Make yourselves as comfortable as you can. Let's get dry and rest, and tomorrow we can take stock and figure out what to do next. For now, at least we're safe."

A low murmur began amongst them all, and Evelyn shuffled closer to Dot and Vita. She thought Bobby might make his way over to Vita, and once he'd moved around the room checking on everyone, he did—only Vita chose to turn and wriggle closer to Evelyn instead. She almost felt sorry for Bobby as he made camp farther away.

"Come on, let's make ourselves comfortable here on our jackets," Evelyn said, her eyes heavy as she thought about sleep. "We can all curl up together to get warm."

As she spoke, her teeth began to chatter, and she wound an arm around Dot, listening to Vita's shallow breathing as she cuddled her from behind. Evelyn had no idea who usually occupied the room—and she didn't have time to wonder for long, as the arms of slumber gently wound around her and she fell asleep.

———— ⬎⬍ ————

When Evelyn woke, she stretched out and immediately curled her legs back in when they connected with someone below her. It all came back to her in a wave, slowly crashing over her until she sat up and opened her eyes, hoping that it had just been a nightmare.

She blinked and looked at all the bodies stretched out on the hard wooden floor around her, the fire having long since died out, leaving the room frigid with cold. There were no windows, so she couldn't even look out to see what the morning was like. Slowly, everyone around her stirred, and Evelyn wished she could just shut her eyes again as she remembered where they were and what had happened.

"Morning," Evelyn whispered.

"Morning," Dot mumbled back.

"What's for breakfast, girls? Scrambled eggs and salmon?"

Trust Vita, always making them laugh even when they least expected it. Evelyn certainly hadn't expected to be laughing so easily, not given the circumstances.

"Morning," Bobby rumbled, a few bodies away from them, his hair standing on end as he sat up and rubbed his eyes with his knuckles. "What's that about scrambled eggs?"

"Oh, that's just Vita's warped sense of humor," Evelyn said. "Trust me, there's no eggs."

"At least we all managed to get some sleep," Vita said. "I was out like a light."

Evelyn glanced at her watch and could hardly believe how long she'd slept. When she'd first lain down, the floor had been so hard she'd barely expected to get a wink of shut-eye, but somehow she'd fallen into an easy slumber. She took her jacket from the ground and slipped her arms in as she started to shiver. Perhaps she'd managed to sleep the night because of the sheer amount of body heat, with them all lying so close together.

"I'm going to go see if I can rustle us up some food," Bobby said, stretching as he stood and looking around the room. "Do your best to keep everyone calm while I'm gone."

He seemed to be directing his statement at her, so she nodded, but it was Vita who Bobby was staring at. Evelyn couldn't help but wonder what was going on between the pair of them, and she hoped that Vita might be more open to giving him a chance now. The poor man was clearly smitten with her, and she was so impressed by how easily he'd stepped into the role of leader.

Evelyn decided she couldn't wait any longer to use the toilet; she just needed to be brave and get on with it. She held out her hands for Dot and Vita. "Come on, I'm not going out there alone and I can't hold it a second longer."

Dot groaned. "Is anyone else just a little nervous about how to, you know, squat that low?"

"Come on, Dot, if I can do it, you can do it," Evelyn said.

Despite the cold, Evelyn smiled as they walked the short distance down the open-air corridor, the first group to leave the room. Even

Dot seemed a little better, although her eyes were bloodshot and Evelyn wondered if she'd managed to get any sleep. The door was slightly ajar, and Evelyn looked at the other two, who just shrugged back at her.

"Knock knock," she called, rapping her knuckles lightly against the timber doorframe before entering.

No one answered so she gently nudged the door fully open and peered in. Flies swarmed the small space and she swatted her hand through the air.

"I'll go first," she said, looking around and realizing there wasn't so much as a scrap of toilet paper. She should have taken a square from her bag; she always kept some with her makeup, but then again she didn't want to use it unless she really needed it.

Evelyn went to shut the door, but the minute she did the room became pitch-black and she couldn't see a thing, so she quickly yanked it back open.

"What is it?" Vita asked.

"I can't see anything with the door closed," Evelyn explained, starting to jump from foot to foot she was so eager to relieve herself. "Can you prop it open for me? Just enough to let a crack of light through?"

Vita nodded and Dot turned her back. "I'll be lookout. Hurry up."

Evelyn hurried to wriggle her trousers down, eyeing the hole and wondering how on earth she'd ever balance on her haunches long enough to empty her bladder. She shut her eyes, finishing as quickly as she could as she pondered over what strong leg muscles the local women must have.

Once she was done, she waited on the door for the other two to take their turns, then they went back and advised the others of the situation.

"I strongly suggest everyone goes in pairs," Evelyn had just explained to the room when Bobby suddenly appeared with Josef behind him.

Just like the day before, a hush passed through the band of survivors at the sight of their rescuer. Evelyn wondered if some of them were starting to think of him as their captor instead.

"Food," Josef announced, standing back and ushering two women through the door. "You very hungry," he added, waving his hands at them all.

The two women wore the same long dresses and head coverings as the women she'd seen the day before, and Evelyn watched them with open curiosity, wishing she knew more about their customs and what might be expected of her group while they were in the village. But the women didn't say anything, just placed the food in the center of the room and backed away, not making eye contact with any of them.

It looked to be some sort of flatbread, and Evelyn found herself salivating as she stared at the plate. It wasn't a lot, but it was something, and it had been more than twenty-four hours since any of them had eaten.

"It's cornbread," Bobby said once Josef had disappeared, along with the women. "He said it's their main source of food here."

"Should I pass it around?" Vita asked.

Bobby nodded his approval and Evelyn tried to ignore the growl of her stomach as she sat cross-legged on the ground beside him and took her tiny portion. It was barely enough for ten of them, let alone thirty. "Any news?" she asked.

He shook his head, his voice low when he spoke. "Nothing. I've entrusted Josef to pass on our whereabouts, and he believes there could be British special operations agents in the area, but I'm not hopeful. It almost sounds farfetched to me."

Evelyn swallowed. "Not hopeful? That he'll help us?" *Was* he their captor?

"Not hopeful that there are British officers working here. But I could easily be wrong."

"And I take it they don't have any form of radio communication?"

Bobby shook his head, sadly, and the reality of their situation washed over her.

"So, let me get this straight," Vita said from behind them. "Our squadron back in Sicily may or may not know that we're missing; there are no Americans on the ground here; and we have no way of communicating with *anyone* who could possibly help us?"

Bobby's eyes were downcast when he took a chunk of bread from Vita, and Evelyn forced herself to eat hers, even though the last thing she felt like doing now was eating. It was as dry as chalk in her mouth, turning to a gluey paste when it mixed with her saliva.

"I'd say you're about right there," Bobby muttered as Vita set down the tray.

"Right about what?" Evelyn asked.

"That we're never going to get out of this hellhole," Vita muttered.

"Oh God, this bread," Dot cried, looking like she was about to fall to pieces. "I can't eat it. It's so dry, I can't swallow."

Evelyn had only taken one mouthful of hers and she had to agree with Dot; it was dry and tasteless. But they had to eat, and if this was the only food on offer, then she was going to force down every single bite.

"Dot, you just need to stay calm," she said, leaning into her. "We're going to be fine if we make the most of what we have, and just imagine the stories you'll have to tell your fiancé once all this is over?"

Dot didn't look convinced, but she did at least start nibbling at her piece of bread again.

A young boy entered the room before anyone else could complain about the food, a flute in his hand and his eyes downcast like he'd been forced to come near them, and they all fell silent again.

"We're going to be alright," Vita said, her voice softer than usual as she shuffled closer to them, the color seeming to have come back into her cheeks as she ate. "I truly believe we're going to be fine, we just have to give it some time. I feel so much better today; my head seems clearer somehow."

But as the boy with the flute sent beautiful melodies floating through the room, taking Evelyn all the way back to her sister's room at home, where she'd often sat and listened to her play an assortment of instruments, Evelyn wondered if perhaps Vita was becoming delusional. Because nothing about their situation was alright; they should have arrived at their destination, transported their patients, and been back at base by now. And Evelyn doubted most of their group could last a few days stranded, let alone the week or more it might take someone to actually find them. She felt worse about their situation than she had the day before.

"Someone's stolen our stuff!"

The yell cut through the room, stifling the soft melody of the flute as everyone rose and shuffled in a hurry toward the door. Evelyn hadn't even noticed they were missing anyone, but one of the medics came bounding into the room, his heavy footfall vibrating through the timber.

"What's gone?" Evelyn asked.

"All the stuff in our bags," he said, out of breath and dropping their bags at their feet. "They've taken almost all our stuff."

Evelyn looked from Vita to Dot and then back to Vita again. Perhaps they were being held captive, after all.

CHAPTER FOURTEEN

VITA

"What's happened?" Dot asked as she stood in the doorway, the flute-playing boy scurrying away, clearly not wanting to be with his American audience any longer.

"Apparently they've stolen all our belongings," Vita muttered. "They've left the bags, but they've taken almost everything out of them." She glared at Evelyn. "I told you we should never have left them down there!"

Evelyn glared straight back at her. "Oh, so this is my fault for following our host's orders?"

"Stop it!" Dot cried. "Just stop it! I can't deal with you two squabbling!"

Vita knew it had been a shallow comment, and she regretted it the minute it came out of her mouth, but before she had time to apologize, Evelyn had turned away and was rifling through her bag.

Given they had no idea when they were going home, losing their possessions felt like the worst possible thing that could happen to them, other than their plane going down in the first place.

"Is there anything at all left in yours?" Evelyn asked.

Vita opened her bag—she didn't care what anyone said, she was keeping hers on her shoulder from now on.

"I still have my makeup and toothpaste, and most of my first-aid kit, except for the scissors," she said with a sigh. "My spare socks, underwear, soap, toothbrush, and clothes have all gone."

"Looks like they took whatever they needed and left the rest," Bobby said, coming up behind her. "We've all lost our razor blades, as well as our soap and clothes," Bobby grunted. "If only we'd all put on our extra socks last night when we were cold, at least we'd still have them."

"What did Josef say?" Evelyn whispered. "Has anyone told him? Does he know our things have been taken?"

Bobby looked furious. "He claims that Albanian people don't steal, because the consequences for theft are so high. He said we must be mistaken."

"So what, we've just imagined that all of our things have gone?" Vita snorted. "How convenient. Did our belongings suddenly grow legs?"

Bobby hung his head, looking dejected for the first time since they'd landed. "We've lost almost everything, including any medical equipment we had."

Vita's heart broke as she looked at him, but as easy as it would have been to go to him, she didn't. She'd been craving his touch, his interest in her, from the moment they'd landed, but she knew she'd never be able to bring herself to make the first move, not after she'd told him she wasn't interested. Besides, she'd given up so much in order to be independent from her family and the marriage they'd organized for her, so it didn't feel right to buckle the moment the going got tough. Didn't she want to prove to herself that she was capable without a man or someone to look after her?

"So, what do we do next?" Vita asked when he finally looked up. "Are we still planning on staying here?"

Bobby nodded. "If we don't stay here, where do we go? None of us know the area, we don't have any local maps, and the partisans we find outside of this village could kill us on sight going by what Josef has told us. To be honest, I'm inclined to believe him. Who would have thought we would end up in a country with two rival parties fighting amongst themselves?"

Vita shuddered and Bobby obviously saw the shift in her, because he cringed.

"Sorry."

"Don't be sorry," she said. "I want the truth, even if it's hard to hear." Her stomach churned at the thought of being lost in the wilderness outside the little village. The room they were in was bad enough, but the forest would be so much worse.

"So, let me get this right," Dot said, shuffling closer. "The partisans are like resistance fighters? And they're fighting over who has control here?"

"That's right," Bobby said. "Their opposition—they're aligned with the Germans from what I can understand, hence us being lucky to have been found by Josef and his friends. These partisans are more aligned with us, so to speak. They see us as friends rather than foes."

"Do you trust him to get word to anyone?" The voice came from the back of the room, near the fire, and Vita turned and saw that Eddie was propped up on one elbow, still lying on the stretcher. She'd forgotten all about him in her haste to use the toilet and check her bag earlier. She instinctively moved over to him, settling on the floor beside him, not wanting him to feel excluded.

"I don't know," Bobby replied. "But once again, I don't see what choice we have. I've asked if Josef will help us make contact with British or American forces, but he said he can't do anything until he visits the leader of the next village to get permission."

"So what you're saying is that we're stuck here, whether we like it or not?" Vita asked. "I thought he already agreed to contact the undercover British agents?"

"Wait, there's British agents here? Why didn't you tell us?" Eddie asked, and some of the other medics looked up, excitement as clear as day on their faces.

"Because it's little more than a rumor at this stage," Bobby replied.

"A possibility, though?" Eddie pressed.

Bobby frowned. "Yes." He cleared his throat. "Vita, a word please?"

She placed her hand over Eddie's for a second, happy to see he had more color in his face than he had earlier, but when she stood to follow Bobby, she saw anger in the pilot's gaze; palpable, red-hot anger.

"What?" she asked, perplexed. "What did I do?"

He gripped her arm tightly, marching her away from everyone else, his voice barely a whisper. "You don't repeat what I tell you privately, do you understand? You don't give them hope there's friendly agents in the area until we know for sure."

She tried to wrestle herself from his grip. "You're hurting me!" she hissed. "Bobby, let go!"

"Are we clear?" he whispered, sharply, still not releasing her. "I need to know I can trust you."

"We're clear," she muttered, finally tugging her arm from him. "But don't you *ever* touch me like that again."

Bobby just gave her a long, hard look, and she turned away from him so he couldn't see the tears stinging her eyes.

The rest of the group started to file back into the room then, the combined murmurs becoming louder and louder, full of complaints about everything that had been taken, which at least took her mind off Bobby. Vita's stomach grumbled, and she wondered when they next might be fed, or if the tiny village would even have enough food to spare for so many visitors.

"Vita."

She crossed back over to Eddie when she heard his call, taking him by the elbow and helping him up into a more comfortable seated position.

"How are you feeling?" she asked. "Is there anything I can get you?"

"Other than a big bowl of hot food and a proper bed?"

She grinned and sat beside him, shoulder to shoulder, easy in his company. "Exactly. Anything other than that."

It still surprised her sometimes how familiar Eddie seemed, the way she was so drawn to him in a completely platonic sense. The kind way he looked at her, the fact she just knew that there was nothing he wouldn't do for her—it made her feel safe in a way only her brother had ever made her feel before.

"You know that poor man is smitten with you, don't you, Vita?"

She laughed. "Oh, stop it. I doubt very much that he's *smitten*."

He grunted. "Trust me, he's smitten. I just wish you'd see that and give him a chance."

"I'm just . . ." She sighed, not sure how to explain how she felt.

Eddie was watching her, she could feel his eyes on her, but she kept looking ahead. "You just what?" he asked.

"It's a long story, trust me," she said. "But let's just say that I gave up a lot to come here, to be part of our squadron, and the last thing I want is my head turned by a handsome man. I want to be more than that." She sighed again. "I know that sounds strange, but it's the only way I can describe it. Besides, I already told him I wasn't interested, and I'm not one to go back on my word."

"Ah, I see," Eddie said. "He's a good man though, Vita. Just remember that, in case you decide that you want to let someone close."

She nodded, still torn over how she actually felt about Bobby.

"You know, I was the last person any of my friends thought would settle down. Then I met my wife, and the way she looked at me . . ." He shook his head. "Let's just say that sometimes you don't go looking for love, but when it comes to the heart, you have to accept that it's outside of your control. Marrying her was the best thing I've ever done."

Vita dropped her head onto Eddie's shoulder then, as tears pricked her eyes again, and as she squeezed them shut, tears slipped down her cheeks as she sat silently and cried. It wasn't just about Bobby, it was everything—the crash, what she'd left behind, knowing she'd never see her brother again, the fact that they might never make it back to America. She would have given anything to be back home right then, to the one place she'd never, ever wanted to return to again. But she didn't even know if she'd be welcome there anymore.

"Vita?" Bobby's soft call pulled her from her thoughts and she quickly wiped her eyes with her knuckles, sniffing as she composed herself, lifting her head from Eddie's shoulder.

"Is something wrong?" she whispered, realizing Eddie was asleep and not wanting to wake him.

Bobby dropped to his haunches in front of her.

"Josef has returned, and he's confirmed there's definitely at least one British SOE agent working locally," Bobby said, his voice low. "It looks like there might be someone who can help us after all, although we still have to find a way to make contact with him."

She nodded, carefully moving away from Eddie so she didn't wake him. "Do you honestly think we're ever going to get out of here? That there's a chance we'll actually be rescued?"

Bobby smiled. "I hope so, Vita. I promise you that I'll do whatever it takes to make that happen, but until we find someone who can help us make contact with our base . . ."

She nodded. "We just have to sit tight," she said, repeating his words from before. "I get it."

"I know yesterday was rough, and it could get worse before it gets better, but I need you to stay strong. I can't have you falling apart on me." He paused. "I need you."

Fear rose within her, but her only tell was the flare of her nostrils; she refused to let Bobby see just how terrified she was.

"You don't have to worry about me," she said, taking his hand. "I'm tougher than I look, I promise."

She stared long and hard at his hand, feeling the weight of his palm cupped to hers, letting him touch her this time instead of following her first instinct, which was to pull away. She might be tougher than she looked, but Bobby was different here, too. He'd shown himself to be both capable and dependable. Which was ironic, given that she'd been drawn to him because he'd seemed more fun than dependable, and certainly more party boy than capable leader.

"Ah, Bobby?" someone called.

She looked past him and saw Ralph standing there, worry etched on his face for all to see.

"Sorry to disturb you, but we have a problem."

Bobby's groan was low, but she heard it. "What kind of problem?" he asked.

"Apparently there's no more food. You any good at hunting?"

Vita squeezed her eyes shut and wished she'd concentrated more at Sunday school so she could recall a useful prayer. Because, right now, no matter what she'd said to Bobby, it felt like it would take a miracle from God himself for them to survive Albania.

"I'm so hungry," Dot whimpered, curled up beside Evelyn with her head nestled in Vita's lap.

Vita was absently stroking her hair, her fingertips moving back and forth over Dot's head in an attempt to soothe her. She vividly remembered wanting her own mother to stroke her like this when she was a child, desperate to feel the love that she saw in other mothers' eyes when they looked at their daughters, but no amount of sidling up to her had gotten Vita so much as a pat on the head.

Dot had been unwell for the past few hours, and Vita had only just brought her back inside after spending much of the afternoon rubbing her back while she was sick.

"I'm not surprised you're so hungry, not after how many times you were sick," Vita murmured. "This is the first time I've ever felt so food-deprived; it's like there's something gnawing at my belly from the inside. It's awful."

"That cornbread might have been bad, but it was better than nothing," Evelyn said with a sigh, leaning her head back against the wall. "Do you think there might be some more soon?"

Vita shrugged, but she wasn't hopeful.

The room was largely silent, despite being filled with so many bodies, and other than the low hum of whispers, there was barely a shuffle. It was strange, because although they were all stranded together, there were some nurses Vita hadn't properly met before, and even more medics she didn't know at all. They'd spent weeks together between Kentucky and Camp Kilmer, but many of them had trained separately prior to that, and other than Dot and Evelyn, she hadn't spent much time with the others. Except for poor Eddie. She glanced over at him, her eyes finding their way back to him regularly, and in the glimmer of the fire, she could see the steady rise and fall of his chest and knew he was still sleeping. She was terrified an infection was going to set in with his leg, and she knew that if it did, there was little they could do for him.

"What are we going to do if Bobby can't make contact with the control towers, and Josef can't make contact with the British operative for us?" Dot asked, pushing up on her elbow beside her. "Is there any way we can actually find our way out of here? Has he said anything to you?"

Vita looked at Evelyn. It was the same question she'd been rolling around in her mind all evening, over and over. Unfortunately, Bobby hadn't confided anything further in her, so she didn't have any more confidence than Dot had in their rescue.

"I refuse to believe that we're going to be stuck here forever," Evelyn said, her whisper full of determination. "If we stay here, with no food and no running water, we'll never survive. There has to be a way of getting home, or to safety at least. I have no intention of giving up."

Vita wanted to believe her, she did, but the fear gnawing at her was as biting as the hunger in her belly. There was a difference between wanting to believe something and knowing it to be true.

"What would you be doing now, if it were a normal day and you were back at home?" Dot suddenly asked.

Vita went to open her mouth, then quickly shut it when Evelyn started to answer. She'd much rather hear someone else's response.

"I'd be singing my little sister to sleep," Evelyn said. "She's found it difficult to sleep for the last few years, since . . ."

Vita watched Evelyn's face change, saw pain there as she rocked back and blinked rapidly.

"Since what?" Dot asked softly.

"Since our mother died," Evelyn whispered. "Losing her was hard enough, but looking after my sisters and my father, giving up everything for them and becoming the matriarch of our family . . ." She cleared her throat. "I always felt like I never got the chance to grieve, because I was so busy looking after everyone else, but now

I can see that holding my little sister was as much a comfort to me as it was to her."

Vita put her arm around Evelyn and hugged her close.

"What about you, Vita?" Evelyn asked softly. "You mentioned losing your brother, but you haven't really told us about him."

She was relieved Evelyn hadn't asked her about her mother. "My older brother," she clarified. "I loved him more than anyone else; we always said it was the two of us against the world, but he didn't even last a month after his deployment. We had plans to defy our mother together, to forge our own paths and do what we wanted with our lives." She paused, not used to sharing her memories. "The worst thing is that my coward little brother is still tucked up safely at home." *Protected by Daddy's money, instead of serving like other men his age.*

Evelyn's smile was warm and her hand even warmer when she reached for her, but Vita vowed to keep the rest of her family story to herself. She didn't want either of them thinking she was a spoiled brat who'd defied her parents just to rebel against her privilege. She had wanted to escape her destiny, but her desire to serve and help had been real, too, and she didn't want anything to overshadow that. For now, she only wanted them to know about her brother, because he was the one family member she'd been close to, the one person she'd always felt was there for her no matter what. They'd spent their childhood racing outside and galloping off on horseback, having adventures that their mother wholeheartedly disapproved of, and she'd naively thought they had so many more adventures still to come.

"You must miss your sisters terribly?" Vita heard Dot ask Evelyn.

"So much. I was so desperate to have a break from parenting them, and frustrated that the older two found it so easy to treat me like the adult and not take on any responsibility while I was there.

But now I'd give anything to be standing at the stove stirring soup for their dinner."

"Sometimes it's the simple things we take for granted, even the things that seem mundane at the time," Dot said. "But at times like this, those moments can seem like the most reassuring memories in the world. I'd do anything for just a few hours of my old life right now."

"Hey, at least you've got your fiancé to look forward to seeing though, right?" Evelyn said to Dot. "All I've got are three sisters who'll be waiting for me to wash their clothes, clean their bedrooms, and cook their meals!"

"I—ah, well, yes," Dot said, stammering. "But actually, girls, while we're opening up to one another, there's something I've been wanting to tell you. To explain, actually."

Dot looked a mess, like she was about to start crying, but as Vita leaned forward to ask her what she meant, the door to the room slammed open with a loud bang. And the shout that came with it sent fear arrowing through Vita in a way she'd never experienced before.

"Quickly! You must get out of here!" It was Josef, and his face was flushed a deep red, his gestures erratic as he thumped repeatedly on the wall, as if he didn't already have their attention. "The Germans are coming! They're coming! You have to go!"

Vita scrambled to stand, hauling Dot up with her and frantically searching the room for Bobby. Where was he? How were they going to get Eddie out in time?

"Grab your bag!" Evelyn urged, and Vita spun around, snatching at the strap and throwing it over her shoulder. She was already wearing her coat, so there was nothing else to look for, and Evelyn was prodding her in the back hard to get her moving.

Nurses and medics were already spilling out the door, a herd of people all desperately fighting to be first out, and just as Evelyn tried to push her farther ahead, a hand fell on her shoulder.

"Bobby! You have to get Eddie, we can't leave him here!"

"Just go, I'll get him out." Bobby's voice was loud, carrying across the crowd. "Run as fast as you can and hide; we'll find each other at first light. Go!"

At first light? He expected her to hide in the dark for the rest of the night? But there was no time to ask questions; as it was, they might not all make it out before they had enemy guns trained on them, and the fear propelled her forward.

"Go!" Vita urged the others around her, watching Bobby only long enough to see him lift one end of Eddie's stretcher.

She'd expected they'd have some light from the moon when they emerged outside, but the sky was covered with a dense layer of cloud, leaving them virtually blind as they shuffled down the stairs, hands colliding as they felt their way along the handrail.

Vita was feeling sure of herself, staying calm, until she heard a shout that turned her blood to ice. She had no idea what was being said, she had no concept of where they were or how close she was to being caught, but she knew for certain that the words were German.

"Run and hide!" she hissed to everyone around her. "We find each other at first light. Run!"

Her words, *Bobby's words*, were repeated amongst the group like a chain letter, and as Vita started to run in the direction of the forest she swore she could feel German soldiers breathing down her neck.

Keep moving, just keep moving and don't stop.

A hand found its way into hers and she knew instinctively that it was Evelyn's; they'd clasped palms so many times in the past forty-eight hours that she would have known her soft skin anywhere. The way she confidently linked their fingers, finding strength together, almost made her believe they would be fine, that they'd all survive the night.

She looked over her shoulder for Dot, but saw only darkness. *She'll be right behind us*, Vita told herself, forcing her feet to go faster even as she tripped and slid on the dirt, scrambling to stay upright.

The farther they went, the faster they traveled, the safer she felt, putting distance between them and the building that had for a short time been their safe haven. And as branches scratched her face and clawed at her hands, she pulled back on Evelyn to make her stop.

"I think that's far enough," she whispered, trusting her instincts. "If we go too far, we could end up lost and separated from the group. We should stay quiet and hide."

Evelyn didn't say anything, her breath heavy as they pressed their shoulders together and leaned back against a tree. They stood like that for some time, as more bodies came closer, their panting audible in the otherwise-silent night air.

It was incredible standing there in the dark, in a forest in a foreign country so far removed from anywhere she'd ever been before, her senses heightened in a way they'd never been. It even smelled different here—the dampness rising off the earth, the grass wet beneath their feet.

"We just have to survive until morning," Evelyn whispered matter-of-factly in her ear. "That's all we have to do."

Vita wanted to believe they could do it, just like she wanted to believe that the villagers who'd taken them in would still be alive come morning, that the Germans wouldn't still be lurking, and that their group would all be intact, but she just wasn't so sure it could be true.

But instead of voicing her concerns, she huddled even closer to Evelyn, wishing Dot was on the other side of her but too afraid to call her name in case it gave them away. For all they knew, enemy soldiers could be within earshot, and she wasn't going to do anything to risk their safety.

"What do you think they'll do to the villagers?" Evelyn whispered. "If they find out they've been hiding us?"

Vita just squeezed her eyes shut. That was something she didn't even want to think about, because whatever happened to those poor people was on them, for putting them in danger in the first place.

CHAPTER FIFTEEN

Dot

Dot tripped on the stairs, her foot slipping and leaving her to tumble, the catch of a hand at her wrist the only thing that stopped her from plummeting down headfirst. She tried to mutter a thank you, to get a word out, but she couldn't make a noise; nothing came out of her other than a gasp.

Help me. She wanted to ask someone for help, for someone to hold her hand and take her with them, because she'd never been so scared in her entire life. Not when her grandparents had passed away, not when she'd turned in circles in their home knowing she was now alone without so much as one living family member; not when Peter had unexpectedly broken off their engagement and left her; and not when their plane had first crashed. This—*this*—was a terror like she'd never known before.

Her foot connected with dirt, the handrail disappearing, and she ran, knowing they had minutes, maybe seconds, before they were caught. The darkness was all-consuming, making it impossible to see anything, and she clutched at her bag with one hand as she ran blindly, wishing she'd packed a flashlight. Not that it would have mattered; it would have been stolen that morning along with almost everything else if she'd had one.

Her panting sounded loud to her own ears, her breath ragged in a way she'd never heard before as she scrambled, one hand held out in front of her. The last thing she wanted was to knock herself out by running into a tree when she reached the start of the forest. From memory she should be out of the clearing soon, away from the one-house village, but she could have been running in circles for all she knew, it was so easy to become disoriented in the dark.

Where was everyone?

"Evelyn," she whispered, knowing she should stay quiet but not wanting to be alone. How had she lost them? How had they become separated so quickly? They were just ahead of her only seconds ago, but she'd become lost in the tightly packed crowd and they'd somehow disappeared in the mayhem.

Dot heard the thump of feet running nearby, knew that someone was close, and fear traced a path across her skin.

"Evelyn?" she whimpered. "Vita?"

She spun around, stifling a scream when her back bumped into something hard, but as she turned and reached out, fingers frantically searching, she realized it was only a tree. She pressed back into it, needing the safety of something solid at her back, something to stop her from going crazy and thinking there was someone or something reaching for her, wanting to grab hold of her.

Everything is going to be fine. Just stay quiet and wait. There's no one here but you, you're just imagining things.

Her body was starting to shiver and she wrapped her arms tightly around herself, trying to stay warm, closing her eyes and wishing she were at home; that she would open her eyes and it would all have been a bad dream.

A scream cut through the silent night air then, a scream so sharp and unexpected that Dot dropped to her haunches, hands over her ears as she rocked back and forth. *No! No, no, no!* This couldn't be happening, this couldn't be real.

Another scream. A woman's scream. She pressed her palms even tighter against the sides of her head, trying desperately to block it all out. But no matter how hard she fought against the noise, nothing could stop the sound of a gun firing.

Peter. Suddenly all she could think of was Peter, what she'd do for him to be at her side, to hold her in his arms and whisper against her forehead that everything would be alright. But Peter wasn't hers anymore, Peter had left her and she needed to remember that. Peter had fallen in love with another woman and chosen to discard her like she'd never meant anything to him in the first place. A tear slipped down her cheek and she dropped her hands, leaning back against the rough bark of the tree as she shut her eyes, trying to push her fears away, the memories that just wouldn't leave her mind.

She had been alone in America, and she was alone here.

Dot opened her eyes then, the memory of what she'd lost fading as she heard what sounded like leaves being crushed beneath a boot.

Run.

She had the most overwhelming feeling that she needed to get farther away, a feeling inside her warning her that she hadn't gone far enough from the village, that the scream had been too loud, too close to her. She needed to find her friends, to stay with them instead of being alone.

Dot stood and turned around, spinning frantically in the dark as she tried to figure out which way to go, as she tried to get her bearings and make sure she was going in the right direction. Why couldn't she figure out which way she'd come from? Which way she was supposed to go?

She wanted to call out, to whisper-scream to someone, to *anyone*, but she didn't make a sound, pulling herself together and believing in her own instincts instead. She needed to move, and fast.

Dot heard a noise then, just the lightest thud of something nearby, but she refused to give in to her fears as she breathed and pointed herself in what she hoped was the right direction. She must be close; the others couldn't be far away.

I can do this.

But something grabbed at her, something that wasn't another tree or a branch clawing at her as she passed. She opened her mouth to scream, to plead for help, as something clamped hard over her mouth and silenced her.

Terror shot through her, paralyzing her as she realized that the something was a hand; a hand so strong and firm that she was powerless to fight against it. A body pressed into hers from behind, rough and hard against her, and her will to survive kicked in the moment she realized she was being held by a man. *A man who could do anything to me if I don't get away!*

She fought, kicking her legs and flailing her arms, fighting to bite down on the hand, but it was useless. The grip wasn't softening and the body was still as hard and rigid as rock.

Dot smelled her captor's breath, her nostrils flaring wildly as she fought to breathe, recoiling at the dirty hands across her face and clamped over her mouth.

I'm going to die. In this forest, at the hands of a stranger, I'm going to take my very last breath.

Dot stopped fighting then. It was useless, and she went limp in the man's arms as he dragged her with him past trees that clawed at her skin, his ironclad grip impossible to break free from.

She wept as she thought of her friends, and as her head thumped against something solid she slipped into a deep black slumber that felt like death.

CHAPTER SIXTEEN

EVELYN

Evelyn opened her eyes and immediately went to rub them, the light burning straight through her. But when she did, she realized her knuckles were caked with dirt, and it was then that she remembered.

We ran in the dead of night. They were coming for us. We could have died.

She sat up, hugging her legs to her chest. She stared at the bodies around her, surprised by how many there were in the forest. She'd been holding Vita's hand as they'd shivered and huddled during the night, each minute dragging like an hour, and they hadn't realized how many other nurses and medics had been close by. They'd all stayed so quiet, all so terrified of what their collective fate might be if they were found.

"Vita." Evelyn nudged Vita with her foot. "Wake up."

She peered around, wondering if it was safe to call out to everyone. Now that they'd survived the night, she couldn't see why not, but then again they had no clue whether they were safe or not. Or whether they'd ever be safe again for that matter.

The screams. She shook her head as if she could get rid of the memory just by blocking it out, but she knew she never would.

There had been two piercing ones, and then a more muffled third cry, but they'd all been female screams, she was sure of it.

"We made it," Vita mumbled, reaching for her as she rose. "I can't believe we survived the night."

It was the first time Evelyn had seen Vita not looking perfectly coiffed. Even the day before, when they'd woken up in the village, she'd looked somehow immaculate, her hair still beautiful and some of her makeup miraculously in place. But today Vita looked like a regular girl, her cheeks smudged with mud, her hair rumpled and knotted, and her eyes strained from lack of sleep. Evelyn instinctively reached out to rub away the mud, but let her hand fall when she realized how filthy her own fingertips were. She'd only make Vita dirtier.

"We need to do some sort of roll call," Evelyn said, trying to remember everyone's names but struggling to make a list of more than twelve in her mind. Her brain felt like she was searching through fog. "Or at least a head count." That was something they could do easily enough, and then it would just be a matter of figuring out who *wasn't* with them.

She did a rough count and only came up with sixteen, including them. But then something caught her eye, and she saw Bobby come crashing through the trees, using the butt of his gun to part the branches in his way. To her relief, he had four others with him.

"You're a sight for sore eyes," he said, looking as exhausted and relieved as she felt.

"How did you find us?" Evelyn asked.

"Flashlight," Bobby replied. "I'd taken it from the plane and had it on me already, so it was the one thing of mine that wasn't stolen. I used it once everything had gone quiet."

"You've been out all night?" Vita asked.

"I wanted to get everyone together, so I've been searching the forest for hours. I got most of this lot here just a couple of hours ago."

Evelyn could see now how tired he was, the fatigue like brackets around his eyes, but he didn't look like he had any intention of stopping.

"How many do you think we're missing?" she asked.

"Ralph is with Eddie maybe five hundred yards away, and there's four more with them. They'll be here soon."

"Are we going back there?" Vita asked, interrupting them, her eyes wide as saucers. "To the village, I mean? Are we safer out here or back there?"

Bobby didn't answer, and Evelyn guessed that it was to avoid having to admit the truth. But he did produce something from his pocket: a crumpled piece of paper.

"What's that?" she asked.

"The flight manifest," he said. "I kept it in case it came in handy."

Evelyn took it gratefully. "It sure will."

He came closer then, stepping over bodies that were starting to rouse, their eyes fearful, looking the same way she'd felt when she'd woken from slumber only minutes earlier, no doubt remembering what had happened the night before.

"I'm guessing you heard those screams last night?" Bobby asked.

Evelyn nodded, numb as she watched his face contort with obvious pain. "We did." She was certain they'd have heard them even if they'd been a hundred miles away.

"I think at least two of our nurses were taken, but I need to do a final head count to be sure," he whispered. "I've only found one bag, but there are two places where we found scuff marks in the

153

dirt, like there'd been a fight or someone dragged away. And with one of them . . ." His voice trailed off.

Evelyn stared at him, waiting, but it was Vita who spoke.

"With one of them, *what?*" she whispered.

Bobby frowned, speaking in a more hushed tone than Vita had. "There was blood," he said. "Something terrible happened there, and until we check through that manifest . . ."

"We won't know who they are," Evelyn finished for him, swallowing quickly as she tried to force down her rising nausea. She cleared her throat, trying to sound calm. "You go get the others you already have, I'll do the manifest." She turned to Vita. "I don't have a pen to check anyone off the list, so you need to keep track of who's not here. Then we'll know for sure who's missing."

Vita didn't reply, and when Evelyn turned around to make certain she'd heard her, she noticed that Vita was hurrying off, bent over and peering at all the sleeping bodies. Most were awake now, and each one looked back curiously as Vita studied them all.

"Vita!" Evelyn called. "Hurry up, I need your help here."

She shook her head, lifting the list and about to start calling out names, when Vita ran back. Evelyn could see that she was shaking, her face eerily white.

"We've lost Dot. She's not here," Vita said, her voice cracking. "She's one of the missing ones."

"Don't be silly, of course she's here. We ran out of the room with her last night." Evelyn's heart started to pound. "I mean, she wouldn't have been able to fall that far behind us, surely . . ."

Evelyn searched all the faces looking back at her. But Vita was right; she couldn't see Dot either.

"I should have said something last night. I reached for her hand but she wasn't there and I just thought . . ." Vita's voice trailed off, her terror palpable as she stared wide-eyed back at her.

"She's probably with the other group," Evelyn said, refusing to believe that something had happened to her, that somehow they'd failed her by leaving her behind. "Let's just do the roll call and wait until they're all here, and then we'll know for sure. Don't forget, she could be with Eddie and the others." She tried to disguise the tremble in her voice, but there was no disguising the one in her hands as she held the manifest and could barely read a name off of it, the paper was shaking so violently. But she could easily be right—Bobby had said there were others, and Dot had taken a special interest in caring for Eddie. It made sense.

Vita stood beside her as she called everyone to attention, reading names off the list and using a lipstick that Vita had given her to put a tiny red dot next to the name of each of those present. She stared at Dot's name and whispered a prayer as Bobby emerged again from deep in the trees, with Eddie being carried on his stretcher between Bobby and his copilot. She held her breath without even realizing it as one nurse appeared from behind the men. It was a woman named Daisy, and although Evelyn was pleased to see her and returned her warm smile, her heart sank as she realized that Vita had been right. Dot was nowhere to be seen.

"Who are we missing?" Bobby asked as he came toward them, walking straight up the middle of where everyone was sitting, a fresh rip through the thigh of his pants exposing a red welt on his skin.

"We're actually missing three nurses," Evelyn said, looking up in disbelief at Vita as the reality of what had happened started to sink in. "But I'll call out all the names again; I'll double-check," she babbled.

This time it was Vita who took charge, taking the list from her and folding it, before passing it back to Bobby.

"We're missing Dot," Vita said. "We lost our Dot, as well as Marcia and Gina. There's no need to read it out again, we didn't make a mistake."

Evelyn swallowed and blinked away the sharp sting of tears. How could they have lost Dot? Darling, sweet Dot, who wouldn't last a day in a prisoner-of-war camp? But she refused to let insidious thoughts of what they might do to Dot inside her head, feeling guilty that she was worrying more about Dot than the other two girls, whom she was certain were lovely, too. But this was Dot they were talking about. *Darling, kind, sweet Dot. Her* Dot.

"We might still find her," Bobby said, no doubt seeing the pain in both her and Vita's eyes. "Don't go giving up hope just yet. She could still be around here hiding."

But as she stared at the others looking back at them, waiting to be told what to do, relying on their pilot leader to get them to something that looked and felt like safety, she already felt her hope fading. Of finding Dot, of getting help, of ever getting home.

It suddenly seemed as impossible as moving a mountain.

———— ⟋⟍ ————

"Do you remember the first time you met Dot?"

Evelyn was lying beneath a tree some hours later, staring up at the branches waving back and forth in the wind. She was so hungry that she was starting to wonder what the bark would taste like, or whether the leaves would be palatable. Earlier she'd chewed on a couple of blades of grass, and she'd started to dream about the dry cornbread from the village, which told her just how desperate she'd become.

"I do remember, actually," Vita finally said—just speaking seeming like an effort. She lifted her head and used her elbow to prop herself up. "It was at training, but she looked as scared as a mouse and didn't speak to me. The first time I met her properly was on the train that day, when we were leaving Kentucky."

"I remember that day," Evelyn said. "I started up a conversation with her about how hot it was, because it was stifling outside and even more so in that cabin, and we bonded over sweat and smoke. And then we bonded over how intimidating we found you."

Vita made a choking sound. "*Intimidating?* Me?"

It felt wrong to be laughing as they talked about Dot, but there was also something nice in talking about her, keeping her in their thoughts. It made it feel like she was somehow still with them.

"You really don't know, do you?" Evelyn asked, lying back down again and going back to staring at the tree. She felt like she didn't have the strength to keep her head up.

The silence stretched between them for a moment, before Evelyn finally filled it.

"You're different than the rest of us," she said softly. "You're elegant and refined in a way that so many of us try to be, but will never master. You're beautiful and confident, like you've been raised to believe in yourself, or perhaps raised with enough money that you've never had to worry about whether there will be food on the table or not."

Vita didn't say anything to contradict her, so she continued.

"Dot was intimidated by you in the beginning, and quite frankly, so was I. No matter how kind you were to us, how friendly, you just seemed so much . . ." She paused. "More," Evelyn continued. "You just seemed to be so much more than us."

Vita's silence made her worry that she'd hurt her feelings. Perhaps she shouldn't have been so forthcoming with the truth, but she'd been thinking it for so long and it had suddenly come out in a rush.

"I think that might have come out wrong." Evelyn's head hurt, as if someone was pounding at her temple with a hammer. She would have done anything for a drink of something cold.

"It's fine. I suppose I know what you mean."

"You do?" Evelyn was surprised Vita wasn't angry with her.

"I . . . well." Vita's sigh was loud, but the voice that followed was quiet. "I've tried so hard to fit in, but I obviously wasn't fooling anyone."

The branches started to wave more ferociously and Evelyn shivered, tucking her icy hands into her deep pockets to try to stay warm. She waited to see if Vita would continue, not sure whether to ask her what she meant or not.

"When I decided to come here, to volunteer as a nurse, I was going against my parents' wishes. They gave me an ultimatum of sorts, thinking I'd stay at home I suppose, but the more they tried to stop me, the more determined I became to defy them."

Evelyn smiled. "Trust me, I don't think you're alone there. There must be mothers all over America who tried to stop their daughters from joining up."

"Oh no, there's nothing normal about my mother—she's a force to be reckoned with." Vita's laugh seemed to be filled with more pain than humor. "She has this misguided notion that women of our social standing shouldn't be getting our hands dirty. That it's beneath us."

And then Evelyn understood—why Vita seemed so different, why she stood taller than everyone else, why she spoke with such confidence, with such a beautiful lilt to her voice.

"Just because you come from a home with significantly more"—Evelyn paused—"*resources* than the other nurses, doesn't make you different from us. You've had the same training as us, held down the same workload, and you've most definitely shown you can get your hands dirty like the rest of us."

Vita's laugh was filled with emotion this time as she held her hands up, and Evelyn could see even from where she was lying a few feet away how filthy her skin was, with dirt caked beneath her nails.

"My mother would actually cry if she saw me like this, with ragged dirty nails instead of a manicure," Vita snorted. "*Peasant* is the word that comes to mind. She'd be more upset about the state of my nails than the fact I haven't eaten properly in days."

They both laughed then, until their humor turned to tears, and Vita shuffled closer to her, reaching out her hand until their fingers brushed. But suddenly all Evelyn could think about was that she didn't even know Dot's fiancé's full name. Even if she could have got word to him, all she knew was that his first name was Peter.

"Thank you for listening," Vita said, her voice low. "I've been keeping my past a secret all this time, but now—well, what's the point?"

"It might have felt like a secret, but our backgrounds have nothing to do with who we are as nurses," Evelyn murmured. "We're all the same at the end of the day; we all do our best for the soldiers in our care. That's the thing when you're serving your country: we're all on an equal footing."

They lay like that for a while longer, the gurgle and rumble of their stomachs the only noise until the crack of branches alerted them to someone coming. They'd positioned themselves slightly away from everyone else, and suddenly Evelyn felt vulnerable as she shuffled even closer to Vita.

But, as they waited, expecting someone to appear, frightened about who it might be, a rabbit emerged, its little nose twitching as it studied them. Evelyn's immediate reaction was that it was cute, and it warmed something inside of her seeing the fluffy animal, but it was immediately replaced with a feeling rooted in survival. If they were going to survive, then they needed to find food, and that fluffy rabbit was one of the few things they could hunt that would nourish them.

"Do you think she's alive?" Vita's question was barely audible, as quiet as the rabbit turning and hopping away, but Evelyn heard it. Maybe it was because she'd been rolling the same question around and around in her mind for so many hours.

"I honestly don't know," she said. "I want to believe she's alive, but maybe that's because I love her and I can't imagine someone could have killed her. That she could actually be gone."

"I'm praying for all three of them," Vita said, and Evelyn saw the tears shining in her eyes. "But I can't help but pray just a little more for Dot, even though that makes me sound like a terrible person."

Evelyn held her hand tighter, wishing there was something they could do. There was nothing she wouldn't do for Dot.

"Do you ever think about our night out in New York?" Evelyn asked, smiling as she remembered Dot all dolled up in her pretty red dress.

"Of course! I'll never forget it so long as I live."

"It was one of the best nights of my life, and I know it was Dot's too," Evelyn confessed. "I just hope she's thinking about it right now, knowing that so many people out here care about her. That *we* care about her."

And as she lay her head back, staving off the cool breeze as she wriggled deeper into her coat, the collar turned up around her chin, she lost herself in the memories of all the fun they'd had. She only wished that she had more memories to make with Dot, because they were supposed to be in this together—the three of them, friends forever. Which was why she felt so responsible for losing Dot after the promises they'd made.

"Vita, we're never going to make it back in time!"

The girls stumbled out onto the road, arms linked as they looked frantically around for some form of transportation. Where was a taxi when they needed one?

Evelyn looked down at her wristwatch, squinting at it but unable to see a thing. It was so dark out, but she had the most terrifying feeling that it was going to be light before they made it back to base.

"If we don't get back by six they'll send us home," Dot cried, clutching tightly to her arm. "Why is everything spinning? Why can't I walk straight?"

Vita was laughing, seemingly unworried by their lateness. "Darling, they're not going to send us home. How many nurses have trained to be in the air? They need us."

Evelyn wasn't quite so sure about them not being sent home; they would be reprimanded in some way if they missed curfew, and she wasn't one to break the rules.

"I don't even think taxis work this late," she muttered. "We might have to start walking, ladies."

She was unsteady on her feet too, having drunk so much champagne to quench her thirst from dancing, and it had most definitely all gone to her head.

A noise from behind made them all turn, and suddenly Bobby and three of his friends spilled out through the iron gates of 21 Club and out onto the sidewalk.

"You ladies need a ride back to base?"

Evelyn's heart leapt. "Yes! Can you take us?"

One of the men jingled a set of keys, and Vita let out a whoop beside her as she dragged her and Dot by the hands to follow them. She imagined they had the same curfew, although they didn't seem in any great hurry.

"Are we going to make it in time?" Dot asked as they piled into the back seat of the car, all bunched up as they tried to fit.

"Honey, we'll make it, don't you worry," one of the men assured her.

"We'll have you walking into your barracks with a minute to spare," Bobby said, glancing back from the passenger seat. He only seemed to have eyes for Vita, although she didn't seem to notice.

Evelyn relaxed as they drove, knowing there was nothing she could do to make them get back to base any faster. She should have kept a better eye on the time, but it had been such a fabulous night. All these years she'd been the one at home, waiting up for her sisters and looking after everyone, but being out with Vita had made her feel more alive than she'd ever felt before.

"Did you have a good night?" Evelyn whispered to Dot.

"The best," Dot said. "Even if we are in trouble when we get back, it was worth it."

Vita kissed her cheek and Evelyn laughed as she leaned into her, pulling Dot in for a hug. They were going to be friends forever, she just knew it.

"We have to find her, Vita," Evelyn whispered as she wiped tears from her face, seeing Dot as clear as day in her mind's eye, pulling herself from her memories. "We promised we'd always be there for one another."

"I know we do," Vita whispered back. "But where do we even start?"

Evelyn clamped her hand over her mouth to stifle her emotions, as Vita sobbed quietly beside her.

Suddenly there was a noise again, this one much louder than before, and they both sat up, backs pressed to the rough bark of the tree behind them.

"It's just me," came the call, and Evelyn breathed a long, unsteady sigh of relief.

Bobby had finally returned, and with him were the five medics he'd taken with him. The rest of them had stayed behind, hiding as best they could for a large group, mostly in pairs, but everyone started to move closer when they realized the men had come back.

"Did you go through the village?" Vita asked him. "Was there any sign of Dot? Had anyone in the village been hurt?"

Evelyn waited, listening, trying to read his face. And she knew before he spoke that it wasn't good news. *Please don't let it be Dot. Anyone but Dot.*

"Josef is coming to join us soon, and they received word from the next village that we can pass through safely," Bobby said. "But there's no sign of Dot or the other two nurses. Josef said he and his group shot and killed three Germans, but the others escaped. He's worried they'll come back, and he wants us long gone. It's a miracle there were no serious injuries or deaths amongst his people."

Evelyn could hear Vita crying, but she didn't reach for her, not yet. She wanted to know more before Josef and his group was with them again; she wanted to focus on what they could do to stay safe. "And the plane? Did you make it back to the crash site?"

They'd all deeply regretted not taking more supplies with them, which was why Bobby and his small group had made the long, arduous journey back there. At the time they'd first left the crash site, they'd all naively expected that help would be on the way sooner rather than later. *If only we'd known how much could change in such a short time.*

"We took everything we could, all the K-rations and as many first-aid kits as we could carry, as well as two parachutes, and then we lit it on fire."

"You lit the entire plane on fire?" she asked. "Won't that be like a beacon for the enemy?"

"We had to destroy it, and besides, they already know we're here," Bobby said, shrugging. "I'm not letting the Germans get so much as a bandage of ours, and I think it's fairly obvious that we're all on our own out here."

Evelyn didn't want to disagree with him in front of the group, because they saw Bobby as their leader and she wasn't going to undermine him, but she most definitely disagreed with what he'd done. They may as well have yelled out to the Germans and waited with their hands raised in surrender.

"Everyone, Josef will be here soon," Bobby said, turning to address the rest of the people gathered behind him. "If you need to relieve yourself, do it now, and then prepare to walk."

"Do you have any idea where the next village is?" Evelyn asked. "Did you ask him whether we could walk out to the coast?"

He didn't meet her gaze then, and she wondered if he simply hadn't heard her.

"Bobby?" she pressed.

"Josef said we'd need permission to travel to the coast, and that we'll be escorted to the next village," Bobby said. "I don't know any more than you do. That's it."

Just then, a group of women appeared, and Evelyn instinctively backed away. The Albanian women they'd met in the village had been dressed so modestly, not showing an inch of skin other than their hands, but these women were different. She eyed the hand grenades they carried, the guns at the ready. *Resistance women who are ready to fight, it seems.* She had no idea what made these women different, why the dress code was so different for them, but she didn't care. Surely women would be sympathetic to them, and they certainly looked as if they could protect them.

As Bobby held up a hand in hello, Evelyn did the same, only she held up both hands to make sure the women knew she wasn't armed and therefore wasn't a threat. But although they looked deeply curious, they never lowered their guns. Not for a moment.

CHAPTER SEVENTEEN

VITA

Vita stood with Bobby and listened to Josef, conscious of how close they were standing. On the one hand, she was becoming more and more drawn to him, but on the other, she couldn't help but want to protect herself. She instinctively took a little step back.

"We cannot help you get to the coast, because it's outside our jurisdiction."

Josef's words were like a knife to her heart, drawing her from her thoughts. How on earth were they supposed to leave if they couldn't get to the coast? She went to whisper her question to Bobby, but she could see that he was ramrod-straight as he listened to Josef.

"Wait—what do you mean, outside your jurisdiction? Another group controls that area? The group you're fighting against?" Bobby asked.

"Correct," Josef said. "You go there and get caught, they kill you. You cannot go to coast."

Sweat trickled from Bobby's head down his temple, and Vita swallowed, hard, seeing him struggle with his composure.

"So where can we go?" he asked through gritted teeth. "What options are we left with?"

"I've had permission to take you on to Berat," Josef continued. "It will take us maybe two days; it will be a long walk for you. But we have protection, you will be kept safe, and there is a smaller village we can stop at on the way."

Vita wondered if Berat was another one-building village, or something more substantial. She didn't want to get her hopes up, but she couldn't help but set her heart on the latter.

"Surely you're not suggesting we travel on to Berat and leave our missing nurses behind?" It was Evelyn asking the question, and Vita was proud that she'd spoken up. She was thinking the same thing, and she expected the other women gathered were, too.

"You don't move, you get taken too," Josef said. "Our village will be burned to the ground if they find out we've hidden Americans. Is that what you want for us?"

There was silence for a long moment, as everyone seemed to digest what he was saying. Vita knew in her heart that, compared to the possible future consequences, sacrificing three nurses would seem inconsequential to the villagers. Tears welled in her eyes. *Inconsequential for them, but not to us. Not to me.*

"Will they do that to any village?" Evelyn asked. "Are you all in danger for taking us in?"

Josef's nod was curt. "Of course. It's why I needed permission from the other village leaders to take you there. The council has to decide, but our custom is to look after visitors, and they did not want to turn you away. You are not our enemy."

Vita knew then that no matter how unfortunate their situation, they were incredibly lucky to have ended up in such friendly territory. Something lit within her again, a strength she'd almost forgotten she possessed, as she comprehended what all of the poor villagers were sacrificing just to keep them out of harm's way. It wasn't fair to judge them for anything.

"Come. We need to start walking and get to the first village by nightfall."

They all silently picked up their bags and helped to carry the extra things Bobby had brought back with him, everyone pitching in so that nothing, and no one, was left behind. And this time when she found herself close to Bobby, Vita took a little step closer.

———— ⊷ ⊶ ————

"Do you have an awful feeling that this is all we're ever going to know?" Vita asked later, keeping her voice low as she walked beside Evelyn. "That any chance of rescue is just some sort of unrealistic dream?"

"My brain is just going around and around in circles," Evelyn whispered back. "One second I'm thinking we're going to die here and never get home, and the next I'm positive we'll survive and somehow get to the coast. And then it starts all over again, a vicious cycle of back and forth."

She stared down at her feet, wiggling her toes as she realized she could barely feel them. They'd gone numb from all the walking and days trapped in shoes; she couldn't even remember the last time she'd taken them off.

"Oh wow, look."

Vita forgot about her toes when she heard the excitement in Evelyn's voice. *Wow* was right. It actually looked like a village. A *proper* village, so different from the first one they'd been in.

"They are preparing a feast for you," Josef said, clapping his hands together. "They will kill a beast in your honor."

Vita's stomach roared at the sound of *feast*, although her hunger immediately dissipated when she saw a poor animal being dragged across the dirt to the center of the village, in the middle of all the houses. Her feet stopped, and she caught Evelyn's hand, the rest of their group also no longer moving around them.

The animal made a moaning noise that sent shivers down her spine, and she watched in horror as two men dragged it along, and another two men pushed it from behind. But it was the sight of another man waiting with a large knife, glinting as he turned it over in his hand, that really made her stomach lurch.

Vita recoiled and averted her gaze. "Suddenly I'm not so hungry," she muttered.

The bellow that erupted from the beast made her flinch, but she saw that Evelyn was standing tall, staring straight ahead instead of looking away.

"I don't know how you can watch," she said.

"We're going to have to be strong if we're going to survive," Evelyn replied. "We want to eat, then animals have to be killed. We're just lucky they're the ones doing it for us, because I certainly don't have the stomach to kill anything myself."

Vita recoiled, but in truth she'd spent her entire life eating meat, she just hadn't ever thought about where it came from, which made her a complete hypocrite.

"Water buffalo," Josef said, as if he could read their minds. "It will feed entire village for next three days."

Perhaps not so much of a feast as we expected, then. Vita knew that once the meat was cooked and presented to her, she'd eat it just as fast as all the others would; it was just the idea of it that was making her queasy.

Then a warm, deep voice cocooned her and made her forget about everything else for a moment. *Bobby.* So much for keeping him at arm's length; they'd held hands once and suddenly she was like a moth drawn to the light.

"How are you holding up?" she asked as he bumped gently into her, his arms full of supplies.

He chuckled. "Better than you if the green tinge of your skin is anything to go by."

She groaned. "It's just seeing that animal hauled to his death like that . . ."

"Sweetheart, I know, it's awful. Just don't look."

Her mouth twisted sideways as she tried not to smile. Part of her so desperately wanted to avoid getting involved with him, but the other part of her was screaming out that they were stranded in the middle of nowhere, and that a little love and laughter weren't going to kill her.

She wanted to ask him about Dot, she wanted to talk to him about how they were going to get to the coast, what his plans were, but instead she stayed silent, just enjoying the sound of his footsteps next to hers and trying not to overthink everything.

"I'm proud of you, Vita," he said, and she caught the glint in his eye as he looked sideways at her. "I thought you were going to fall to pieces out here, but you haven't."

"You thought I was a princess—is that what you're saying?"

"I think we both thought of each other as a lot of fun," he said truthfully. "I honestly didn't ever expect . . ."

"I know," she said, her cheeks heating as he glanced at her again. "It feels different here, doesn't it?"

His smile was sweet. "Yeah, it does."

They were almost at the village now, and she kept watching Bobby so she didn't have to glimpse the buffalo.

"It's nice to see what you're really like, that's all. I suppose what I'm trying to say is that I like this girl just as much as I liked the party girl back in New York."

"So you weren't smitten with me from the start then?" she teased, wishing Eddie could hear their conversation so she could prove him wrong.

"You were fun at the start," he said, his voice dropping lower. "But now—now you're something else, Vita. Something real special."

Tears filled Vita's eyes; it might just have been the most romantic thing anyone had ever said to her. One thing Eddie had been right about was what a good man Bobby was. She looked around then and realized how far they'd dropped back from the rest of the group.

"I like seeing you like this, too," she replied. "You're a lot more than I ever gave you credit for. I thought you were just a fun spin on the dance floor."

Bobby's smile was warm, and as they stopped walking he bent down, hovering with his face near hers, his lips inches from her own as he shuffled closer. Vita had the chance to move away—she could have smiled and stepped back or turned her cheek—but suddenly, kissing Bobby seemed like the best idea she'd ever had.

His lips brushed so gently over hers, the touch so light that it left her open-mouthed and desperate for more, but his lips only returned for one slow, final second before he straightened to full height again.

She knew barely anything about Bobby, other than the fact he was usually the life of the party and made all the nurses swoon. But this—*this* was the real man behind the smile, and for the first time she saw him as more than a fun fling. She saw him as a man capable of looking after her. A man who might just be worth risking her independence for.

"Keep the faith, Vita," he whispered, moving the parachute he was carrying to under his arm so his hand was free. He gently rubbed at her face with his thumb, smooth against her cheek. "We'll get home, one way or another. Just keep the faith."

She raised her hand to touch her mouth as he walked away, leaving her standing alone. As she slowly became more aware of her

170

surroundings, she realized that some of the medics were bent low to a stream up ahead, and she touched her own water canteen in her bag, knowing it was perilously close to being empty. But there was no way any of them should be drinking that water—it was brown and it was too close to the village, although she doubted anyone would bother listening to her if she told them. They were already guzzling the stuff down, and only a handful of them were taking the time to dilute their chlorine tablets in it.

"I see you've finally started to take my advice."

The mutter came from behind her, but Vita didn't need to see his face to know it was Eddie. She laughed as he was carried past, having thought the entire rest of the group was ahead of them when she'd let Bobby kiss her.

"Trust you to see that," she said.

"Hey, I've got nothing else to do here."

She heard the jest in his voice, but it wasn't enough to disguise the pain bracketing his eyes or the sweat beading his forehead. Eddie needed a hospital faster than they could get him to one, and she slowly fell into step beside the men carrying him, just wanting him to know she was there.

———— ❧ ❧ ————

Four hours later, they all sat at two long tables in what Vita could only describe as a hall. The seats were made of wood and terribly uncomfortable, but the smell of food had them all salivating. Although, when one enormous bowl was presented to Bobby alone, along with a single spoon, Vita knew she wasn't the only one perplexed—she was just glad she wasn't the first to be served.

She was sitting to Bobby's right, and she had no idea why he was the only one given food, and Josef had disappeared so there were no villagers who understood English and could help them.

They were all communicating with an ad-hoc sign language that wasn't proving to be particularly useful.

Bobby looked at her for help, but all she could do was shrug. After some minutes of the soup's delicious smell wafting through the air around them, the man beside Bobby took the bowl and dipped the spoon in, taking a sip and then passing it back to him, gesturing around the table. She'd been surprised there were no local women joining them, and she wondered if women usually shared meals with men, but she didn't know enough about their customs and none of the men seemed concerned they were all together. Perhaps the rules for guests were different.

"I think you're supposed to take a sip and then pass it on," Vita whispered under her breath.

Bobby gave her a confused look but did as she'd suggested, taking a spoonful and then passing it to her. Two of the villagers clapped their hands together and smiled, so Vita did the same thing, putting the spoon in and taking a welcome gulp. It was the most delicious thing she'd ever tasted—the broth flavorsome, with little bits of meat or something floating in it—and it took all her willpower not to take another spoonful of the sweet liquid before relinquishing it. She passed it on to Evelyn and watched her eyes widen at the taste, knowing her friend was enjoying it just as much as she had. The bowl continued around the table, before being passed over to the next one and then making its way back around and past her again. In the end she had three spoons in total, and she would have done anything for her own bowl to devour.

Cornbread was brought out then, once again by women wearing black clothes that covered every inch of them, so at odds with the partisan fighting women they'd met earlier. Josef had told Bobby they were all of Muslim faith, but she didn't know enough about their faith or culture to understand the difference. She could only guess it was their choice, or perhaps their husbands' choice, whether to dress modestly or not, and whether to join the fighting.

"It's so unusual, sitting with so many strangers and eating together like this," she murmured to Bobby as his hand fell to her leg. She let it rest there, liking the weight of his touch.

"Not to me," he replied.

She glanced at him. "What do you mean? Are you trying to tell me you've been stranded in a village before?"

His smile was there, but it didn't reach all the way to his eyes, not like usual. "I, ah, spent some time in an orphanage when I was little, so every night it was a big table just like this and not a lot of food to go around. I was very young but I still remember some things."

He could have blown her over with a feather she was so shocked. "An orphanage?" she repeated. "You were an orphan?"

"I was adopted when I was about four, so the memories are murky," he said. "No one knows where I came from. I was left outside a church and taken in."

"And your parents? Your adoptive parents, I mean—are you close to them?" she asked, thinking of her own parents and how much she hated them, even though they were her own flesh and blood.

"They're incredible, just genuinely good people. They'd do anything for anyone, but even so, I think I've spent my entire life trying to prove to them that I'm worthy of saving. It's why I became a pilot, I suppose." He paused. "They lost a son in an accident—he was the same age as I was when they adopted me—and it's why they went looking for a boy to take in."

It all made sense now: why he was so eager to be everyone's friend, why he relished the attention of women. He'd spent time alone, unloved in an orphanage, so of course he wanted to be loved now, wanted to show everyone that he was worthy.

Their conversation came to an abrupt end because Josef reappeared, and Bobby was summoned away with some of the older men from the village. But one person caught Vita's eye: a woman who was lingering in the doorway, her eyes flitting around the room. Vita stood, reaching for the empty bowl and carrying it to her, wondering if she was waiting to clear the table. She hoped the women had all had some too and they weren't expecting any of the soup to be left over for them.

"Hello," she said, holding out the bowl.

The woman smiled shyly and repeated a heavily accented "hello" back to her.

"Have you eaten?" Vita asked, pretending she had something in her hand and eating it, not sure if she'd understand her.

The woman smiled. "Yes, have food."

Vita had no idea how this woman had come to learn English, but it was nice to converse with her.

"You know Josef?" she asked, pointing to the door he'd disappeared through.

The woman nodded. "Josef. Yes."

Vita curiously studied her face, realizing she most likely wasn't a partisan fighter, even though she hadn't covered her face and hair. She was dressed in a very simple hessian-looking long dress, with a wrap of sorts around her shoulders, and her hair was pulled back severely from her face. Vita wished she could ask more about their culture, but she feared her questions might come out wrong.

"How did he become the leader?" Vita asked.

That made the woman laugh. "He kill most Germans," she said. "That's how you become leader in village."

That wasn't what Vita had been expecting to hear, but the woman just patted her arm and walked away, leaving Vita to help the others from her group push the tables up against the walls to make space, as they prepared for yet another night of sleeping rough on the floor.

And less than thirty minutes later, she felt a touch on her shoulder, and it was Bobby, curling up beside her as she struggled to get to sleep. They were fully clothed, still wearing their boots and coats, but she immediately felt the warmth of his body as she tucked herself into him. Since he'd kissed her, she was suddenly craving his touch.

"I'll keep you safe, Vita," he whispered in her ear. "I promise."

Before she could reply, before she could even think of anything to say or do other than clasp his hand closer to her chest, he was asleep. The poor man must have been exhausted.

The way she felt about him, the way he sent spirals of warmth through her, the fact that he would do anything to keep her safe— a promise she knew he'd do anything to keep—it all told her that she'd been right in refusing to marry the man her parents had chosen for her. She and Bobby might be from different worlds—she an heiress and he a former orphan—but she'd rather sacrifice it all if it meant avoiding a loveless marriage to a wet fish of a man. Her almost betrothed had been nice enough to her, but he'd also been like an overeager puppy where her parents were concerned, and as she used Bobby's arm as a pillow, she knew that she'd choose him in a heartbeat over the man who'd been chosen for her.

CHAPTER EIGHTEEN

VITA

Vita was starting to realize just how fortunate she'd been all her life. It was morning, a full ten hours since they'd eaten with the villagers, but her three sips of soup, slice of cornbread, and two mouthfuls of water buffalo from the night before seemed like a distant memory. And unless the villagers had all eaten in secret, it seemed their dinner was supposed to sustain them for the morning, too. What she'd give to eat breakfast! She had no idea how they survived on so little.

"Come, my dears, come!" Josef was calling to them from outside the largest building in the village, and Vita looked to Bobby before following the others. He was striding across the hard-packed dirt with Josef in his sights, and she scurried to follow him.

Josef's smile was broad as he gestured to the men behind him, and she guessed they were the village elders or leaders. She wondered if they, too, had gained their status because of all the Germans they'd killed. She shuddered at the thought, still worried about how easily they'd put all their trust in a stranger.

"Today, we move on to the next village," Josef declared. "And we've been given a mule for your injured man."

Vita's eyes widened and she scanned the crowd for Evelyn. She found her and smiled at the look on her friend's face, at the relief she saw etched there.

"Thank you," Bobby said loudly. "Thank you all for your kindness. We will never forget it."

"We leave now," Josef said. "We have long trip to get there, much walking, many hours."

"How safe will it be?" Evelyn asked. "And has anyone heard news of our missing nurses? Has there been any word at all?"

Josef's expression darkened, and Vita stared sharply at Evelyn, willing her to stop asking questions. They were all wondering the same thing, of course they were, but Josef's patience looked to have grown thin.

"You forget about those nurses. Enough!" he berated her. "We all start walking now—you all lucky to be alive."

Vita didn't miss the warning look from Bobby to Evelyn, and she knew the warning extended to all of them. She waited a moment, until the men had moved away, before scurrying over to her.

"I know we have to keep moving, but I just can't stand the fact that we're moving on without her," Evelyn whispered as tears streamed down her cheeks. "What if she's hiding somewhere or waiting for us to come, and we just . . ."

"Turn our backs and leave her?" Vita asked. "I know, trust me, the same question keeps circling in my mind, too."

"Come on, let's go," Bobby ordered everyone, rounding them all up. "Josef says move, we move. We can't risk all being here in the open like this."

Vita watched him, saw the tight set of his mouth and the hardness in his gaze. He didn't even seem to notice her as he passed, so focused on his job of getting everyone moving, which gave her time to truly study him. She swung between wanting to give in to the way she felt about him and keeping him at arm's length—although maybe she was only feeling that way because he was their leader. She saw him in a completely different light now, the way he'd risen to the challenge and shown just how capable he was. But did that mean she should give in to her feelings for him? He'd made it clear he was interested, and part of her wondered if they'd be stuck in Albania forever, which meant she may as well just enjoy being with him.

She sighed. Everything was so messed up in her mind; sleep deprivation, starvation, and desperation seemed to have transformed her brain into a place of turmoil instead of steadiness, and she was starting to doubt her own thoughts.

This time when they started walking, she settled into a slow, steady rhythm more easily, eyes downcast as she stared at her feet. The terrain was rocky in some parts, slippery in others, and dusty the rest of the way, and the last thing she wanted was to fall. And it wasn't only her who was silent; there wasn't a murmur amongst the rest of the group either. They were all too hungry, tired, shell-shocked, unwell, or a combination of everything to talk. The only sound was the thumping of their boots, sometimes in unison but most often not.

Maybe two hours later, or perhaps more like four, with sweat curling down her neck and leaving her hair damp, and feet so sore they felt like they were covered in fresh blisters, she heard a command.

"Stop."

They all halted at Josef's command. And as she looked around at their group, she barely recognized the faces staring back at her. Nurses who usually had perfectly pinned hair and warm smiles now looked sad and bedraggled, and the men looked like the fight had been knocked straight out of them. Their little feast seemed like a lifetime ago, and Vita knew the faint, spinning feeling in her head was likely from a severe lack of food and water. Thinking of water, she took her canteen from her bag and sipped, forcing herself to go slowly and savor every mouthful.

"We need to go very carefully now," Josef told them. "We have to cross airfield to get to next village."

"*An airfield?*" Vita gasped.

"Airfield, yes. We go in small groups, running across to the other side."

Silence stretched between them all, and it was Bobby who finally spoke up.

"You said all the airfields were under German occupation," he said. "Is that why we need to be so careful? Because there are Nazis out there?"

Josef nodded. "Yes."

Vita's heart dropped, and she could feel the slumping of shoulders around her, a sense of defeat that was impossible not to detect. Was it even feasible for their group to pass through an enemy-occupied airfield without being seen? Emotion welled inside her as she dug her nails into her palms, fists balled as she fought the urge to fall to her knees.

What was the point? Had they been wrong all along in following so blindly? Should they have refused? Were they going to die anyway, despite their suffering and determination? Despite everything they'd been through?

"Something doesn't feel right about this." Evelyn was beside her now, her voice low.

"I agree."

Evelyn's eyes were wide when she turned to face her. "Should we say something? I mean, I've put my faith in Bobby without question until now, but . . ."

Vita listened to her friend's whispered words, blinking back at her. "I don't know. I honestly, I just . . ." She took a breath, swallowing hard. "I just want it all to be over."

"I know. Trust me, I know, because so do I."

Vita just blew out a breath, trying not to cry. But it wasn't easy. Nothing about crash-landing in Albania was easy, and suddenly she couldn't keep up her veneer of confidence any longer. She was scared.

"I suppose we have to do as we're told, because we can't exactly just turn around and go back, can we?" Vita murmured. She looked back at Eddie, strapped onto the mule, so helpless. When Evelyn put an arm around her, she gratefully leaned into her, never having needed human contact so badly.

"Want me to tell you something funny?" Evelyn whispered, leaning in close as they started to walk again, following behind the others. "I promise it'll make you laugh."

"Go on then." Vita turned her attention back to Evelyn. Just seeing her smile made her feel better.

"I had to go to the toilet before, and I'm already out of paper, so I had to rip a page from my book! My beloved copy of *A Tree Grows in Brooklyn* that my father gave me!"

Vita did laugh, she laughed so hard she received a sharp "shhh" from those ahead of them, and she had to clamp her hand over her mouth.

"Somehow, even in desperation, there is light," Evelyn whispered. "We need to remember that, always."

Evelyn slung an arm around her neck and, despite all the misery, Vita at least knew she had a friend in her; a friend capable of cheering her up despite it all.

"Stay low," Bobby called out from up ahead, and Vita did as he said, dropping low so she was crouching in the long grass. "We're going to follow Josef's orders, so we need to listen to him very carefully."

He didn't need to tell them it was life or death; it was quite clearly implied.

As she studied all the other faces around her, Vita realized how familiar they'd all become—even those she didn't know well had become almost like family to her, as they all fought to survive. *Family.* She pushed the word from her mind. She doubted her own family would even be concerned for her, if they'd been notified at all. And if she ever did make it home, the first words out of her mother's mouth would be "I told you so." She'd almost choose being stranded in Albania over that fate.

"We go just a few at a time once we get to the airfield," Bobby whispered, just ahead of her. "We could be waiting for some time for the coast to be clear, maybe hours, but Josef is confident this is the only way to get us to safety."

They shuffled forward, down low, hands and knees hard against the dirt, until the trees cleared and the airfield was visible. Vita was surprised when she saw it—a stretch of concrete and a lonely building, on the edge of the forest. They were able to lie low in the long grass, but when she looked back she saw that Eddie was still slumped on the mule, which didn't exactly help their ability to camouflage.

A loud rumble vibrated through the earth then, and Vita held her breath as a roar sounded out, tearing through the sky. She peered over the person in front of her, craning her neck and pushing up and away from the earth. And then she froze.

The place was crawling with Germans! How in God's name were they ever supposed to pass through undetected?

She was about to tell Bobby how ridiculous the plan was, to point out that he must be able to see with his own two eyes that the mission was akin to suicide, but before she could, Josef spoke again.

She could taste her own fear, the metallic tang in the back of her throat impossible to swallow away, as she stared at the soldiers running back and forth across the runway. She should have told Evelyn to say something, they should have voiced their concern instead of just whispering to one another. *Any moment now. They'll see us any moment now and we'll be powerless to fight back. A few partisans will be no match for the mighty German army.*

"When they are distracted, we run," Josef said, his voice carrying between them all. "We have done this many times, so there is nothing to fear."

Bobby reached back for her, and she let him take her hand. She had to trust in him; they all did.

"Run!" Josef's sharp command suddenly saw the row of people in front of her leap to their feet and sprint fast through the long grass, their legs disappearing in the foliage. Vita held her breath, her hands fallen and now hanging at her sides, as they crossed the airstrip, all running in the oddest way with their bodies hunched over, as if by folding themselves in half they wouldn't be seen. But a German plane hadn't long ago landed, and all the soldiers appeared busy, caught up in their work. Although all it would take was one man to turn, one man whose attention was caught, and it would be over for all of them.

But that's not what happened. Within seconds, the little group was safe, or at least they were out of eyeshot. And then it was her shuffling to the front with the others who were preparing to run next. Bobby nodded at her, and she did the same back, and although it felt like the longest wait of her life, it was probably less than fifteen minutes. And suddenly the order came for them.

Vita's body felt like it was on fire. Her lungs screamed as she gulped for air, running blindly toward the other side of the airstrip. She knew the Germans were within earshot, knew that any mistake from anyone in their group would signal the end, but she pushed it all out of her mind. All she could see was the other side. Her only focus was on running as fast and as hard as she could, to get to safety.

She could taste the wind on her lips, could smell the fuel from the plane, feel the terror in the air. But still she didn't slow down.

Until her foot slid beneath her.

"No!" she gasped as she tripped, falling to the dirt as the others kept running, just when she'd thought she was going to make it. Fear clawed her throat as she tried to scramble up, as pain shot through her ankle, making it almost impossible to run.

"I've got you." Hands caught her around the waist, lifting her up, half carrying her, half pulling her along. Strong hands that gave her no doubt that she was going to make it across after all.

Bobby. Bobby had come back for her.

She fought with everything she had to keep moving, and then suddenly they'd made it and she was left panting, staring up at Bobby as he eased her onto two feet.

"Can you bear weight?" he asked.

She nodded, staring at Bobby, clasping his hand tightly as she tried to process the enormity of his actions. Without him, she'd be dead.

"You risked your own life to save me," she whispered. "You came back for me."

His eyes met hers. "I'll never leave you behind, Vita. Never."

Vita threw her arms around him, holding him tight. She had no idea how she'd ever thank him enough, how she could ever tell him how much his actions meant to her. But when she stepped back and saw the tears in his eyes, she realized she didn't have to tell him; he already knew.

Bobby cleared his throat and turned to check the rest of their group, and she glimpsed Evelyn nearby, seeing the same panicked relief in her gaze, too. Thank God they'd both made it.

"We need to keep moving," Bobby ordered, his hand finding hers and holding tight.

"Why can't we wait until everyone is across safely?" she asked. "It doesn't seem right to leave them."

"Because we have a long, treacherous walk ahead of us," he replied, pulling his hand from hers to rub at his stubbled cheeks. "Josef told me we were to make a start, that we'd be safer in two smaller groups."

"I agree with Vita. It doesn't feel right." Evelyn's quiet statement made Bobby turn.

"Look, if I'm honest I don't feel right about it either," he muttered. "But Josef knows this area better than anyone, and—"

An explosion rang out like a bomb going off, reverberating through the trees. The noise of an aircraft flying over low was deafening, as was the unmistakable sound of gunfire.

Everyone started to panic then, scattering and falling out of line, but it was the pain on Josef's face that Vita found the most alarming as she caught sight of him, running as fast as he could, so close behind them yet so far away. He looked . . . *terrified.* This man who'd gotten his reputation from killing so many Germans looked absolutely terrified, and that in turn terrified her. What hope did they have if he couldn't survive?

She ran after Bobby to an incline, exposing themselves more than they would have otherwise, but they needed to see what was happening. Vita could see some of the group running across still, the last of them, but they could also see the German planes flying low. And it was the last of the partisans the aircraft were aiming at, firing at them, and it looked like there was little chance of escape. Once again, they'd put the locals in danger, and they were likely going to die trying to save them.

A tree exploded, flames instantly licking up the trunk, and still the plane continued to fly low, continued to fire at people who had treated them as friends. People who'd walked side by side with them, shoulder to shoulder, treating them more kindly than they ever could have hoped for. Who'd all shared what little they had.

"I'm sorry," Bobby said, to no one and everyone, and she saw the pain in his gaze, the devastation easy to read as it spread across his face as he cried. She instinctively reached for him, her arms wrapping around him as he let out an inhuman, guttural cry at the carnage before them. It was the first time she'd seen Bobby broken since they'd crashed; the one man who'd been unflappable, who'd refused to give up. And if Bobby was broken? She gulped, squeezing his shoulders in her arms. Then they were all going to break.

"Bobby!" Evelyn yelled from the back of the group, standing farthest away from the devastation. "Bobby, we need to move! There's no time to wait!"

Vita's arms fell away from him then as he stood taller, like Evelyn's call had brought him back to the present, to the responsibility he had to get the rest of them to safety. His shoulders squared, he turned to face their group, their faces a combination of terror and exhaustion.

"We keep walking," Bobby said grimly, his voice husky as he addressed them, clearing his throat. "We do not stop, we do not look back, we keep walking for as long as we can."

"Come on, you all heard him!" Evelyn yelled. "Get moving!"

"Where's Eddie?" Vita asked, spinning around and looking for him. "Has anyone seen Eddie?" Panic rose inside of her until Bobby moved and she saw him, her heart catching as she realized he'd made it. They didn't have the mule, but they did have the man, and that was all that mattered. She looked back at the scene they were leaving behind one last time, defying orders as Bobby and another man prepared to heft Eddie behind them on a parachute they'd saved from the plane. She couldn't believe their Albanian friends had been killed, or that their group had survived.

That could have been us. That could have been us gunned down here, and no one would ever know how or where we even died.

The shots became louder, the plane coming closer yet again, circling back for them.

"Run!" Bobby yelled. "Run as fast as you can and don't look back!"

Vita tripped and stumbled, righting herself as she fought to scramble along beside Eddie.

"How's the pain?" she asked, gasping when her foot connected with a sharp rock, her ankle weak from her fall earlier.

"It's like my entire leg has just been set on fire," Eddie replied, his voice strained and husky. "But I'm alive, and that's what matters."

She wished she could stop and reach for his hand, to whisper something comforting to him, but all she could do was keep pace with the rest of the group, and pray that they were heading in the right direction.

Where are we? Vita heard moaning, and she looked around, off-balance and queasy. It was like when she'd had too much to drink, only instead of a room spinning around her, it was the sky. She looked up, the gray clouds visible when she tilted right back to look up where the trees parted, and suddenly the branches seemed to be reaching out to her, trying to touch her.

She shut her eyes and gulped air as if she were greedily swallowing water. It had been a few days since they'd crossed the airfield, or maybe it had been a week; she'd lost track of time. They'd left most of the group behind—hidden in dense forest and too weak to continue—while they looked for help, but now she had the feeling they were terribly, horribly lost. They'd gone in search of the next

186

village, of somewhere safe with food and shelter, and instead they'd found nothing.

"Girls." Bobby's voice was hoarse, and she turned to see him beckoning for them to follow.

She did, because it was easier to follow than try to think what to do herself.

It was just her and Vita, along with Bobby and Ralph—they were the only ones who hadn't come down with a severe case of the GIs, although Bobby was starting to look a little off-color. She felt delirious herself, Bobby swimming before her as she tried to fix her gaze.

"Come on, we have to keep going. Have to," Bobby grunted, "find the village."

She heard the moaning sound again, but when she looked across at Evelyn and saw that her friend's mouth was shut, that she was silent, she realized it must have come from her.

"I don't think I can," she whispered, not sure whether anyone else would even hear her. Was she speaking aloud, or was it only in her head? Confusion shimmied through her as she tried to focus. She reached for her canteen again, unscrewing the lid and tipping it up, hoping for just a drop that she might have missed before. But, of course, it was still bone dry.

"Oh shit!" she swore, lurching forward but stopping short of falling over.

Her boots had stuck in mud, mud she hadn't even seen, and she quickly realized that the others had fallen into the same trap. And the more she tried to move, the more stuck she became, until the mud was almost up to her knees.

When she dropped her canteen, her tears began, and nothing she could do would stop them. She wept as she stood; stuck, bedraggled, and so hungry and thirsty she would have given her right arm for something to eat and drink.

But despite her sobs, she still heard the click.

Vita froze.

"Hands up," Bobby muttered, and as Vita lifted her head and her hands, slowly looking around, she saw where the click had come from.

A man stood, his rifle pointed straight at them, partially concealed by the undergrowth. As he stepped out, Vita ran her eyes over him, taking in his clothes and the way he approached them. He wasn't fooling anyone if he was trying to look like a local—it appeared he was wearing some kind of uniform, though with a scarf tied around his throat and something else tied around his middle that looked to be Albanian.

"You the Americans?"

She watched in silence as Bobby replied, hoping for the second time since they'd crashed that he was right in trusting his instincts and telling this man the truth about who they were.

"Yes."

"Your plane came down?" the man asked, walking closer still, his gun trained on them.

"Yes, that's us," Bobby said, his hands still raised. Although it wasn't like they were going anywhere—they were well and truly up to their knees in mud. "I'm Captain Bobby Redfern, United States Air Force, and I still have the manifest if you want to check it."

The weapon lowered and the man's smile changed his face, made Vita want to run to him and throw her arms around him in gratitude for finding them. *If only I could get out of the damn mud.*

"I'm James Millard, British SOE agent," he said with a smile. "You'd think a bunch of Americans would be easier to find, but I've been looking for you lot for days."

CHAPTER NINETEEN

DOT

Dot crouched low, huddled with her arms wrapped around herself, straining as she listened to the German soldiers speaking above. She could only hear them faintly, and she barely knew any German, but still she listened, frozen in place. The air in the basement was musty, the floor hard-packed dirt, which left a thick, unpleasant taste in the back of her throat. She knew that when she finally emerged she'd be caked in a layer of dust, embedded in her shoes and skin.

When she couldn't stay on her haunches any longer, her ankles aching and her knees creaking, she sat down, her back against the stone wall. *I can do this. I'm going to be fine. Everything is going to be fine.*

Only she didn't believe her own words. She tucked her knees up to her chin and started to rock, silently listening, silently waiting, knowing that eventually the boots would stop thudding and she'd be able to come out.

But what if I can't come out? What if . . . She pushed the thought away, refusing to let her mind wander. She was alive, and there was no reason she couldn't stay alive.

Knock, knock, knock.

Dot froze. She held her breath, not wanting to make a noise as she strained to listen, to make sure she'd heard right. And just as she was about to gasp for air, as she thought maybe she'd imagined it, the sound came again.

Knock, knock, knock.

Dot quickly turned over onto her hands and knees and shuffled forward, crawling across the damp dirt as quickly as she could, keeping her head low so she didn't hit it as she moved into the tunnel. She reached out, feeling her way along in the dark, wishing she had a light as she struggled to see where she was going. The tunnel was narrow, but big enough for her to crawl through. And it was something she'd done before, so she knew what to do and how long it would take her.

She breathed evenly to keep herself calm as she struggled to turn around and pull the cover over the end. They'd used a barrel there to disguise the entrance, and she'd have to push another away at the other end, once she'd wriggled the small distance along the crudely dug tunnel.

Soon she was shuffling forward again, her knees aching, reaching for the other end with her hand extended, and she pushed to move the other barrel out of the way, starting to feel claustrophobic in the confined dark space. She pushed and pushed again, but nothing happened.

I'm going to die in here. Oh Lord, I'm going to die!

She started to panic, clawing to get the thing out of the way as she started to hyperventilate.

Come on, come on! Her tears started then, falling furiously as she tried to push one more time.

But this time, she needn't have worried. Hands reached for her, warm, familiar hands, and suddenly she could see again, her eyes straining as she clumsily tripped her way out of the tunnel.

"Dot? What's wrong?"

"I'm fine," she whispered, keeping hold of the warm hand that had found her. "Just scared for a moment, that's all."

She smiled at Marti in the dark, even though it was almost impossible to see one another. When she'd first arrived, it had been Marti who'd made her feel safe, her warm smile and kind gaze reminding Dot of her friends. And when Marti had wrapped her in her arms to welcome her, instinctively seeing how scared she must have been, she'd known she was safe.

"What did they say?" Dot asked, whispering as they put the barrel back in place and then huddled together, shoulder to shoulder, knee to knee, on the basement floor.

"They're looking for Americans," Marti replied. "They know about the crash."

Dot swallowed. *Of course they know.* It shouldn't have come as a surprise, the crash had happened . . . She tried to walk back the days in her mind and found she couldn't. It could have been one week, it might have been two. The days had all begun to blur into one another.

"Did they say anything else?" she asked.

Marti squeezed her hand. "You are safe here. We keep you safe."

Dot squeezed back. As far as Albania went, she *was* safe. How many houses would be built side by side, with men prepared to dig a tunnel between to keep their houseguest from harm? It meant she could be in one house, and then magically appear in the house next door without anyone knowing. She'd learned to be as quiet as a mouse, and she never went near the little windows in the house for fear someone might see her and give away her whereabouts. She might trust Marti and her family, but she didn't naturally extend that trust to everyone else in the village. And now that the Germans and the opposing party had taken control . . .

Dot pushed away her fear. All she could do was be careful and not make a mistake. There had been a lot of German military activity nearby, and originally they'd decided that if Germans were coming, she was to hide—but now anyone who came to the door warranted a fast escape down to the wine cellar for her. Ever since the fighting had begun, things had changed, and she kept thinking about the first time she'd been down in the wine cellar, only a few days after she'd been rescued.

They all sat, huddled together in the tiny wine cellar, cringing as loud booms echoed overhead and vibrated through the house violently enough to make the wine bottles clink together.

They were strangers to her, but she'd felt part of the family since the moment she'd arrived. Marti was younger than her, perhaps only seventeen, but her brother, Stefa, was older, she guessed at least twenty-five. It was Stefa who'd taken her that night, his hand over her mouth, terrifying her, making her believe she was about to die at the hands of the enemy. He'd dragged her like that, one hand holding down her arms and the other clamped over her mouth so tightly, she'd had to fight to breathe through her nose.

But when he'd finally let her go, lighting a candle in the dark and holding it to his face, she'd known that he would never hurt her. His eyes were kind—it was the first thing she'd noticed about him—and before she'd had the chance to back away and flee into the night, he'd held out his hand and said his name.

"Stefa," he said, touching his chest. "We will keep you safe. I won't hurt you."

His English was almost as good as Josef's—the only other English-speaking man she'd met in Albania.

"Dot," she said, touching her own chest and moving closer instead of away, which had been her first instinct. But this man with the warm brown gaze felt far safer than anything else around her.

"Come," he said, gesturing with his head. "Trust me."

And she followed willingly, because when she looked over her shoulder into the pitch-black of night, she knew she didn't really have any other choice. There was nowhere left to go, not when she had no idea where her friends were. In the morning she could search for them, but not tonight.

But morning never dawned in the way she'd expected it to. The sun came up, but with it came the Germans, searching Stefa's village, clearly not having found what they were looking for. By the time they moved on, it had been too late. Stefa had gone looking, and he'd asked around as best he could, but by all accounts her group had left without her.

She'd mourned in the beginning, hurt that Vita and Evelyn would let everyone move on, but she also knew in her heart they wouldn't have done it if there were another option. She also didn't know how many of them had even survived.

And then the fighting had begun.

Nani and Goni were the kindest couple she'd ever met, and even though they spoke barely a word of English, they had already become like surrogate parents to her. Dot had sat beside Nani in the cellar that first night, listening to her singing softly in her native tongue, the melody comforting even though she didn't have a clue what the older woman was singing about.

Nani's brother lived in the house next door with his children, and it was he who'd taught Marti and Stefa how to speak English. He'd worked in an English hotel for some years before returning to Albania, and he'd brought books home with him that were dog-eared from all the hours Marti and her brother had spent reading them.

Marti was tucked tight into Dot on her other side as gunfire continued above them, the attack seeming to go on and on. And once they'd sat in silence for perhaps an hour, Marti had taken her hand and pulled her to her feet, as everyone had slowly trudged up the narrow stairs from the cellar back up to the house.

When the house vibrated yet again, long after they'd made their way back upstairs, Dot braced herself for another attack. But it was worse than that. As she stood shoulder to shoulder with Marti on one side and Stefa on the other, they watched in horror as German vehicles rumbled along the main road of the town. They pressed their noses to the glass and stared.

Nani said something under her breath, and Dot looked to Marti, waiting for the translation.

"What is it?" she asked, when the translation never came.

Marti's eyes were full of tears when she turned to her. "She said the Germans and the BK have won."

"The BK?" Dot asked. "What does that mean? Who are they?"

"They control this area. The Albanians you met when you first crashed, they fight against the BK," Stefa explained. "Those partisans, they are fighting for a different Albania."

Dot understood. They'd been told in the very beginning that there were two groups fighting for territory within Albania; and that the opposing group would have slit all their throats if they'd been the ones to find them. That particular comment had rattled around in her mind constantly from the moment she'd heard it. She instinctively shuffled closer to Stefa.

"Are they so bad?" she asked. "This BK party?"

Stefa shook his head. "They are not so bad to us. But then we are not fighting against them."

"What do you think has happened to the rest of my group? To the other Americans?" she asked.

She watched as Marti asked Nani, but she didn't need any translation of her sad frown and the slow shake of her head. Perhaps Dot didn't want to know what had happened to them; it was far better imagining they'd escaped and were safely on their way back to Italy, however far-fetched that might be. Even if they'd had to leave her, she still hoped they made it to safety.

"Goni will try to find out," Marti whispered to her as they slowly backed away from the windows. "If they are alive, someone will know."

She waited as something else was translated for her, as Goni spoke to Marti, looking at her every few seconds.

"What's wrong?" she asked.

Marti sighed.

"Please, if it's too dangerous with me here, I can go. I don't want to put you or your family in harm's way," Dot said, holding back her tears. The idea of leaving was terrifying, but she'd do it if it meant keeping this family safe. "I can go."

Marti spoke to her family and they crowded around her, shaking their heads.

"They say no," Marti said.

Dot breathed a sigh of relief.

"Goni said that he is going to start digging tomorrow, with my uncle. They're going to dig you a tunnel, between the houses. Underground."

She could have blown Dot over with a feather. "They're going to dig a tunnel, just for me?"

"To keep you safe," Marti said. "Then if the Germans come, you can crawl next door and no one will know you're here."

"Thank you," Dot whispered, throwing her arms around Marti. "Thank you all so much."

She did cry then, unable to dampen down her emotion at how kind these people were being to her, to a complete stranger. They were risking everything for her, and she had no way to repay them.

"Thank you," she said, opening her arms to Nani and hugging her. To the men, she put her hands together as if in prayer and gave them a little bow, still whispering "thank you" and hoping they understood the depth of her gratitude.

When she turned, it was Stefa who was staring at her, his eyes catching hers. And somehow he didn't have to say anything; she just knew that he'd do anything in his power to keep her safe.

She shut her eyes as she thought about Stefa, waiting for him to come down to get them. There was something about him, something that made her smile whenever he came near, and she had a feeling that he felt it, too. He was shy around his family, but in the few moments they'd been alone together, he'd looked at her in a way that Peter never had. In fact, he made her wonder if she'd ever actually been in love with Peter at all, because he'd certainly never made her heart flutter like Stefa could with barely a smile in her direction.

"I think that's him," Marti whispered, and they waited for the familiar *tap, tap, tap* that Stefa would do again.

When the taps came once more, they listened to make sure there were definitely no Germans upstairs, to make sure it wasn't a ruse, before Marti opened the trapdoor and light flooded down into the cellar. It was a basic house, with no indoor plumbing at all and very basic cooking facilities, which made their well-filled wine cellar all the more surprising. Dot looked back at the wine now that it was partly illuminated, and wished she could uncork a bottle and drink it to help with the shock.

Marti disappeared after giving her a quick backward glance, and she was surprised to see Stefa move into the open entrance to the cellar. As he held out a hand and pulled her up, she gratefully took it. But this time he didn't let go. Stefa kept hold of her hand, his fingers warm against hers, his breath even warmer when she leaned in slightly so that their cheeks were almost touching.

They stood like that for what seemed like forever but was maybe less than a minute, his fingers still intertwined in hers, and his other hand slowly lifting, stroking her hair back from her face.

And then he nudged her cheek softly so that her eyes were forced to meet his, his gaze searching, before he slowly pressed his lips to hers.

It was a chaste kiss, just the most simple, soft glide of his lips against hers, but it felt like the most intimate caress of her life.

"You're safe," he whispered against her lips, before a noise behind them made him step back.

Her hand was still in his, their arms outstretched, until their fingertips slowly lost contact. And then Marti came looking for her, a cup of tea in hand and her eyes searching Dot's.

"What's wrong?" Marti asked.

Dot smiled, hoping her flushed cheeks didn't give her away. "Nothing's wrong. I'm just happy to be here with you, that's all."

If only Vita could see me now. Dot took the tea from Marti and followed her into the little living room, avoiding Stefa's gaze but smiling and nodding at both his parents. She'd been alone for so long, so desperate to be part of a family, and somehow she'd found what she'd been looking for in a country she hadn't even heard of until their plane had gone down.

CHAPTER TWENTY

EVELYN

Evelyn stared at the man. After days of feeling like it was all over for them, like it was their predetermined fate to die in Albania, she couldn't believe there was a British man in front of them who might actually be able to save them. A British man who looked well-fed, strong, and completely in charge of the situation. His dark hair was brushed back neatly off his face, his smile warm as he stared at them, and she couldn't imagine what a sight they all must look.

"Come on, let's get you all out of that mud and turned around in the opposite direction."

"Why?" she croaked, her throat so dry the word barely came out. "Why do we need to turn around?"

"Because you're headed toward a German-occupied village, which is the last place on earth you want to end up. Trust me. If you want to live, we go this way."

His tone was grim but his demeanor was encouraging, and despite being untrusting since they'd crashed, Evelyn had the most overwhelming feeling that this man was someone she needed to listen to. She had no reason to doubt he was who he said he was, and it wasn't like they had anyone else to help them now that Josef was gone.

"We need to turn around and retrace your steps, find the rest of your group, and then head immediately for a safe village."

"We thought that's where we were heading," Bobby admitted, and Evelyn watched as he fought to get out of the mud, step by torturous step. She did the same, only she wasn't quite so successful, her body so weak it was almost impossible to find the energy to lift her feet. "You think we can find somewhere safe to rest?"

"Yes, we'll be safe there, for a night or two at least," James said, reaching out a hand. She clasped it, grateful for the help, but she waited before moving, extending her own hand back to Vita.

When they finally found themselves back on drier land, Vita flung her arms around her, and Evelyn hugged her back fiercely, not bothering to fight her emotion. Vita shook violently in her arms, and Evelyn's shoulder was soon soaked through with her friend's tears.

"Is he real?" Vita asked.

"He's most definitely real," Evelyn replied, looking at the man as he talked with Bobby, although she could barely believe it either. "I almost wonder if I'm imagining it, but no, he's most definitely real."

"I can't do this any longer, I can't," Vita cried. "If he can't get us out of here, if we have to be out here any longer . . ."

Evelyn held her tighter, worried Vita was at breaking point; that perhaps they were all at breaking point after everything they'd been through.

She slowly released Vita when James stepped closer, self-conscious about how dreadful she must look at he stood before her. He was unshaven, but with only a few days' growth, compared to the men they were with who'd already grown beards in the time since the crash. His hair was combed, his clothes were clean, and he had the sort of spark in his eyes that told her he wasn't suffering from starvation and dehydration like they were. And that, alone, was enough to give her hope.

"James," he said, holding out his hand and offering her his water canteen in the other. "Only drink a little, we have to preserve it."

"Evelyn," she said, taking his hand and staring at his clean skin and clipped nails against her dirt-crusted hand. But instead of recoiling in embarrassment, she stood tall and took the canteen from him. He knew they'd been stranded for—she tried to count back; how many days had it even been? She actually had no idea how long they'd been in Albania now, she'd lost track, but however long it had been, he would likely know. Which meant that he was probably impressed they were alive at all, and wouldn't give a damn about how they looked. She took a small sip, and then another, even though her instincts told her to guzzle every last drop.

"This is Vita," she said, gesturing behind her, but she saw that Vita wasn't exactly looking up to introductions. She had her arms wound around herself, bent forward, so far removed from the Vita she knew. How could she even begin to describe what Vita was usually like, in comparison to this shell of a woman?

"You're both nurses?" he asked, as he pointed in the direction they were to walk.

Evelyn followed his lead, walking beside him as Bobby went to Vita and took her hand. Evelyn relaxed knowing that Bobby was taking care of her and passed him the water, surprised she'd found the energy to keep walking.

"Yes, we're all nurses. You know about our flight? About what we were doing?"

James nodded. "Yes. I was notified by local intelligence that an American plane had gone down, and I pieced it together from there." His smile was warm, and she didn't know if she was drawn to him because he was their rescuer or because she would have liked him regardless. There was something about him, something that told her he was dependable, that he could handle himself. She eyed the pistol at his waist. Or maybe it was simply because he was armed and looked strong that was making her want to stick to him like glue.

"I understand you were on a charter flight to transport injured soldiers," he said. "Is that correct?"

"Yes," she replied. "It was the first time so many of us have ever been sent up together. We usually work in teams of two or three per flight, but this time they sent twenty-six of us."

"Well, I dare say it was a failed experiment," he said with a chuckle. "I doubt they'll be making that mistake again."

She stared at him, not sure whether to laugh at his joke or slap him for being so cavalier about what had happened to them. She decided to let it go, and watched as Bobby passed the water back to him.

"I understand you've recently lost two nurses," James continued, his voice more somber this time. "I'm very sorry for your loss."

Evelyn stopped walking. "Three," she said. "We're missing three nurses, not two, and when you say you're sorry for our loss . . ." She could tell from the look on his face, from the way he'd said it, that they weren't just *lost*. He knew more than they did.

"I know nothing of a third nurse," he said, standing a few feet from her as he addressed them all. "But there are reports of two nurses being killed by the Germans. Their bodies were found."

Vita's sob was so loud it cut through her, but Evelyn just stood silently, breathing, feeling the wind on her face as she took a moment. Deep down, she'd known they were gone, but it still packed a punch that threatened to steal the air from her lungs. Her only hope was that Dot hadn't faced the same fate, that she was the third nurse, the one who was still unaccounted for.

"You didn't know they were dead, did you?" James asked.

She shook her head, forcing her feet to start moving again. "No, we didn't know for sure." *If we don't keep moving, then we'll be dead too.*

"And this third nurse—"

"Dot," Vita said from behind. "Her name is Dot."

Vita spoke as if the third nurse, the one that was still alive, was definitely Dot. And although Evelyn hoped it was, she knew that there was just as much chance that it wasn't her, too.

"She went missing the same time as the other two?" James asked, sounding surprised.

"Yes, the same night," Evelyn told him, hoping that Vita was right, that the third one *was* Dot. "We only heard two screams that evening, but Dot was one of the missing. She was right behind us and then . . ." She could still see Dot behind her, could see her in the room with the rest of them before they'd run. *If only I'd taken her hand. If only I'd kept hold of her.* "And then she just wasn't anymore."

"If she's alive, I'll find her," James said, and he spoke with such conviction she believed him. "But the first thing we need to do is find the rest of your group and get you to safety. What state are they all in?"

Evelyn didn't know how to answer that, but thankfully Bobby spoke up. "Most of them are suffering from chronic diarrhea, although we haven't eaten in days so you'd wonder how anything is even passing through them. And we've run out of louse powder."

"When did they last eat or drink?" he asked. "Have they had any sustenance at all?"

"No," Evelyn said. "We used the last of our K-rations days ago, and we've been out of water for at least two days. I think it was the water that made them so sick."

"Most likely," James said. "But if we can just get them to the village, they'll survive, and the best thing about the people here is

202

how accommodating they are to visitors. They don't have a lot, but what they do have, they'll share. They're very special people."

"And this place," Evelyn asked. "Is it the same as the other villages or . . ."

"It's a proper village, not like most of the others you will have passed through," James said, as if he knew exactly what she meant. "I think you'll be pleasantly surprised."

They walked in silence for some time, and despite her fatigue and deep-set hunger, Evelyn managed to settle into a steady rhythm, in time with the rise and fall of James's boots. And when she finally spoke again, it was to ask a question that had bubbled within her from the moment he'd introduced himself.

"James, if I ask you something, can you promise to answer honestly?"

He glanced at her, and when he held her gaze, she knew that she could trust him.

He gave her a quick nod. "Of course."

"Is there actually any chance of us getting out of here?" she asked. "Of us ever making it home? I need to know whether it's a possibility or not, or whether we need to give up on the idea completely."

"Yes," he said, without hesitation. "There is a high probability that I'll be able to get you out of here, but what I can't do is tell you how long that might take. It could be days, it could be weeks."

Warmth spread through her as she digested his words. "I needed to hear that, more than you could ever imagine." She didn't care about how long, she just needed to know it was a possibility—that seeing her sisters and her father again wasn't merely a fantasy—and she had no reason not to believe him.

And then he did something that took her so by surprise she almost tripped over. He reached over to her and took her hand, his fingers clasping hers tightly for a moment.

"You can trust me, Evelyn," he said. "I'm not letting a bunch of Allied nurses perish on my watch, are we clear? You have my word."

She stared at their connected hands before looking up at him as his fingers fell away from hers. For a moment she forgot all about her hunger and fatigue, so surprised by the easy way he'd touched her, by the way he was looking at her.

"We're clear," she whispered back.

Hope filled her, and she found the strength to walk faster, to keep up with him as he lengthened his stride. They *were* going to make it home now, she just knew it. This man, there was something about him; something about the way he walked, the way he talked . . . she just knew. If they were ever going to make it, he was going to be the one to make it happen.

"They're worse than I expected." James's expression was grim as he studied their group, and Evelyn stood beside him, seeing them through his eyes now that they'd reunited with everyone again. They'd all been together so long now, the days blurring together, and the way they looked had blurred, too. But now, she could see how bad things were. Not eating had taken its toll, the strain obvious on their faces, the weakness so blatant in the way they moved. James had found them just in time.

"How far do you think they can walk?" James asked. "I'd hoped we could make the village before dark, but . . ."

Bobby had come to stand with them, but he was clutching his stomach now and Evelyn instinctively took a step back, not wanting to catch whatever was spreading through the group like wildfire.

"We're going to be slow," Bobby said. "I'm worried about hygiene, too; everyone is so sick and we don't exactly have the right, ah . . ." His voice failed for a moment. ". . . *facilities.*"

James grunted. "You've been drinking water without chlorinating it, haven't you?"

Bobby nodded. "Most of us have. We ran out of chlorine tabs after the first week."

Evelyn raised her hand. "Not me," she said. "I haven't drunk in two days."

James surprised her by taking his own canteen out again and offering it to her immediately. "Take a couple more sips," he said. "There's no point being the only one without the GIs and ending up dying of dehydration."

She took it gratefully, careful again to only drink a small amount, before passing it back to him.

"Why don't you take the strongest and leave the rest of us behind for now?" Bobby suggested.

Evelyn immediately searched for Vita, seeing her on the ground, trembling, beside Eddie. He was looking better than she expected, his leg starting to heal well despite the conditions. Unfortunately, without the mule and with all the men so weak, she didn't know who was going to be able to carry him, and he still couldn't put enough weight on his leg to walk.

"No," she said, surprising herself with the strength in her voice. "We're not leaving anyone behind."

James nodded. "I respect that. I would say the same thing if they were my men."

"So what do we do?" she asked.

"We go slowly, and we stop when the weakest person can't walk any farther. Then we reassess our plan."

"When do we leave?"

"Now," he said. "There's no time to waste. A case of the GIs can turn serious without hydration, and the longer it takes us to get there . . ." He cleared his throat.

"The more likely we could end up with some seriously sick friends," she finished for him.

"Exactly."

"Well, let's get this show on the road then, shall we?"

Evelyn started to move around the group, touching the tops of heads and whispering comforting words. The water had given her a renewed strength, given her the incentive she needed to pull herself together again. She saw James crouch down next to Eddie and left him to it, focusing on the women in the group. They'd started to look up to her, and she knew they liked the way she'd taken charge; even though all she wanted to do was drop to her knees alongside them, she didn't. It was time to get to safety.

"Come on, girls, you have to get up."

She received groans in response, and she noticed that two of them were scratching their heads. Vita had become obsessed with using her louse powder, terrified of any bugs making their way to her scalp, and just seeing them scratch made Evelyn instantly itchy herself. It didn't help that they'd run out of powder now, which meant they had no way to treat it, either.

When only a few of the nurses rose, wobbly on their legs, anger started to rise within her, and she folded her arms as she stared down at them.

"I'm going to be blunt with you, girls," she said. "We stay sitting here, we don't ever make it home. All those dreams of making it back to America? They're a fantasy unless we get to the next village, and that man there"—she pointed over at James, who was watching her curiously—"is our best chance at finding help. So you either stay here and fend for yourselves, or you draw on something deep inside and get the hell up."

Breathing heavily, she didn't take her eyes off them.

"Now!" she ordered, with a commanding tone she hadn't even known she possessed.

And, like clockwork, they started to move. Evelyn reached for hands and took hold of arms, helping some of the women to their feet, determined to make sure every last one of them made it. She might have been bossy, but it was from a place of love and she hoped they all knew it.

"Who is he?" she heard one of the women whisper.

"He's British operative, James Millard," James said from behind her.

Evelyn turned, and despite everything she smiled at the way he was looking at her. Perhaps it was just the water that had affected her after all.

"And if you all know what's good for you, you'll do whatever she says," he added.

Now *that* she hadn't been expecting. But she'd gotten everyone upright, and right now, that was quite the accomplishment as far as she was concerned.

"What are we going to do with Eddie?" she asked, directing her question at James.

"You let me worry about your injured man," he said. "Just get this lot walking in that direction, and don't stop unless I tell you to." He pointed into the tree line to the left, and she breathed deeply, feeling a familiar tremor of fear run through her as she stared into the unknown. "And I'll follow up behind with your man."

"He's not my man," she corrected.

James laughed. "Well, you know what I mean."

She laughed too, something she hadn't done in so long. It made her cheeks ache, as if her muscle memory had forgotten how to create the movement, but somehow it still felt good.

Evelyn stretched out, completely stark naked, and made a starfish shape in the bed. She started to laugh, the sound hiccupping out of her as she luxuriated in the feeling.

"Did you ever imagine that sheets could feel so good?" Vita asked from the adjoining bed.

"Honestly?" Evelyn sighed. "Nothing has ever felt so good in all my life. Actually, I take that back, the little hot-water bath we had was pretty darn amazing too."

"And the cornbread when we arrived—somehow that tasted like the best thing I'd ever eaten," one of the other nurses called out. "I'm almost starting to like the stuff, and that's saying a lot."

Evelyn doubted she would ever like it, but she did appreciate the sustenance. They'd travelled for four days in the end with James, although it had felt like a lifetime. He'd kept them going, refusing to let anyone stop, and they'd maintained a slow plod through the forest, first to a small village where they were able to rest for a few hours and refill their water canteens. And now they'd finally reached their intended destination, they'd been billeted into local homes after being given somewhat of a hero's welcome with singing and flowers thrown at them, and it was nothing like the remote villages they'd been in up until that point. *And the sheets. Oh, the sheets!* She doubted she'd ever take the feel of sheets against her skin for granted again.

"I like James," Vita said, surprising her.

Evelyn smiled to herself in the almost dark, thinking of their suave, handsome rescuer. "It just so happens I like him too."

"Something changed when he found us," Vita continued, almost as if she were speaking her thoughts out loud without thinking. "There's something about him that made me hope all over again, like he lifted all our spirits just with his presence. I don't think anyone actually believed we were going to survive until he came along."

Evelyn lay her head down, eyes shutting as she saw James in her mind. He had certainly given her hope; she only *hoped* she hadn't misplaced her trust in him getting them safely out of the country. She also wished she didn't feel so unsure, as scared of the idea of James touching her as she was terrified that he might not do it again.

———— ◌ৎ৵ঔৎ ————

The next morning, she rose before the others, hastily making her bed and then dressing in her tattered clothes. She refused to dwell on how filthy her uniform was, despite having been cleaned in the river, although she promised herself that if she ever did make it home, she was burning everything, right down to her underwear. She never wanted to set sight on anything related to this ordeal ever again in her lifetime.

Evelyn tiptoed across the bare floorboards, hoping not to wake anyone in her host family, although she imagined they rose early to carry out their chores. She went to the toilet, a basic facility in an outhouse, and heard something, or someone, moving outside the structure.

"Hello?" she whispered. She strained to hear as she stood by the outhouse door.

"It's only me."

James. "What are you doing up so early?" She hadn't expected to see him, not when she was out on her own. Her stomach twisted into knots.

"I could ask the same of you." He stepped into her line of sight then, holding a gun. She recoiled, but he slid it into his waistband as soon as he saw her reaction.

"Sorry, I've just had one too many guns pointed at me since we crashed here."

He nodded. "Understood. Would you feel better if you were the one holding it?"

"Me? Hold one?" Evelyn laughed. "I don't think so."

James took a few steps away, and she wondered if he'd heard something or if he was just being cautious, checking to see if anyone else was up. She looked around at the white homes with their matching red-tiled roofs to her left, and then at the large river to her right, but saw nothing out of the ordinary that might have caught his attention.

"Evelyn, I'm used to working alone, but this assignment is different. My role is usually to gather intelligence, not to single-handedly move more than two dozen people through enemy territory."

She didn't have an answer for him, and she guessed he didn't expect one, so she just stood silently and waited for him to continue.

His eyes were warm and soft—they reminded her of the hot cocoa she made for her sisters at home—and she liked the way he watched her. She didn't doubt that if a rogue German appeared behind her, he'd shoot him without a second thought to save her life, but with her he was easy-going and thoughtful to be around.

"What I'm trying to say is that I can't work alone on this one. I need someone I can count on, someone who can use a weapon if they need to."

"Oh," she said, nodding in understanding. "Bobby seems comfortable with a gun, if you'd like I can—"

"I don't mean Bobby," he said, staring at her, not blinking as he seemed to wait for her to understand. "He already has his own weapon, and a role as group leader. I need someone else."

Holy hell, he means me. She blinked for the both of them, so rapidly her eyes watered. "Me? You want that person to be *me*?"

"I saw the way you rallied your people together, and I have a feeling that I can trust you," James said. "You need to believe me that I always follow my gut instincts, and my gut is telling me—"

"I can't shoot a gun," she blurted out. "There's no way. I mean . . ." She looked around her, as if perhaps he was actually talking to someone other than her and she'd made a mistake. "I've never even held one."

"Evelyn," he said, stepping toward her, slowly, until he was only a couple of feet away. She could feel his gaze on her, heating her skin just from his proximity to her, and as he lifted his hand, she gulped, not wanting him to touch her but desperate for it all the same. "Hold it for a moment. Feel the cool of the metal, and take a slow, deep breath."

James placed the pistol in her palm, his fingers uncurling hers and then curling them around it.

"Is it loaded?" she stammered.

"Yes," he said. "This is war, Evelyn, not make-believe."

She cringed, but his next words somehow sent a rod of steel down her spine.

"If you know how to use this, you can protect yourself and your friends," he murmured. "You only have to be scared if you can't take the shot, if you don't know how to use it."

She didn't need his fingers to hold hers in place any longer. Evelyn took a breath and squared her shoulders. *If I'd been able to defend us, maybe Dot would still be here.*

"Alright," she said, meeting his gaze, her body relaxing even though she still held the weapon. "You show me how to use it, and I'll be your person." *I can do this. There's no reason why I can't. Just because he's a handsome man doesn't mean I can't be confident around him.*

He smiled as she passed him back the gun, before stepping away. "I knew from the moment I saw you getting all those people up off the ground and convincing them to walk that I could count on you."

She didn't acknowledge the compliment outwardly, but inside she beamed. "Shall we start now?"

"Give me a minute, I need to clear it with the village leaders first." He grinned. "The last thing I want is for them to mobilize their little village army and come charging for us when they hear the echo of a gunshot!"

Evelyn stared after him as he walked away, and just like that she was standing watching her family disappear all over again.

"The soldiers need me, Katie. They need nurses like me."

"But I need you," Katie whispered, tears raining down her little cheeks. "Please don't leave me."

———— ❦ ————

Evelyn wiped her face with the back of her hand as she heard James's heavy footsteps again, signaling his return. She'd made that promise to her sister so easily, not knowing at the time just how false her solemn oath to return home had been. But this man, this soldier, could be the one to help her keep her word.

When James stood in front of her again, on the same patch of earth he'd occupied perhaps ten minutes earlier, he gave her a long, steady kind of look.

"You ready?" he asked.

She'd been expecting him to comment on her tear-stained face or ask if she was alright, and the fact that he didn't made her like him all the more.

"Yeah," she said, clearing her throat. "I'm ready."

He started to walk and she followed his lead, silently walking behind him until he stopped in a small clearing just outside of the village, the forest surrounding them. She'd come to fear the dense trees that she'd spent so long trekking through, but standing beside

James, she felt as if they were providing a protective buffer, shielding them somehow.

"Here," he said, passing her the pistol. "I want you to hold it, get a feel for the weight of it in your hand."

She took it from him, steadying her breath as she felt the gun's weight. She lifted it slightly, clasping and then unclasping her fingers, and moving her hand from side to side.

"You only need to fear a gun if it's aimed at you, or if you don't know how to use the one you're holding," James said, taking another gun from just under his trouser leg.

He obviously saw her surprise, because he lifted his other trouser leg to show off the glint of something else. "I always have two pistols and a knife on me."

In another life she might have been nervous, but it only made her feel safer with him; something she hadn't felt since their plane had crashed.

"I don't think I want to know how to use the knife," she said.

"Fair enough." He chuckled. "But let's get you up to speed with that gun, shall we?"

Evelyn stood dead still as he came closer to her, feeling her pulse pick up its rhythm at his proximity.

"May I?" he asked.

She nodded, seeing that he was staring at her hand. He moved when her head tipped up and down, standing behind her and lifting her arm, until it was outstretched and aiming straight ahead. She wasn't used to a man touching her, nor being so close, and she hoped her hand wouldn't start to shake from nerves.

"Take a breath," he said, his voice low.

She inhaled, hearing it tremble and hoping he didn't notice. She fought the urge to shut her eyes, nervous about what he was going to ask of her.

"Slowly let your breath go," he murmured, "and at the same time, curl your finger gently around the trigger."

Evelyn followed his instructions, the tiny hairs prickling on the back of her neck as his breath grazed her skin.

"The next time you breathe, I want you to squeeze the trigger on the exhale," he whispered. "You're going to aim for that tree."

She wanted to whisper back, but no sound came out of her, other than the gentle rise of her breath, and then the slightly louder hiss as it exhaled between her lips.

Crack.

"Well done," he murmured, putting pressure on her arm again to steady her, as if he could feel the erratic, fast beating of her heart as it almost exploded from her chest. "Do it again."

This time, she inhaled more slowly, forcing herself not to rush, no longer scared despite the jolt of adrenalin that had surged through her only seconds before.

James's hand fell away from her arm, but his body was solid and strong behind her, so close she could have leaned back and been pressing against his chest. But she didn't, because as she released her breath, as his hands touched her shoulders and gently pressed them down, forcing her to relax, she squeezed the trigger again.

She grinned, not even half closing her eyes this time.

I did it. I shot the damn tree!

Evelyn spun around, forgetting in her excitement that she was still holding a loaded gun. "I did it!"

"Whoa!" James grabbed the pistol and lowered it. "You did good, but don't go shooting the teacher. You only ever point if you want to shoot."

She grimaced. "Sorry. I just . . ."

He grinned when she didn't finish her sentence. "It feels good though, doesn't it?"

Evelyn sighed. "It feels so good to be in control of something, after all this time being stranded here and feeling so useless," she said. "Does that sound strange?"

"No," he said, shaking his head. "It doesn't. Not when you consider how out of control and helpless you must have felt these past few weeks."

She stared at the gun, wondering how her attitude toward it could have changed so rapidly.

"It's one thing to shoot a tree," James said, as if he could sense what she was thinking. "But it's another thing entirely to shoot a man."

Her gaze lifted from the pistol to him. "You've killed before?"

"I have," he replied, without hesitation, and she saw the way his eyes changed, the softness she'd been so fond of earlier hardening. "But when it comes to war, it's kill or be killed. We have to forget the person we were before the war if we're to survive."

Evelyn realized how close they were still standing, and even though she knew the proper thing to do would be to take a step back, she didn't. *Couldn't.* There was something about being close to James, like being under an umbrella shielded from the rain, and she wasn't ready to step out from under it just yet.

"So you weren't a soldier, before the war?" she asked, swallowing uncertainly as she tried to pretend she wasn't nervous just being around him.

He chuckled. "I was a bank manager, actually. You could say I've had quite the change in career, but I suppose that's the same with almost everyone fighting for their country, isn't it?"

She supposed he was right, even though she couldn't imagine him working in a bank.

"What about you? Were you a nurse before the war?"

She smiled. "No, I was just a girl living at home, up to her armpits in dishes and wading through her sisters' laundry. Then

I went to train as a nurse and I was eventually accepted into the Medical Air Evacuation Transport Squadron."

"So you were Cinderella then?" he asked, his mouth twisting as he fought a smile.

Evelyn laughed. "Yes, just without the evil stepmother."

She caught herself then, leaning toward him, her skin flushed as they shared the joke, their foreheads too close, and he must have sensed it too, because he suddenly took a step back, the umbrella moment over as swiftly as it had begun.

"We should, ah, be getting back," James said, gruffly.

Evelyn wrapped her arms around herself, a shiver running the length of her. What had she been thinking? Had she been *flirting* with him? She knew the answer to that without having to ask herself. "Yes, of course."

He nodded and put more distance between them, any spark she thought they'd had well and truly disappearing.

How embarrassing. The poor man is probably horrified with me!

"Thank you for the lesson," she said, trying to pretend like the air hadn't completely changed between them.

"We'll need to practice again," he said gruffly. "I'll need to show you how to load the gun, but I think my instincts were right about you being capable."

"Well, thank you." And then she was hurrying to keep up with his long, loping stride as they made their way back toward the village. She might have overstepped personally, but nothing could take away the feeling she'd had holding that gun, when she'd aimed at that tree and managed to put a bullet straight into the trunk.

But he was right; aiming at a human was going to be another story altogether, one that she wouldn't know the ending of until it happened.

"James, can I ask you a question?"

He stopped, turning back to face her, but she noticed that he still didn't come any closer. She'd clearly misread how he felt about her. "Of course."

"Why were the villagers so happy to see us when we arrived? It was like they knew to expect us."

"They did know you were coming, they'd received word—only, they thought you were part of an Allied force sent to liberate them."

"*Us?*" She choked on the word. "They thought a disheveled group of men and women were going to be part of a liberation? From who?"

"The Germans," he said. "They're used to women fighting with their partisan armies, so it's not such a far-fetched idea as it might sound. Some of the villagers are very conservative, but others are not, and around here they certainly think of America as a friendly country."

"What a terrible disappointment we must have been," she muttered.

His laughter was warm. "They seemed heartened by the fact that I was with you, though, so that helped soften the blow."

James strode ahead again and she followed behind, pleased he was at least talking to her even if she was still mortified that she'd made it so clear how much she liked him. She had such little experience around men, and the fact that she'd even tried to flirt with him . . . Evelyn groaned. She only hoped she hadn't made too much of a fool of herself.

CHAPTER
TWENTY-ONE

DOT

"I have a surprise for you."

Dot looked up when Stefa entered the room, smiling as soon as she saw him.

"What is it?"

"They know you're here," he said, his hands in his pockets as he stood in the doorway. "And they've given me clearance to take you for a drive."

"Who has?" Fear rose in Dot's throat. "Who knows I'm here?"

"The commander of the controlling BK group," Stefa said, still smiling. "He said he knew there was a nurse in the village, he'd heard the Americans were looking for someone, and I told him that you had come to our home seeking refuge."

"Stefa!" Marti scolded him from across the room, and Dot froze, barely able to believe his words.

"Won't they punish you?" she gasped. "Won't they come for me?"

"No, they won't," he said. "They've told me I can take you for a drive, that you'll be safe. The Germans can't know you're here, we need to be careful, but he said it's safe to take you out right now."

He paused. "I was with my uncle, and he is very important to them. His business with them is worth more than any one life."

Dot looked from Stefa to Marti and back again. She was allowed to go for a drive? It didn't seem real. After so long being housebound, trying to keep busy with housework and cooking, but going slowly crazy between the four walls, it seemed unbelievable that she was allowed to walk out the front door.

Marti spoke rapidly in Albanian and Dot had no idea what they were saying, other than understanding they were arguing. She looked around the room. The living room was the main room in the house, and at night they spread their pallets out and all slept in the one space together where it was warmest. In the morning, they rolled them up and cleaned the space; this one big room was both her prison and her refuge. Dot let her gaze lift to the window, to the sun shining in, and she could barely imagine what the fresh air would feel like.

"Will you come?" he asked. "I want to show you how beautiful Albania is. Please."

Dot should have hesitated—she knew she should be more cautious—but the happiness in Stefa's gaze was contagious. Going outside and feeling the simple pleasure of the wind on her face was her idea of a dream.

"Yes," she said. "I'll go."

"Now?" Marti asked. "But I have to help with dinner preparations, and—"

"We'll be fine without you," Stefa said. "I'll look after her."

Marti muttered something else Dot couldn't understand, before stalking out of the room. And, after a quick glance at his parents and a nod of acceptance, Dot found herself tying a simple scarf around her head and putting a navy-blue jacket over her shoulders, both items borrowed from Marti. She couldn't disguise

219

her blue eyes, but she could make herself more like a local woman than an American.

"Come," Stefa said, holding out his hand.

Dot took it, and she barely managed a breath before they burst out the door together, a beaten-up jeep parked outside, waiting for them.

"I borrowed this," he said with a shrug.

Stefa opened the door for her, but Dot couldn't move. She lifted her face to the late afternoon sun, smiling as the wind brushed her cheeks. After so long inside, pacing like a caged lion, she finally felt free.

"Does it feel good, after so long inside?" Stefa asked.

Dot opened her eyes, grinning at him. "Better than good. It feels incredible."

She finally got into the jeep, following Stefa's orders to keep her eyes downcast, so they didn't draw attention, her scarf demurely covering her hair. When he reached for her hand, she let him, their fingers colliding in a warm, comfortable hold that seemed more natural to her than anything else in the world. The way she felt about him had taken her by surprise, but she hadn't tried to fight it. Everything else about her existence felt so impossibly hard; except for Stefa.

"Are you sure we can do this?"

He looked down at their hands and she laughed.

"Not that!" she muttered. "Are you sure we can be out here? What if someone sees?" She should have been more nervous at the idea of anyone seeing them, but for the first time in her life, she found she didn't really care.

"We supply wine to the Germans and the BK group," he explained. "We have to be very careful, but the commander is a friend to us, and he said that today we would be safe. He said it must be very difficult for you to never leave the house, and he wanted to make sure you were being looked after. We still need to remain vigilant about the Germans and any raids, but we can trust this man."

"Why?" she asked, holding his hand tighter as they drove along the dirt road. "Why is everyone so kind here?"

Stefa didn't answer her, concentrating on driving and pulling off-road and onto the grass. She braced herself as they bumped along, feeling like her teeth were going to rattle from her jaw, until finally they came to a stop. He still didn't say anything as he cut the engine and stepped out, coming around to open her door.

She took his hand and stood, following him as he led her out to a clearing, beckoning for her to sit on the grass, looking out at the most beautiful view she'd ever seen.

"It will be dark soon," Stefa said, "and it's even more beautiful in the moonlight."

Dot looked at the hills around them, at the endless stretches of green, so lush and different to the type of landscape she was used to in America.

"It is beautiful," she said. "I think you live in one of the most beautiful countries in the world."

They sat in silence for some time, close but not quite touching, and Dot placed her hand on the ground between them, hoping he might cover her hand with his. Her scarf had slipped down now, exposing her hair, and she saw the way he turned to look at her, with an almost open curiosity in his gaze.

"You asked before why everyone is so kind here," he said. "We are bound by *besa*. It is like our—how do you say—code of honor."

She turned to watch him as he spoke. "A code of honor?"

He smiled. "It means to keep the promise. If an Albanian gives you his word, or makes a promise, it is a matter of honor that we keep you safe."

"I see," she said. "Well, you have certainly done that."

"We are a proud people, and *besa* means everything to us," he explained. "It's why we never turned Jews over to the Germans. They made the order upon occupation, but we told our Jewish families we would keep them from harm, and we mean what we say. They are safe here, so long as we are all here to protect them. Any of us would open our door to them."

Dot blinked away tears as she thought how such a small country could be so brave, their people so kind and honorable. "It's not like that through the rest of Europe," she told him. "What is happening to the Jews, the way they're being taken to camps, it's just awful."

"We have many religions here, but we are all Albanian," he said. "Our people fight each other over politics, the partisans fight the BK, but it is not about religion for us."

When Stefa's fingers finally found hers, Dot let her head fall to his shoulder, noticing the way his breath quickened when she did so. It reminded her of sitting with Vita, side by side, shoulder to shoulder, but it was also like nothing she'd ever felt before. And it was then, in that moment, she realized just how long it had been since she'd thought of Peter, and the realization brought a smile to her face. Instinctively she reached for her necklace, but not as a comfort. This time, letting go of Stefa's hand, she undid the clasp, letting it fall and then holding it for barely a second in her palm before discarding it on the grass behind her. It was a memory of her past she no longer wanted; but it had taken until this moment to be truly brave enough to discard it.

When she felt Stefa turn, his body angling toward hers, she tipped her head back and stared up at him, brazenly meeting his gaze, so much more confident than she'd ever been before. And when his hand cupped her cheek, so gentle and soft, she leaned into him and didn't hesitate to move her lips against his when he dipped his head to kiss her.

They'd barely had a minute alone at the house, but here, in the open, they had a blissful moment, just the two of them, with only the birds singing their final song before dark as company. Dot gulped, as terrified as she was excited. She'd barely kissed Peter; he'd been warm but not overly interested in being intimate, other than the odd chaste peck on the lips. But Stefa . . . Her breath shuddered out of her. Stefa made her want to kiss him again and again and again.

Stefa pulled back and looked down at her, an open question in his gaze, and she nodded in reply, instinctively knowing he was asking for her permission to touch her, to kiss her again.

And as the wind brushed against her cheeks, Stefa's lips warmed her body and left her desperately, unashamedly, longing for more.

CHAPTER TWENTY-TWO

DECEMBER 1943

EVELYN

Evelyn sat with Vita, both cross-legged, fashioning little decorations as best they could from what they'd found in the forest, adding some little red ribbons that someone had given them. It was almost Christmas, and there wasn't a single member of their group not struggling with being so far away from home, although she was trying her best not to think about her family. They'd continued to move from village to village, with James not wanting them to stay in one place for too long, although it seemed like they might be staying where they were for a little longer this time. *Unless the Germans start to move closer again.*

Her stomach was growling, but Evelyn could no longer feel the pain; it was like she'd become numb to it, used to only eating such small amounts, and her body felt different now. Her movements were slower, her arms weaker, her chest heaving if she tried to walk too far.

Since they'd had to move on to a smaller, more remote mountain village, meals were few and far between. They simply didn't have enough to go around, although the villagers were so kind and shared whatever they did have. Her only relief was that there was a river to bathe in, so she at least felt clean.

Evelyn leaned back as Bobby approached their group, watching as he took Vita's hand and led her away, saying something under his breath to her that Evelyn couldn't hear. She'd wondered, deep down, if Bobby and Vita would still be together by the end of it all, if there ever *was* an end, but she could see now that something had changed between them. Something that had made them stronger.

"Penny for them?"

Evelyn looked up and found herself looking into James's eyes. "Honestly? I'm thinking of home," she said.

"Home is dangerous," he said, lowering himself beside her so that his back was against the wall and his gaze on the sparsely decorated branches in front of them. She found herself staring at his booted feet, crossed at the ankles, and then comparing her own boots, with holes forming in the toes. If she could see the soles, she'd be looking at the wear there, too.

"There was a cobbler in Berat," he said, as if he could read her mind.

"Shame we're not in Berat then." He laughed, and she realized how rude she'd sounded. "Sorry."

"Nothing to be sorry about," he said, still chuckling. "I'm just amazed you still have the energy to joke."

She smiled, despite it all, liking the easy feeling that had resumed between them. "James, I know you can only do so much, but have you heard anything at all about the missing nurse?" She held her breath, glancing at him, seeing the slight clench of his jaw. She'd been about to say "Dot," but of course they didn't know if she was actually the missing one or if she'd been killed, so Evelyn refrained from naming her. "It's just I've seen you poring over maps these past few days, and I wondered . . ."

"You're right, I have been, in part because I need to find us a way out of here, but I have been trying to pinpoint a location for her."

"And?"

He shook his head. "I don't have anything for you yet. When I do, you'll be the first to know."

Someone ran toward them, a young man she'd seen conversing with James before, and he held something out in his hand. Evelyn sat still, looking away slightly so he didn't think she was listening, even though she most definitely was.

"This just arrived?" James asked.

James reached into his pocket, taking some money out. She saw the man's grateful smile as he nodded; and, as soon as his back was turned, James opening a piece of paper.

He read the words in seconds, before screwing the paper up into a ball and shoving it into his pocket as he stood and stalked away. Evelyn didn't need to think twice—she jumped to her feet and moved faster than she had in days, hurrying after him.

He wasn't slowing down, though, and she broke into a run, touching his back when he was finally within reach.

"James!" she gasped, surprised when he spun around, his face full of fury. His brow was furrowed, his eyes like thunderclouds as he glared down at her. "James, what did it say? Was it bad news?"

He grunted, his shoulders rising and then slowly falling. "It was worse than bad," he said.

She swallowed, waiting for him to continue.

"What did it say?" she asked again when he stayed silent.

"There is a planned drop, food and other supplies, plus feminine items for the women."

She breathed a sigh of relief. "Well, that doesn't sound so bad." *Not that any of us need the feminine items—periods are a thing of the past now we're all so malnourished.* But she didn't tell him that.

"They also said that men are expendable, but planes are not."

Evelyn ran the words over in her mind, not sure she understood what he was saying. "So they're doing a drop, or they're not?"

He was staring away into the distance now, and she studied his face, how serious he looked, how *pained* he looked.

"What does it mean, James?" She reached for his arm, hesitating before letting her fingers fall over his forearm, holding on to him.

"It means that London has decided you're not worth rescuing, because their goddamn planes are too valuable to risk," he ground out. "They'll drop some supplies, but there's no one coming to save you. They won't risk a landing here."

Evelyn's fingers tightened on his arm. "They won't come at all? Even now they know we're alive?"

James turned to face her, glancing at her hand on him, before looking her in the eyes. "I'm so sorry, Evelyn, truly I am."

A fire lit within her, powering her, fueling something she hadn't even known she was capable of.

"Well, make them come!" she said. "If no one is coming, they'll all give up! Every single one of them! There's no way I can convince them all to keep believing we'll make it home if—"

"Dammit, Evelyn, don't you think I know all that?" he shouted.

She recoiled, snatching her hand back and glaring at him. "Contact the United States Army," she said. "Just because Britain has refused it doesn't mean America won't come for us. I know they will."

"You just want to me to contact the US armed forces and demand that, do you?"

"Yes, I damn well do!" she said, folding her arms across her chest. "And if you won't do it, then I will."

"You're bloody unbelievable," he muttered as he stormed away from her.

"James," she called, rushing forward to pick up something he'd dropped. She turned the small square over, surprised to find she was holding a photo of a beautiful woman. Evelyn looked up, seeing that James hadn't bothered to turn, and her eyes found their way back to the photo again.

What a fool she'd been.

His heart clearly belonged to another, which meant she'd made an even bigger idiot of herself than she'd realized when she thought they'd had a moment weeks ago. No wonder he'd been avoiding her. She tucked the photo into her pocket, burning with anger. He'd had ample opportunities to tell her he was married, and if he wasn't being honest about that, then what else was he hiding from her?

――― ∽◦∾ ―――

Evelyn was shaking, and this time it wasn't from the cold or hunger. She kept to herself, talking to some of the other nurses and trying to keep one eye out for James. Because he was going to be furious with her when he found out what she'd done, and she intended on making herself scarce when he returned. He'd left her with one of his pistols and instructions to protect the village at all costs while he did some reconnaissance, assuring her that if there was a gunshot he'd be back as fast as he could.

Although she'd taken his orders very seriously, the gun tucked into her waistband, she'd also done something that was going to make him see red. But she wasn't going to apologize for what she'd done; she'd only done what he wouldn't.

She held the note, trying to stop the quiver in her hand as she waited to see the man she'd come for. The same man she'd seen James converse with so many times, the man who'd brought the note advising him that the Brits weren't coming to save them.

She waited, not sure whether he spoke much English, and praying that he believed her. Although, she reassured herself, he'd seen her so many times with James that he didn't have reason to doubt her. And all he did was make sure the note reached someone else, presumably someone James was working with who had a radio transmitter.

When he appeared, she gave him a beaming smile. "This is from James," she said, passing him the paper. Paper she'd stolen from his belongings, along with money to pay the man.

He just stared at her, one eyebrow raised.

"He's had to leave the village on urgent business, but he needs this transmitted immediately. Please make sure his contact receives it."

She was starting to wonder if he just didn't speak English, until he finally broke his silence.

"Mr. James wants me to take this?" he asked. "To his contact? He said that?"

Evelyn smiled and reached into her pocket, taking out some money. "He also said to give you this. It's very important this message is received as quickly as possible."

The money changed the man's face, and he tucked it into his pocket along with the note, nodding at her and turning. She had no idea where he was going with it, or if it would even work, but she had no access to a radio herself and she didn't know what else to do. And although a voice in her head told her to follow him to see who the radio transmitter was and where he was based, she knew it wasn't the right thing to do, not if she wanted him to believe James had sent her.

Evelyn heard a noise then and saw James, as angry-looking as a bull, marching past the little Christmas tree they'd decorated. She touched Vita's shoulder as she crouched down.

"Cover for me, will you?" she asked. "Tell James you haven't seen me."

Vita frowned, but Evelyn didn't explain further.

She hurried away, darting between the trees in an effort to avoid the man looking for her, but when a strong hand caught her wrist in a vicelike grip, she knew he'd outsmarted her.

"Where are you going?" he asked, his breath on her neck he was so close.

She gulped. "Ah, just to the toilet," she replied, as calmly as she could. "And you're hurting me, so could you please let me go?"

His fingers only curled tighter. "You thought I wouldn't find out?" he muttered. "You thought I wouldn't know what you'd done?"

Her eyes flickered up to him, and she saw anger there like she'd never seen reflected in his face before.

"I only did what you wouldn't," she said, lifting her chin defiantly.

"You could have jeopardized everything, Evelyn!" He suddenly let go of her and she held her wrist close to her body, protectively. "You have no idea what you've done."

"All I've done is ask for the Americans to come for us, something *you* should have done immediately when you knew the Brits weren't coming!"

He was clearly seething, but there was nothing she could do. She was tired, beyond hungry, and sick of being stuck in Albania, and she wasn't going to apologize for doing something to help change that. As far as she was concerned, he'd forced her to do what he wouldn't.

"I've been trying to figure out the best way forward, so don't make out like I've been sitting around doing nothing. I can't just make rash decisions, and we limit communications to keep everyone safe. We have to follow protocol." He sighed. "Dammit, Evelyn, you need to trust me. We need to be honest with each other."

"Oh, you're a fine one to talk about being honest!" She reached into her pocket and threw the photo at him, hating how angry she was, how hurt she felt.

"How did you get this?" he asked, his hand shaking as he held the photo, staring at her in disbelief.

"You dropped it," she muttered.

"This is my wife," he said, looking at the photo before carefully tucking it into his jacket pocket.

"Why didn't you tell me?" she asked. "You let me think you . . ." Her voice disappeared. She didn't want to say it. "You should have told me you were married."

"I'm a widower," he said, taking a step closer to her, his voice only just loud enough for her to hear. "She's no longer with us."

"She's dead?" Evelyn's heart was beating so loud she swore she could hear it pounding.

"I didn't tell you because I don't tell anyone. It's one of those things that I keep close to my chest." He patted the photo there and gave her a sad smile. "Literally."

What a fool she'd been. Again.

"You left me with no choice before, James," she whispered. "Wife or not, I had to do it."

"We always have a choice," he replied. "Don't pretend like you didn't have a choice, Evelyn, although I'm sorry you had to find out like that."

They stood, staring at each other, both breathing but not saying anything.

"Would you believe the air drop went ahead, but that it was raided," he finally said, sounding defeated as he rubbed his temples with the heels of his hands. "It's been so picked over, there's barely anything left, and they missed the coordinates entirely. It's what I went to find."

Evelyn deflated; they'd all been desperate for it to arrive. "So there's no food at all coming?" she asked. The K-rations they sent might be awful, but they were something. She thought of what Josef had said all those weeks ago about Albanians not stealing.

"I'm afraid not."

"I know you're angry with me for what I did, but can you not see that—"

"You'd do well not to keep talking, Evelyn. Impersonating me in a message to authorities and lying to my local courier goes well beyond me being angry."

She turned away from him slightly, so used to doing the right thing all her life that she was struggling with going against the grain, but in this case she knew in her heart that what she'd done was right.

"So what do we do next?" she finally asked.

"*We* don't do anything next," he replied, sounding exasperated. "*I* will wait to see what response we get."

"So you're not going to send another message telling them?"

"Evelyn, if I admit what you've done, then my head would roll. So no, I'm not going to do anything other than wait. What you've done—you may well have caused a breach of confidential information. You . . ." He raked his fingers through his hair. "Goddamn it, Evelyn! I don't know whether to be ridiculously impressed with your ingenuity or put you in handcuffs for your insubordination."

Her cheeks burned, but the way he was looking at her, that burned too. In a completely different way. "Could you choose impressed?"

James shook his head. "Honestly, Evelyn."

"I'm sorry if you hate me, but . . ."

He moved closer, and although she saw anger there still, she saw something else too, a softening, a warmth that he couldn't hide. "I don't hate you," he muttered. "I could never hate you."

She swallowed, studying his face, hating how her body seemed to betray her whenever he was close.

"If I'm completely honest, I'm ridiculously impressed with you. You're not what I expected, Evelyn. In fact, you're far from it."

Evelyn's heart started to race, her eyes flitting as she tried to look him in the eye, not sure what to do or how to take the way he was looking at her. She'd misread him before and he'd blown cold toward her ever since, but this time . . . She swallowed. She'd been the one at home, while her sisters had grown up and started to go off to dances and to have fun. She was the one waiting up for them, making sure they had what they needed, caring for Katie; as if she were the grown-up, the mother. But although she'd taken to the domestic duties, she'd missed all that, so there'd been no sweethearts or dancing with young men, leaving her highly inexperienced when it came to the opposite sex. She only hoped she was good enough at maintaining her facade of confidence, so that James would never guess how inept she felt around him.

"You're so like my bloody wife," he said, shaking his head. "She's the only other woman I know who'd have the nerve to do something like this."

"Honestly?" Evelyn asked, trying not to smile.

His shoulders trembled then, his face breaking into a smile that she hadn't expected. He was laughing! "Yes," he admitted. "This is exactly the kind of thing she would have done. She would have given me the look, the look that said she was disappointed in me, or perhaps even a sweet smile that didn't tell me anything—just to put me off the scent—and then she'd have gone and done whatever she'd wanted to in the first place."

"Now I understand why you don't hate me, then." Evelyn grinned. "Because you're used to women not obeying you."

"Oh, that I am." He shook his head. "And if I'm honest, I miss it. It was nice having someone in my life who didn't have to obey my orders. She didn't care if she ruffled my feathers, because she knew that most of the time, she was right."

"My mother was like that," Evelyn said. "My father is always in charge at work, but when it came to our home, he always looked to her. She ran a tight ship, so when she died, it was like we'd lost our captain, and even all this time later, he's still lost without her."

They both stood, both knowing loss and both knowing there was no point in saying empty words that wouldn't fill the void.

"How about we go find something to eat?" James said. "And I'll decide what to do with you when we get a response to your message."

"We need to break it to the others that there's no delivery drop," she said with a sigh.

The others still didn't know the British weren't coming for them, though, and she knew it was only a matter of time before they started asking questions. Which meant they had to pray her risk paid off.

James gave her a sideways glance that set her skin on fire, and she wondered if perhaps he might just have feelings for her after all.

—— ❧ ——

Evelyn saw the man coming before James did. She'd been helping to cart water with some of the local women, even though her legs felt so spindly and weak it had taken every ounce of effort to do so, but she still noticed the man when he walked into the village. It was cold, and she blew on her fingers to keep them warm, thinking of the woolen gloves she'd always worn during winter at home. What she wouldn't give to wear them right now.

She stayed where she was and tracked him with her eyes, seeing him eventually stop near the basic hut where James and the other men slept each night. And then James came to the door, and she watched the exchange, still not moving. She'd been on tenterhooks for two days, waiting for something, *anything*, to be sent back to James, but until now there'd been nothing. And she expected either a bellow of anger to erupt from him within the next few seconds, or a whoop of excitement.

She was disappointed to get neither of those reactions, and wondered if it was perhaps a message about something else entirely. Until she saw him look up, and even from a distance could see the slight upturn of his lips.

Evelyn hurried down to him, not going to wait any longer; the anticipation was far too great.

"You've heard, haven't you?" she said, skidding in the dirt in front of him, reaching for the paper. "What does it say?"

"Uh-uh," he said, holding it high, out of her reach. "This is official government correspondence."

She groaned. "James, please!"

He didn't give the paper to her, but he did lower it. She wanted to grab it from him, but she wasn't confident enough to get that close to him—not yet.

"Tell me what it says."

"Well, in fact, it says they're coming for you," he said, ducking his head as he whispered the next part. "The Americans *and* the British. It seems they've had a change of heart."

"They're coming?" she gasped. "Help is actually coming?"

"Yes, Evelyn, help is coming." He laughed. "I'm as shocked as you are, trust me! You must have been rather convincing, whatever you said. And I dare say the Brits were railroaded into helping once the Americans became involved."

She squealed and threw her arms around him, launching off the ground as she hugged him. James laughed with her, swinging her in the air, the note going flying in the wind, which made him drop her as quickly as he'd gathered her up in order to chase it.

"Go," he said, as he caught it in midair. "Go and tell everyone the good news while I check the coordinates and figure out where we have to be in two days' time."

Two days. Our rescue plane is coming in two days' time!

Evelyn was about to leave, but something deep inside of her made her turn. James's smile was wide, his eyes so bright, like they'd been that very first day when he'd found them stuck in mud up to their knees.

She crossed back to him, refusing to second-guess herself as she pressed a kiss to his cheek. "Thank you," she murmured. "Thank you a hundred times over."

"Hey, you've only got yourself to thank for this one. You've impressed me, Evelyn, more than I could ever tell you."

"James, without you—"

"Enough with the praise," he said gruffly. "Now go and spread that news. Lift morale."

She didn't need to be told twice, but she did see something else pass across his face, something she couldn't quite read. "There's something else, isn't there?" she asked.

"The part for my broken radio; I finally have it," he said.

"Which means you can communicate directly now without using a middle person?" she asked.

"Exactly."

"That's wonderful news."

Her head was spinning; there was suddenly so much to be grateful for, and things were looking so much more positive than they had only minutes before. And as much as she wanted to run and tell her friends, she also would have done anything to stay with James, to have a few more moments basking in his attention. But she had to go.

"Vita!" she called, taking her leave. "Vita! Come quickly!"

Vita's eyes were hollow, with dark circles beneath them, her hair pulled back into a severe bun that was so different to her usual big, coiffed hair, but there was still something about her that made her stand out from the other girls.

Evelyn raced over to Vita, surprised by her sudden burst of energy, catching her friend's hand and pulling her close. "We're being rescued, Vita! The Americans and the British are both coming for us, in two days' time. We're going home!"

Vita's eyes widened. "Home?" she whispered. "Someone's actually coming?"

"Yes." She touched her head to Vita's, taking a deep, shuddering breath as she did so, barely able to believe it herself. "They're really coming, we're getting out of here."

Vita clutched her hand, and they stood like that for a long moment before Evelyn finally pulled away.

"Will you tell Bobby? He'll need to see James and coordinate everything with him," she said. "I'll go tell the others."

Vita nodded, but before she moved she cried out and flung her arms around Evelyn, the emotion of finally seeing a way home shuddering through her friend.

"I can't believe it's almost over," Vita whispered into her ear. "I just want this nightmare to end."

"Me too," Evelyn murmured as she rubbed big circles on Vita's back. "Me too."

She only wished that when she woke from her nightmare, she could keep James with her, even for just a bit longer, instead of knowing he would disappear from her life forever the moment she set foot on that rescue plane. But in the end, she'd sacrifice it all to see her family again.

I'm coming home, Katie. I'll be tucking you into bed again before you know it.

CHAPTER
TWENTY-THREE

EVELYN

"I've translated the message," James said, tugging his fingers through his hair, "and their communications are coming through loud and clear . . ."

"But they can't seem to hear yours still," Evelyn finished for him, tucking her knees up to her chin as she sat on the dirt floor with Vita on her other side. She was facing James, and Bobby was the only other person in the small room. James had wanted everything to remain on a need-to-know basis, believing that anyone from outside their group could betray them, and he certainly didn't want anyone other than the four of them knowing the coordinates.

"Try again," Bobby muttered, without breaking his stride as he paced the room. "You have to keep trying."

The wind howled outside, snow falling in wispy flurries as Evelyn stared out. In twenty-four hours, her elation had turned to desperation, and she knew in her heart there was no way their rescue flight could land in such terrible conditions. Albania was a rugged, mountainous country that was as harsh as it was beautiful, and the snow was adding an entirely different dimension. So far it had been difficult to survive—but now? She wondered if it would be downright impossible.

"Bobby, scribble down the message," James ordered, as the signal came to life again, and he stared at the message he'd already decoded.

It sounded to Evelyn like the same thing being repeated again, but she sat quietly, moving a little closer to James as his brow furrowed, staring down at the page.

He read the message out under his breath. "Arrangements hold for Yanks. Pick up between 1100 GMT and 1300 GMT tomorrow. Have party ready at SE corner of field. Permit no person within mile of airfield except your party and strong partisan guards. Confirm OK. QRZ at GMT tonight."

"What does QRZ mean?" Vita asked, leaning closer to Evelyn. She'd been about to ask the same thing.

"It's a Q code. It tells me when they'll call again."

"And if we don't respond?" Evelyn asked.

James went back to staring at the message he'd decoded, as if it might hold all the answers. "It means we've missed our opportunity to confirm the pickup," he said, quietly.

"So we'll just have to stay here?" Vita whispered, her voice cracking. "We'll just forget that the rescue was ever going to happen?"

"No," James suddenly said, looking up at them both. "We keep trying. I'll repeat our confirmation all night if I have to, hoping they hear it, and then we still proceed with our plans. There's a chance this will still go ahead, that our message will be heard."

"What about the weather?" Evelyn asked. "Could this snow derail the entire thing?"

"We pray all night for a clear morning," he said, picking up the radio again and giving Evelyn a quick look, even though he hadn't really answered her question. "I'm not giving up on this rescue. It was a miracle they said yes in the first place, and we might not get a second chance."

"Is there anything I can do?" Evelyn asked as she rose.

"You can urge the partisans to do a patrol for German activity," James said. "Tell them you're acting on orders from me."

He gave her a little smile and she raised her eyebrows at him. At least this time she didn't have to pretend.

"Come on," she said to Vita, pleased to see that her friend was up on her feet already. "We've got work to do."

As they walked away, out into the almost dark, Vita gripped her hand so tightly it hurt, but Evelyn didn't pull away. There were so many questions, so many what-ifs hanging between them about their fate, but neither of them said a word, they just kept holding hands and went looking for the partisans.

—————— ⚬❧⚬ ——————

"I need you all to listen," James said early the next day, standing in front of their group. They were a ragtag bunch now, with their overgrown hair and tattered clothes, so unlike the well-groomed, impeccably uniformed group they'd once been. But everyone stood to attention, not muttering so much as a word as James spoke.

"We are to wait in position at the coordinates that have been sent to me," James said. "Someone up there is looking out for us, because I thought there was no hope of the weather clearing, but it's fine enough for a landing to take place. Everything is lining up to make this rescue possible."

Evelyn shivered. It *was* like someone was looking out for them, although she knew it wasn't quite so straightforward as James was making out. He had no idea if his confirmation had even been received—it was as if the radio was working one way and not the other—but he was taking a chance on the fact that it had been heard, or that they'd come anyway, knowing how difficult communication was in Albania. Only he wasn't making this particular fact public knowledge.

She pushed the thought out of her mind, refusing to give in to the worry when there was nothing she could do about it.

"If I'm happy with the conditions, we mark the ground with a cross using those parachute panels over there. I need you to decide on your four strongest members and they will be in charge of making the mark," James continued. "I know you were all disappointed when the airdrop was picked apart by locals, but we need to thank our lucky stars that they didn't bother taking these panels. They're our most important resource right now."

A murmur began then amongst the group, rippling through them, and Evelyn relaxed as she saw all their smiles. No matter how fatigued or unwell they were, she knew in her heart that every single one of them would make it up the hill to the pickup point, even if they had to crawl to get there. She watched James, studying him, so unsure of how she felt or how he felt in return. They'd had moments, and there was something that kept pulling them together, but every time she felt they'd become closer, he seemed to take a step away.

"I'm going up now to maintain surveillance until pickup, and the rest of you will come up later this morning under the leadership of Bobby. It's only a few miles, but I know it's going to feel like a marathon to some of you right now, so he'll allow plenty of time," James said, before softening somewhat as he seemed to consider individuals within the group. Then his eyes found hers. "Today will mark fifty-two days since your crash, and I certainly hope you won't be seeing a fifty-third."

Tears filled Evelyn's eyes, but she kept staring back at James, wishing she didn't have to say goodbye to him in order to get home.

She stayed standing as the rest of the group dispersed, and although she didn't expect it, James came over to her.

"You're alright?" he asked, glancing over her as if to check. "Shoes okay, blisters not too painful?"

She looked down at her feet. "I'm better than most," she replied. "You don't have to worry about me."

James's gaze was soft, his hands were hanging by his sides, and she almost hugged him. *Almost.*

"Evelyn," he said, staring down at her, so close but still seeming so far away.

She nodded, waiting, hoping he was going to say something to tell her how he felt. But then his face changed, his jaw tightening.

"I'll see you soon," he said, but still he stood, as if he were waiting for her to do or say something. Or maybe he was wrestling with his own thoughts of what was appropriate. *Was that truly all he wanted to say?*

"Yes, I'll see you soon," she whispered back.

James smiled, his hand moving just a little. He was holding something, but two of his fingers reached out and touched hers, so lightly she could only just feel them. Evelyn shut her eyes for a moment, straining her fingers to press back into his, and when she opened her eyes, James was gone.

"What is it?"

Evelyn crawled up the hillside to position herself beside James. She'd come the rest of the way up to him on all fours, staying low to make sure no one saw her. It was the closest she'd ever been to him, but when Bobby joined them, she noticed that he was positioned almost as close to James, which made her feel less self-conscious.

Her leg was pressed to his, from thigh to knee, and her elbow was beside his as she propped herself up to look down the hill toward the airfield. He passed her his binoculars, and she lifted them to her eyes, staring down as disbelief coursed through her.

The weather might have turned in their favor, but it seemed like nothing else had.

"The place is alive with bloody Germans," James muttered. "Tanks, trucks, troops, you name it, it's down there. I can't believe it."

"So what do we do?" Evelyn asked, passing him back his binoculars. She wanted to lean her forehead into the dirt and pretend it was all a bad dream, but she kept her chin up, refusing to crumble.

"What's the time?" James asked.

"We have thirty minutes until arrival," Bobby replied.

James lifted his binoculars again. "Then we wait," he muttered. "We wait until the last moment, and then I'll decide."

Evelyn stared down into the valley, even though she couldn't make out the activity without the binoculars. But she could still see it in her mind.

"We're not being rescued today, are we?" she asked, trying to swallow the lump in her throat. *It's over before we even had a chance.*

"No," James said, without lowering his binoculars. "I'm so sorry, Evelyn, but I don't think you are."

Evelyn looked at Bobby over the top of James's head and he looked back at her, and she'd never seen such defeat in their brave pilot's gaze. Tears shone in his eyes, and they just stared at one another for the longest time.

They resumed their positions then, with Bobby giving time updates every five minutes, until the faintest roar became audible in the distance. Evelyn froze.

"That's them," Bobby said, his eyes wide as he started to rise but was pulled violently back down by James. "They're coming!"

"But they aren't landing," James said, his tone low and authoritative. "Not today."

Bobby looked defiant for all of five seconds, before understanding passed over his face.

"We let them land, it's a suicide mission for the pilots and you know it," James said. "I'm not authorizing it, and you'd be wise to respect that decision."

"So we just sit and watch them?" Evelyn asked, incredulous. She'd still been holding out hope, still been so sure that if the planes came, they'd get another chance. It was like a bad dream.

"Who tells the others?" Bobby asked.

James tucked his binoculars away and started to crawl backward as the sound of the planes became slightly more audible, even though they were still a way off.

"I will," he said. "I'm the one making the call, so this is on me."

Evelyn blinked away her tears. It was unbelievable. They'd defied all the odds, they'd stayed alive, the weather had cleared, the planes had been sent despite the communications problem—and still they weren't going to make it home.

She reached boldly for James's hand once they were standing, no longer caring whether it was the right or wrong thing to do. She needed to draw on his strength so she didn't collapse to the ground, and she wasn't going to wait for him to be the one to reach for her, not this time.

He looked at her hand, but it only took him a second to clasp it tightly back.

They made their way back to the others, running now, heads low until they were at the meeting point and had reached the group of excited faces; faces full of anticipation, of hope, of desperation. But it was Vita's face Evelyn found the hardest to look at; Vita, who'd once been so strong and vivacious, and who now looked so weak. So desperate.

"They're coming!" someone whispered. "I can hear them."

Vita's eyes widened as Evelyn kept staring at her, wishing things were different, that they weren't all about to be as crushed as she already felt. And then James pulled her with him toward the parachutes, hidden beneath some foliage so as not to draw any attention, just as the sky came to life above them.

There were four men, all medics, waiting in position near the parachutes, ready to move out as soon as James gave the order. But it never came.

"I'm so sorry, but we can't let them land," he ground out, still holding her hand. "The closest airfield has been taken by Germans. No Allied planes are landing here today."

It's over.

James pulled her into his arms then, her face against his chest, his arms bracketing her as she cried, as she tried to breathe past the pain in her heart.

CHAPTER
TWENTY-FOUR

VITA

They're coming for us. They're actually coming for us!

Vita wriggled forward, past Bobby, staring up at the sky as the sudden roar of planes filled the air above them. Tears slipped down her cheeks and she didn't bother to wipe them away, wanting to scream with excitement as she watched three P-38 Lightning fighters flying so low over the hill they were huddled on, she could actually see the pilots' faces.

"We're actually going to make it out of here," she whispered to Bobby, holding tight to his hand as she dragged him forward with her. "It's over. It's over!"

When she looked back at him, unable to stop smiling, she was surprised to see a frown on his face, the complete opposite of the elation she felt. And then she saw the tears in his eyes.

"What is it? Why do you look as sad as a wet cat?" she asked, tugging at his hand. "We're going home! Bobby, this is it!"

As he opened his mouth to speak, the sudden, all-consuming drone of a Wellington roared overhead, seeming to appear out of nowhere, its machine guns visible as it followed two smaller planes. And then more of the twin-engine fighters came screaming over them, in threes, until, as Vita stared up in disbelief, twenty-one Allied planes filled the sky.

"Bobby, the Americans *and* the British have come for us!" she cried. "Look at them all!"

But when she saw the now-somber look on his face, she froze. Vita turned to see what he was looking at, and a terrified shiver ran through her as she watched the grim line of James's mouth and the sad shake of Evelyn's head. Why weren't they marking the ground for the rescue planes to land? Why were they packing everything away? What was going on?

"Evelyn!" Vita screamed, over the deafening roar of aircraft. "Evelyn, what are you doing?"

"Vita, come back here." Bobby's hand reached for her wrist, but she pulled away and his fingers slid across her skin.

"No!" she cried, disbelief coursing through her. "No!"

Arms encircled her but she refused to let Bobby hold her back, fighting against him.

"You mark that spot! You let those planes land!" she screamed.

Bobby's grip tightened, but she continued to fight, refusing to believe that they were going to let the planes go, that they weren't going to let them land. This was their only chance!

"Vita, it's too dangerous, they need to get out of here. We can't let them land."

"No, *we* need to get out of here!" she sobbed, pushing against him, turning in his arms then to beat against his chest, thrashing so hard that he eventually let her slip away. "What are you doing? Help them mark the spot!"

"It would be suicide for those pilots," he murmured as his grip on her loosened, his hands falling away from her.

Vita ran headfirst at Evelyn and James, not listening to Bobby, scrambling for the parachutes, prepared to mark the spot herself if she had to.

"Help me!" she cried to anyone who would listen, frantically looking up to watch the planes, to make sure she still had time, that she could still show the pilots where to land. "Someone help me!"

Why was no one helping her? Why could no one see that this was their only chance of escape?

"It's too late, Vita."

Evelyn's voice washed over her as she continued to run, her heart pounding, head spinning as she looked up, watching the last of the planes disappear beyond the hill.

"No! No, you do *not* get to decide that for us. I'm getting on that plane!" she screamed.

They've gone.

And any chance they had of making it home had just gone with them.

Vita screamed and kept going, kept pulling at one of the parachute panels and running with it, flattening it out on the ground and then running back for another, and another. Everyone else was either standing crying or dropped to their knees, defeated, but Vita wasn't going to stop. She couldn't stop.

"Help me!"

Bobby ran to her, and she reached for him, believing he was going to help her, that he was finally on her side, but when he touched her, it was to restrain her again.

"Vita, you need to stop," he murmured, his arms vicelike, not letting her move an inch.

She watched in horror as James collected the pieces of parachute she'd spread out, commanding the men to gather up the rest of it as the roar of aircraft became only a distant hum.

"No!" she cried. "Get them back! You have to get them to come back!"

She started to kick and scream, fighting against Bobby's hold, only stopping when James and Evelyn came closer.

"This is all your fault!" she yelled as Bobby almost lost his grip on her, catching her around the waist and drawing her back in. "You did this to us! You should have let them land. You had no right to send them away!"

James just stared at her, and Evelyn's mouth opened but nothing came out. It was Bobby who spoke, Bobby who comforted her as her world fell apart.

"They couldn't land, Vita," he said, his voice barely louder than a whisper. "It was the right call. We couldn't let them land here."

"No!" she repeated as she started to sob, her tears hiccupping out of her as her body gave way. "You get them back here, you tell them to come back for us!"

Bobby's arms were strong around her, holding her up, his mouth against her hair as he soothed her. Her shoulders sagged, her body on the verge of giving up.

I'll never forgive you, she thought, seeing Evelyn and James standing there together, staring at her as if she were deranged. *I'll never, ever forgive you.*

They were going to be stuck in Albania forever, she just knew it.

And still, she could see all those planes circling, all those planes that'd been sent to save them. Planes that were now going home without them.

CHAPTER TWENTY-FIVE

DOT

Dot trembled, listening to the roar of aircraft overhead. Part of her wanted to hide in the corner or even down below in the cellar, hands over her ears to block out the noise, but the other part of her needed to see. She resisted, her fingers creeping closer to her ears, but when Marti burst into the room, her eyes wide with excitement rather than fear, Dot dropped her hands.

"Look. Look!" Marti cried, grabbing hold of her and dragging her over to the window.

She'd spent so long hidden, not wanting anyone to see her, shrinking from sight every time there was a noise, to suddenly having her nose pressed to the glass as Marti pushed her forward. Stefa had managed to take her out for three late-afternoon outings, but when German activity had suddenly increased in the area, their little sojourns had abruptly come to an end.

"What are you so excited about?" she asked.

Marti just pointed, and as Dot craned her neck she wondered why she'd want to look at the Luftwaffe circling. Even for someone as bored as her, she didn't want to see them.

"Look!" Marti urged.

She almost stopped breathing. *No. It can't be.*

"I don't believe it," she whispered, laughing as she stared up at a sky filled with American aircraft—more than she could count. "What are they all doing here?"

She couldn't help but be excited; it was her first sighting of anyone or anything American since she'd lost the group. If she'd followed her heart, she'd have grabbed a sheet or something colorful and run outside onto the road, screaming and hollering as she waved to get at least one of the pilots' attention. She wanted to yell out that she was an American, that they needed to take her with them, even though she knew it was ridiculous to expect a pilot to land in the middle of nowhere. Hell, it would be ridiculous to expect them to know she was American. But the fact they were so close she could almost reach out to touch them . . .

She wrapped her arms tightly around herself instead. If they found her, she'd have to leave Stefa. And his family. She dropped her gaze from the sky. Being with Stefa and his family had made her feel whole again—even housebound and bored out of her mind. It had reminded her of what she'd lost and what she'd so desperately wanted: to belong and be loved. And with Stefa . . . She instinctively touched her stomach. There was a change in her body, she could feel it—*sense* that something was different. There was some part of her that wondered if perhaps she could be pregnant with Stefa's child. All those years of trying to be the perfect young woman, trying to fit in and do what society dictated, and yet here, even with the prospect of being unwed and pregnant, she'd never felt more like herself.

"I think they're here for you," Marti said. "For all you Americans."

Dot's mouth opened but she didn't speak, not straight away. She had no idea whether her friends were even alive or not; whether they'd managed to make contact with base; whether they were even in Albania still. Had these planes come for them?

"Dot?" Marti asked again.

"Maybe," she whispered. "Maybe they've come for us, but they're not going to find me hidden here, are they?"

Marti's arm wound around her, and she leaned into her, their heads bent together as the sky continued to swarm with activity. The planes were loud and bold, and a little voice inside her head told her they *were* here for a rescue mission, no matter how far-fetched that sounded even to her own ears.

Tears slid down her face, wetting Marti's shoulder, but if she noticed the dampness, she certainly didn't complain. Besides, Marti would think she was crying about not being rescued, not because she was heartbroken at the thought of leaving her and Stefa.

"What's it like there, Dot?"

"In America?"

"Yes, in America."

Dot sighed, letting herself remember, going back in time in her mind.

"It's different from here, so very different," she replied. "Where I come from, we don't have villages so much as we have towns and cities, full of houses and tall buildings." She had no idea whether all of Albania was rugged and rural, but from what she'd seen it was like chalk and cheese comparing it to America.

"Is it like that everywhere in America? Where do you grow your food?"

Dot smiled. "Oh, well, we have farmland, plenty of it, and those farmers and ranchers have their own plots of land. But they're usually within driving distance of a town or city, where they can do their shopping and so forth."

Marti was silent a beat, and Dot looked up again to watch as the aircraft slowly started to disperse until they'd completely disappeared from her line of sight. But the two women still stood there quietly, side by side, staring out the window.

"And who do you live with?" Marti asked. "Who will you go home to?"

Dot could have answered any other question without faltering but this one . . . She cleared her throat, placing her hands on the window and leaning forward, looking down at the road.

"No one is waiting for me," Dot whispered. "I have no one."

"But your family?" Marti asked, moving closer to her again.

Dot turned to face Marti, swallowing, about to say the words she'd uttered to not one person since she'd received the news.

"They're all dead," she said, her voice shaking. "First my parents, and then my grandparents. I'm all alone there."

Marti stared at her a moment before opening her arms and embracing her, kissing Dot's head as she held her close.

"I'm so sorry."

She let Marti hold her, craving the contact.

"Well, you're part of our family now. I'm your sister," Marti said with a grin. "I always wanted a sister."

"Me too." Dot was telling the truth, she had always wanted a sister—had fantasized sometimes about what it would be like to have a sibling—and as the idea of ever making it back home began to seem more of a dream than reality, she found she was no longer horrified by the prospect of remaining in Albania.

"I'm sure they're not here for me or the others," Dot said, staring at the sky one last time before turning her back to the window. "It was probably just a show of force to the Germans."

"I don't think so."

Stefa was standing in the doorway, his hands pushed into his simple peasant trousers, so coarse they could have been made from old sacks. His eyes tracked her, curious, as he stood, as if he was trying to figure out what she was thinking. Her breath caught in her throat as it always did when she saw him, their time alone so rare that she found herself always hoping for just a moment together.

"Why?" Marti asked him.

"Because they would have fired at the German-controlled airfields," he said. "They've come here for their people, I'm sure of it."

Dot digested his words, not sure what to believe, even though she agreed with him in principle. Why would they come and not shoot the enemy? They were at war, and if they were sending aircraft into occupied territory, especially so many planes, it must have been much more than a simple reconnaissance mission.

"Even if my group were still alive . . ." she began, shaking her head, not sure what she even meant to say next.

"Tell her," Marti said.

Dot looked from Stefa to Marti and back again. "Tell me what?"

Marti took her hand. Did she know something about her group? Something bad?

"Please, just tell me. What do you know?"

"I heard my father whispering with my uncle, just last night," Stefa said. "I wanted to make sure before I told you, before I got your hopes up."

"Any news, good or bad, you can tell me," Dot said. "I just want to know what it is, whatever you know."

"They said that your group is still alive," Marti said for him. "A big group has been through a village, all Americans. That's what he heard. He thinks they might try to head for the coast."

"They're alive?" Dot gasped, a weight lifting from her shoulders that she hadn't known was so heavy. "That's wonderful news. How far is the coast?"

Stefa's sad expression caught her attention then, and once again she looked between him and Marti.

"Should they not be heading for the coast? Is it too dangerous?"

"It means they're far away from here by now," Marti said. "The BK control so much of the land there, and if they even make it . . ."

Dot understood. Her friends were already heading for the coast, without her, and there was no way she was ever going to catch up to them. Just like there was no way they were ever coming back for her. No regiment or rescue mission was going to be deployed for one lone nurse; she'd been sacrificed for the good of the group. It was bittersweet.

"Did they say . . ." she started, clearing her throat as her voice caught. "Did they say how many were in the group?"

Those screams she'd heard that night, the confusion as everyone had disbanded in the dark, it still haunted her. She relived it every single night, when the house had long fallen silent and the other bodies slumbered; she went over it again and again, wondering what had happened.

"They said it was a very large group, that's all," Marti said. "They were all American survivors."

Dot had expected to feel a crushing sense of loneliness, that she had been left behind, but she didn't. If they were gone, then her decision was made for her. She would stay with Stefa and his family.

"I'm sorry," Stefa said.

Dot smiled at him, trying to push away thoughts of that night. She shut her eyes and saw herself spinning in the pitch-dark, branches brushing her skin, shuffles in the silence scaring her, a scream cutting through the stillness. She quickly opened them again, not wanting to see, not wanting to acknowledge that she'd been saved when someone else, or more than one someone, had faced a terrible end.

Without Stefa, she knew in her heart she'd already be dead.

"Dot, I'm sorry. We shouldn't have told you," Marti apologized, reaching out to her.

"I'm pleased you did. I needed to know," she said.

"Would you like some tea?" Marti asked, as Stefa went back to standing in the doorway.

She glanced at him, knowing this might be their only chance to be alone.

"Yes. Please. That would be lovely."

Marti touched her as she passed, and when she'd disappeared, Stefa stepped forward and she quickly fled into his arms. His lips fell to the top of her head, his hold on her warm and strong, and she inhaled the now-familiar, earthy scent of him.

"I'm sorry," he whispered.

She looked up at him, knowing they only had minutes, maybe less, before Marti returned.

"Stefa, I think . . ." she started, not sure how to tell him, not even sure if she was right.

"What is it?" He dropped a kiss to her lips, warm and tender.

When he finally pulled back and searched her eyes, his hands on either side of her face, she found the courage to say the words.

"I think I could be pregnant," she whispered.

His face first broke into a smile, before his brow furrowed, worry creasing his face as he wrapped her in his arms again. He didn't say anything, but he didn't need to. All his worries were the same as hers; she could feel the fear and love radiating off him as she tucked herself into him.

"I love you," he murmured into her hair.

They heard a noise then and she stepped back, her eyes blurry from tears as Marti entered the room.

"I love you, too," she mouthed.

Stefa placed his hand over his heart, and then he was gone. And as Marti left to retrieve something she'd forgotten, Dot crouched down and huddled beneath the window, arms tight around her knees as she shut her eyes and mourned what she'd lost.

She loved Stefa, more than she'd ever loved Peter—in a raw, deep, primitive way that she'd never understood until now. But she also loved her friends, friends she might never, ever see again.

What she wouldn't give to hear Vita's laugh one more time, or feel Evelyn's shoulder pressed to hers as they laughed and talked lying on their bed in Sicily. She only wished she'd had the chance to tell them the truth about Peter, because after everything she'd been through now, after being so easily accepted by Stefa and his family, she no longer understood why she'd kept it from them in the first place.

"Darling, when you said you hadn't drunk alcohol before . . ."

Dot was sick over the boat railings as Evelyn held back her hair, as she'd done for her only hours earlier, and Vita laughed about how much the fish were enjoying their breakfast. Dot would have kicked her if she'd had the energy, but when she was finally upright again, all she cared about was keeping what was left of her breakfast down.

"Look, the Statue of Liberty!" Evelyn said beside her. "Isn't she beautiful?"

Dot leaned back and looked up as they passed. Evelyn was right, she was indeed beautiful, and not something Dot had ever expected to see from the water before. Or at all.

"I thought we were going to get caught last night, or locked out," Vita said with a grin. "I only just slithered through that door with seconds to spare."

"I just wish I hadn't had that last glass of champagne," Dot groaned.

"Or perhaps the last two?" Evelyn teased. "Or three?"

"Stop, stop!" Dot shook her head as she started to turn green again, the ship moving out into deeper waters and starting to move faster.

It contributed to a more intense motion, which was not helping her stomach any.

"Sweetheart, that night out is going to give us something to talk about for months," Vita said. "It was one of the best nights of my life."

"Why?" Evelyn asked. "Because we're such great company?"

Vita made a snorting sound and Dot laughed, despite the commotion in her stomach.

"Well, yes, actually, that and the fact that I felt free," Vita said. "It was like I'd been liberated. There was no one to worry about, nothing to think about, I was just able to be me."

"I know the feeling," Evelyn said. "I haven't felt like myself in such a long time."

Dot watched them both, her fingers on her necklace, wanting to tell them, needing to say something about Peter, to tell them the truth. But the words never came. How could she tell them now that he'd discarded her like a pair of old socks?

"Here comes the fish food again!" Vita cried, as Dot launched forward, wishing all over again that she'd never, ever said yes to downing champagne like it was water.

She opened her eyes when she felt Marti's hand on her back, smoothing her hair from her face where it had caught in her tears.

"We'll look after you, Dot. It will all be fine, you'll see."

She let Marti hold her, wishing she had the courage to tell this new friend how she truly felt.

That leaving her and Stefa would be even more painful than knowing my friends have left without me.

CHAPTER TWENTY-SIX

VITA

Vita's boots felt as if they were full of lead, every step a Herculean effort, her shoulders slumped and her neck barely able to hold her head up. But it wasn't the hunger, thirst or exhaustion making this trek impossible; it was the sense of defeat.

It was as if there were a rain cloud above them, making them miserable, following them wherever they went, and there was a little voice in her head telling her to just stop. Telling her there was no use continuing on, that it was pointless to keep on trudging when they were never, ever going to make it to safety.

But still they walked.

"We need to keep going, Vita. Don't slow down," Bobby said, waiting for her and matching his stride to hers.

"What's the point, though?" she whispered back to him, wishing she hadn't said it the moment the words slipped from her mouth.

The look he gave her was one of desperation. "Because we have to keep on fighting, that's why."

She stared at Evelyn's back, just ahead of her, all of her hate directed toward her. "It's their fault we're still here. We'd be—"

"Shot down from the sky, most likely," Bobby interrupted. "Is that what you'd prefer? To be dead? Or to have seen the pilots trying to rescue us dead?"

"Of course not," she muttered.

"Well that's what would have happened. You think Evelyn wants to stay here? You think she doesn't want to get back to her family? You think *I* would have accepted James's decision if it weren't the right one to make? Do you truly think that little of me?"

She didn't bother answering him. It didn't matter what he said. All those planes had come just for them, and she didn't believe they would have been shot down. There was a chance, sure, that they could have come under fire, but there was every chance they'd all be back in Italy by now, too.

She seethed as she looked at Evelyn with her head bent toward James, talking about something. Probably making plans about what they were going to do, as if they were the only ones capable of making a decision.

"You look flushed," Bobby said, frowning as he stopped and took her hand, his fingers going to her pulse. "Do you feel alright?"

"I'm fine," she snapped. But he was right, she was feeling hot.

"You might have a temperature."

"Or I could just be fuming that we're still stuck here," she said.

"Here, have some water." He passed her his canteen and she took it, gratefully taking a few long sips.

She looked ahead to the rest of the group, some stumbling and others looking like walking skeletons, hunched forward as if they could barely take another step, and she wondered how the hell they'd all survive if they had to be there another fifty-three days. The thought alone made her want to scream.

"Vita, you know I love you, but you need to get it the hell out of your head that Evelyn and James are the villains here," Bobby said, giving her a stern look. "James is doing everything in his power to get us out of here, and Evelyn is—"

"Evelyn's what?" she interrupted. "Because as far as I understand it, Evelyn is qualified to be a nurse, not to decide what's best for us."

Bobby shook his head. "You're unbelievable, you know that? You're acting like a princess."

"A *princess*?" She almost choked on the word. "Don't you ever call me that, Bobby. One thing I'm not is a princess."

Her *mother* was the princess, not her. She was the one who'd rolled her sleeves up and gotten dirt beneath her nails; she was the one who'd turned her back on her privileged life when she could have so easily stayed home.

"You might not like it, but the way you're behaving now shows very clearly how used you are to getting your own way," Bobby said. "So stew for a bit and stomp away from me, but then get your head on straight and focus on being a part of this team. Because there's no room for behavior like yours, not here."

She stopped, staring back at him, hardly believing the way he was speaking to her.

"And then apologize to your friend," he said. "Because you're being a real piece of work and she doesn't deserve it."

Bobby left her then, and she tried to stop her jaw from dropping.

"Bobby!" she demanded. "Bobby!" How dare he walk away from her like that!

But he didn't turn, and she had no other option but to keep on marching with the group to wherever the hell James was taking them.

He said he loved me. Instead of arguing with him and being every inch the princess he was accusing her of being, she should have just told him that she loved him back.

"He's right, you know."

She turned and saw Eddie with a makeshift pair of crutches, trying his best to hobble along. Most of the time the others had tried to carry him, but he was a big man and they were all so weak that it was an almost impossible task now.

"I don't recall asking your opinion," she snapped.

He shrugged, wiping at the beads of perspiration on his forehead with one forearm. "You can be angry all you like, but it's not going to help."

"Those planes . . ." she started.

"Those planes were sent for us, but it was the right call not to let them land. We'd all be dead by now, and you know it as well as I do."

She stared back at him.

"If anyone wanted those planes to land, it's me. I'm living through the worst pain of my life, every minute of every day is excruciating, and yet you're the one acting like what happened today is your own personal injustice."

Vita held her tongue.

"Bobby doesn't deserve your anger, and neither does Evelyn. But hey, feel free to unleash on me and get it all off your chest. Go full princess if you need to and have a right little hissy fit."

She laughed. She actually laughed. "You're a real bastard, Eddie, you know that?"

"Not the first time I've been called one. Is that all you've got?" He grinned at her and she walked over to him, settling into a slow pace beside him.

"Using those crutches must be hell."

"You're not wrong."

They kept ambling along, before he stopped and stared at her. "You know when I told you to give Bobby a chance?"

She nodded.

"Was I right about that?"

"Yes," she said, sighing. "You were."

"So when I tell you that you need to make things right with Evelyn?"

Vita took a deep breath and nodded, and they fell back into their slow amble. Eddie was right. Again. She just needed some time to collect her thoughts and figure out how to ask for Evelyn's forgiveness.

That night, after almost six hours of walking that had tested the best of them, Vita huddled close to Bobby. Although he hadn't come back for her while they were walking, he hadn't objected when she'd come to sit beside him at their makeshift campsite either.

"Where's he going?" she asked, as James said something to Evelyn and then left, his bag over his shoulder.

"To find a better place to radio from," Bobby told her. "The trees are so dense here, he thinks it's affecting the signal."

She nodded, watching Evelyn as she sat alone, cross-legged, so close and yet somehow so far away. Even though she was still cross, Bobby's and then Eddie's words had dampened her anger, and now she was feeling stupid for behaving so hysterically. She just hadn't worked out what to say to Evelyn yet, other than *sorry.*

"Let's try to get some sleep," Bobby said, stretching out beside her. "It's going to be a long walk again tomorrow, I imagine."

Evelyn looked at Vita then, her eyes finding hers across the way, and Vita stared back, smiling and hoping Evelyn could sense how stupid she felt. She lowered herself beside Bobby, promising herself that she'd apologize come morning.

The rustle that woke her sent a shiver through her entire body, although she didn't move. Vita stayed still, her eyes shut, as she listened, her ears pricked.

There it was again. Vita's heart was pounding so loudly she could hear it, and as she opened her eyes, about to push herself up to sitting position, a scream died in her throat.

Standing in the moonlight, barely a few feet from her, was a German soldier, his rifle raised and pointed in her direction.

This time, her throat didn't suffocate her scream. This time she screamed so loud it was like a siren cutting through the air, as she stared straight at the soldier.

She shut her eyes, waiting for the pain, waiting to hear the crack of his rifle, to feel the searing-hot pain of the bullet entering her body, knowing she was about to die. But when the sound of a single gunshot rang out through the night air, Vita didn't feel a thing.

Her eyes flew open, her hands on her body, checking for the wet stain of blood, but then her eyes registered what had happened. She looked up in horror.

Evelyn was standing there, pistol still raised, the German soldier lying on the ground, his rifle thrust away from his body. Blood was pooling already, dark and inky, illuminated by the moon.

Evelyn just saved my life.

Vita's legs were as unsteady as a foal's as she tried to stand, collapsing beneath her. She stared at Evelyn, trying to get to her, seeing the way her friend's body had started to shake uncontrollably. She was still holding the pistol, still in the same position she'd been in when she took the shot, frozen in place as if she couldn't believe what she'd done.

"Evelyn," Vita called as she stumbled toward her, wanting to fold her in her arms and whisper *thank you* over and over again for saving her life.

But it was James who got to Evelyn first. It was James who wrapped his hands around the gun and forced it down, who took it from her and pushed it into his own waistband, who whispered to her and wrapped her in his arms.

Vita stood helplessly on her own, watching on, as James held Evelyn, rocking her back and forth.

She saved my life. Evelyn shot that man dead and saved my life.

Arms circled her from behind and she turned into Bobby's protective hold, expecting to cry into his chest but finding her eyes dry, her emotion stuck inside of her just like her first scream had been.

Bobby was whispering to her but she couldn't hear what he was saying, couldn't register the words. All she could hear was the sound of her own scream splitting the air as the soldier had aimed his rifle at her.

"Everyone, I want your attention!"

Bobby nudged her and turned her forward in his arms, and she stood numbly listening as James addressed them all. There was movement around them, shuffling and snuffling, and slowly more of their group came to stand close to James, huddled in a tight circle.

Vita wasn't sure if the moonlight was a good thing or not, because although it illuminated James and meant they could see one another, it also made them visible to anyone else who might be lurking.

"We leave for the coast immediately," James said, one arm still around Evelyn as he spoke, with a look on his face that said he'd murder anyone with his bare hands who dared to touch her. "He may have been the first of many, which means we're sitting ducks if we stay here."

She heard some of their group groan and others start to protest, but James's next words made every single one of them fall silent.

"I was able to make radio contact again," he said. "If I can get you to the coast within the week, there'll be a rescue boat deployed to get you out of here."

We might actually still make it out of Albania? Her heart started to skip a beat, hope surging through her all over again.

"The journey is going to be tough, and although we'll have one night in a safe house, the rest of the time we'll be sleeping rough, for only a few hours here and there."

Vita found herself nodding, ready to do anything she needed to do.

"You have five minutes to gather your things, then we move on. And there's no time for stragglers, so you keep up or you get left behind," James said sternly. "If a German patrol sees us, we're all as good as dead."

But before James could turn back to Evelyn, Bobby called out from behind Vita.

"How do you think he found us? Was it coincidence?" he asked.

James shook his head. "I very much doubt it. More likely a local back at the village betrayed us. This hillside could be crawling with Germans, but we won't know until we start to move. I suggest you pick up the Nazi's gun and be prepared to use it."

Vita clasped Bobby's hand tightly, but she was forced to let it go as he retrieved the rifle.

"Bobby, can you help me move the body?" James asked. "We need it tucked away out of sight, just to give us some time in case someone comes looking for him."

Vita's stomach lurched but she marched right along beside Bobby to help, lifting one of the dead soldier's arms even as she recoiled and her stomach lurched, threatening to betray her. She heaved, trying as hard as she could to pull him even as her arms screamed in pain.

Are you alright, was what she wanted to say, followed by: *I'm so sorry*. But Evelyn wasn't looking at her, standing angled away from the body, and the divide between them felt so great she didn't know how to breach it.

"Did you hear that?" someone whispered.

James stood, pistol in his hand, pack already on his back. "Let's go."

And not a single person disobeyed his order.

CHAPTER TWENTY-SEVEN

EVELYN

Evelyn stared down at her hands. They were shaking so violently it was as if they had a mind of their own. She tucked them tight under her armpits, partly to stave off the cold and partly to stop the tremble.

I killed a man.

The words kept repeating over and over in her mind, and no matter how hard she tried to push them away, they wouldn't stop.

Crack.

She shuddered, her feet stopping as a wave of nausea took hold, seeing it all over again, feeling the shock reverberate through her body as she squeezed the trigger, as she saw the soldier crumple in front of her.

I did that. I took his life. He'd still be breathing if it weren't for me.

"Evelyn."

The arm around her was warm, the touch soft, but still she recoiled.

"Evelyn, it's me."

James's deep, calm voice soothed her, and this time when his arm circled her, when he tugged her close, she gave in and went to him. She pushed hard against him and he let her, drawing her in and taking a big breath that somehow steadied her as she listened to it, her ear against his chest.

"The first is the worst," he murmured to her, standing still as if they had nowhere else in the world to be, as if they weren't fleeing an enemy that might or might not be hunting them. "You need to remember why you did it. If you hadn't killed him, Vita would be dead, and he wouldn't have stopped at just her. This is what I trained you for."

Her breathing slowed as she listened to him, as she digested what he was saying. She knew he was right, that in war it was kill or be killed, but she still couldn't stop seeing it, she couldn't stop thinking that she'd taken the life of someone. It had been one thing training with James, but to actually put that training into practice? She was scared at how easily she'd lifted the gun, as if by instinct.

"Evelyn, we need to keep moving," he said as his arm released her, just slightly. He still hadn't relinquished his hold, and she was tempted to snag her fingers around his waist to keep him there. But she didn't. She didn't do anything because, when she uncurled her fingers, her hand, like the rest of her body, started to tremble again.

"If I could I'd hold you all night, Evelyn, I promise I would, but it's not safe here," he said. "We need to put as much distance between them and us as we can."

She swallowed, her mouth so dry she could barely move her tongue. "You truly think there's more?" she asked.

"I know there's more," he muttered. "We were betrayed, and there's no way one German soldier was sent after us, just like there's no way it's a coincidence he found us. An entire unit will be coming soon."

She nodded. Once she started, it was almost impossible to stop the movement.

James seemed to notice, even in the barely there light, and he tucked his fingers beneath her chin, as if to stop it from bobbing. She stared up at him.

"I'm going to look after you," he murmured. "We're going to get to the coast, and you're going home."

She took a breath.

"Do you trust me?" he asked.

"Yes," she whispered, without a second of doubt.

"Then hold my hand and don't stop walking until I tell you to. Can you do that?"

"Yes," she repeated.

"Right, then let's get going," he said, starting to walk, her hand clasped in his just as he'd promised. "I've had new intel that there are some SOE agents at the caves on the coastline, and there are also two American agents who've been sent in to help. So this time, no matter what, I'm going to get you all out of here. There will be no more dress rehearsals, alright?"

She wanted to ask him how long the walk would take, how he knew about the other agents, why he was certain they'd make it to the coast and then out of Albania entirely, but she didn't. Her tongue felt like it was stuck to the roof of her mouth, and all she could do was keep hold of James's hand and keep on stumbling forward. Roots and rocks slammed into her feet, her shoes broken and providing her with little protection, but she knew that she could walk for days if she had to. Anything to put distance between them and another soldier like the one she'd shot.

She wondered where Vita was then, how she was holding up after coming so close to losing her life, but clouds must have drifted in front of the moon because all of a sudden she couldn't see a thing around her.

"Evelyn?"

She turned to look at James again, seeing the pain in his face as he held tightly to her hand.

"I know I've pushed you away before, that I might have been hard to read, but the truth is . . ."

Evelyn wanted to tell him to stop, that he didn't need to explain himself, but she didn't.

"What I'm trying to say is that I care about you—deeply, in fact. I don't think I've ever met a woman quite like you."

She squeezed his hand, blinking away a fresh wave of tears at his outpouring of emotion.

"That's why I know you're going to be fine. You just need to trust me."

There was no time for more words or even an embrace; they needed to start walking and there was no time to waste.

―――― ✦ ――――

They hadn't stopped for hours, other than a brief stop for everyone to catch their breath and to fill up their water canteens in a fast-flowing stream, and although Evelyn had thought she could walk for days on end, she was starting to realize how broken her body was. It had stopped shaking, but every ounce of energy had drained out of her, and they had absolutely nothing to eat. She stared at the grass, tendrils of green shimmering with raindrops, and she wondered if it was worth eating it just to experience the feeling of something in her mouth, something for her teeth to chew.

"We push on," James ordered everyone. "We'll stop at dusk, which means we have at least a few hours still to go."

There was crying and moaning—sobbing from some of the nurses, and cries coming from some of the men—but when James barked at them a second time, ordering them to get to their feet, everyone eventually obeyed. His tone made Evelyn cringe, but she knew that he was only trying to save everyone, just like she knew that it wasn't a tone he'd ever use with her.

She caught sight of Vita then, walking with Bobby, and when their eyes met, Vita lifted her hand in a small wave, her lips moving ever so slightly into a smile. Evelyn raised her hand in return, aching for her friend and wishing they had time to stop and talk, to just be together. James had been an incredible comfort to her, but she'd been through so much with Vita, and she hadn't realized how much she'd missed her.

Vita might have behaved badly, but Evelyn could understand; emotions had been running high and she'd felt the same crushing disappointment her friend had felt, even if Vita hadn't recognized it at the time.

But the moment passed, Vita merging with the rest of the group, and so Evelyn fell into step with James again, leading the group, never leaving his side. He wasn't holding her hand now, but they walked close enough to bump hips or brush arms, and she liked knowing that he was there, that his body was so close. Something had changed between them; there was a deepness that had been lurking but suppressed until now, and it gave her the strength to keep walking beside him.

Rain started to fall as they continued to walk, dripping from her hair down her face and slowly down inside the collar of her coat. It sent a shiver through her, but she ignored it, her feet marching a comforting beat as they kept up a steady pace.

"We rest here," James eventually said, once they'd walked in silence for what felt like forever.

Evelyn looked back, counting heads in the thick drizzle, squinting to make sure she could see everyone.

"I want you all to find somewhere sheltered—tuck beneath a tree out of the direct rain while I secure the perimeter."

Evelyn's eyes leapt to his, but still she didn't say anything.

272

"Do you want to rest or come with me?" James asked.

She was so tired she could have fallen asleep on her feet, but she had the most overwhelming feeling she didn't want to be without him. The last thing she wanted was to be alone.

"I can stay, if I need to," she replied, her eyes dropping to the gun at his waist, the one he'd taken off her.

Please don't say yes. Please don't tell me I need to hold that pistol again.

"You don't need to stay." She watched as he left her for a moment and had a word with Bobby, gesturing and talking about something. When he came back, the dreaded pistol was gone, although he was still armed with his other one and the knife she knew he always kept strapped to his lower leg.

It started to pelt down, and she followed blindly behind James, blinking away the rain mixed with tears that filled her eyes. They walked the perimeter together, and then he beckoned for her to come with him beneath the cover of some trees that had grown to form something of an umbrella, although rain still dripped sporadically between the leaves.

"We're taking first shift to keep lookout," he said, and she watched as he shuffled back against the tree. "We listen and watch as best we can, and then Bobby will take the second shift."

She moved closer to him, her back against the neighboring tree trunk.

"You feeling better?"

She nodded. "Somewhat. I think it's just the shock of it all."

"I've seen men crumble after their first kill, so you're doing just fine if you ask me," he said.

Evelyn studied him, committed the profile of his face to memory. There was something about James, something that meant he could draw her in fast, could make her feel at ease in a split second.

"When did you lose your wife?" she blurted out, not sure how the words even left her mouth but suddenly needing to know what had happened to this man she felt so deeply about.

"At the very beginning of the Blitz in London," he answered, without missing a beat. "Late 1940."

So he'd lost his wife before she'd even signed up to be a nurse.

"I'm sorry," she said, not sure what else she *could* say, especially after being so nosey.

"You're asking because of what I said the other day, about you being like her, aren't you?"

She smiled. Why was she not surprised how easily he'd guessed where her interest came from? "Yes, I suppose I am."

"Well, I wasn't lying, if that's what you're wondering," he said, his voice low and deep, words meant just for her as they stayed quiet, tucked away from the world. "She was determined and spirited; she had a smile as wide as could be; and when she looked at me, it was as if she could see nobody else *but* me." He sighed. "That doesn't even make sense."

"No, it does," she whispered back. "Because it's the way my father used to look at my mother."

James gave her a sad half-smile.

"She died a bit before your wife did," Evelyn told him. "And he never recovered. Without her light cast on him, I suppose he just didn't know how to shine anymore."

"And now?" James asked, turning to her.

She looked away, blinking back her tears. "I doubt he'll ever shine again."

"Maybe you're wrong," he said. "Maybe something will happen, or someone will come into his life, and you'll see that again one day."

She was about to answer when she saw something, a flicker, pass across his face. Before she could say anything, James had caught her hand.

"You've made me smile again, Evelyn," he murmured. "That's why I know your dad isn't a lost cause, not yet."

She wanted to tell him that her father had daughters, that they should be enough to make him want to be happy again, but the way James was looking at her stole the words from her. Her heart picked up its rhythm and she felt the weight of his hand against hers.

"You truly mean that?" she asked, trying not to laugh. "Some exhausted, malnourished, desperate nurse in Albania has made you smile again?"

His chuckle was as warm as his smile. "If only you could see what I see," he said. "Hell, I'd almost keep us going in circles out here just to get an extra day with you."

The rain became harder then, falling heavily from the dense leaves and branches crisscrossing above them. But when James's hand lifted to her face, his wet fingers splayed against her cheek as he waited for her to lean in, she forgot all about the weather.

Evelyn leaned forward, just a little, her breath coming in little pants as his mouth moved closer, as his lips widened into a smile before slowly meeting hers. Rain slipped against their skin and between them, moistening their lips and making them slippery, but Evelyn ignored it all as James's mouth moved against hers, brushing it so softly.

And when he finally pulled away, leaving her breathless, she reached for the back of his head and pulled him straight in again. She pressed her body against his as his arms wound around her, tugging her closer, his chest warm and hard against hers, kissing one more time, and then another, and another, until finally she paused for air.

Evelyn caught her breath as James stroked her face, so tenderly she could barely feel the back of his knuckles against her damp skin. And then he dropped his forehead to hers, staying like that a moment before straightening and pressing a kiss to her temple.

"We need to keep watch," he muttered. "Although, trust me, I'd much rather do *that* all night."

Evelyn didn't answer. She just wanted to absorb the feeling of him against her, of the way his arm was tucked so protectively around her as she turned in his arms. She wriggled back into him, cocooned in his embrace, his chin resting on the top of her head as they stared out into the creeping darkness.

"I'll find you, once this war is over," James whispered. "If you want me to find you, I will."

"Yes," she whispered in reply, hugging his arms tight to her front. "I want you to find me, James. There's nothing I want more in the world than for us to be together once all this is over."

He kissed the top of her head before placing his chin there again, and Evelyn shut her eyes, certain she could sleep upright in his arms she was so bone-achingly tired.

"James," she whispered.

"Mmm-hmm," he replied.

"How long do we all have to stay alive? How long will it actually take us to get to the coast?"

"A week, maybe a little longer. Why's that?"

"I honestly don't know if everyone is going to last that long," she admitted.

"It's time you let someone else do the worrying for once," he said, stroking her arm. "You've done your part to keep everyone alive, and now it's my turn."

A few days ago, she would have argued with him, wanted to know more details to decide if he was making the right judgment calls, but now all she wanted was to be told what to do. She didn't know how to keep them all alive, but James did.

"She was a worrier too," he said quietly. "Always worried about other people, wanting to make sure everyone was alright. It's how she died during the Blitz; she stayed behind to help a woman in labor rather than going to the underground shelter."

"I'm so sorry," Evelyn said, feeling him shift behind her, wondering if he was about to let her go.

"It's why I fell in love with her in the first place—that big heart of hers," he said, before clearing his throat. "It's one of the things that reminds me of her when I'm with you. When I saw you that day, that look of determination on your face when I confronted you about sending that message." He laughed. "I thought there's only one other woman I've ever met who would have the balls to do something like that. Honestly, I never thought I'd be fortunate enough to encounter a second."

She leaned her head back into him and smiled, even though she doubted he could see it in the dark. But he must have sensed it, because those warm, pliable lips found hers again for the most delicious moment.

Evelyn sighed when she was finally forced to straighten. It had been a night of firsts; first kill and first real kiss. She only hoped the dreams about the latter would outweigh the inevitable nightmares about the first.

"Were you running away from your life, after your wife died?" she whispered.

James stiffened behind her. "I'm still running."

Maybe that was the difference between them: they'd both been running from something, it's how they'd both ended up in Albania, but he was still running and she would have given her right arm to run headfirst into what she'd left behind.

Although she wouldn't say no to one more night standing in the cocoon of James's arms, even in the middle of the forest, in a country she hoped to never visit again in her lifetime.

CHAPTER
TWENTY-EIGHT

EVELYN

Evelyn's legs were ready to buckle, but she gritted her teeth and kept forcing each step as they trekked up the mountain. The night before, they'd stayed in a modest safe house, barely big enough for them all to cram in, with James letting them all rest to recover their strength. But tonight they weren't going to be sleeping—James wanted them walking in the dark, emphatic in his desire to move them up the mountain before sunrise. She knew he was worried about how close they were to German territory, and if they moved during daylight hours, they could be spotted from the road.

The hike had been grueling; Evelyn's lower legs were burning from the exertion and her breath was rasping in her throat, but she refused to stop moving, terrified that if she stopped she wouldn't be able to start again. *We're almost there, I can feel it in my bones. We're so close.*

As she hauled herself up the steepest part of the trail yet, the temperature seemed to fall even lower, with remnants of snow underfoot. She saw lights in the near distance and her heart began to beat faster—not from the exhaustion now but from anticipation.

It could only mean they were almost there. The coast was in their sights!

Evelyn picked up her pace, walking faster as they ascended the top of the mountain just as the sun rose, the shining, luminous waters of the Adriatic glimmering back at her as she watched.

They still had to get down the mountain, but they were there, and that's what mattered. Home was in their sights.

"I'm going down to warn them of our arrival," James called out, slightly ahead of her. She'd fallen back from him as he led the group, helped by a local they'd collected at the safe house the night before—a guide who apparently knew the mountains and the coastline like the back of his hand.

She watched James go, more settled than she'd been at the start of their journey, and more at peace with what she'd done along the way to keep them safe. Talking with James, and walking, had given her perspective, and she knew she had so much to be grateful for when it came to the time she'd spent with him. She only wished the idea of leaving him wasn't so torturous. They'd lain together in bed, fully clothed with their legs intertwined to stay warm, and she'd tried to absorb every moment, commit every second to memory.

"I'll never forget you, Evelyn," he whispered in the dark, stroking her hair as he spoke. "War took everything from me, but somehow it's also given me something beautiful, too."

She leaned into his touch, closing her eyes as his hand skimmed her cheek.

"Do you promise to find me?" she whispered back. "You're not going to forget about me the moment I'm gone?"

His lips were against her forehead then, his arms cocooning her, as if to show her how much he wanted her near.

"If we both survive this war, nothing will be able to keep us apart."

Fatigue clawed at her, begging her to give in to sleep, and eventually the steady sound of James's breath, his arms so warm around her, made it impossible to fight. She'd wanted to stay awake, to spend what might be their last night together awake and present, but in the end it was a battle she simply couldn't win.

Evelyn could almost feel James's arms around her still, and when she opened her eyes after catching her breath, she hated that he wasn't there beside her. She looked around at everyone—all of them collapsed on the ground despite the snow seeping through and wetting their clothes—and they eventually stood and prepared to make their way down the mountain, with their guide taking the lead. Evelyn found herself passing Vita, the other woman limping as she shuffle-walked.

Vita moved closer to her and gave her a small nod, and Evelyn went straight to her, not hesitating in taking her hand as they both started to cry, holding on to each other as they stood, on top of the mountain, looking down at the sea.

"Thank you," Vita whispered, clutching her hand so fiercely Evelyn feared she might break it. "I should have said it days ago, but thank you."

Evelyn stared at the sea, losing herself in the blue shining so vividly back at her.

"You saved my life back there, Evelyn. I don't know what to say. I wish I'd said so sooner, because even though I was hideous to you and blamed the botched rescue on you, you still saved me."

Evelyn laughed, despite how horrific everything was, despite the fact Vita had almost died. "Well, you weren't so hideous that I considered not saving you."

Vita laughed too, although her laughter rapidly turned to tears. "You're a good friend, you know that? You're a better friend to me than I've ever been to you."

"Don't say that," Evelyn said, shaking her head and turning to face Vita, opening her arms to envelope her in a warm, strong hug. "You've been a great friend to me; you've held me when I cried, and held my hand as we grieved for Dot. This place has tested us in ways we could never have prepared for."

"Well, I'm sorry, and I should have said it long before now," Vita said softly, stepping out of Evelyn's embrace. "You're amazing, Evelyn. You stepped up and did what had to be done for the greater good, for all of us, but I couldn't see past my own desperation that day."

Evelyn sighed. "Well, you're forgiven. We've all been through a lot, and we don't ever need to talk about that day again."

Bobby had moved closer to them, giving them a quick glance before beckoning for them to follow, and follow they did. They made their way like billy goats down the mountain, gripping each other's arm as they slid and slipped in the snow, their shoes beyond the point of affording them any grip on the mountainside.

Evelyn felt lighter, and it wasn't because she had nothing to carry, with their musette bags being left behind at the safe house so as not to slow them down. This had more to do with Vita; having her friend back, the rift between them mended as if it had never existed in the first place, made her feel like herself again. She'd missed Vita terribly this past week, and it had almost been too much to bear on top of losing Dot.

And then James appeared at the foot of the mountain, and that lightness was replaced with a twist in her stomach that made her want to retch. He was smiling at their group, but when his gaze met hers, she saw only sadness, which could only mean one thing: they were going home.

She should have been rejoicing, she should have wanted to drop to her knees and cry tears of relief, but all she could feel was pain; the pain of knowing they were about to say goodbye.

"You'll see him again," Vita said. "You have to believe that."

It was as if she'd read her mind. "But will I ever see him again?" she asked. "He's from England, and by all accounts we'll be sent home to America as soon as we're cleared for discharge. There's no way I'll ever cross paths with him again, no matter how many times he tells me that he'll find me."

"If it's meant to be, it'll be," Vita insisted. "Have a little faith, Evelyn. We've survived sixty-three days in Albania despite all the odds being stacked against us."

Evelyn's heart lifted. "You really think so?"

"I know so," Vita said, but as she spoke she half fell, grunting as Evelyn roughly caught her before she hit the ground.

"Are you alright?" Evelyn searched Vita's body, looking for injuries and remembering her limp from earlier.

"I'm fine," Vita said, pushing her away. "Go to him. You have forever to worry about me."

Evelyn hesitated. It went against all her instincts to leave her friend, but when she saw Bobby coming closer, she decided to listen to Vita, the pull toward James stronger than anything she'd ever felt before. A little voice told her it was because he'd saved them, that she was somehow infatuated with the man because of what he'd done for her, but inside she knew that wasn't true. She liked James not because of what he'd done, but because of who he was. Because of how he made her feel when she was with him.

"How are you holding up?"

His voice wrapped around her, giving her strength, drawing her closer.

"I'm fine," she said, but his eyes told her he didn't believe her.

"Come with me," he said, leading her toward the caves that were largely hidden from view.

She was aware the others were trailing behind them, following their leader, but when he held out his hand for her, she clasped it as if it were only the two of them—although she was quick to drop it when two men came toward them, stepping out of the shadows.

"Evelyn, these are your fellow Americans, Lieutenant Carter and Captain Kennedy," James said. "And out the other side on his radio is British Lieutenant Craig Johnson."

"It's such an honor to meet you," Evelyn said, holding out her hand and shaking Carter's and then Kennedy's hands. "Thank you for helping us."

"Hey, when you hear there are thirteen of our nurses missing in the middle of nowhere, you don't muck around."

Tears welled in her eyes. "Well, unfortunately you only have ten of us," she said, clearing her throat as she fought her emotions. "But we're all very grateful."

James took her hand again, as Carter and Kennedy both welcomed the rest of the group, passing out cigarettes and chocolate as Evelyn and James found themselves a quiet corner near the other side of the cave. Evelyn turned to him as he sat across from her, staring out at the ocean.

"So, what happens next?" she asked.

He ignored her question and instead moved to squat down in front of her, taking her booted foot into his hand and untying the laces, slowly removing them as she winced. It was as if her skin had imbedded itself into the leather and a layer of it was being removed along with the boot.

"Why didn't you tell me your shoes were this bad?"

She shrugged. "I didn't want you to feel you had to carry me."

"Evelyn," he cautioned, carefully taking her sock off and then staring at her foot. "You've got some of the worst blisters I've ever seen—infected by the looks of it. How on earth did you even keep walking?"

"Because I wanted to live," she said, staring at her foot cradled so gently in his hands. "It's as simple as that."

His eyes were so warm, his touch so soft, and although she was mortified that he was looking at her skin when it was in such a state, she refused to pull away from him. It wasn't often someone put their own needs aside to care for her, and it felt nice.

"You didn't answer my question before, about what happens next," she said.

He took something from his pack, a type of ointment, and unscrewed the top, resting her foot on his knees. "Johnson will confirm contact with the ship waiting to transport you back to Bari, and then when it comes close, they'll send rowboats out to take you all to safety."

"And you? What will happen to you?"

He dabbed ointment onto her skin, before removing her other boot and repeating the process while she tried not to wince. The pain sent spasms through her foot and up her leg, but she gritted her teeth and refused to cry.

"I'll go back to doing my job," he said. "Until the war is over, or I'm reassigned."

"Can I ask you something?" She hissed as he touched a painful blister on her big toe.

"Ask away."

"Did you volunteer to come here—to Albania specifically I mean—or were you sent?"

He didn't answer her immediately, studying her foot and taking great care as he moved it from side to side. It wasn't until he was finished that he finally looked up and spoke again.

"This was a dangerous posting, and I offered to come here," he said, his voice low. "I was one of the only men with no family, with nothing waiting for me at home. Until very recently, I didn't have anyone to live for, so I felt like this type of job was made for me."

She swallowed. James blinked, but he never looked away.

"Do you have someone to live for now?" she asked.

His fingers brushed the arch of her foot. "I do, actually. I'm just hoping she still wants me to find her once all this is over, if we both make it out the other side alive."

Evelyn's skin flushed, her body temperature rising. "I'd like that," she stammered. "I'd like that a lot. I just don't see how—"

"Don't you worry about the how. Where there's a will, there's a way."

James put her foot down gently, leaning forward, but just as she slipped her arms around his shoulders, they were interrupted by a sharp call. Their eyes were still locked, despite the interruption, but James had his head cocked to listen.

"Sir, we've made contact with Bari!" the man announced. "Ship will be in our sights by 2200 hours, unless the moonlight is too bright, and then they'll try again tomorrow night."

James grinned at her, passing her socks to her as he stood.

"Thank you for the update, Johnson. Get Carter to keep watch, and we'll deploy the flares once he sees them or has confirmation they're in position."

Evelyn was carefully putting her socks back on when James's hands touched her shoulders from behind.

"It's almost time to go home, Evelyn. This nightmare is almost over."

She shut her eyes, basking in the feel of his hands on her, the warmth radiating from his palms. And for a moment, in her mind's eye, she could see him sitting in her kitchen at home, laughing and playing cards with her father as she cooked for them; calling her sisters down for dinner; feeling the brush of James's hand against her back as she set his dinner down in front of him and he looked up to thank her.

As his palms lifted, she tenderly replaced her shoes and caught her breath, as her mind continued to play tricks on her and show her a dream that she knew might never come true.

"It's time."

James's words sounded so final. Evelyn lifted her head. She'd been standing at his side for the past hour or so, stoically staring at the sea and waiting for the moment when they'd see the ship. Their shoulders were close enough to bump, their fingers brushing every now and again until Evelyn had eventually wound her little finger around James's, just to feel him beside her.

She cleared her throat as he reached for the flare guns, looking at her before passing her one.

"Hold it out like this," he instructed, guiding her with his own. "Just like you're shooting it normally, but pointed toward the sky. Yours are red, mine are yellow."

She took a deep breath before holding her hand out for the pistol, trying not to think about what had happened the last time she'd held one. The rest of their group was asleep or resting still, either in the cots dotted throughout the caves for the American and British undercover agents who used them regularly, or curled on stones that still held the last of the sun's heat. And she was about to do something, to send up a signal with James that would see them in real beds with real food by first light, if not sooner.

She held the gun out, following his instructions, before shooting and sending a bright plume of red out that lit up the sky, at the same time as Johnson beside them started to radio and James shot his yellow flare. She listened as Johnson repeated "one, two, three" in German, and within seconds the radio crackled to life and they heard the same message relayed backwards.

"*Drei, zwei, eins.*"

Everything is going perfectly to plan. This is actually going to work. This is not like last time.

Evelyn stared at the flares as they slowly fell through the night sky, listening to the same message being repeated again, and she knew what James was about to say before he even said it.

"It's time to walk down. Let's rouse everyone."

"We have trouble!"

On the heels of James's words, Carter came running, skidding in front of them.

"What is it?" James asked.

Oh my God, we're not getting out of here. It's happening all over again. Just when it seems failsafe, when it seems like nothing could stop us, it's all going to end in heartache again.

"We've got men under fire, there's been a German attack and the safe house you were in has been compromised. They're too close for comfort."

"But we have spies in every damn village!" James cursed. "Were there any reports of the Germans coming—any warning at all?"

Carter shook his head. "Nothing. But we need to get down there and provide cover. And James"—he cleared his throat—"one of our men is badly injured. We need to get him out of there."

James looked conflicted, and Evelyn instinctively reached for him. "You can leave. I can get everyone down to the beach." She smiled bravely. "It's going to be fine. We're too close for this to fall apart now."

But when his eyes met hers, she knew that wasn't going to be an option.

"I'm seeing you all onto those boats myself," he ground out.

She didn't argue with him, standing back as he spoke to the other men.

"Prepare for immediate departure. As soon as the group is safely at sea and we get radio confirmation they're all on board, we leave."

Evelyn's stomach swirled at the thought of James going directly into the conflict like that, but she also knew it was his job. Nothing she said or did could change that, and it wasn't as if he could just go with her and sail away to Italy without any repercussions.

"I'll go wake everyone," she said, putting some distance between them, even though it went against all her instincts.

"Come on, let's go," she called out inside the cave. Some had already woken at the sound of flares and raised voices; others were still asleep, or passed out from starvation. "It's time to go, hurry up!"

Bobby was already on his feet and rousing as many of the men as he could, nudging their shoulders and yanking some onto their feet by their collars, and she did the same to the women, only without the yanking. Even if she'd wanted to, she didn't have the strength.

An excited hum began as everyone realized what was happening, and soon their homeless-looking group was assembled. She left Bobby to do a quick headcount and went to find James again. He was poring over a map, a light held low over it, but he turned when he heard her behind him.

"Ready?" he asked.

"As we'll ever be."

He led the way down to the beach, and they all skidded and tripped their way for almost an hour until the ground changed beneath their feet, going from rough and rocky to a much softer sand. But the patch of beach was barely big enough for them all to stand on, and as James shot another two yellow flares into the sky, Evelyn's eyes widened at the sight of three men in an inflatable boat suddenly appearing in the water before them. With barely any moon, it was impossible to see without the flares, and yet they'd been so close it was a wonder they hadn't heard them. She only hoped there were no Germans looking for them, because those flares weren't exactly discreet.

"Come on, let's take the women first," James said. "Five at a time, in you go."

As the first of the nurses, crying with relief, hurried through the water and were hauled over the sides of the inflatable by two of the men, Evelyn edged closer to James. It was almost time, and she had no idea what to say, or *how* to say goodbye to a man who'd come to mean so much to her.

The little boat left, leaving them in the dark again, and she had the most overwhelming feeling that something terrible was going to happen. That it was all a farce, too good to be true, and that any moment now guns were going to start firing or a German plane would light them up from above.

But nothing happened. The only noise was the gentle lapping of water at their feet, and the excited whispers of the next women lined up to go. Only, she was supposed to be one of those women.

"I'll wait until the end," she whispered to the group. "Take Eddie this time."

She stood like that, beside James, for almost two hours, not yet ready to let him go. And not ready to let go of Dot, either. Her darling friend who, even if she'd miraculously survived, was never going to make it home. Evelyn shuddered just thinking about how she'd have to tell her friend's fiancé, if she ever managed to find him.

After four loads, though, she knew roughly how long it would take to return, and the nerves bubbling up in her throat signaled to her that it was time for their final goodbye, whether she was ready or not.

James's arm went awkwardly around her, like a distant cousin hugging her out of duty, but Evelyn ignored it and spun around, wrapping her arms fiercely around him. It seemed to be all the encouragement he needed, because his hold on her changed in a heartbeat, and he tucked her beneath his chin as his chest shuddered against her.

"You survive this darn war, you hear me?" she demanded.

"I will," he whispered into her ear, his lips caressing her hair as he held her even tighter. "I have something to live for now, so I'll be damned if I'm going to die."

Evelyn inhaled, committing the smell of him to memory, her palms remembering the feel of him as she heard movement behind her. James started to let her go, his fingers sliding against her coat, but then he drew her back in, his lips finding hers in the dark, crushing against hers as her tears fell, for one last kiss.

And just before she stepped away, before her last goodbye, he whispered in her ear, and tears ran down her cheeks as his warm breath brushed her skin one final time.

CHAPTER
TWENTY-NINE
Dot

Dot's breath sounded so loud in the silence as she waited for Stefa to come to her. Everyone else was asleep, but she knew he would come, like he always did. She turned on her pallet in the living room where they all slept every night, the only room that was warm enough to combat the cold evenings with its cozy little fire.

She heard the shuffle of his covers, and within seconds he was nudging her in the dark and lying beside her. She reached for him as his arms came around her, warming her and comforting her at the same time.

"How are you feeling?" he asked, so quietly she could only just make out what he was saying.

"I'm fine. A little sick, but fine," she replied.

She lifted her head and tried to make out his features in the dark.

"It's time to tell everyone," he whispered, leaning up to kiss her, his soft lips brushing against hers. "They will understand."

She certainly hoped so, because the last thing she wanted was to upset his family. They'd been so kind and accepting of her, and although she suspected Marti had guessed there was something going on between her and Stefa for some time, she'd never said anything.

"I know this isn't the future you imagined," he whispered.

Dot held him fiercely, not wanting him to feel that way, wishing he could understand how she felt about him.

"Don't say that," she said. "I love you."

"And I love you, too," he murmured, his palm finding her stomach and splaying across her, telling her all she needed to know.

There was a rustle of covers then and Stefa tensed, kissing her quickly before rising. She lay there after that, wondering how she'd managed to fall in love with a man she should never have crossed paths with in her lifetime.

If only she wasn't so terrified of giving birth in Albania.

CHAPTER THIRTY

VITA

Vita trembled as she climbed high up the side of the boat, her fingers knotted in the netting, her toes curled in her broken shoes to stop from slipping into the murky, dark waters below. When her feet finally connected with the deck, as arms caught her and guided her away from the edge of the huge ship, she staggered a few feet before collapsing. Her breath was ragged, the sheer adrenalin of riding the waves in the rubber boat, being propelled away from the coast and toward safety, finally catching up on her.

We're safe! We're actually safe! She couldn't believe it.

"He the last one?" someone called.

"No, there's one more load."

She waited, pushing the hair from her forehead and squinting to see in the dark. Her stomach was growling with the deepest hunger she'd ever known, and her body was aching, but she ignored it all as she waited. There would be no justice if they didn't all make it safely onto the boat, or if they didn't manage to make it out of Albania when they'd come so close. There was the faint sound of gunshots in the distance, traveling on the wind, and the idea of encountering enemy fire made the hunger in her belly turn to a gnawing fear instead.

Please don't let this be like last time.

Vita pushed up on her elbows as someone eventually called out, and Bobby suddenly clambered over the sidings along with three others, the last not even clear before someone yelled "All aboard!" and the ship lurched forward. They weren't waiting around; the captain was obviously determined to get as far away from Albania as quickly as he could, and she couldn't blame him.

"Come on," Bobby said, suddenly appearing beside her and holding out a hand. "I hear there's food, hot tea, and blankets waiting for us below deck."

Vita clasped his hand and let him pull her up, watching the way he smiled at her, his eyes shining down at her just as they had the night they'd met, although his face was so different, and so much had changed. His beard was scraggy, hiding his chin and half his cheeks, and his hair had grown long, to the point he'd had to start pushing it off his face constantly and tucking it behind his ears. But she liked it; he still looked as handsome as ever, if a little thinner and aged by his facial hair. She held no regrets about deciding to be with him; Albania had given her the gift of seeing Bobby for who he really was, and for that she was grateful.

But as she held his hand, something, or rather *someone*, caught her eye. *Evelyn.* She was standing alone, staring back at the land that was impossible to see as everyone else disappeared below deck. She must have been one of the last to arrive, and it was only because the clouds had parted and the moon was shining through that Vita could even see her at all.

"Can you believe we actually made it?" Bobby asked with a chuckle, his beard brushing her cheek as he kissed her.

"No," she replied honestly. "I can't."

"Come on then, let's go get something to eat before there's nothing left."

Vita stared at her hand tucked into Bobby's, and as much as she wanted to go with him, she couldn't. "I'll catch up to you," she said. "There's something I need to do first."

She looked back toward Evelyn and knew he'd followed her gaze when he gave her hand a squeeze.

"She needs me," Vita said.

"I'll see you soon."

He took his leave and Vita made her way over to Evelyn, stopping before she was beside her. She could feel her friend's pain, knew how close she'd become to James and how difficult it must have been to say goodbye to him, and she could see her shoulders shaking as she stood, crying, on her own.

"I'm sorry you had to say goodbye to him like that," Vita said. "I can't imagine how hard that must have been."

She heard Evelyn's deep inhale, watched as her shoulders moved, but still she didn't turn around.

Vita stood awkwardly, not sure whether to leave Evelyn or embrace her, but after deliberating for a moment she stepped forward and slid an arm around her friend's waist, pulling them hip to hip and slowly dropping her head to her shoulder.

"Are you thinking about James or Dot?" she whispered.

Evelyn's head touched hers. "Both."

They stood in silence a moment longer, the sway of the boat soothing in its rhythm.

"He told me, just as the rowboats arrived, he whispered to me that he'd heard the missing nurse was still alive," Evelyn said. "He promised me that if the intelligence was correct, he'd stop at nothing to save her, and I just know it's her. Or maybe I just want it to be her so badly."

Vita froze. "You honestly think she could be alive? After all this time?"

"I don't think he'd have told me if he didn't believe it." Evelyn cried, and Vita held her tighter. All those weeks in Albania, and she'd barely seen Evelyn cry, never seen her break down like this or show any signs of weakness other than when she'd shot the German soldier. But she was sobbing now, and Vita knew that if she wasn't holding her, she could slide straight to the deck.

She opened her arms, letting Evelyn turn, holding her as emotion shuddered through her, rubbing big, warming circles on her back.

"We're safe now," she whispered, as if she were soothing a child. "You're safe now. Everything's going to be fine." She stifled her own tears, waiting until they'd passed before she spoke again. "It doesn't seem right to be leaving without Dot, but if she's truly alive, then there's no one better than James to find her and get her to safety."

Evelyn didn't say another word, but her sobbing slowly subsided and eventually she stood breathing heavily as she composed herself. Vita gently wiped her tear-streaked cheeks and took her hand, seeing the way Evelyn looked back one more time, perhaps hoping to catch a final glimpse of James even though there was nothing to see in the darkness.

"Come on, we both need a hot cup of anything and something to eat," Vita said. "James is one of the most capable men I know, so you don't need to worry about him. He can take care of himself."

Evelyn nodded, and Vita kept hold of her hand as they slowly made their way across the vast deck and down below, to a raucous, happy scene in the officers' quarters. She led Evelyn to the table, which was already covered in crumbs and sticky to the touch, and she gratefully took the crackers passed to her, along with a jar of jam and a spoon.

She spread one for Evelyn first, even though she was beyond starving, before doing one for herself. As the sweet strawberry jam dissolved on her tongue, she shut her eyes, never having appreciated anything in her life as much as she did that first bite of food.

"Good luck eating any more," Bobby said as he came to join them, the others already lying in the surrounding bunkbeds. "The most anyone ate was four crackers; it's like our stomachs have shrunk to a quarter of their original size."

He gave Vita a look that she replied to with a smile, and she appreciated the way he never commented on Evelyn's drawn expression. It was like everyone else had come back to life after being dormant for so long, yet Evelyn's transformation had been reversed.

Vita spread another cracker with jam and passed it to Evelyn, pleased that she took it, then had another herself. "Nothing has ever tasted so good," she confessed, licking her fingers.

"Wait till you climb into that bunkbed," Bobby said with a grin. "Nothing has ever *felt* so good, either."

Vita looked over and saw that there was only one spare, with a few men already spread out on the floor, and it was as if Bobby had read her mind.

"You and Evelyn take it," he whispered. "I'm fine sleeping rough for a bit longer."

"You're sure?" she asked.

He nodded. "Trust me, we'll be back at base in no time. You girls enjoy the rest."

She'd fallen in love with him many times since the crash, but this single act of kindness toward her and Evelyn was enough to tell her just what kind of man he was. That she hadn't been wrong in opening up to him or letting him close.

"Thank you," she whispered, rising to hug him and kiss his cheek.

"Quickly, have another cracker before I change my mind," he said, gruffly, and she laughed and followed his advice, dragging her eyes from him as she turned her attention back to Evelyn.

"Come on, it's time for some rest before we arrive back in Italy," she said, noticing that the color had returned to Evelyn's face now, her cheeks pink again and her eyes no longer so lost. And although she still took her hand to guide her to the single bunk they were going to share, she knew instinctively that Evelyn was going to be fine. They all were.

Well, all of us except for Dot, that is.

———— ❧ ————

If the trip by boat back to Italy had been surreal, then Vita had no way to describe what it felt like to be in an army truck, being driven to the 26th General Hospital. She dropped her head back as they bumped along the road, still amazed that she was being transported somewhere by vehicle rather than having to walk, after so long of having nothing in the way of luxury.

When the truck eventually rumbled to a halt, she reached out for Evelyn, but it was Bobby who caught her eye. He was standing at the rear of the truck, and there was a stern-faced soldier standing there saying something to him. She strained to hear, but couldn't make out a thing.

"Just wait," Evelyn said. "He won't leave without saying goodbye."

Her friend had read her mind; she only hoped that she was right about Bobby not leaving. She'd expected they would stay together, that no one would dare separate them, but she could see now how naive that had been. Once he was cleaned up, he'd probably be questioned and then sent elsewhere; he could be back up in the air again within weeks. The thought sent a violent shudder through her.

Most of the others disembarked from the truck, but Bobby seemed to be having a heated exchange now with the soldier as they stood near the exit, before turning his back and coming over to her. Evelyn's hand slipped from hers, leaving her with Bobby.

The last few remaining passengers moved around them, but Vita stared up at him, knowing instinctively that it was the end for them.

"I have to go," he whispered, holding her hands as he lifted them to his lips and kissed them. "Ralph and I are going to be debriefed, but I'll see you again in the hospital, alright? I think we'll all be spending some time there recovering."

She nodded, wondering if he would end up taking the blame for what had happened, for the crash. "Of course. I'll see you soon."

Bobby leaned forward and pressed a quick kiss to her lips, before lifting one finger to her cheek and tracing a love heart against her skin. It almost broke her—such a tender display of affection as they were about to be parted.

"If we're separated, I'll find you," he murmured. "If we can survive Albania, we can survive anything."

She swallowed, refusing to cry as he backed away and then disappeared out the back of the truck. In her heart, she had the most unusual feeling, something she'd never experienced before.

You've got a broken heart, you fool, she told herself. She'd never let herself love before, never let herself get close to anyone, but Bobby was something else. Bobby had changed everything.

"Nurse, we need you off the vehicle."

She realized it was her they were waiting on, and she hurried to the back, taking the soldier's hand to help her down as she ran to catch up with the rest of her group. As she ran, she caught a final glimpse of Bobby's back as he disappeared into a tent.

"Everything alright?" Evelyn asked when she caught up to her.

"I just have the strangest feeling that I've said goodbye to him for the last time," she confessed. "I don't think I'm ever going to see him again."

"Don't be silly, that's not possible," Evelyn said, brusquely, as if she were so certain of her words. "It's probably just being parted from him that has you worried. We've all been together for two months now; it's understandable you don't like being separated from him."

Vita understood what she was saying, but she still had a heavy feeling inside her that she couldn't explain away. And she was suddenly acutely aware of the way Evelyn must have felt saying goodbye to James.

"You two, over here," someone called out.

Vita wouldn't have even noticed she was being spoken to if Evelyn hadn't hauled her along with her.

"Where are we going?" she asked.

"I'm your escort," the soldier said. "You're to be debriefed in the interrogation room by Lieutenant Colonel Brandon."

"I'm sorry, did you say *interrogation* room?" Vita gasped.

"Nothing to worry about," he said. "It's routine procedure for anyone who's been across enemy lines. Now, I just need you both to sign here."

Vita scanned the words on the page, her eyes blurry. She blinked furiously, glancing at Evelyn and seeing that her piece of paper was shaking in her hand, too.

"I'm sorry, could you read this for us please?" Vita asked. "I usually have reading glasses." It was a lie, but she couldn't think of anything else to say. Had her eyesight deteriorated in Albania, or was her body just too exhausted to function properly?

He nodded. "Fair enough. It says that you understand you must not reveal to anyone, other than those in the interrogation room, where you have been or who helped you from the time you crashed until you were rescued. This is to protect the identity of all involved, and to protect your benefactors and future downed troops. Do you both understand?"

"So we can't even tell our families where we've been? What happened to us?" Vita asked. She'd been planning on telling her mother exactly what kind of an ordeal she'd been through!

"No, ma'am. The only person you're to speak to about the matter is the lieutenant colonel."

Vita nodded and glanced at Evelyn, who was also nodding. Did they suspect them of some wrongdoing in Albania, or was it truly just to keep others safe? She decided not to ask the soldier accompanying them and save her questions for when she was in the room.

"Once you've been debriefed, you'll be taken to one of two separate hospital wards, joining the rest of your group. Do you have any questions?"

"No," Vita muttered, reaching for the pen to sign the paper. "Let's just get this over with."

She followed him and Evelyn into a tent well away from the hospital—and, she supposed, well away from prying ears. Inside, there was a large map spread out on a table, and a stern-faced man in uniform sitting on the other side of it. He rose, saluting the soldier escorting them, before sitting down and pointing to the map.

Vita's head was starting to pound; all she wanted was to go to sleep. But from his very first question, she knew it was going to be a very, very long night.

———— ❧ ————

A week later, when Vita stepped off the plane that had chartered them from the hospital base to their headquarters in Catania, her legs were trembling so violently she could barely keep one foot moving in front of the other.

"How you holding up?" It was Evelyn, and her voice sounded as shaky as Vita's legs felt after being on a plane again.

"I feel like vomiting up my breakfast," she admitted. "All three mouthfuls of it."

Evelyn laughed. "It's crazy, isn't it? I'm so darn hungry but I still can't manage more than a few mouthfuls of anything. I imagined we'd be eating like horses if we were ever rescued!"

It wasn't until they were in hospital that Vita had realized just how thin they'd all become. The women were in one ward, the men in the other; and suddenly, without having to worry about their survival, she'd been able to study not only her body but the other nurses' bodies, too. Their shoulder bones and hips were all protruding, they'd all stopped having their monthly visit, and they'd all been covered in red-raw infected bites, not to mention the abscessed blisters on their feet—and two of the medics were suffering from infectious hepatitis. But their smiles had remained, and from the moment they were propped up in their hospital beds, they'd all managed to keep their spirits up. They were safe, and that meant they had everything to be grateful for.

And now they were heading back to their old headquarters and their villas they'd left over two months ago—thinking they'd be back within a couple of days—before going to a party in their honor.

"It doesn't feel right, does it?" Evelyn asked, as the rest of the 807th that hadn't gone up on their flight emerged from the building up ahead, all forming a line and clapping for them. "Celebrating when Dot is still missing."

Vita sighed. "I know. I don't want to celebrate anything until we know for sure whether she's . . ." She swallowed. Hard.

Evelyn took her hand and they walked together toward the small crowd cheering. She forced herself to flash a smile, wondering how much anyone here even knew about what they'd been through, but thankfully the crowd parted for them and they all walked into the building. The very same building where they'd initially been briefed about their roles with the MAETS and what their schedule would look like, only a few months earlier. *It feels like a lifetime ago.*

"Welcome, the returned 807th!" someone boomed, as Vita spun around and took in the room, so different to how she remembered it.

Someone had tried to make it look festive, with handmade signs hanging from the rafters, and against the far wall there was a table with a cake as well as plates of other food.

"Wow—all this is for us?" Evelyn muttered. "I thought our ordeal was supposed to be secret?"

"My guess is that they've been told we were missing, but not where. They would have had to come up with a cover for why we were gone so long."

Evelyn was still holding her hand as they crossed the room, watching the other nurses and medics, some of the men still sporting mustaches and beards, albeit trimmed ones, as reminders of their time in Albania. Only Eddie wasn't with them; his leg injury hadn't healed properly and he'd developed a painful abscess as well, which was still being treated back at the hospital.

"Have a piece of cake, and then the returned 807th is invited to the officers' villa on the hill," someone yelled out. "It's time to celebrate!"

There was plenty of excitement, and Vita understood it; heck, she would have loved to be part of the revelry. But it was as if she'd left part of her heart in Albania with Dot, and unlike many of the others she wasn't so excited about the prospect of returning home to America earlier than expected.

In the end, they nibbled their pieces of cake before boarding a truck to go up the hill, their old villa seeming to wave to them, calling them back as they passed. And if it hadn't been for Evelyn, Vita would have insisted the truck stop and drop her off there so she could just crawl into bed.

"I'm not ready to go back there, not yet," Evelyn whispered to her.

"I just want to curl into a ball and sleep."

"There are too many reminders of Dot, though," Evelyn said, flatly, her eyes cold as she stared out the back of the truck.

Vita watched her stare and saw what Evelyn was seeing, could imagine Dot standing at the window, the curtains parted, staring out at them. She shivered. It was as if Dot was right there with them, her breath warm against Vita's cheek as she leaned into her, as they laughed together.

"She's coming back to us, I just know it," Vita said, hoping she sounded more confident than she felt. "And we'll all be tucked up in that villa again, staring out at the ocean and thinking it's the most beautiful view we've ever seen."

"I hope you're right," Evelyn murmured. "I really, really do."

Soon they were at the officers' villa, and Vita became a ghost; or at least she felt like one. It was as if she were floating above the party—she could see and hear the revelry, but she wasn't part of it. She, the girl who was always the life of the party, who loved nothing more than to drink and dance and be merry, felt sick in the pit of her stomach just being there at all.

"Come on, darlin', let's dance!" A handsome officer crossed the room and held out his hand, his smile wide and his eyes bright, but she recoiled when he touched her hand.

"No," she stammered. "No, thank you."

Evelyn must have seen the look on her face—or perhaps she instinctively knew how she felt, because the same sadness, the same emptiness, was probably inside of her, too. "We've had a harrowing few days; some of us are still a bit too tired to dance," she apologized, her arm looping around Vita's waist. "Maybe just let us catch our breath, and then we'll come find you."

He seemed disappointed but let them pass all the same, as music filled the room and more nurses and medics spilled in to fill the space. As much as Vita wanted to enjoy it, wished she could shut her eyes for a moment and imagine her pain and worry away, she knew it was no use. But she shut them anyway, inhaled deeply through her nostrils, tipped her head back a little. Suddenly she was back in that first village room, sitting huddled on the floor, with Evelyn on one side and Dot on the other, their feet nudging together, connected, making sure they were close.

Her eyes flew open, halting the memory as quickly as it had appeared.

"Why don't I get us a drink?" Evelyn whispered to her. "Maybe we could go sit outside, or find a quieter room or something."

Vita nodded, numb, resisting the urge to drop to her knees and cry, to collapse right there in the middle of the party. She'd never felt so vulnerable before, in so much pain.

And then there was Bobby. She shuddered and started to suck back deep lungfuls of air, certain there wasn't enough oxygen in the room for her, let alone all the officers and her squadron. She wanted Bobby back just as much as she wanted Dot.

Vita pushed past everyone in her way, blind in her desperation to get away from it all. It wasn't right that they were all celebrating, forgetting that they'd left three of their squadron behind. Dot might make it, but the other two nurses who'd been so brutally killed? But in truth, even if one nurse *had* survived, there was no guarantee it was Dot. It was little more than wishful thinking and she knew it.

"I'm sorry, I . . ." She stumbled over her words and her feet. "Please, please let me through."

When she burst through the door and swallowed the fresh air as if it were water, she started to relax, to breath more calmly, and she felt her pulse finally begin to slow. And then Evelyn was there, her gaze understanding as she passed her a glass of something. Vita didn't need to know what it was; she took it gratefully and took a sip, liking the way it warmed her immediately from the inside.

"Where do you think Bobby is?" she asked, the question suddenly spilling out of her.

"I suppose he had a separate debriefing since he wasn't part of the 807th," Evelyn said. "I'm confident there's nothing to worry about. It will be something to do with him being Air Force."

Vita stared up at the sky, remembering Bobby's touch, the way his smile lit up his eyes when he looked at her, the way he'd kissed her before she'd said goodbye to him. Two of the people she loved the most were gone, and she didn't know if she'd ever see either of them again. She'd been so careful to protect herself from being hurt, and yet she'd opened herself up to Bobby and ended up hurting all over again, albeit in a different kind of way. *I wouldn't give up my time with either of them. Even to avoid the pain. I will never regret a moment I spent loving them.*

"We shouldn't be out here," Evelyn mused. "If we're found out—"

"We plead ignorance," Vita said with a shrug. "They're sending us home anyway, aren't they?"

Before Evelyn could reply, a deep, mature voice cut through the otherwise silent, early-evening air.

"I'm sorry to interrupt, ladies, but I'm told you girls are nurses with the returned 807th?"

Vita stared at the bushy-mustached older gentleman standing a few feet from them. He was in full dress uniform, and she thought that he was at least as old as her father.

"We are," Vita replied. "Is there a reason you're looking for us?"

He cleared his throat. "I was only wanting to share some good news with you," he said, taking a few steps closer. "May I?"

He came to stand beside them and Vita nodded. "Of course."

"I'm General Fred Bluebridge, British Army," he said, taking a flask from inside his breast pocket. They watched as he unscrewed the lid and took a quick sip.

"I'm Vita, and this is Evelyn."

He passed her the flask and she took it, taking a little sip and then passing it on to Evelyn, who hesitated but eventually lifted it to her lips.

"I expect you were friends with a nurse called Dorothy?" he asked.

"Dot?" Vita replied. "You must be talking about our Dot."

He smiled. "That's the one. I shared a bunker with her, the second day the 807th were on the ground in North Africa, before you moved on to your permanent base in Bari. She was such a charming young lady."

"That was our first air raid," Evelyn said. "I remember so well because the sky was suddenly alive and all we could see were those red flares up in the air. We had nowhere to go because we hadn't dug our foxholes, and we all had to squeeze in wherever we could."

"Well, Dorothy found the best spot on the beach," he said with a chuckle. "I'd taken over an old German bunker, so mine was equipped with a cot and chairs, and a perfectly disguised hole where some of my men were shooting anti-aircraft guns. She was so timid, so I offered her a glass of my finest wine, and by the end of the evening I'd decided she was the most charming young lady I'd ever met."

Vita shut her eyes, imagining Dot down there, wondering how she'd never heard the story herself before, why Dot had never mentioned it.

"She's not here with us," Vita whispered. "We've had no word of her specifically since we left—ah . . ." Her voice trailed off. "Since soon after our crash."

"Oh, she's alive alright," the general said. "I've received uncon-firmed news that she's been found. We sent the very best to look for her, and if he's found her, he'll see to it that she gets home. I know all about where you've been."

"You're talking about James, aren't you?" Evelyn asked. "I know we're not supposed to speak of it, but surely you know—"

"How do you think James was assigned to find you in the first place?" the general asked with a grin. "I personally put the call in to redirect him to search for you when I heard about the crash, and then I ensured that no expense was spared in bringing all the 807th MAETS home."

"You did that?" Vita gasped.

"Let's just say that young Dorothy made quite an impression on me. I refused to accept that Britain wouldn't search for you, which is why British aircraft ended up coming with the US to find you. I was only sorry it wasn't a success."

"She reminded you of someone, didn't she?" Evelyn said quietly.

The general sipped from his flask again, before tucking it away in his pocket. "She did. My daughter, actually. We lost her to influ-enza when she was barely sixteen, but something about Dorothy made me remember—reminded me so much of her kind heart."

"You definitely think she's alive? That this nurse is actually her?" Evelyn asked. "And, ah, that James is still alive, too?"

The general winked at her. "James clearly made an impression on you, hmm?"

Evelyn looked mortified so Vita answered for her. "He made an impression on all of us. Without him, we'd still be up to our knees in mud or dead in the snow, so it's no exaggeration to say that we all owe him our lives."

"Right you are. Well, it was nice meeting you both," he said, standing and giving them a hearty smile. "You give my love to

Dorothy when you see her, won't you? And tell her that I'll always remember her."

"We will," Vita replied, waiting until he was out of earshot before turning to Evelyn.

"What do you think?" she whispered.

"I think that James was being truthful when he told me there were reports of Dot being alive and that he'd do anything to find her," Evelyn said. "Though the more time that passes, the less likely I've thought it could still be true, if I'm completely honest."

She dropped her head to Vita's shoulder, and Vita tipped her own head down, too, just like they had that day on the boat as they'd stood and stared back at Albania. Only this time, they stayed like that until late into the evening, staring up at the sky, as Vita wondered if Dot was somewhere in Albania with James, looking up at the same canopy of stars and dreaming of home.

You're going to make it, Dot. I just know you are.

CHAPTER
THIRTY-ONE

DOT

The knock at the door had sent Dot diving for cover. One minute she'd been singing in the kitchen, cooking alongside Nani as they listened to the radio. The next, she'd dropped the wooden spoon she'd been holding and run down into the cellar, terror surging through her as she retreated to the wall where the tunnel was. She placed her hand against her stomach and rubbed in wide circles, taking comfort from her baby hidden in there, but also wondering how long she'd be able to fit in the tunnel on her hands and knees. It was fine now when she was barely showing, but what about in a few months' time?

She strained to hear, but what sound she could make out was muffled at best, and so she sat and waited. There had been no warning, no German raid in the village or sudden attack, which was almost worse—because who was at the door? Someone had found out her identity, she just knew it. All this time of staying hidden, of being so careful, and someone had found her.

It felt like an hour had passed, but it could easily have been much less; she had no way of knowing. Every second was torturous, filled only with her own breath that seemed to rasp louder and louder with each exhale. And then there was a thud.

"Tell her to come out," a man called.

After so long of not being able to make out a word, she heard this as if it were spoken directly to her. His English was perfect, although it wasn't an American accent, and she froze, not sure what to do. But in the end, Dot rocked forward and made for the tunnel. She wasn't going to sit there and be taken, and she wasn't going to put Stefa's family at risk if they were found to be harboring an American. She'd told them she'd leave, she'd told them she'd never put them in danger, and she'd also insist that they had no idea she was even hiding down here if anyone asked.

She quickly cleared the entrance to the tunnel, scurrying in, swallowing her fear. It was a tight fit, the musty smell of earth hitting the back of her throat as she crawled between the houses. Another thud echoed out, the cellar door opening, but she kept going without pulling the disguise over the entrance. There was no time.

Dot groaned as she struggled to move forward, but she finally made it out to the other side as a man shouted behind her. She pushed her way out at the other end, fighting against all the odds and ends that had been piled up against the exit and falling out into the next-door cellar.

Goni and his brother were both winemakers, there was nothing suspicious about them having such large underground cellars, but she doubted they'd be able to explain the tunnel away so easily. But if she were found hidden here . . . She gulped, gasping for air as she hurried to the cellar door, yanking on it to get it to open.

The door jammed as she slammed her palm against it.

"Open!" she cried. "Damn you!"

She gave it one more thrust and fell straight into the adjoining cellar, landing on the floor on her hands and knees.

"Dot?"

She heard Stefa's aunt call to her, but she didn't respond. She didn't have time. Dot scrambled to her feet and ran through the house to the door, pulling it open and doing something she hadn't done in weeks. Or maybe it was months, she didn't even know anymore.

The cool air outside was like a slap to her cheeks, stealing her breath away, her first taste of fresh air since her secret outings with Stefa. She gulped it down, the light bright to her eyes, before she remembered why she was there. *I have to run.*

Dot glanced down the road, relieved there were no trucks.

"Stop right there."

The words were spoken as a command, with the authority of a soldier, but instead of acquiescing to him, she refused to turn, and kept on walking, trying her hardest not to run. She was just a woman walking down the street, she had no reason to think he was talking to her.

"I said stop." Only this time it was followed by the distinctive click of a gun.

Dot turned, raising both hands as she slowly pivoted to face whoever was after her.

Surprised didn't even come close to what she was thinking as she set eyes on the man. He had a closely cropped beard and hair that needed a cut, but his dark brown eyes were warm and he was most definitely *not* a German officer.

"Get back in the house. Now." He pointed with his gun and inclined his head, and she did as she was told, seeing Marti and her mother peering at her from behind parted curtains. She prayed she hadn't put them in more danger by fleeing outside.

"Quickly, before you're seen," he muttered, walking close behind her and hurrying her into the house.

Dot turned once she was inside, surprised to see him push his pistol into his pants and hold up his own hands, as if to reassure her that he wasn't going to hurt her. She watched, cautious, not ready to trust anyone despite the gun no longer being trained on her.

"I'm not going to hurt you," he said evenly, stopping to peer out the window before pulling the curtains tightly together.

"Who are you?" she croaked, backing up until she was standing beside Marti and Nani. She saw Marti's father move into the room as well, glancing at her, looking every bit as worried as she felt, before Stefa burst through the door, his face flushed and his breathing ragged. His eyes met hers and it made her even more terrified of what could happen. She glanced at the gun in the man's waistband and prayed Stefa wouldn't do anything stupid.

"First of all, you can wipe that terrified look off your face," the man said, looking weary as he crossed the room and took his bag from his back before slumping down into a chair. The timber groaned beneath his weight. "I'm here to get you home."

"Home?" she laughed, balling her fists. "I'm sorry, who did you say you were?" As they all stood, watching him, wide-eyed and trembling, he made it appear like the most natural thing in the world to be sitting in someone else's home, telling a stranger in a foreign land that he was about to take her home.

"James Millard. I'm a British SOE."

Her jaw went slack. "*You're* the British agent?"

"I've been searching for you for weeks," he said, rubbing his eyes, and it was then she noticed how weary he looked. There were dark shadows beneath his eyes, and he rubbed at his temples with the heels of his hands. "But we can talk once we start walking. We need to head for the coast within the hour."

"The hour?" Dot looked at Marti. "No, I'm not leaving here! I have no idea if you even are who you say you are."

He grunted. "Fair point. But your friend Evelyn told me you might need convincing, so she told me to say that she can't wait to go drinking and dancing with you in New York again once this is all over. Something about a twelve-hour pass and you feeding the fish over the railings."

Her heart started to race. "You've been with Evelyn? Is she safe? What about Vita and the others?"

His smile was warm, and the air changed in the small room just from her knowing he'd been with her friend. "Last I saw, they were all on a ship headed for Italy. I managed to walk them all to the coast, and that's exactly what we need to do now. There's no other way, and I want to go before the local situation changes again. I was careful getting here today, but after that little scene outside just before . . ."

She'd been so desperate to keep Stefa and his family safe, and in the end she might have done the one thing to put them, and her, in even more danger. Dot moved closer to James, until she was standing almost beside his chair, trying to push aside her guilt as she came to terms with leaving. She'd not long accepted the fact that Albania was the only country she'd ever know again, but now . . .

I can't leave him.

She wrapped her arms around herself as she addressed James. "I appreciate you coming for me, I do, but I'm not leaving," she said. "I've found a home here."

James looked surprised, but it was Stefa who spoke, who came rushing to her side.

"Dot, you have to go," he said, taking her hand and placing it over her stomach, so that both of their palms were splayed there. "You'll be safe in America. Our baby will be safe," he whispered.

Tears stung her eyes. "No! I'm not leaving you. I can't."

Stefa was still holding her hand when he turned to James.

"Tell me what your plan is," he said. "Tell me how you're going to get her there safely."

James turned his attention to his bag, not seeming at all surprised by her closeness to Stefa. Before she knew it, he was passing her identification papers. "I've arranged safe passage through the mountains for both myself and Dot. I have a contact within the BK, and he's given me the letter we need to pass through safely. You're to be a Muslim housewife, who's trained as a nurse."

"And you're certain you can trust this contact?" Stefa asked. "You're certain it's safe?"

"I'm certain," James said. "Everything's arranged. I've been working here for months now, I know the lay of the land as well as many of the locals. I'm her only chance at getting out of here."

Dot started to pick at her nails, a nervous trait she'd had since childhood, as she listened to the men speak.

"Stefa, please don't make me go," she whispered. "Please, I can't leave you. *We* can't leave you!"

He wrapped his arms around her and she held him, not caring who was watching. *Can I leave? Can I actually do this?*

"This is the only way we can keep our baby safe," he murmured to her, against her hair. "This might be the only chance we get, and I don't know how long we can keep you hidden, how long you will be safe here."

She stared up at him, in his arms, tears slipping down her cheeks as she stared into his eyes. He was right, she knew he was right, but it didn't make her decision any easier.

Dot's breath shuddered out of her as Stefa nodded, smiling at her even though tears shone in his eyes, too.

"One day, after the war, we will find a way to be together again," he whispered. "You keep our baby safe. He's all that matters."

She pressed her cheek to his chest and held him, steadying herself, catching her breath, before finally extracting herself and turning to face James. She didn't dare look at Marti, she couldn't, not without losing her composure.

"I'll go with you," she said, each word almost impossible to utter. "What do I need to do?"

"These are for you—take them," James said, pressing the papers into her hand. "You need to show these in case we're stopped, and I need you to change into local clothes. Perhaps we could buy some from your friends here? I want you to look every inch a Muslim woman, and you must keep your eyes downcast if ever we're stopped. I don't want anyone noticing those big blue eyes of yours."

She tried not to become overwhelmed with all the instructions, and finally turned to Marti, knowing she would oblige. They were a similar size, and she'd already been kind enough to share with her.

"Here." James placed some money on the table and nodded toward the men in the room. "For your troubles and your silence. The quicker we get out of here, the more chance I have of keeping my promise."

"What promise was that?" Dot asked, seeing the way Stefa smarted at the offer of money.

"I promised Evelyn that I wouldn't stop until I found you, and she made me swear that I'd get you to the coast, too. Trust me when I say that I have no intention of breaking my word to her." He pushed up from his chair. "Now, you go and get changed and be ready to leave in fifteen minutes."

Dot stood and watched him, not moving.

"Dot? Did you hear me?" he asked. "We need—"

"Thank you," she whispered. "Thank you for coming back for me. I know it seems like I'm not grateful, but I am. It's only that I found a family here who've loved me like their own, and I'd come to terms with never leaving."

"Well, like I said, Evelyn was insistent, and I don't have any intention of leaving a United States nurse behind. Now, could anyone rustle me up a cup of tea? I'd be most obliged."

She hurried off with Marti then as Stefa translated for his mother that their guest wanted tea, his eyes catching her as she passed, sending a fresh wave of emotion through her.

"I'm going to miss you so much," Marti said the moment they were out of sight, enveloping her in a big hug. "You'll always be my sister. I only wish you'd told me that you were in love with my brother."

Dot hugged her back, crying as she held on to Marti. All she'd wanted was to get out of Albania, and now her heart was breaking at the thought of never seeing Marti and her family again. Of never learning more of their songs or singing along with them as they did housework, of never sitting up late listening to the radio or lying together on their floor mats side by side each night.

"I'm sorry," she said. "I love you both."

"Oh, I knew," Marti said, laughing. "You were terrible at hiding it. I just wish you'd told me, that's all."

Stefa appeared then, tapping on the wall to get their attention, pulling her from her thoughts.

Dot broke away from Marti and walked over to him, knowing it was the last time she'd do so, her heart breaking into a hundred pieces as she ran her hands over his shoulders and inhaled the scent of him one last time.

"Thank you," she said, through her tears. "Thank you for saving me that night. I will never forget what you did for me." She hesitated. "Or how much you've loved me."

"This is the right thing to do," he said, his fingers finding her chin and tilting her face up to him, kissing her passionately, with so much love that it almost made her change her mind all over again.

But as quickly as he kissed her it was over, with a final kiss to her forehead before he disappeared so she could get changed.

Dot hurriedly put on Marti's clothes, dressing in a long skirt and top, and letting Marti tie a scarf around her head. She stood silently while Marti tucked her hair behind the coarse fabric, but when her friend finally stopped fussing and looked up at her, she saw her eyes were swimming.

"I'm going to miss you so much," Dot whispered.

Marti burst into tears, even though she was clearly trying so hard to keep her emotion in check. If James was successful in getting her to the coast, she was never going to see Marti again, and the pain of that realization stole a piece of her heart.

"Come on, it's time to go," Marti said, taking her hand and leading her out of the room. "Be brave, and tell that baby all about his aunty when he's born."

Dot didn't bother to act surprised that Marti knew; she'd clearly seen the protective way Stefa had touched her stomach before. She had no possessions, nothing to take with her, and James never asked when she stood there with her hands empty. But he did stand quietly as she said a final farewell to those she'd come to love, who'd kept her safe despite the danger. Without them, she'd have been long dead by now, and she'd never forget the kindness they'd shown her.

Stefa wrapped his arms around her again, kissing her lips, her cheeks, her forehead, as if he was committing every part of her to memory. And despite the pain in her heart, she forced herself to walk away the moment his lips left her skin.

"Goodbye," she cried as James opened the door, beckoning for her to join him.

She tucked in close to his side, looking back one last time at the family she'd come to think of as her own, at the man she loved more than she'd ever loved anyone in her life before.

A little part of her wondered whether she should have stayed, although she knew that was her fear talking: fear of not having her own family to go home to, and fear of the unknown. She wasn't safe in Albania, which meant her baby wasn't safe there, which meant she'd been left with no choice. It was her heart or her baby, and she knew that, from that day forward, every decision she made was going to be to keep her and Stefa's child from harm.

CHAPTER THIRTY-TWO

VITA

"Dot?" Vita squinted as she saw someone through the window, and she ran forward, thrusting the door open, so surprised she may as well have seen a ghost. "Oh, Dot."

She didn't know whether to cry for her or smile. When she'd heard Dot was pregnant it had come as a huge shock, and seeing her pregnant was an even bigger one.

"I don't know what to say," Vita said, opening her arms and giving Dot a big hug. "But it's so, so good to see you."

"Is she here?" Evelyn called out, before appearing in the hallway.

Vita recognized the look on Evelyn's face; it was how she'd felt only minutes before. Evelyn had turned as white as a sheet as she stared at their long-lost friend, wringing her hands together and hurrying to greet Dot.

"Dot, you're here! You're actually here!" Evelyn cried, moving past Vita to embrace their friend. "I honestly didn't believe it when I heard you were coming. I still can't believe you made it back, after everything, after . . ."

Vita cleared her throat as Evelyn's gaze dropped to Dot's rounded stomach. Dot had written to them and said she was expecting, but promised to explain it all when she saw them, and Vita had fretted ever since, wondering what had happened to her between the day she'd gone missing and when James found her.

Dot looked nervous, her eyes as wide as saucers, and Vita quickly took her arm. "It's so good to have you here. Come on, the coffee's brewing and I can't wait to have a cup."

"That'd be lovely," Dot said, and Vita hugged her arm as they walked, not wanting Dot to feel embarrassed. Whatever had happened to her, they were going to look after her, and the last thing Vita wanted was for her to feel uncomfortable. She hadn't been able to shake her own memories from Albania, falling into the same repetitive dream night after night, always being on the run, always having someone chasing her. And it was always that German soldier, his rifle glinting in the moonlight. So she hated to think what ran through Dot's mind whenever she closed her eyes.

"Dot," Evelyn said as they all stood in the living room. "Dot, I . . ." She looked to Vita, who just nodded her encouragement. Evelyn was more tactful, and they'd already decided that she was going to be the one asking the questions.

"When you wrote to us, telling us you were expecting, we didn't know whether to be happy for you or heartbroken. We couldn't figure out if it was your fiancé's baby, or . . ."

"He's not my fiancé anymore," Dot said, her voice small as she sat.

Vita dropped onto the sofa beside her, glancing at Evelyn, who was hovering near them. She looked at Dot's neck and realized the necklace she'd always worn no longer hung there, and that her ring finger was bare.

"He finished with you when he found out you were pregnant?" Vita gasped.

Dot shook her head, taking out a handkerchief and dabbing at her eyes. "The night before I went missing, I started to tell you both the truth, but . . ."

Vita reached out and took her hand. "What are you talking about, Dot? What truth?"

"Peter finished with me before I joined the MAETS," she said, her eyes downcast. "I suppose I wanted to believe that it wasn't true, that maybe he would feel differently after the war ended. I kept thinking that if I just kept believing, if I didn't admit it to anyone . . . So I lied. I'm so sorry, I only hope that you'll both forgive me."

Vita laughed. She couldn't help it. "You honestly believed I'd think less of you for not being engaged? Dot, I ran away from an engagement! Trust me when I say that I couldn't have cared less!"

Dot smiled when she looked up, her handkerchief clutched in her hands. "Looking back, I can see how foolish it was. But I'd spent my whole life trying to fit in, desperately wanting a family of my own." Vita's eyes followed Dot's hands as they moved to cover her stomach. "I think it's fair to say things didn't exactly go to plan."

"And the father?" Evelyn asked, moving to sit on the sofa next to Dot.

Dot smiled, her eyes glistening with tears. "That night I disappeared, I was taken in by a beautiful, loving family. And that's where I met Stefa."

Vita exhaled. "So your baby wasn't . . ."

Dot was blushing now. "The baby is Stefa's. We fell in love, Vita, and leaving him behind was the hardest thing I've ever done in my life."

"I'm so sorry," Vita said, holding Dot's hand again. "I had so many awful thoughts about what might have happened to you . . ." She swallowed, banishing the hideous worries she'd had about Dot during the time they'd been parted.

"Tell us about Stefa," Evelyn said, rising and moving into the kitchen to pour the coffee. "We want to know all about this beautiful man."

Dot was quiet for a long moment, taking her coffee when Evelyn returned with it and staring into the cup.

"He was everything Peter wasn't, and yet it took being in his arms to see that," Dot said. "I only hope that we get to see him again, because the thought of living my life, of raising our child, without him—"

"Don't say that," Vita interrupted. "You have to believe that you'll be reunited one day, otherwise it'll be too much to bear."

"I hope you're right, Vita," Dot said, smiling through her tears. "Because this little one needs to know what a special man his father is."

They sat in silence a while, each sipping their coffee, until Vita finally spoke.

"What you said before, about not telling us about Peter, about believing it couldn't be true?" She took a deep breath. "Well, I know the feeling. I did the same thing when we received the telegram about my brother. I refused to believe it. I was convinced he wasn't actually gone, that he'd somehow only been injured and would find his way to a hospital or something." She shook her head. "It's why I volunteered to be a nurse in the first place, although by the time I started my training I knew I had to admit that he was gone."

"You definitely have nothing to apologize for, or worry about with us," Evelyn said quietly. "And if he hadn't called things off with you . . ."

"I never would have been with Stefa," Dot said, her hand resting protectively over her stomach. "I have this baby to look forward to now, and that's all that matters."

Dot had started to cry, and Vita put an arm around her at the same time as Evelyn did. "This baby is going to be so loved," she

323

told her, stroking her hair as she held her. "We can help you to raise him, or her. You're not in this alone, I promise you that."

"Vita's right, we're here for you. We're your family now, Dot," Evelyn said.

"Are you alright for money?" Vita finally asked. "Because if there's anything you need, if there's anything I can do for you, you only have to ask."

"I'm fine, actually," Dot said, clearing her throat. "My grandparents left everything to me, so I have a lovely home and enough money not to worry about expenses. But I don't know how I'm going to actually raise a child alone, so if you both mean it . . ."

"I'll move in with you if you need me to," Vita said. "I mean, I've never even liked babies all that much, but I know I'll love yours."

They all laughed, and Evelyn shook her head at her like she thought she was mad, but Vita meant it. She would do anything for Dot, even if it meant rocking her baby to sleep every night and holding her hand through labor.

They all sat in silence for a moment as Dot wiped her tears, the three of them sitting side by side on the sofa. It was like there was so much left unsaid between them all, so much they could be talking about—the shared experiences that no one else could ever understand.

"So, tell me about you both," Dot said. "Do either of you have any news?"

"Actually, yes," Evelyn said. "I had a letter from James. We, ah, write to each other every now and again."

"You know, he did tell me when he came for me that he'd made you a promise. I just didn't realize it was more than—"

"Oh, well, I wouldn't say that it's—"

"Evelyn! We all know!" Vita rolled her eyes. "There's no need to pretend, not to us."

Evelyn blushed a deep red, and Vita stifled her laugh.

"Well, he's definitely special to me, if that's what you're insinuating." But her smile gave her away, and Vita had no interest in embarrassing her more. "He actually received the Distinguished Service Award for extraordinary heroism from the British Army when he returned to England, so I think we should all be raising our glasses to him." She laughed. "Well, in this case, our coffee cups."

They all laughed and raised their cups high, clinking them together.

"I wish we were all together, toasting him with champagne," Vita declared, sighing as she took a gulp of her coffee and leaned back. "Wouldn't it be marvelous?"

"It certainly would, although I'm much better on coffee than alcohol," Dot scoffed.

They sat in silence again, and Vita felt herself being pulled back into the past, certain that the same thing was happening to the other two as well. It was like a movie reel: her time in Camp Kilmer, the night in New York, the trip across the ocean, the day they climbed on board the enormous Skytrooper, laughing and chatting, all excited to be traveling together for the first time. It wouldn't stop playing on repeat, over and over again.

"Do you ever wonder what would have happened to us if it hadn't been for James?" Vita asked, shuddering as she considered the possibility. "Would we have had any chance at making it out of there at all?" She'd broken her own rule of not bringing up Albania.

Evelyn shook her head. "No, not a chance. There's no way we could have gotten to the coast without him, and even if we had, how would we have found a way to leave from there? We were up to our knees in mud, half-starved and completely lost when he found us. I think for certain we would have died there."

"I would have lived," Dot whispered, and Vita's eyes were drawn to her as she spoke. "I was part of an Albanian family by that point, and they were so kind to me. I'd resigned myself to the fact that it was going to be my home, and even though I wasn't safe, I had Stefa." Tears slipped down Dot's cheeks as she smiled at them. "I've never loved anyone as much as I love him, which made being rescued so bittersweet for me."

"You didn't know whether you wanted James to rescue you?" Evelyn asked. "Is that what you're saying?"

"At first," Dot said. "But in the end, I knew it was the only choice I could make, no matter how I felt."

"I owe him everything," Vita whispered, trying not to choke, absorbing what Dot was saying but also pulled deep into her own pain, into how desperate she'd been to be rescued. "I know that I'd be long gone if he hadn't tracked us down. He deserves that medal and anything else the army decide to give him. I just wish we could tell the world about what happened to us and what he did."

"Will you stay in touch with him?" Dot asked.

Vita grinned. "You're asking the wrong person."

Evelyn went red again and Vita waggled her eyebrows at her, receiving a death stare in reply.

"He's asked if he can keep writing to me, if that's what you're asking," Evelyn replied, shaking her head at Vita. "In fact, if I'm perfectly honest, I—"

"She's in love with him and can't wait until the war ends," Vita said for her. "So they can get married and have perfect little James babies."

"Vita!" Evelyn scolded.

Vita only shrugged, liking the game, but Dot was laughing so hard she had tears running down her cheeks again, from laughter this time instead of sadness.

"I'd forgotten what it was like, being with you two. It's like being the little sister and watching my two older siblings banter." Dot smiled. "I've missed it, but until today I hadn't realized just how much."

A sudden click of the door and footsteps echoing out alerted them to the fact they weren't alone any longer, leaving them to wipe their eyes and clear their throats. That was the one thing Vita had struggled with the most since the crash: the emotions. Before Albania, she'd barely ever cried, but since then, she'd been able to cry at the drop of a hat.

"Girls, are you in here?"

Within seconds, Bobby's blond head appeared in the doorway, and Vita stood up to greet him, never taking for granted that she could step into his arms and kiss him. After everything they'd been through, she'd doubted their relationship would make it, or that they'd both live to get back home at all.

Bobby kissed her back, running his hand through her hair and staring at her in that long, loving way he had since the night he'd returned home, and then he crossed the room to greet the other two women. Their smiles were as warm as his, and Vita watched on as he kissed first Evelyn on the cheek and then turned to Dot, holding her at arm's length before embracing her. It was the first time Bobby had seen her alive since Albania, too—and, bless him, he didn't miss a beat when he saw her rounded stomach.

"Dot, it's so good to see you," he said, finally letting go of her, and Vita could tell that seeing them all together had taken him back there, too. "I want you to know that there wasn't a night we didn't lie awake and try to figure out a way of going back for you, but—"

"I understand," Dot said, interrupting him. "We're all four here now, and that's what matters. There's nothing to feel bad about, we all just did what we needed to do to survive."

"So can a guy take three gorgeous girls out for dinner then?" he asked, and Vita saw a flicker of that old charm, the charm that had sent her head over heels in love with him the very first night they'd met.

"You most certainly can," Vita said, rising and indicating for the others to join them.

"Come on then, ladies. I'm taking you to a little corner restaurant a few minutes' walk away. I think we all need a drink, am I right?"

Vita took his arm and smiled at her friends, a sensation of warmth spreading through her as she looked first at Dot and then at Evelyn.

"Dot, you do realize that we're your family now, don't you?" she asked. "Your baby is going to have two bonus mothers in me and Evelyn, although I'm sure I'll be the favorite."

Evelyn laughed. "Vita! You don't even like babies!"

Vita shrugged. "Well, it just so happens that I already like this one."

She leaned past Bobby and reached for Dot's hand, surprised by how tightly she grasped hers back. They'd all survived, despite the odds, and this little baby on the way was the biggest miracle of all.

EPILOGUE

EVELYN

Evelyn sat across from James on the plane, staring at the piece of yellow fabric in his hand. She reached out to touch it, instinctively knowing how it would feel, what it would smell like, the emotion that would surge through her just from seeing it again. And when she looked up at James, she knew he understood; all these years, he'd been one of the only ones to ever understand.

"I never thought we'd be coming back here," he said, his fingers closing over hers. "Who would have thought, after all these years?"

She smiled at him, finding strength in his touch as she always did, even though his hands were no longer smooth and tanned. Now, they were marked with sunspots, his knuckles gnarled with arthritis, but they were still the same hands that had reached for her in Albania. *And reached for her ever since.*

She inhaled deeply as the plane descended, the thud sending a ripple through her that she hadn't experienced before as they finally hit the runway. It had been fifty years ago but the memory of that landing, of what it felt like to crash, was as fresh in her mind as it had ever been.

"Mom, are you okay?"

She smiled over at her son, Max, his face creased with concern. He'd been reluctant for them to travel at all, so shocked by the discovery of his parents' secret after all these years. But it hadn't been until recently they'd been able to share their story at all, to protect those who'd risked so much to save them. She didn't blame him for finding it all hard to digest.

"I'm fine, darling," she assured him.

"What are you holding?" Max asked, as the seatbelt signs continued to flash, the plane slowly coming to a stop on the runway.

Evelyn wrapped her fingers around the fabric before leaning over James and passing it to him. Max took it, looking curiously at the small yellow square.

"It's a piece of parachute that I've kept all these years. My one little keepsake from our survival," she explained. "It came in a drop that your father organized, when almost everything was stolen except for the parachutes."

She watched as he turned it over in his hands, fingering the fabric before looking up at her. "I still can't believe it. All these years, not really knowing how you and Dad met."

Evelyn took James's hand, clasping their palms together as she dropped her head to his shoulder. "I owe your father my life," she murmured, closing her eyes as all the lights in the cabin came on and the flight attendant announced that it was time to disembark. "Without him, none of us would have made it home alive."

When she opened her eyes, she took the fabric from Max as he stood to take down their luggage from the overhead lockers. When she finally rose, she saw Dot already waiting in the aisle. Her daughter, Mary, stood behind her, and she shot Evelyn a curious smile.

Evelyn smiled back. Mary had been like a daughter to her—to both her and Vita—from the moment she was born. *Our little miracle*, that's what they'd always called her, all infatuated by the raven-haired, brown-eyed little girl who'd had all three of them wrapped around her little finger, not to mention her doting uncles who'd have done anything for her.

Evelyn blinked away tears as she thought of Vita. They'd been as close as sisters since their return to America, never going more than a few days without seeing one another or talking on the telephone, but she'd passed away before their file had been declassified. And then Bobby, Vita's darling Bobby, who'd doted on her ever since they'd arrived back in America all those years ago, had died only a few weeks later. She and Dot were convinced the poor man had died of a broken heart.

As they all began to shuffle forward, in line to exit the plane, Evelyn only hoped that there wasn't more heartache to come.

"You sure you're ready for this?" James asked, beside her.

She turned and pressed her ear to his chest and listened to the steady beat of his heart, just like she had as they'd stood on the beach in their last minutes together in Albania.

"I'll find you," he whispered. "Wherever you are, whatever happens, I'll find you once all this is over."

"How? How will you find me?"

"Evelyn, I'm an operative for the British Army. It's my job to find people."

She stared up at him, his face thick with beard now, his eyes tired, crinkled at the corners as he smiled down at her.

"I never thought I'd be saying this to a woman who wasn't my wife, but I love you," he whispered. "And I will find you. When all this is over, we can begin our life together."

She curled into him, pressing her body tightly to his as they stood on the sand, until his arms guided her into the little lifeboat.

Everything had changed since that night. Everything except the steady, comforting beat of her husband's heart.

"Yes, my love, I'm ready. Are you?"

His smile told her everything she needed to know.

DOT

Dot gripped her daughter's hand tightly as they walked through the airport, pulling their bags behind them as they searched for their guide. He'd told them he'd be waiting for them, ready to take them where they needed to go, and she was busy scanning every man standing with a placard, announcing who they were waiting for. "There!" Mary said. "He's there!"

They hurried toward him, flanked by Evelyn, James, and Max, and Dot's heart beat so fast she worried she might be on the verge of a heart attack.

"Dorothy?" he asked, a big smile forming beneath his mustache.

"Yes, that's me," she said, clearing her croaky throat.

"I have a vehicle outside waiting," he said. "Come with me."

"Please," she said, touching his arm to stop him from walking away. "Please, do you have news for me? Were you able to locate those who helped us?"

He shook his head, and her breath caught in her throat at the sadness in his gaze.

"Unfortunately, we received news about the family of Hasan Josef, the man you said saved you," he said. "I recently received confirmation that his father was tortured, as punishment for Josef helping you, and other villagers were executed by the Germans for their role in hiding your group. I'm so sorry."

Dot turned, instinctively reaching for Evelyn, for the hand she'd held so many times in Albania and over the years since. She looked sadly to her left, wishing Vita was there with them. It didn't feel right not to have her by her side.

"And what of Stefa and Marti? Were you able to find them?" she whispered, barely able to utter the words.

The man's face broke out into a smile then. "Yes! Oh yes, I was. They are the wine family."

She squeezed Evelyn's hand as her heart started to pound again. "They are alive?"

"Yes, they are alive. We are going to see them tomorrow."

Dot's legs buckled and suddenly her daughter had her arms around her, helping her to her feet.

"Mom, this is all too much. I—"

"Stefa," she whispered. "All these years, and my Stefa is still alive."

Mary's arms braced her as they started to walk slowly through the airport again, but she shrugged her daughter away, taking hold of her hand instead.

"I'm stronger than I look," she muttered.

A snort behind her made her laugh. "That's funny, because I recall Evelyn saying those exact words to me the last time we were here together."

They all laughed at James, and although she knew their children thought they were mad for wanting to come back, she knew in her heart it was the best thing she'd ever done.

———— ❧ ⚘ ————

Dot could barely breathe. Part of her was certain that there had been a mistake, that her guide had found someone else, that it wouldn't be Stefa and Marti waiting for her but someone else entirely. But then another little part of her, an optimistic voice that kept whispering to her, told her that she *was* about to see them again.

"Not far now," the guide said. "We just need to go down this next hill and then we should be—"

"We're here." The words came out as a gasp as Dot pressed her nose to the window. There was the hill he'd taken her to, the place they'd spent three blissful afternoons together, alone. It was all crystal-clear in her mind, despite the years that had passed.

"Mom? Are you okay?"

"We're here," she repeated, seeing the same hope she felt inside reflected in her daughter's eyes. "This is the right place."

She hadn't expected to recognize his village, had thought so much would have changed and wondered if her mind had muddled some of her memories, but this part of Albania seemed untouched by the decades since she'd last seen it. The grass was still lush, the village appearing only slightly larger and more populous than she remembered.

And then she saw him.

Their four-wheel drive came to a halt on the road, but Dot didn't wait for the driver to come and open her door. She stepped out, dust swirling around her shoes as she blinked, wondering if her mind was playing tricks on her.

It's not.

The man had thick hair, only it was snow-white now instead of a lustrous black. His body was slightly stooped, but his shoulders were still square and strong—and those eyes . . . She shook her head as he started to walk toward her, his arms outstretched.

I've never forgotten those eyes, not even after all these years.

"Dot?" His voice was raspier than she remembered it, but just hearing him say her name swept her back in time, and she broke into a run as his face creased into a smile.

"Stefa!" she cried, falling into his arms, her cheek to his chest, feeling like she was twenty-five again and not seventy-five.

She cried as he held her, his lips finding her hair again just like they always had, his hands warm on her back as he cried with her. Dot had forgotten they were on the side of the road, that anyone could see them; all she could see was her Stefa.

"Let me look at you," he said, holding her at arm's length and staring down at her.

His cheeks were damp and she lifted her hand to gently wipe them, smiling through her own tears as she watched him.

"All these years, and somehow you're still beautiful," he said, in his thickly accented English.

"I never thought I'd see you again," she whispered. "Even when they said they'd found you, I still didn't believe it was true."

She heard someone clear their throat behind them and turned, realizing when she saw Mary standing awkwardly with the guide that she'd forgotten about her poor daughter.

"Sweetheart, come here," she said, stepping away from Stefa and holding out her hand. "There's someone very special I'd like to introduce you to."

Mary was a woman of almost fifty now, but in that moment, the way her face broke into a smile, Dot saw her as the little girl who'd asked so often after her father, wondering why she'd never met him. Why he wasn't part of their lives.

"Oh, Dot, it's not . . ." Stefa said, holding his hand to his mouth as he let out a cry. "This is—"

"Our daughter," she finished for him, watching as Mary stepped forward with open arms to embrace her father.

Stefa held her like she was the most precious thing in the world, his arms around Mary, folding her against him as he whispered something over and over in Albanian that she couldn't understand.

"She's beautiful," he said, laughing as he held out an arm for her to join them. "She's so beautiful, just like her mother."

Dot looked around then, wondering where Marti was. There was no one with Stefa, he'd been standing alone, and she glanced over at his house and wondered if she was in there.

"Where's Marti?" she asked. "I've been looking forward to seeing her almost as much as seeing you."

Stefa shook his head, sadly, and he didn't have to say anything. She knew.

"When?" she asked.

"Barely a month ago," he replied.

I only missed her by a month.

Dot nodded. It had been optimistic at best to think she'd be able to see both of them again.

"All these years," Stefa said, speaking to Mary even though he was looking between them. "I've wondered what you were like, whether I had a son or a daughter, whether I'd ever find a way to see you. And now, here you are."

They all stood in the street for some time, staring at one another, before Stefa waved his hands and invited them in.

"Later, I'll take you to pay your respects to my family," he said, linking one arm through Dot's and the other through Mary's. "But now, we drink wine and celebrate. This," he cried, pulling her even closer and pressing a kiss to her cheek, "this is the happiest day of my life."

Later that night, when Mary had retired to bed and it was just her and Stefa, Dot moved closer to him, sitting side by side at the table, shoulder to shoulder, their hands resting on glasses half full with wine.

"Tell me what happened, after I left," she said. "Was everyone safe?"

He nodded, his arm snaking around her and holding her close. "Life went on as normal once you'd gone," he said. "Some of our neighbors knew we'd been hiding you, but there were no retaliations and we just kept our heads down and kept supplying our wine to the Germans, to keep them happy."

She listened to him, pressing a kiss to his hand as it fell over her shoulder.

"And the past fifty years?" she asked. "I half expected to find you married."

"I was," he said. "I waited ten years, believing that somehow I'd find a way to be with you, but eventually I gave up. We had thirty happy years together. She was a kind, generous woman." He paused. "But she wasn't you."

"I married, too," Dot said. "He was a good man, but I always held something back, and he couldn't stand it. We divorced after seven years, and since then it's just been me and Mary." She smiled. "As a child, I told her many bedtime tales of Albania. She knows we loved her so much before she was even born, that we chose to break our hearts to keep her safe."

They sat in silence a while longer, sipping their wine as rain started to fall on the roof, reminding her of all those nights she'd lain on her pallet, with Stefa on one side and Marti on the other, wondering whether she'd ever make it home alive.

"Marti always told me we'd be together again. She never stopped hoping."

"I never stopped hoping either," Dot whispered.

"Are you still a nurse?" he asked.

She laughed. "No, I'm not. I'm a doctor now, would you believe?"

He put down his wine and turned to face her. "You're a doctor? My Dot is a doctor?"

She nodded. "I am. I put myself through medical school when Mary was five years old, and I've dedicated my life to helping people. I refused to let my second chance at life be for nothing."

He reached for her hand then, standing and pulling her up with him. His arms were warm around her, and as she stepped tightly into his embrace, she found she still fitted perfectly to his frame. The last time she'd stood like this had been when he'd said goodbye to her—but this time, she wasn't ever going to walk away from him.

"Stefa," she whispered, too scared to look up at him, choosing to keep her face to his chest instead.

"What is it?"

In that moment, she felt like they were young again. The way her heart thudded in her chest, the way his hands rubbed up and down her back, it took her back decades.

"Stefa, will you come home to America with me?" she asked.

He was silent, and she shut her eyes, willing him to say yes.

"Or I will stay here," she murmured. "If you won't leave your country, I'll stay here with you this time. But I can't walk away without you, not again."

"Yes," he said, his words whispered straight into her ear. "Yes, my love. I will go home with you and our daughter. It's time for us to finally be a family."

Dot tipped back in his arms, staring up at him, seeing not the white-haired gentleman watching her back, but the young, strong, raven-haired Stefa she'd fallen for so many years ago. The man who'd saved her life, who'd bravely come for her in the dark of night, who'd risked everything to keep her safe.

And when his lips touched hers, it was the same intoxicating kiss of youth that told her anything was possible.

Albania had stolen a piece of her heart, but this time she was taking her piece of Albania with her.

AUTHOR'S NOTE

I came across the nurses and medics of the MAETS when I was researching another book on World War Two nurses, and I quickly became obsessed with finding out everything I could about the 807th Squadron when I heard about what they'd been through. I found it almost impossible to believe that twenty-six Army Air Force flight nurses and medics, along with their pilots and flight crew, had crashed in Albania and spent so much time lost there, and that their file was classified for so many years! I also couldn't believe that they'd all survived; it seemed surreal that all thirty men and women could have made it out of enemy territory alive. And although communism did end in Albania in the early 1990s, it was many more years before the story of the 807th was shared with the world.

Despite it being a work of fiction, much of this novel is based on fact, including the MAETS training and the crash itself, as well as some of the villages and types of people the group encountered, and the scene when the US and British aircraft arrive to save the group and ultimately have to leave without them. I also tried to make the scene when the group was rescued as authentic as possible, including what it was like in the caves and their boat trip back to Italy, as well as their debriefing and hospital care.

The one part of this book that isn't true at all to history is when the three nurses become separated from the group. In reality, three nurses did go missing, but they actually all survived and were kept in a house similar to the one Dot was hidden in, by a wine-making family who dug a hole between their underground wine cellars so the girls could crawl from house to house in case of a German raid. For my novel, I decided to have only one character saved by a local family, but I still wanted to show a genuine glimpse of what it was actually like for those three women.

Also, there was indeed a British special operations lieutenant (in addition to other operatives) who was instrumental in saving the main group, and who found them up to their knees in mud, riddled with lice and severely emaciated, although he wasn't the only one to help rescue the group.

I must make it clear that all the characters in my books are entirely fictional, however I would like to make special mention of all the nurses, medics, and pilots who survived those difficult 63 days in Albania, as well as the three nurses who were there for an unbelievable 135 days. It truly is a miracle that no one died in the plane crash, and that they all survived their ordeal. With this novel, I wanted to create a fictional story that was inspired by these real historical events—to give my readers a taste of what it must have been like for those heroic nurses and medics so many years ago.

This is my eighth historical fiction novel, and with each one I become more and more passionate about telling the stories of women during World War Two. I am continually amazed at not only the roles women played during the war, but the situations they endured. I hope that in reading this book, you feel as proud of these women as I do, and inspired by their strength.

If you'd like to find out more about the true story of the 807th Squadron who survived Albania, make sure you follow my Facebook page or join my reading group on Facebook, where I'll be sharing photos and behind-the-scenes information with my readers. There are also some fantastic articles and non-fiction books written about the survivors and their journey, if you'd like to read more.

And one last note that I feel compelled to share . . . in the novel I mention that the Albanian people refused to comply with an order to turn over lists of Jewish people during German occupation in 1943. In fact, they protected and hid Jewish families, loyal to the promises they made to keep them safe, with various government agencies even providing them with fake documentation! Incredibly, there were many more Jewish families living in Albania after the war than before—they not only protected Jewish Albanians, they also provided sanctuary for any Jewish refugees. Albania had a majority Muslim population, but they welcomed and showed compassion for religions different to their own, and succeeding in protecting the Jewish people where other European nations failed. That tells me a lot about what it meant to be Albanian, and is a part of my research I will never, ever forget.

I love to hear from readers, and the best way to connect with me is via my Facebook page @SorayaLaneAuthor or by signing up for my newsletter via my website.

ACKNOWLEDGMENTS

Writing during the era of COVID isn't easy. Our lives have changed in ways we never imagined, and sometimes it feels like life will never be the same again. But the one thing I've found comfort in is books. In writing this novel, I hope that I've managed to distract you from the real world for a short time, as my favorite authors have done for me.

I do have a core group of people I need to thank—they are so incredibly special to me and I am so privileged to continue working with them. First, I owe deep gratitude to my long-time editor Sammia Hamer, who I've worked with on all but one of my historical novels. Sammia, thank you for all your encouragement, all your wonderful feedback, and for being such a champion of my work—I feel so incredibly grateful to be working with you. I also owe huge thanks again to the wonderful Sophie Wilson, who is always instrumental in helping to take my work to the next level during structural edits.

My editing team has expanded this year, though, and I'd like to pay a very special thanks to editor Victoria Oundjian. It's terrifying as an author working with a new editor, but from the moment I first spoke to Victoria I knew we were the perfect fit. So, enormous thanks go to both Sophie and Victoria for helping to shape this novel—your ideas, enthusiasm, and belief in my ability made editing this book such an enjoyable process. Victoria, you have officially joined the "dream team"! My gratitude also extends to copyeditor Gemma Wain—thank you!

I have an incredible extended team at Amazon Publishing that stretches well beyond editorial, so thanks also to everyone in the UK office for your ongoing support. I'd especially like to make mention of my author relations managers, Nicole Wagner and Bekah Graham.

Thanks and gratitude also to my agent, Laura Bradford. Laura, we've worked together for a decade now, and I appreciate all your advice and for being my advocate—thank you.

I must also make special mention of my amazing writing friends—Yvonne Lindsay, Natalie Anderson, and Nicola Marsh. You ladies are so special to me, and I deeply appreciate your daily support and friendship. And the amazing authors over at Blue Sky Book Chat on Facebook—thank you for inviting me into the fold and making me feel so welcome!

And to you, my amazing readers, I wouldn't have been able to write this book without your support. Because of you, I'm able to continue writing the novels I love, and I thank you for all the books of mine you've purchased over the years. If you don't already follow my Facebook page/Facebook reader group, please do so, as it's the best place to connect with me. Also, if you want me to "zoom" call into your next Book Club meeting, all you have to do is ask!

Soraya x

ABOUT THE AUTHOR

Photo © 2019 Martin Hunter

Soraya M. Lane graduated with a law degree before realizing that law wasn't the career for her and that her future was in writing. She is the author of historical and contemporary women's fiction, and her novel *Wives of War* was an Amazon Charts bestseller. Soraya lives on a small farm in her native New Zealand with her husband, their two young sons, and a collection of four-legged friends. When she's not writing, she loves to be outside playing make-believe with her children or snuggled up inside reading. For more information about Soraya and her books, visit www.sorayalane.com or www.facebook.com/SorayaLaneAuthor, or follow her on Twitter: @Soraya_Lane.